"It's not often that my e... but completely blown o... the case with this finale. While *Salvation* and *Salvation Lost* were about the back story and build-up, *The Saints of Salvation* is all about the payoff. However, when you put the three novels together it's clear that this is simply one big story, and the Salvation Sequence is perhaps Peter's best yet, and certainly his most accessible. . . . In fact, this will be my first recommendation to anyone new to Hamilton's work going forward. In short, the Salvation Sequence shows a writer that is the master of his genre, delivering everything expected, and more. —*SFF World*

"A stirring finale . . . Peter F. Hamilton brings his Salvation trilogy to a satisfying climax with *The Saints of Salvation* [which includes] fabulous technology and some mind-spinning science—as well as cataclysmic battle scenes and, despite the often bleak premise of a human race besieged by overwhelmingly superior forces, some characteristic optimism." —*The Guardian*

"Hamilton concludes his Salvation Sequence trilogy with a rousing, action-packed space opera that further cements his reputation as a master of the genre. . . . Hamilton keeps the pages turning with riveting action and intrigue, making the hefty page count fly by. Fans will be thrilled to see this series go out on a high note."
—*Publishers Weekly* (starred review)

Praise for
SALVATION LOST

"Action-oriented hardcore science fiction at its page-turning best . . . Hamilton excels at interweaving the narratives of multiple viewpoint characters without once relaxing narrative impetus, combining time-lines to great dramatic effect and telling a tense hi-tech story that never loses sight of the human element." —*The Guardian*

"This is bold and fearless plotting, and I anticipate just as many thrilling revelations and stunning reversals in the concluding book three, *The Saints of Salvation.* . . . So long as there are writers like Hamilton who can blend the core and eternal human bits with the ultrahuman visionary stuff, science fiction will flourish." —Paul Di Filippo, *Locus*

"[An] epic galaxy-spanning conflict . . . Told in a quick-reading style with humor, a depth of character, and a cunning plot, *Salvation Lost* nicely sets up the conflict for the series finale." —*Booklist*

"The pacing is swift, with spectacular action, thoughtful strategies, eye-popping ideas, and Hamilton's usual attention to detail, all woven into a taut, gripping narrative."
—*Kirkus Reviews*

"Everything readers of *Salvation* will have hoped for. A series emerging as a modern classic." —Stephen Baxter

"Savage, brilliant, and compelling . . . a masterclass in tension and spectacle." —Gareth L. Powell

"I found myself gripped by *Salvation Lost*, as I devoured it right to the scintillating end. Earth-invaded/Humanity-enslaved stories usually put Homo-Sapiens through the wringer—and Hamilton ratchets that up and then some. This is vertiginous in its scale, covering vast tracts of time and space, and mind-bending as it examines new frontiers of human physicality. This is a dazzling tale of humanity face-to-face and toe-to-toe with the ultimate enemy!"
—Michael Cobley

Praise for

SALVATION

"Dynamic, multifaceted characters, strong mind-expanding concepts, and an impressive flair for language [make *Salvation* a] rare celestial event. . . . One of Britain's bestselling sci-fi authors has launched an addictive new book as the initial stage of what is sure to be an intriguing new series." —*SyFy*

"How far 'space opera' has come! The Old Masters of sci-fi would admire the scope and sweep of *Salvation*, but marvel even more at the amount of thought that now has to go into making futures plausible." —*The Wall Street Journal*

"[A] vast, intricate sci-fi showstopper . . . the journey grips as hard as the reveal." —*Daily Mail*

"Peter Hamilton just keeps getting better and better with each book, more assured and more craftsmanly adroit, and more inventive. [*Salvation* is] a bravura performance from start to finish.. . . . Hamilton is juggling chainsaws while simultaneously doing needlepoint over a shark tank. It's a virtuoso treat, and I for one can hardly wait for *Salvation Lost*." —Paul Di Filippo, *Locus*

"Peter F. Hamilton is known as one of the world's greatest sci-fi writers for a reason. . . . *Salvation* is well worth the effort and a great introduction to some good old-fashioned space opera." —*Fantasy Book Review*

"Packs a teeth-rattling wallop . . . Hamilton expertly keeps his audience coming back for more." —*Kirkus Reviews*

"An engaging collection of tales." —*Booklist*

"Exciting, wildly imaginative and quite possibly Hamilton's best book to date." —*SFX*

"Hamilton's possible worlds are grist to the mill of humanity's evolution." —Mark Stevenson

THE SAINTS
OF SALVATION

THE SAINTS
OF SALVATION

Book Three of The Salvation Sequence

PETER F. HAMILTON

NEW YORK

The Saints of Salvation is a work of fiction. Names, characters,
places, and incidents either are products of the author's imagination
or are used fictitiously. Any resemblance to actual persons,
living or dead, events, or locales is entirely coincidental.

2021 Del Rey Mass Market Edition

Published in the United States by Del Rey,
an imprint of Random House, a division of
Penguin Random House LLC, New York.

DEL REY is a registered trademark and the CIRCLE colophon
is a trademark of Penguin Random House LLC.

Originally published in hardcover in the United States by Del Rey,
an imprint of Random House, a division of Penguin Random House LLC,
New York, and in the United Kingdom by Pan, an imprint of
Pan Macmillan, London, in 2020.

ISBN 978-0-399-17890-0
Ebook ISBN 978-0-399-17889-4

Printed in the United States of America

randomhousebooks.com

4 6 8 9 7 5 3

Del Rey mass market edition: July 2021

The Salvation Sequence is dedicated to The Americans,
with my gratitude and thanks.

In order of appearance:

Anthony Gardner

Betsy Mitchell

Jaime Levine

David Pomerico

Anne Groell

JULOSS FALLING

Ahead of the Neána insertion ship, Juloss glowed like a sapphire pearl, its vast oceans and small continents wrapped in long, tranquil streamers of cloud. Space around it was speckled with diamond-dust glimmers as sunlight bounced off the orbital forts that guarded this precious world against invasion.

The insertion ship flew in south of the ecliptic, shedding cold mass in irregular bursts like a black comet. By the time it was on its final approach to the unsuspecting planet, it was down to twenty-five meters in diameter. It had no magnetic field and its outer shell was radiation-absorbent, rendering it invisible. Fully stealthed, it eluded the vigilance of the orbital forts to slip past them, discarding the last of its reaction mass in its final deceleration maneuver. Now it was basically falling toward the western edge of the largest continent, where a tall mountain range sank into the sea. Tiny course correction ejecta continued to refine the ship's descent vector, steering it toward the coast, which was still thirty minutes from greeting the dawn. Inland, perched on undulating foothills, lights from the lonely city of Afrata shone brightly across the lush valley.

As it hit the upper atmosphere, the insertion ship peeled apart into six pear-shaped segments. They plunged downward, aerobraking with increasing severity as the atmosphere thickened around them. The segments were aimed close to a thin spit of land whose rocky coastline was covered in a tangle of vegetation.

A hundred meters from the shore, six large splash plumes shot up into the air like thick geysers, crowning and splattering down amidst the startled seabirds flying out to catch the first fish of the day.

The Neána swam ashore. Creatures out of every human's dark ancestral nightmare, risen out of banishment to stalk the land once more—formidable reptilian bodies moving fast on multiple sinewy limbs, razor claws snapping continuously. They climbed the cliffs at the foot of the mountains and set off in search of their prey.

Dellian knew the Neána pack was closing on him. He was in Afrata's downtown district, lurking in the shadows of a deserted plaza as the hot sun shone down vertically. The creepers that were colonizing the lower floors of the crystal and carbon skyscrapers trailed long strands like a verdant waterfall. It was good cover. He stole through the dangling vegetation, letting their silky leaves slither over his bare face—a sensation akin to a shower of fine dust.

Somewhere along the avenue he was approaching a flock of birds took flight, wings pumping hard to create a swirl of bright colors, blotting out the sky. He peered forward, seeing long shadows slink between the ferns that had conquered the pavements. A fast clattering was just audible above the dumb squawking of the fleeing birds: the gullet rattle Neána packs used to communicate when they were hunting.

Dellian spun around the corner of the building, raising his bow. The lead Neána was closer than he would have liked. When the diabolical *thing* saw him it started a kill run. Muscles as thick as his torso flexed along its hind limbs, pounding it forward, two sets of upper body limbs extended, claws snapping. Its victorious ululation was deafening. Dellian stood still for a second, keeping the bow stable. He let the iron-tipped arrow fly. It split the air like a black laser beam and pierced the Neána's gullet.

The monster lurched to the ground, bile-colored blood

pumping from the wound, momentum tumbling it forward. The others screamed their fury and charged him, but Dellian was already gone, racing for the other side of the avenue and the tangle of creepers skirting the skyscraper. Dappled darkness closed around him, and the rough leaves clung to his bulky bulletproof vest, slowing his flight. His boots crunched the fronds beneath his feet as he headed for cover behind the skyscraper's entrance portico. Behind him, the Neána were calling to one another, their stark twig-drum rattle reverberating across the plaza.

He reached the portico and crouched down. His breathing was heavy in his ears, heart pounding as he waited . . . but nothing attacked him. He eased his metal helmet up a fraction and snuck a quick glance around the wall. Two of the Neána were stalking along his side of the plaza, with three more scouring the buildings beyond the central fountain pond.

Dellian gripped his assault rifle tightly and slowly moved clear of the portico, dependent on just a few wispy vines to shield him from the aliens. He brought the muzzle up and opened fire in a blaze of flame and thunderous noise. Recoil hammered into his shoulder, but he kept his aim steady and watched the slugs tear a line through the first Neána's flesh. The one behind it hesitated, as if cowed by the violence, then it pulled what looked like a bazooka out of its harness.

"Fucking Saints!" Dellian yelled. He sprinted forward, firing as he went, spraying bullets in the general direction of the second Neána. The creature fired its weapon, and the portico exploded behind him.

A blast wave slammed into him, sending him sprawling. The armor suit's reactive carapace absorbed the brunt of the force while he curled up to roll through the impact. Adaptive musculature brought him back up to his feet *fast*, and sensor graphics swept across his optik, tracking enemy targets. The micro-missile launch pod snapped up out of his backpack, ready for acquisition data. Four Neána were powering into the plaza, wearing gray carbon exoskeletons with multiple weapon attachments. Electronic warfare systems went active, blitzing the plaza in a digital haze.

Dellian was about to fire his missiles when the sky overhead began to brighten. His sensor view flipped to vertical. High above, a brilliant golden fireball was punching down through the atmosphere, a rigid amber pillar of overheated air stretching out behind it. He took an instinctive step backward as the fireball seemed to accelerate. Its radiance flooded the plaza, turning his vision monochrome.

"Oh, crap—" He turned to run.

The fireball struck the fountain, and light detonated out, overwhelming everything.

Dellian blinked the glare away and stared through the high fence that guarded the perimeter of the Immerle estate. Twenty-five kilometers away, on the other side of the jungle-clad valley, Afrata shone like the sun, every building gleaming as if it contained a solar flare. He shrugged and jogged on toward the sports fields where his yeargroup should be waiting. They were due to play a soccer match against the Ansaru clan that afternoon. Personally, Dellian couldn't wait another eight months until they all reached their tenth birthday, when Alexandre had promised them that they could start training in the orbital arena. He just loved the idea of them flying around in zero gee, somersaulting in slowmo, bouncing off walls to soar like a bird . . .

A lokak screeched out its hunting cry. Dellian stopped again, scanning the fence. That had sounded very close.

"There's nothing there, you know."

He spun around to see Yirella standing behind him. But this Yirella was fully grown, easily twice his height, and she didn't have hair anymore. Even so, she was wearing a t-shirt and sports shorts, just like him. Yirella always did join the boys on the pitch to play their games, unlike Tilliana and Ellici. He gawped at her for a moment; somehow, this older Yirella was even more captivating than the one he knew . . . although he knew this one as well. *I don't understand.*

"Then what was that sound?" he asked, smug that he'd outsmarted her of all people.

"A memory." She went down on her knees, putting her big head level with his, and held both hands toward him. "Do you trust me, Del?"

Outside the fence, a whole chorus of lokak screeches began, rising in pitch and ferocity. He knew that meant they were gathering, ready to assault the estate at the bidding of the Neána. Always the Neána, the eternal enemy, tricksters and betrayers.

"Yes," Dellian said nervously, trying to look at her and not out at the tangled jungle beyond the fence.

"Good." She took his hands. Her fingers were cool and dry and immensely strong. Yirella's presence always made him content, but this time the physical touch was profound. It wasn't just his skin that was feeling her; the sensation of touch was sinking deep into his flesh, cooling and relaxing his muscles. He hadn't realized he was so tense.

"This is important, Del. None of this, what you're seeing—the estate, Juloss—none of it is real."

"What?" He turned his head a fraction.

"No. Look at me, Del. Keep looking."

Her eyes were wide with love and concern. The emotion was so strong that it was all he could do just to stop his eyes from watering. "I don't understand," he said miserably.

"There is one thing I know you do understand: I am here, Del. I am with you. And I will never leave you. Not ever, because I love you."

The world behind her was vibrating, as if he were shaking his head frantically. But he wasn't; no way could he shift his gaze from her beautiful eyes.

"This is like a game, Del. I want you to play it with me. Will you do that?"

"Yes," he whispered, scared now. The world was shaking so badly he didn't know why he couldn't feel it.

"There are bad things out there, but they're not the beasts we were always warned about. These bad things are like nightmare monsters, and they invade your head to fill it with really evil ideas. But I'm here with you now, so together we can fight them off."

"I don't want to fight. I want to go home."

"We are home, Del. That's why we're here in the estate. This is so *you*—the very start of you, so fundamental they can't corrupt it like everything else. You belong here."

"Yes."

"So we have to take away the abuse they're suffocating you in. Do you remember your yeargroup?"

"Yes."

"They're your squad now, aren't they?"

He closed his eyes briefly, seeing the laughing faces of his yeargroup, their features distorting as if they were reflecting off a buckled mirror, changing and aging. Except—

"Rello," he groaned as his friend's face blackened, cracks splitting open to ooze slimy blood before the vision shrank away to nothing.

"I know," Yirella said gently. "He's gone."

"We killed him. It's our fault. We're nothing more than prisoners. They chained us at birth."

"Nobody chained us, Dellian. We're free."

"No. It's the Saints. They did this to us, they took away our choice." He snarled. "I'm glad they're dead."

"What?"

He stared at her shocked face. "I'm glad," he told her truthfully. The world around them stopped shaking. A reassuring gray crept into the colors, toning down the harshness of the tropical landscape. The so-called Saints had been killed; he remembered seeing it so vividly. The Olyix had shared their memory of the time when the revered *Salvation of Life* had arrived back at the gateway star system. The *Avenging Heretic*, the Saints' stolen transport ship—which had stowed away on board the arkship for the whole voyage home—had made a sudden dash for freedom, shooting without warning at the harmless Olyix ships nearby. They had no choice but to regretfully return fire, just to protect themselves from such senseless aggression. It remained so vivid in his mind, exploding in nuclear violence, its radiance shimmering off the gateway's opalescent splendor. So painful, knowing how much he had been lied to—

"Damn it," Yirella snapped. "That memory route left you open. Sorry, my fault. Dellian, focus, please. Focus on me."

He smiled weakly at her as the grayness grew around them.

"I love you, Dellian. Do you remember that?"

"Of course I do."

They kissed as the grayness eclipsed the universe. And they fell—

—into the orbital arena. A place he adored—such a simple place, a padded cylinder seventy meters long with a diameter of a hundred. Above him, drifting through the air, were thirty hurdles: hazard-orange polyhedrons—as familiar as star formations in the night. Oh, the games they'd played in here. The fun; the wins and losses. And so early on he'd broken every rule to attack another boy who was going to hurt Yirella . . .

"Oh, yes," he exhaled. And when he looked at Yirella, she was sharing the thrill of all those memories that came swirling out of their shared youth.

Then she let go.

"No!" he exclaimed.

Still smiling, she fell away from him. The arena wall behind her attenuated, showing him Juloss far below. It was under attack. Thousands of big Olyix Resolution ships raced in toward it, glowing hazy amber as they cut through the upper atmosphere at terrific velocity. Mushroom clouds seethed upward from the surface as cities and estates were obliterated.

"No!" he yelled. "This is not what happened. The Olyix are our friends. They didn't do this."

"I've got the flagball," Yirella shouted back joyfully. "I'm going for the goal hoop."

Dellian squinted, seeing her in a protective bodysuit, grinning wildly as she clutched the flashing flagball. The opposing team's goal hoop hung in space, halfway toward the burning planet. The speed she was traveling at was frightening.

"Careful," he said.

She laughed delightedly, on course to score the winning goal.

He didn't see the number eight player streaking toward her. Except it wasn't the number eight anymore, it was an Olyix huntsphere accelerating hard, targeting systems aligning on Yirella's lanky body as she flew effortlessly toward the goal hoop.

"No!" Dellian cried. His armor suit powered him toward

the huntsphere. He struck it hard, knocking it off course. His talon-tipped gauntlets scrabbled against the shiny sphere, scoring long marks in the tough shell. Then it began to flex, with bulges pushing up—as if whatever it contained were trying to reach out and wrestle with him. He strengthened his hold, attempting to crush it in his arms. The sphere responded by softening against his chest, letting him merge inward. He would fit it perfectly, he knew.

Ahead of them, Juloss split open, revealing the end of the universe, where the silver remnants of stars formed elegant rivers of twilight and fell into the nothingness at the heart. Beside it, a golden light was shining, calling him onward.

Yirella landed on the surface of the huntsphere, legs apart, ebony skin alive with scarlet hieroglyphs. "This is going to hurt," she said sternly.

"What? Yi, don't—" Somehow Dellian was looking down on himself, the huntsphere, with Yirella balancing perfectly on him, reaching down. Her hand punctured the shell, and the pain was incredible. His scream made the dying universe tremble.

The damage she'd caused had opened up long cracks in the sphere. She tore at them, prying up jagged sections and sending them spinning off into the void. He began to struggle, writhing frantically to escape her merciless fingers.

"Trust me," she said. "Don't fight this, Del. I'm stripping out the neurovirus."

"What?" He was sobbing now, the pain was so intense, burning along every nerve to punish his quaking brain.

"I love you, Del, you know that. Nothing can take that out of you."

"Yes."

"Then say it!" she demanded.

"I love you."

Her hands ripped apart the last of the huntsphere shell to reveal his Olyix quint body.

"I can't be that," he wailed.

"I love you, Del. Forever. No matter where that takes us."

"Help me," he pleaded.

The end of the universe was curving around them, its

final fragments forming a fetid vortex that was pulling them down into the death of eternity and the golden god at its side—the one waiting for them. Yirella's hands sliced into the quint flesh.

Dellian felt fingers closing around his arm. She pulled. Quint flesh stretched like slippery rubber, clinging to him, merging to give him strength. Now he was struggling against it, the foreign thoughts of devotion to the God at the End of Time tearing free in agonizing ruptures.

"Yirella! Don't let go."

The universe rushed to extinction, the vortex walls spinning past in a lethal whirl of nightmares and demons.

"Please," he begged.

Yirella tugged hard, crying out wordlessly at the terrible exertion. Slowly, with stringy alien goop clutching at every centimeter of his skin, she pulled him out of the quint body. He came free with an excruciating tear. The extinct universe vanished.

Dellian juddered wildly. Bright light flared around him. Everything hurt—but nothing like as bad as it had mere instants before. He was waving his limbs around—proper *human* limbs—though they were wrapped in wires and fibers as if someone had scooped him up in a net. His short hair was on fire as something pulled every last follicle out of his scalp.

His flailing stopped as he ran out of strength, and he flopped down onto the bed. There was no air in his lungs, and his chest heaved desperately, trying to get a breath down his throat. The surroundings swam dizzyingly in and out of view. People in medical robes clustered around, worried faces peering down, talking incoherently fast. There was a curving glass wall three meters away, with the whole squad pressed up against it—mouths open to shout, eyes wet with tears. Janc was pounding on the glass; Uret had sunk to his knees. Tilliana was weeping.

"What the fuck?" The words were a rasp. He turned his head.

Yirella was on the couch next to his, propped up on her shoulders, her scalp invisible beneath a fur of silky white strands finer than any hair. Tears trickled down her cheeks as she stared at him.

"Del?"

"I love you," he said. Then the memories crashed back with the power of a tsunami, knocking him back down onto the mattress. "The Saints are dead," he told everyone and burst into tears.

LONDON

DECEMBER 8, 2206

The time icon flashed up in Ollie's tarsus lens: the image of an old Seiko wristwatch with hands that clicked around in combination with Tye, his altme, supplying a tiny *tick* of clockwork in his audio peripheral. Ancient watches were popular these days—not that anyone went short of power for an altme processor peripheral; they all worked off body heat. But still, it was an understandable fad given London's chronic shortage of electricity and how quirky solnet was nowadays. Trouble was, Ollie had spent his first twenty-four years immersed in purely digital displays, so analogue messed him up. It took him a second to work out that the way the hands were pointing meant it was six o'clock. Which was actually eighteen hundred hours, so it was officially evening. In the time before what every Londoner now called Blitz2, people would have known it was evening—the biggest clue being that the sun used to set every night. But now that clue was no more.

Presumably it still did set—not that Ollie trusted the government to tell anyone if the Olyix had stopped that from happening as well. When he glanced up at the London shield, all he saw was the devil-sky, same as it had been for the last two years: an eerie violet glare seething kilometers overhead. Sometimes, if he squinted against the intensity, he thought he could make out patterns writhing against the thick barrier of artificially solidified air protecting the city—milk-clouds in coffee, but sped up to hypersonic velocity.

The atmosphere outside was completely ruined now, decimated by the grotesque amount of energy the Olyix Deliverance ships were firing at thousands of city shields across the globe. They'd heated up the air to a point where ocean evaporation had reached a previously unknown peak. Climatologists on the remnant of solnet were talking about a "Venus-tipping-point," but all Ollie knew was that the air outside had degraded to a constant blast of hot fog. Plants simply couldn't survive the hostile temperatures and humidity. As for animals, they were dying in a catastrophe that surpassed the Pacific Rim firestorms back in 2056.

A few months ago, he and Lolo had traveled to the edge of the shield out at Epsom, just to see if it really was as bad as everyone said. There in the deserted suburbs, the overhead violet glare condensed into slender ribbons of lightning that crackled around the rim, allowing the foolhardy to glimpse what lay outside. They'd seen the Surrey hills through the short breaks in the turbulent mantle of smog. Lying beyond the vast dead marsh that now throttled London, silhouettes of the ragged slopes rose to a bleak hellscape of steaming ground matted with the slushy remnants of vegetation. Any evidence of human habitation—the ancient towns and elegant villages dating back to the time of mythical kings, the new carbon sink forests triumphantly planted throughout the twenty-second century—had all been vanquished in the backlash of the invaders' assault.

What they'd witnessed left him depressed, yes, but it was the guilt that had inflamed his anger and determination. *The Olyix have killed Earth, and I helped them. I didn't mean to. I didn't know.* But that made no difference to the shame.

He gave the devil-sky a last hateful glance and went back into the small industrial building that was now home—a fancy description for a brick-wall shed with a carbon-panel roof. They'd found it just off Bellenden Road, squeezed in between the nice houses of Holly Grove and the old railway line. He'd been reluctant to use it at first; the railway arches were too similar to the ones that his old gang, the Southwark Legion, had used. So not only were there painful memory triggers facing him every time he walked outside, there was also the danger of pattern recognition. He was still on Special Branch's most-wanted list, so their G8Turings would have profiled him. What if they'd decided he was emotionally weak, needing to cling to familiarity? They would have him reading those shabby, ivy-smothered brick arches as a psychological crutch.

Or . . . "You're so paranoid about the police," as Lolo told him every time he mentioned the possibility.

Ollie's rational brain knew sie was right. From what he could gain from his cautious and intermittent access to the remnants of solnet, he was still high up on the authorities' list of wanted suspects; they were never going to forgive and forget the Legion's involvement in the Croydon raid, nor the disaster that was Litchfield Road. Not that the Specials would mount surveillance along every stretch of London's disused railway arches just in case he was so pathetic he needed a familiar landscape for reassurance. Besides, even two years into Blitz2, the government was providing the city's residents with minimal support. Their whole effort was devoted to maintaining the shield and keeping the population fed. Everything else was secondary—or so they said. But Ollie wasn't so sure. The authorities had been *very* keen to find him.

Inside, the building's long main section was basic, naked brick walls with misted-over windows that allowed a weak glimmer of the shield's light to penetrate—a perfect setting for a small-scale industrial enterprise. The last one had been a bespoke ceramic crafts manufacturer that had shut down over a decade ago. But the kilns were still in place—five of them lined up along the middle of the floor, electricity-hungry brutes that fired artistically colorful glazes at temperatures well over a thousand degrees. Their doors were all shut tight, but Ollie smelled wood smoke in the dank air as he walked past them and muttered a curse.

He'd spent more than a month modifying the kilns, covering the internal firebricks with high-efficiency thermocouples to extract energy from anything burned inside. Any fire was now strictly illegal in London, as in all of Earth's cities that remained under siege from the Olyix. Fire was the one thing that unified every citizen these days, consuming the precious limited oxygen that people needed to breathe. See it—report it—and more often than not give the arsonist a good kicking before the police and firefighters arrived. Ollie could still remember the first time he'd seen a fire engine race past in the street: a magnificent ground vehicle out of history with lights blazing and siren screaming. He and Lolo had been mesmerized at its appearance, then cheered it on, waving at the crew like a pair of awestruck schoolkids. Dozens of the big machines had been brought out of museums and renovated since Blitz2 began.

So burning wood in the kilns was a precarious project that had to be well hidden from the neighbors. After fitting the thermocouples, Ollie had stripped the ancient air-conditioning ducts from the rafters and rerouted them. Fans sucked air through the kilns, maintaining a good flow over the logs they burned, before extracting it and sending it down into the old railway storm sewer where it could dissipate harmlessly among the fatbergs and rats.

On a bench at the end of the kilns, a one-hundred-twenty-centimeter model of the *Nightstar* starship shone a weird silver from the devil-sky light coming through the windows. Ollie had never even heard of the sci-fi show until a couple of months back, but Hong Kong had released a hundred interactive episodes back in 2130, sponsored by a fashion house that had long since vanished. Before Blitz2, he would have accessed solnet for every fact about it, but solnet was a bad idea these days for anything other than basic comms. Too much self-adaptive darkware was loose in the network, left over from the Olyix sabotage.

He'd heard about the model from a contact in the Rye Lane market not long after he'd started asking about collectibles. Adults paying ridiculous money for weird old trash fiction memorabilia was a whole genre he hadn't ever known existed until he'd discovered Karno Larson—his golden link to Nikolaj and vengeance.

He didn't even need to steal the model. Nobody paid anything for hobby stuff like that these days, so the owner had been happy to hand it over in exchange for a fully charged domestic quantum cell. Once Ollie got it home, in a trailer behind a bicycle he pedaled all the way back from Pimlico, he'd had to admit it was superb. *Nightstar* looked like it had been designed by an insect race tripping on heavy-duty nark, and this was a handcrafted one-off, which elevated it to a genuine piece of art. He half expected it to lift off and vanish into hyperspace with a blaze of twisted starlight.

"Time to go," Ollie called.

"I know," Lolo replied from the room at the far end; it had been the ceramic company's office and now served as their bedroom and living room. For Ollie it was a place to crash and have sex, but for Lolo it was their home, their honeymoon suite, their fortress castle sheltering them from the horrors of Blitz2. Which was why Ollie put up with the strips of white gauzy linen sie'd strung up around the bed and the little candles with mock flames that sprayed out a sweet musky scent to add to the romance, as well as rugs and pearl-and-jade trinkets and the antique black-lacquer furniture they'd acquired from a deserted house farther along the street.

Lolo came out and smiled broadly. Sie was dressed as if they were going out to dinner in one of London's restaurants from the time before. Given sie was in hir female cycle, sie'd chosen a purple-and-white flower-pattern dress with a plunging neckline. Hir face was expertly dusted with highlighter and rouge, with the devil-sky light shining on high-gloss cherry-red lipstick, hir hair in a peacock-blue Mohawk. Just looking at how gorgeous sie was, Ollie felt himself stiffening.

"You look grand," he said.

"Thank you."

A quick kiss accompanied by strong perfume, and a smiling Lolo was holding up a basket with a gingham cloth draped across it. "Let's go."

Ollie gave his fleshmask a quick check in the mirror. As faces went, it was okay. He wasn't happy with the rounded chin, nor the longer nose, and he still wasn't sure about having white skin, but the dimples were nice. And the fleshmask responded well when it came to showing his expressions, although the creams he'd been applying to his own skin did inhibit the subtler emotions. He was strict with himself about keeping the fleshmask on the whole time, avoiding G8Turings zeroing in on him with feature recognition. But that freedom came with the price of inflammation and dry skin and some horrific outbreaks of tinea. For Ollie, who had always taken superb care with his appearance in the time before, that was almost unbearable. Fortunately, moisturizer and other basic skin creams could solve the crises—for a price.

He performed a few exaggerated grimaces as a final test. "Good to go," he announced.

"I wish you didn't have to wear that thing all the time. You have a lovely face. I adore looking at you."

"I wish you didn't wear a bra all the time, but hey, those are the breaks."

"Turds! Don't you binaries ever think about anything else?"

Laughing, Ollie put his arm around hir, and they went outside together. Sunglasses on in unison. Ollie's were like ski goggles—hardly the kind of stylish image he wanted, but their thick rims didn't allow the light from the devil-sky around the edges. Even with the additional protection afforded by his tarsus lenses, too much direct exposure always left him with a migraine.

It wasn't far to Reedham Street, where the government nutrition agency had set up a public kitchen in the community center. Plenty of people were walking toward it. Ollie recognized most of them from the daily visit and nodded occasionally. Saying anything was pointless, thanks to the constant background buzz from the shield straining to hold back the perpetual energy bombardment from the Olyix ships as they attempted to overload the shield generators. Consequently, conversations these days tended to be up close and loud.

"I saw Mark today," Lolo said.

"Right," Ollie acknowledged as they passed the end of Chadwick Road. One of the big old plane trees halfway along had survived since the siege began, but in the last couple of months it too had succumbed to the absence of rain and the eternal devil-sky. Ollie was mildly sad to see it was finally shedding its yellowed leaves. "Who's Mark?"

"He's the one who always brings the mushrooms."

"Ah, okay."

"Anyway, his friend Sharon has a sister who works at the defense ministry. She said one of the seismologist techs told someone in her office that the Olyix aren't tunneling under the shield anymore. They're playing the long game now. Their ships are heading for the settled star systems, and when they get there they'll cut the power those planets are feeding back to Earth, and the interstellar portals will die. We won't have any food pellets for the printers, or electricity to run them. So they'll starve us out."

Ollie did his best not to sigh. For someone who had been educated in the supposedly excellent egalitarian school system of Delta Pavonis, Lolo could be fucking stupid at times. "That's a load of bollocks. You've got to stop living off gossip. What you just said is a paradox. I'm sure the Olyix are heading for the settled worlds, but if they cut the power that's coming to us from Delta Pavonis and New Washington and all the others, Earth's city shields will fail." His finger pointed up at the devil-sky. "And *that* mothermonster will come crashing down, just like it did last month in Berlin. We'll all die—which is exactly what they can't afford. Not after the effort they've put into beating us down."

"Berlin's shield fail didn't kill everyone." Lolo pouted. "Just the ones the storm hit when it burst down." Sie paused for a second. "And the ones who drowned when the river Spree flooded back in."

"Thankfully for everyone else, the Olyix flew in real fast and converted them into cocoons, so they got to live on, sort of," Ollie scoffed. "Lucky them. They get to see what the universe is like at the end of time."

"You can be such a downer."

"Most like, when the power does get cut from the settled worlds, the Olyix will just starve us out. We'll walk meekly into the arkship two million by two million."

"We wouldn't! People are better than that."

"Face it, if there's a choice between dying in a tsunami of ruined supercharged toxic atmosphere or taking your chance as a mutated freak cocoon that's on a trillion-year pilgrimage to meet an alien god, what do you do?"

"Well, I'm not going to give in. I'm going to make a stand."

That statement was a wide opening into a world of snark that Ollie wasn't prepared to enter. Not tonight. "And I'll be standing right there beside you."

Lolo gave him a happy hug.

The Bellenden Community Center was a civic hall built eighty years ago on the site of an old school. Its composite panels had been printed to resemble traditional London brick, though that had faded over the decades so they now looked like walls made of a kid's fraying building blocks. There was a constant stream of people walking through the entrance arch, most of them carrying bags full of cold dishes they'd printed out at home to accompany their hot meal. Nearly half of them were refugees who'd poured into the city when the Olyix started their invasion. Everybody who lived in the countryside or the ribbontowns had come, seeking safety under the shields, boosting the population toward eleven million. They were crammed into old deserted buildings, with few amenities. *Communal* was how most people lived these days. Ollie didn't mind; it allowed for plenty of anonymity.

The scent of cooking filled the air as they went up the community center steps. Inside, the main hall had been laid out like a makeshift café that no one had quite got around to regularizing, with a jumble of various tables and chairs taking up most of the floor, and long stainless steel canteen counters along one side. Rations were served from a hatchway that had two light-armored police standing on either side. You could either choose to have the rations cooked in the center or take them home. Most people ate in the hall, as electricity was scarce in this part of town. Who had enough kilowatts to heat food every day? Ollie queued up and held out his R-token for the woman inside the hatch. Registering for it had been surprisingly easy. Just after the siege started, he'd stolen Davis Mohan's identity—one of his old neighbors from Copeland Road. When he and Lolo had begun exploring the nearby houses, they'd found Davis lying on his kitchen floor in an advanced stage of cocooning, his body a barrel of modified organs, limbs almost gone, fading in and out of consciousness. For Ollie, a fake identity was a simple enough task—one he'd done dozens of times before while he was in the Southwark Legion. If anything, this was even easier. When rationing was introduced in those chaotic early days, solnet was reduced to a Dark Ages version of itself, and the checks were childish.

The woman behind the hatchway scanned his R-token and handed him a ribbon of pellet bags and a packet of assorted texture powders.

Lolo stepped up. "Any salmon powder?"

"Sorry, sweetie, not today. Got some blueberry powder if you want. It's quite good if you mix it with water and let it set in a mold. An ice cube tray is best."

"That's so lovely of you, thank you." Lolo pulled a small jar out from under the basket's gingham cloth. "Almond-flavored marshmallows. I've been experimenting. Let me know what you think."

They exchanged a smile. Ollie thought the ribbon of pellet bags she gave Lolo was a lot longer than the one he'd got. He shook his head in bemusement. "Is there anyone in here you don't flirt with?"

"I'm not flirting," sie exclaimed in an indignant tone. "I'm just nice and talk to people. It wouldn't hurt you to try it sometime. We're all in this together, you know."

"I talk to people. The ones I need to."

"Ooh, storm a-brewing. You're so hot when you do that moody Mr. Serious Voice."

"Oh, for fuck's sake."

"Mind your mouth, boyfriend. There are children in here."

They went and stood in line at the counter. At the first station, they handed over a couple of the pellet bags each. Ollie looked at the labels on the powders he'd been given and dropped the one for butter chicken on the counter.

"You'll smell of that all night," Lolo complained.

"Stop whinging. It won't smell or taste anything like butter chicken."

A couple of minutes later they'd made it down to the serving station. Lolo took a pair of plates out of the basket. Ollie watched with an impassive face as the bloke behind the counter ladled a pile of gingerish slop onto his plate. *It doesn't matter; this is just what you have to do so you can rescue Bik and Gran,* he told himself.

They sat down at one of the tables. Lolo made a show of taking the additional dishes sie'd prepared out of the basket, all peppy and cheerful as each one was announced. "I made some salad, look, and some naan bread—though to be honest, it's more like a pizza base. And some chocolate mousse for pudding." Sie produced a bottle with what Ollie really hoped was apple juice, because it looked too yellow for his liking. Besides, alcoholic drinks were banned from the community center.

"Thanks," he said.

"It's not easy, you know. I could do with some more electricity."

"Can't spare any. Sorry."

Lolo gave a martyred sigh. "Right."

"Look, I'm close, okay? Tonight should give me Larson."

"I don't want you to get hurt."

"I cause the hurt, remember?"

"Ollie, please—"

"Don't worry, I'm careful. You know it." Ollie picked up one of the leaves from the salad dish. That was a mistake. It was basically a thin green biscuit that tasted like what he imagined raw seaweed would when it grew next to a sewer outlet.

The tables around them started to fill up, and with it the volume of conversation rose. Kids started to run around, and older people were helped to tables by younger relatives. Several Civic Health Agency nurses worked their way along the hall, checking up on their patients, asking families if the youngsters were okay.

One couple was carrying a newborn, which Ollie frowned at. "How could they do that? How could they have a kid in this place?"

"Gedd and Lillie-D? They're sweet people, and their baby's a real cutie. I've cuddled him a few times."

"Why? I mean, don't they understand what's happening? Our two chances of getting out of Blitz2 are none and fuck all. How could they bring a kid into this world?"

"Because we can't afford to give up hope. Just look at

him; he's so adorable. We need babies to remind us why we're alive."

"That's not hope, that's being stupid and selfish." Shaking his head, he bit into another salad leaf and tried not to pull a face.

"Evening, guys, how's it going?"

Ollie looked up to find Horatio Seymore standing at the end of the table. The senior manager helped run a half dozen district food operations in this part of London. He'd been some kind of hotshot with the Benjamin charity in the time before. Ollie had even encountered him a few times when social agency outreach workers had tried to get Bik and his parkour équipe to come along to a youth gym. Then one other time: an unnerving not-quite-encounter along the Thames just after the last of Ollie's Legion friends had been killed.

Which made Horatio someone who actually knew Ollie's real face. Every time he turned up at the Bellenden Community Center, with his neutral smile and non-judgmental attitude, Ollie's nerves kicked in. He knew that was stupid. The fleshmask was flawless. But still . . .

"We're good, thanks," Lolo said. "Would you like some lemon squash?"

"It's lemon?" Ollie blurted.

"Ignore my friend, he's such a philistine."

Horatio's smile became more genuine. "No thanks. So you're all right? Got something to do in the day?"

"We trade," Lolo said. "We do all right."

"Nothing too illegal, I hope?"

"Absolutely not. I'm into food textures. If you've got some watts left in a quantum battery, that's my payment; I can work you up most flavors. Vegetables are a speciality— no offense to the people in here, of course."

"Of course," Horatio said. "Glad to hear it. But if you do ever need help, you can always call on me. I'm not official, not part of the council or police, okay?"

"That's very kind," Lolo said. "We need more people like you."

Horatio nodded affably and moved on to the next table.

Ollie spooned up some more of the not-butter-chicken goop. "I don't like him."

"He's a good man," Lolo protested. "You're just horribly biased against authority. Not everyone in government is automatically a corrupt fascist, you know. And anyway, you heard him—he's not actually officialdom."

"Then what's he doing here?"

"Helping people." Lolo gestured around exuberantly. "Without people like him, people who care about others, where would we be?"

"Breaking through the barriers the bastard Zangaris have built across the interstellar portals and getting offworld to where we'd be safe."

"Nowhere in the galaxy is safe from the Olyix."

"The exodus habitats will be. Not that we'll ever make it there."

"We will," Lolo insisted. "Once you find Larson, we'll have ourselves some real trading power."

"Oh, so *now* you want me to go after him?"

"Don't be such a trash king. I love you, Ollie. I've literally given you my life because I believe in you."

Which wasn't a responsibility Ollie had wanted at all. But he had to admit, for all hir stupid opinions and neurotic nerves and fragile mien, Lolo made this purgatory just about bearable. "I'll find him. Don't worry. I'm real close now."

A couple of hours after the evening meal, Ollie pedaled up the north end of Rye Lane. The east side was taken up with a big old shopping center that had been derelict for thirty years. Behind its boarded-up façade, it had been decaying sluggishly, attracting layers of gloffiti and moss while developers negotiated with the local council and the mayor's office about turning the big site into luxury apartments. Since the siege started and solnet commerce failed, traders had found their own use for it. Stalls had set up in the old shops—some no more than an overoptimistic kid sitting on a chair hawking a box of scavenged junk, while the more realistic merchants had metal-meshed kiosks and some tough fellas on either side to protect the commodities. By now Ollie had good relationships with several of them. He wheeled the bike up to Rebecca The-L, who was in her usual Gothic black lace dress, with druid-purple dreadlocks hanging down to her waist.

"Davis," she drawled, "looking gooood."

"Not so trash yourself."

"You bring me some wholesome K's?"

"Very wholesome." Ollie took three quantum batteries out of the bike's panniers.

Rebecca The-L's nark-drifter smile lifted as she took them from him and slipped the first into a charge port on the kiosk. She let out a soft whistle of appreciation as she quickly read how many kilowatts he'd brought. "Impressive. Have you got a cable direct to Delta Pavonis?"

"Something like that. So are we in business?"

"Davis, I appreciate quality, and you never fail me."

"You have them?"

She gestured to one of her tough fellas. He produced a small aluminum case from inside the kiosk and gave Ollie a disapproving look.

"Go ahead," Rebecca The-L said as her dreamy composure returned.

Ollie slipped the catches and opened the lid a crack. Inside, two synth slugs the size of his little finger rested in protective foam, their dark skin glistening as if dusted with a sprinkling of tiny stars. Designed in some black lab using eight-letter DNA to craft unnatural components into their basic body, they had a bioprocessor cluster instead of a natural slug's nerve cells. He told Tye, his altme, to ping them. Data splashed into his tarsus lens, confirming their functionality. "Be seeing you," he told her.

"You don't look dangerous, Davis. You have a pleasant face, guile-free. But it's your eyes that give you away. When I look into them, I see only a depth that comes from darkness."

"Er, right. Catch you later." Ollie could feel Rebecca watching him as he wheeled his bike away. It took plenty of self-control not to look back.

The next kiosk belonged to Angus Ti, who claimed he traded whatever you wanted but didn't have the kind of connections Rebecca The-L had. Ollie offered him a couple of quantum batteries he'd charged up from the kilns. "I don't know where you keep getting electricity from," Angus said, "but this makes you my most valuable supplier."

"Happy to help. Now what are you offering?"

After a relatively good-natured haggle, he wound up with nine tubs of food pellets and a jumble of texture powders, plus a bag full of empty quantum batteries. "I get first refusal when they're full," Angus said as he passed them over. "You know I give the best deals around."

"Sure thing." Ollie held his hand out. "So . . ."

Angus handed over the main event—a packet of zero-nark pads.

"More like it." Ollie hadn't used nark since the siege began, but Lolo hadn't stopped. Sie had made an effort to cut down, but hir dependency was starting to worry Ollie. "Hey, can you throw in some duct tape, too?"

Angus gave him a calculating look, then produced a half roll from under the counter. "You want anything else? My shoes? My girlfriend to bang?"

Laughing, Ollie grabbed the roll. "Tape's fine. Be seeing you."

"Sure. What you want that for, anyway?"

"Thought maybe I'd see if I'm into bondage."

"You take that shit easy, kid. People can get hurt."

"Thanks." Ollie turned away from the kiosk. "Voice of experience." He could guess the hand gesture Angus was making behind his back.

It took Ollie nearly an hour to cycle from Rye Lane up to Dulwich; these days the clear path was anything but. Two years on and still nobody had moved the broken taxez and cabez and bagez that cluttered the concrete, and now it was getting worse as people started tipping their rubbish wherever they felt like. And of course most of his route seemed to be uphill, leaving him sweating heavily, which was going to play hell on his face again. He'd never even thought about Connexion's London metrohub network in any of the time before; it just *was*. Now, distance had become achingly real again—a handicap of effort, sweat, and time. As he pedaled away with straining legs, all he could think about was stepping onto his old boardez and rolling along effortlessly one last time. It wasn't like he didn't have the electricity to power it up again, but that kind of profligacy would draw way too much attention.

He reached the end of Lordship Lane and turned west onto the A205. The road cut through sports pitches that were now just desert-dry soil as hard as stone, enclosed by prickly dead hedges. But the goalposts were still standing, their scabbed white paint gleaming oddly under the radiant devil-sky.

Past the playing fields, the hedges changed to high brick walls, guarding big houses. Ollie stopped pedaling and free-wheeled along slowly until he came to a nouveau-riche three-story cylindrical house, complete with mock-Tudor façade, that belonged to one Brandon Schumder. The gates at the end of a short gravel drive were tall, topped with spikes that weren't entirely ornamental. He didn't expect them to be a problem. In fact, he felt a rush of satisfaction that he'd finally arrived here.

Without solnet, it had taken two years of dealing in markets, building contacts, paying in kilowatt hours or nark, and trading his own information, all with one goal: finding Nikolaj. Ollie still didn't have her, but he knew for certain now that Nikolaj and Jade worked for the Paynor family, one of the major crime families operating out of North London. That just left him with trying to find a way to reach the Paynors. They were a tight bunch—and even tighter nowadays. But that was what he was good at: planning. It was like his superpower, one of the main reasons the Southwark Legion had never been caught. He just needed an angle no one would expect.

More quiet questions, and he had heard the name Karno Larson, who among other things had acted as the Paynor family's money man in the time before, laundering illegal wattdollars clean and loading them into the legitimate banking system. There was plenty of cheap talk about Karno, but solid details—like his location—were hard to find. A couple of small-timers suggested Brandon Schumder might know.

Ollie stared at the gates from the other side of the clear path and raised his arm, running a scan. He'd salvaged several systems from the old stealth suit he used to wear on raids with the Legion. There was no point putting it on now; not even its hazy gray fabric could conceal him under the insistent light of the devil-sky. So, in a marathon whinge session, Lolo had hand-stitched some of its systems into his leather biker's jacket, along with a layer of armor fabric.

Tye splashed the results, showing zero power in the gates—and specifically the lock. So not even Brandon Schumder had the wealth for that kind of wattage these days. Ollie's tarsus lens zoomed in, revealing a slim chain holding the two gates together, with a padlock dangling down, its shiny brass casing almost a shout for attention.

"Too easy," he muttered suspiciously. But no, a scan of the house's curving wall revealed no active electrical circuits. A sign of the times. Before Blitz2, only the seriously wealthy could've afforded this house, but material things weren't a measure of wealth anymore. Therefore personal security wasn't currently high on anyone's priority list.

Ollie fingered his insurance collar—a black band with a lace trim that fitted so perfectly around his neck that it could have been a tattoo. A silly nervous gesture; its icon was a solid unchanging splash in his tarsus lens. But given who he was going up against, checking wasn't paranoia. If Nikolaj was as good as everyone said, she might have heard he was asking questions.

He went over to the gates and pressed a small ball of thermon onto the padlock's hoop. There was an amber flare, and the metal melted away. The sensor splash showed him there was no one on the road or lurking behind the desiccated bushes. Technically, it was nighttime. Hard to judge, but with the sun below the horizon, the purple gleam from above was maybe slightly dimmer. He could see a couple of lights on in the house, shining out of second-floor windows.

He shut the gate behind him and walked up to the front door. Not a long walk, but the sensation it gave him let loose a whole slew of bittersweet memories. He'd always had the Legion to back him up when they went on raids or burglaries. Now it was their phantom faces that accompanied him down the drive. Tye splashed data about the house's network. Signal strength was low, but it provided connectivity with the remnants of solnet. Ollie launched a darkware package into the node.

The front door was another faux Tudor monstrosity—all bulky panels with iron bolts driven through them. He took a strip of charge tape out of the cycle's pannier, ready to apply it to the lock, when Tye reported the darkware had gained full control over the house network. Ollie drew his nerve-block pistol and ordered the front door to unlock. A soft click confirmed it had obeyed, and he kicked it open. Bursting in like some goon out of a Sumiko interactive pumped up his exhilaration. Nothing like the buzz he used to get on Legion raids, but still his confidence and focus were high.

The wood-paneled hall was dark and long, ending in a broad, curving staircase. "Hey, motherfucker," he bellowed. "Come out. Now! I wanna talk to you."

Tye told him someone's altme was connecting to a house network node upstairs, requesting an emergency link to the police G8Turing. "Response insertion," he ordered his altme. The icons changed, confirming he was the only response Schumder was going to get.

"Dick move, Brandon Schumder," he said. "Even if you'd got through to the cops, my dark-ops team inside your house right now could slaughter any tactical squad before they reached the front door. Now get your arse downstairs like a good boy, or there will be consequences." The phantom faces escorting him smiled their approval as he imagined Schumder's reaction to his panicked call for help.

"Don't shoot," a voice called from upstairs. "Please, we're not armed."

Brandon Schumder shuffled into view at the top of the stairs. He was taller than Lolo, and so thin Ollie thought he might be ill. But then Mensi, his wife, was standing behind him, and she was almost as tall and equally thin. Ollie never could get over the way rich people lived. Cosmetics and anti-aging procedures, sure—who wouldn't if you had the money?—but shit like this was just creepy.

"Get down here," he ordered.

"Yes, yes," Schumder said anxiously. He put a foot on the

first step as if he expected it to electrocute him. "Take anything you want. Anything. We'll open the safe for you."

"Keep coming."

Schumder was four steps from the bottom when Ollie shot Mensi with the nerve-block pistol. She juddered helplessly, a forced gagging sound coming from her throat, and started to collapse.

"No!" Schumder cried, and struggled to catch her. He made it to the hall floor, the two of them going down in a tangle as Mensi's weight drove him to his knees. Ollie shot him, too.

Five minutes later, he'd used the duct tape to secure Mensi to a heavy dining room chair, while Brandon was taped spread-eagled on the table. Ollie had run out of duct tape before the last leg was secured, so he had to cut off a curtain cord and use that. He waited until the nerve block had faded and they'd started to recover. Mensi began a miserable wailing until he went and stood in front of her, pressing the pistol to her temple.

"This is a nerve blocker. It's meant to incapacitate your body if I shoot you from a distance," he explained. "If I fire it now, at zero range, I might just as well be dropping your brain into a food blender. It will turn you into a zombie, and not the good kind. So be quiet. Understand?"

She gave him a petrified look, the tears streaming down her face. But she clenched her jaw tightly shut.

Ollie went back to the table and looked down at Brandon.

"You don't have to do this," Brandon said. "I told you to take anything you want. Just please don't hurt us."

"Okay," Ollie said. "You sound like a reasonable man. We both want to get this over as quickly as possible, with minimal pain, so this should be easy. You know, if my friend Lars was here, he'd enjoy beating seven types of crap out of you."

Brandon tensed up, a whimper escaping from his lips.

"But Lars is dead."

"I'm sorry."

"Why?" Ollie taunted. "You didn't know him. Or did you?"

"I don't think so. No."

"No. But I'm trying to find the person I hold responsible,

THE SAINTS OF SALVATION   29

so you'll understand why I'm anxious to get the right information."

"Yes."

"You're in banking, right? To be exact, the Reindal Commerzebank?"

"Yes."

"Good, then I've got the right person." Ollie leaned over, putting his face centimeters from Brandon's. "Where does Karno Larson live?"

"Who?"

"Oh, shit. Wrong answer."

"But I don't know—"

Ollie stuffed a napkin into Brandon's mouth, forcing a lot of the linen down. Brandon strained against it, making muffled gasps.

"Remember," Ollie told Mensi. "One word from you and—" He made a pistol with two fingers and shot her with it.

She whimpered in terror.

This was the part Ollie had kept telling himself—*promising* himself—he could do.

Right from the start he'd known that Brandon would be difficult. This was the kind of man who would've been given security counter-training by the bank, and there'd be fear, too—fear of giving up Karno, and what would happen to him if he did. Making him talk needed a whole new approach—and attitude. Ollie had never done that before.

The Legion had concentrated on scams and raids. No one had got hurt—well, apart from the ones Lars had beaten to a pulp. But even Lars didn't do this kind of thing. Tronde could have done it without hesitation, him with that unnervingly cold streak, and maybe Piotr, too. But they were dead, so it was all down to Ollie.

He put the case he'd got from Rebecca The-L on the table next to Brandon and opened the lid. Brandon stopped moaning and tried to get a look at what was inside. Ollie slipped on the protective gloves and picked up the first synth slug. Its strange grainy coating sparkled in the weak light filtering through the windows.

"Do you know what this is?" Ollie asked.

Brandon shook his head, his muted voice trying to protest.

"It's a synth slug." Ollie held it up as if seeing it for the first time. "And that sparkle is the artificial diamond bristles it grows, the same as we grow hair. You know what they say about diamonds, apart from being a girl's best friend? The hardest natural substance there is. Cuts through anything. Really. *Cuts*."

Brandon froze, his chest heaving as he tried to yell in protest.

"The slug doesn't have a brain," Ollie said, "but it does have a bioprocessor cluster which allows me to control it." He pressed it against the sole of Brandon's foot.

This was it—the point where he'd either chicken out, or . . . He closed his eyes. Instead of Tye's splash in his tarsus lens, all he could see were two cocoons: his brother Bik, and Gran.

For a long moment he stood perfectly still. Then he activated the synth slug's control icon. It started to wriggle against Brandon's foot. The tiny diamond fibers gnawed through the skin, and blood began to seep out. Brandon was desperately trying to scream, the cords on his neck standing proud as he struggled against the tape holding him down.

Ollie took out the second synth slug and pressed it to Brandon's other foot. It squirmed about, chewing its way into the flesh.

"The best thing about them is they can grind their way up through you very precisely," Ollie explained to a frantic, tormented Brandon. "To start with, I'll get them to stay inside the bone, munching their way up the marrow. After all, I don't want them to cut an artery or something critical; that way you'd bleed out and die before you told me what I want to know. And I really want to know where Karno Larson lives. But you're a big, strong, determined bloke, aintcha? Not some pussy who'll squeal and give it up. So it's going to take a while. After they've chewed all the leg marrow into soup, I'll steer them into your rib cage. Don't worry; I'll keep them out of your spine. Gotta leave all those nerves intact so you can feel what's happening, yeah?"

On the table, Brandon looked like he was having a heart

attack, writhing around so badly the tape was cutting into his wrists. Ollie ordered the slugs to pause. They were barely a centimeter inside Brandon's feet, with blood and pulverized bone running out of the holes they'd gouged. He leaned over, staring down at his captive.

"Did you wanna say something?"

Brandon was shouting so hard he even managed to dislodge the napkin slightly.

Ollie put his finger to his lips. "Before I take the napkin out, I'm going to repeat the question: Where does Karno Larson live? If you say anything other than that—if you start swearing or threatening me—I won't let you speak again until the slugs have reached your hip bones via your balls. Understand?"

A near-hysterical Brandon nodded feverishly.

So slowly it was a taunt, Ollie pulled the napkin out of Brandon's mouth.

"Docklands!" Brandon yelled. "Karno's in Docklands. Royal Victoria Docks, the Icona apartment block. Third floor. I promise! He never leaves anymore, not since Blitz2 started. He'll be there."

"Cheers, fella," Ollie said, and stuffed the napkin back in. He retrieved the synth slugs and dropped them back in the case. He grinned cheerfully at a weeping Mensi and walked out through the front door. He managed to take five steps along the drive before he doubled over and threw up onto the gravel.

DELTA PAVONIS

DECEMBER 9, 2206

Eight AUs beyond the star's outer cometary belt, the rim of the circular portal glowed a rich cobalt blue as it expanded out to fifty meters in diameter. An Olyix midlevel transport ship flew out of the opening—a truncated cone sixty meters long and thirty wide, its fuselage a dark burgundy color that absorbed what little light there was. Thin purple ion plumes gusted out of gill-like vents near the rear, and it began to accelerate at a steady one point three gees.

"Gravitonic drive at seventy percent," Jessika Mye announced cheerfully.

Sitting opposite her in the pearl-gray virtual chamber that was the *Avenging Heretic*'s bridge, Callum saw her lips twitch in amusement. He wondered just how much of that was real. The nervecapture routine could be adjusted for reaction sensitivity, either toning down or emphasizing every expression and tic his emotional state produced. Like Alik and Yuri, Callum couldn't be arsed with it; faffing about with crap like that was just a higher resolution version of choosing an expresme icon for solnet comms. He'd stopped doing that when he was fifteen.

Same with the bridge, which was as basic as you could get. Five consoles with wraparound screens, and flight controls so simple they could have come from the late twentieth century. They didn't exist, of course; this virtual was being fed into his brain via a cortical interface. Soćko had designed it for them, warning it was dangerous. If the Olyix ever gained access to the *Avenging Heretic*'s network, the onemind could subvert their minds with a neurovirus.

"So we'd better not get caught," Alik had replied levelly at the planning meeting; that had been eighteen months ago.

Callum watched the data on his console screen, the colorful wave motions of graphs and icons similar to a tarsus lens splash. When he focused on them, the rest of the bridge drifted away, leaving him at the center of pure information. Space this far out from Delta Pavonis was relatively clear, confirmed by the minimal impacts against the protective distortion field around the ship. Mass sensors confirmed there was nothing other than hydrogen atoms and a few grains of carbon within a thousand kilometers of the hull. Power flow from the fusion generators into the systems seemed to be okay, and the network was glitch free.

"Who's first?" Jessika asked.

The information fell back into the console screen, and Callum was looking around at the other four chairs. They were laid out in a simple pentagon, with Kandara on his right, then Jessika, Alik, and Yuri. All of them had spent the last year training for the flight, trying to get their heads around the gravitonic drive and wormhole theory. Their collective age didn't help; new concepts didn't sit well in old brain cells. But slowly they'd come to control the simulations without screwing up too badly.

"I'll go," Callum said.

Alik laughed. "You owe me fifty," he told Yuri.

Yuri looked glum.

"What?" Callum asked.

"Mr. Save-the-world-twice-before-lunch," Alik gloated. "Of course you'd want to fly this fucker. Feel the glory again."

"Hey, I was in Emergency Detox for eight years, a century ago. I gave up my adrenaline junkie days when I left. I want to get this right because we have to. And I didn't hear you two pussies racing to volunteer."

Kandara rolled her eyes. "Boys, boys."

Callum didn't think her nervecapture routine was turned up, either.

"Take it, Callum," Jessika said. She and Kandara exchanged a smirk.

The control columns on Callum's console went active. He placed his hands on them. It was a strange feeling. He wasn't holding the ergonomic handles, which was the vision being fed into his mind. Instead his nerves sensed patterns like slow-moving currents of water. The screen's information closed in on him again, and he shifted the patterns, perceiving the gravitonic drive's energies reformatting. The *Avenging Heretic*'s vector altered. Navigational data expanded, and he started plotting a new course, shifting a shoal of cursors by thought alone. *Is my visual focus doing that?*

Reassigning his perception and responses to integrate with the ship's network was still a work in progress. Jessika had said that eventually they wouldn't even need the bridge simulacrum; control would be an autonomic thought. Callum considered she might have been a bit generous in her assessment of how adaptive they were.

The variable portal they'd come through was now three thousand kilometers behind them. Eighteen thousand kilometers away, a dark rubble pile asteroid was tumbling along its lonely orbit. Acceleration vectors materialized in the navigation data, and Callum began to shape the drive patterns to match them, putting the ship on a course that would end in a rendezvous.

"Nicely done," Yuri said.

The *Avenging Heretic* accelerated up to two point two gees. There were some fluctuations in the thrust, which Callum did his best to get under control. His manipulation of the patterns wasn't as proficient as he'd like.

"Don't overcompensate," Jessika said. "Keep the alterations smaller and smoother. The routines are adaptive; they'll learn your style."

Callum did his best to squash an instinctive defensiveness; she was advising, not criticizing. The oscillations in the drive leveled out.

They took it in turns to fly the *Avenging Heretic*: Yuri decelerating for rendezvous; Kandara maneuvering around the frozen asteroid; Alik taking them back to the portal. Callum felt Alik had a way to go before he was as proficient as the others but didn't say anything.

Jessika brought them back through the portal and onto the cradle in Kruse Station. Atmosphere began to vent back into the big chamber.

Callum looked around the bridge, and suddenly the effort of de-tanking was depressing. "We could just stay here until the next test flight."

"No way," Kandara said. "We're going to be spending a long time in these tanks. And I, for one, am not adding to that." Her image imploded in a silent cloud of pixels.

"The design crew needs to run analysis on the tanks," Jessika said. "This is the first time they've been used on an actual flight. Simulation runs can only tell us so much." She shrugged and vanished.

Yuri's grin was so wide he had to have his nervecapture routine turned up to eleven.

"Disengage the suspension tank," Callum told Apollo, his altme. The neural interface routines were now good enough to read his vocalization impulses directly. Besides, he couldn't use his voice peripheral—not with an oxygen nozzle filling his mouth.

Feeling seeped back into his brain, along with the thick, gurgling sound of fluid draining out of the suspension tank. The frame holding him juddered slightly, and then there was a solid floor under his feet. A long strip of green and amber medical icons splashed across his tarsus lens, and he blinked his eyes open.

Directly ahead of him was the curving glass wall of the tank, smeared in clear fluid. With full body sensation returned, he could feel the droplets all over his skin and sneezed them out of his nose. The tube in his mouth wriggled outward, creating a moment of panic. *Serpent down my throat.* He started to gag as the end pulled free of his lips, dripping goo around his feet. More icons flashed and turned green. Umbilicals disconnected from his navel sockets with popping sounds. The metallic tubes coiled away into the top of the tank. Then he was trying not to grimace as the waste pipes withdrew.

Final icon warning, and he braced his feet. The frame released him, and the glass wall parted to let him out. He was standing on a metal grid in the *Avenging Heretic*'s central chamber—a cylinder twenty meters high, divided into three sections by the grid floors. The ship had been heavily modified from its Olyix design and refitted with five suspension chambers. Human equipment and materials had supplanted the original walls, producing a metallic tube cluttered with blank system cabinets that made Callum think of a twentieth-century submarine. The emphasis was on function rather than the élan of twenty-third-century design, while the disturbingly coffin-like tanks seemed to have been resurrected from the period of history occupied by the Inquisition.

"You were in a hurry to get out of there," Callum said to Kandara as they waited for Alik and Yuri to climb down the ladder to the lower deck.

"And you're okay in that white bubble?" she asked curiously.

"Sure."

"I'm not. We need to refine it. A lot."

"It does its job."

"Callum, we're going to be spending years together in the bridge simulacrum. I need to not get spooked every time."

"We can add some texture. Like you say, we'll have plenty of time to try out new designs."

"And the smell?"

"What smell?"

"Exactly, there isn't one. Or hadn't you noticed?"

"I . . . No," he admitted.

"Well, that's one nerve impulse the interface hasn't mastered." She glanced down the ladder as Jessika followed Alik below. "I wonder if the Neána forgot to build a sense of smell into their metahuman bodies?"

"I doubt it. I remember Jessika being quite the wine connoisseur when we were working on security after the Cancer operation."

Kandara's eyebrows rose gleefully. "You two dated?"

"No! Strictly work social events. Two teams getting properly acquainted."

"Okaaaay . . ."

"Hey—"

But she was gone, sliding down the ladder with a grace he could never match.

The lower deck housed the gym, the G8Turing medical bay, and the common washroom. Standing in the shower, Callum checked the umbilical sockets clustered around his navel, where the skin was still red and tender. He'd have to mention that to the medical team. The implants should have healed fully by now.

Like the others, he'd spent the last ten months in and out of the station's clinic having extensive body modifications to prepare him for the mission. His stomach was new: a biologic organ grown in a Neána-style initiator, allowing him to digest a direct nutrient feed from the suspension-tank systems. Then his bones had all been reinforced with high-density fibers at the same time as his internal membranes had undergone gene therapy to strengthen them—all with the goal of making him more resilient to high acceleration forces. After an organ audit, the doctors had gone on to announce they were going to grow him new kidneys, a prostate, and a left eye, and would replace a meter of lower intestine—"just to be safe. You're going to undergo some unique physiological stresses a long way from any medical help."

Hearing that news was as depressing as the memory of all the time he'd spent convalescing after the first tranche of procedures. He'd always kept himself in good shape. But he did get some malicious satisfaction from knowing that Yuri had even more replacements scheduled—starting with his liver, which was only twenty years old anyway. The doctors kept on telling him to stop drinking, which Yuri kept on ignoring. And then there was poor old Alik, who'd had to give up his peripherals. "They won't do well in the tank," Jessika told him sternly. So he sulked off to DC for a week to some classified government clinic to have his even more classified spy gizmos extracted.

Kandara, to no one's surprise, needed the least remedial work. However, like Alik, she had to have a small armory's worth of weapon peripherals removed. "It's like being naked on my high school prom dance floor," she confessed at dinner after the technicians had finished taking them out.

Callum had nearly made a smartarse comment, but decided cowardice was the best option. Besides, Jessika had later confided that Kandara had some initiator-made peripherals put back in—and told him not to tell Alik.

Lankin came in as they were all getting dressed. The Connexion science director had been appointed as the *Avenging Heretic*'s mission controller, marrying the technological requirements with the mission objective. Callum was glad someone with that level of experience and ability was overseeing the flight. Although he was only in his fifties, Lankin was damn good at his job.

"You're all needed at a full Council meeting," Lankin told them.

"When?" Alik asked.

"As soon as you're dressed."

Callum exchanged a glance with Yuri. That Lankin had come in person to tell them was significant.

"Was something going critical before we left?" Kandara asked.

"If it was, I didn't know," Alik said gruffly.

There was no formal title, nothing in any legitimate record; they were just known as the Council. Officially they advised the Sol Senate security office, who implemented any policy or action. In reality, they'd been tasked with formulating the plan to strike back against the Olyix, no matter what the cost and how long it took.

The Kruse Station conference room was windowless, as if to emphasize its ultra-secure location somewhere in the Delta Pavonis system. A large table carved from dark-red rock took up the center, with a vase of white and orange chrysanthemums sitting on its polished surface.

Callum smelled the flowers as soon as he came in and glanced over at Kandara, who was laughing at something Alik said. Now that she'd mentioned the lack of a smell in the interface simulation, he knew he was doomed to notice it constantly.

Ainsley Zangari III was already sitting on one of the leather chairs, along with his sister, Danuta. It had been a while since Ainsley Zangari himself had attended a meeting of the Council. Kruse Station rumor had it that the founder of Connexion was undergoing a lot of therapy to help him cope with the fact that his decades-old paranoia about the Olyix had finally become real.

"How's your grandfather?" Alik asked politely.

"He's managing, thank you," Ainsley III said.

Callum nodded sagely. *Managing. No mention of recovering.* He sat down at the table, greeting his aide, Eldlund, who was sitting next to Loi in the corner of the room.

"How did it go?" Eldlund asked keenly.

"I got to fly it," Callum said modestly.

"Wow!"

"I'm not the greatest pilot, but the G8Turing handles the flight specifics. It's more like giving directions."

"And the cortical interface?"

"Good, but interpretation could be better. We just need time to get used to the system."

Eldlund and Loi exchanged a glance.

"What?" Callum asked.

"Time has never been our ally," Loi said.

Callum was going to ask his aide what he'd heard when Emilja Jurich and Adjutant-General Johnstone came in together. They sat down without ceremony. Last to arrive was Soćko, accompanied by Captain Tral, who as always was wearing hir gray uniform.

"Let's get started," Emilja said. "Soćko?"

"There is a squadron of dangerous ships flying down the wormhole to the Sol system," the human Neána said. "I sensed it in the *Salvation of Life* onemind three hours ago, as soon as a transport ship arrived from the enclave with the information. The onemind seems very confident."

"You mean these new ships are going to be more dangerous than the Deliverance ships?" Alik said. "Are they the Resolution ships you're always warning us about?"

"No. These are not Resolution ships."

"So what sort of ships are we talking about?" Ainsley III asked.

"A new type. I don't have a classification for them, as the Neána have not been aware of them before, but I did see their purpose in the onemind's thoughts. They're carrying some kind of gravitonic generator. I'm not sure how it works, but presumably it's a variant on the gravitonic drive. However, the intent was very clear in the onemind's thoughts: The enclave had provided them specifically to wreck the city generators."

"How can a gravity drive wreck the generators?" Danuta asked.

"If they can focus the gravity, make a coherent beam of it, which is what I think they're doing, they'll pull the shield generator away from the ground. Literally rip it free and suck it up into the air."

"Hellfire, how sure are you?" Emilja asked.

Soćko gave her a regretful shrug. "I can't give you percentages. Reading the onemind's thought streams is like standing in a waterfall and trying to make out individual droplets. If I put my hand out to catch one, it disturbs the flow and they'll know I'm there. But there are some droplets—the important ones, the ones it keeps focusing on—that repeat constantly. It has been reviewing the information and capabilities ever since the transport ship arrived. I think the Olyix must have made them specifically to end the siege."

"How long until they arrive?" Johnstone asked.

"Ten days."

"Fuck," Callum grunted.

"What the hell do we do now?" Ainsley III demanded.

"Bring S-Day forward," Johnstone said. "Nothing else we can do."

Emilja gave him a startled look. "Are we ready for Strikeback?"

"No. It's scheduled for six months' time: June of next year. But we still won't be ready then—or not ready in a sense that I can guarantee success. Right now we have built up sufficient attack ships and Calmissiles to hit the *Salvation of Life* hard enough to force it back down the wormhole. What we don't have yet is the ability to hit the current crop of city siege ships as well."

"Do we need to?" Ainsley III asked.

"It's part of the plan," Yuri said reasonably.

"Not really," Danuta countered. "It's a hugely desirable part of the plan, sure, but the core is to get you inside the Olyix enclave. Everything else is secondary to that objective."

"Our Trojan mission, *and* the exodus habitats," Yuri said. "Both parts have to work for the plan to have any meaning. And frankly, we're just the cherry on the cake."

"What will happen with the cities if we do force the *Salvation* to retreat sometime in the next week?" Kandara queried. "There must be a contingency plan."

"Not a plan specifically," Johnstone said. "More a calculation. If we do hit the *Salvation of Life* hard enough—and in the right way—we're hopeful the Deliverance ships on Earth will launch and try to get into the wormhole before the Olyix close it behind them. For any that are left, we use every warship we have to chase them all the way to hell. Any that don't leave . . . Well, that means they're an easy target."

"You'll let nukes off in Earth's atmosphere? Seriously?"

"What's left of Earth's atmosphere, sure, if that's what it takes to end their attack. They've ruined our world. Even if we started to re-terraform it tomorrow, it would take millennia to recover just to the stage where we could start to regenerate the biosphere. And probably longer than that for the polar ice cap to re form. As for glaciers, that's for our great-great-great-grandchildren."

"I don't think the five of us can really concern ourselves with Earth anymore," Yuri said. "What happens to Earth and the exodus habitats after we leave is what happens. We just need to concentrate on getting our part right."

"That's brutal," Callum protested.

"Eighty-three cities have fallen since the siege started, thanks to screwups, crap maintenance, and sabotage," Yuri replied. "That's practically one a week. Our life is brutal now, and it's never going to get better—not for us. You need to face that."

"Yeah, fuck you, too, pal. We only get one shot at this, so it has to be right. No, it has to be *perfection*. You were on that test flight. We were mediocre at best."

"But it worked," Kandara said. "We flew. First time out! The equipment works, we worked. So the rest of us aren't as good as Jessika when it comes to piloting, but we sure as hell function as a team. And precision piloting isn't half as critical as the rest of the mission coming together."

"Okay," Emilja said. "Do any of the five of you have a substantial doubt that you can get into the *Salvation of Life* if we initiate Strikeback?"

If he was being honest with himself, Callum had to admit his doubts were all down to nerves. There were so many interlocking factors, every one of which had to play out perfectly, and the stakes were insane. But . . . "Yeah, I think we can do it." He looked around at Loi and Eldlund. "What about you two? Your role is pretty damn essential."

"Find us an Olyix transport ship in the right place, and we'll be fine," Loi said.

"General?" Ainsley III asked.

"The Olyix transport ships are always on the move. But we can track them. If one is on course for a suitable position, we'll know."

"Any possibilities coming up?"

"Yes. Unfortunately. Two of the Salt Lake City shield generators are losing efficiency; it looks like minor component burnout. They all have multiple redundancy built in, of course, but the tolerances are getting close to redline levels."

"Surely that's a simple replacement issue?" Danuta said.

"Maybe. But the fact that two generators are glitching at the same time is suspicious. We have replacement generators scheduled, but we're also worried about Paris and London."

"More sabotage?"

"Yes," Soćko said. "Nikolaj's team has infiltrated a shield generator compound in London; they launched creeper-drones, which have chewed their way into the generator auxiliary systems. In Paris, Edouard's people have almost penetrated the perimeter to the power supply portal from New Washington. So we can expect a concentration of transport ships outside those three cities over the next few days."

"For Christ's sake," Danuta protested. "If we know about the sabotage teams, we need to exterminate them. And I still can't believe anyone is dumb or desperate enough to work for an Olyix agent."

"This is the problem we've faced right from the start," Alik said. "We can't let the Olyix know we're plugged into the *Salvation of Life*'s onemind. And if we start taking out their operatives on Earth, they'll realize quickly enough."

"Yeah, yeah, but people helping them? That's fucking disgusting."

"Most of the sabotage is carried out by drones and synth creatures," Yuri said. "The dark market suppliers don't realize what their products are being used for."

"I still think we should take them out. We know all of them by now, don't we? So what if the onemind realizes?"

"It might affect our Trojan flight," Jessika said. "We need to be able to fool the onemind about the identity of the *Avenging Heretic*. We cannot risk it discovering that we can perceive its thoughtstream, and—by implication—deceive it."

"But we can't let more cities fall! Damnit, Berlin was bad. Nobody expected that. The people trapped under those shields need some good news."

"We're looking for other angles to come at the Olyix agents," Alik said. "If there's another way, we'll find it."

"The Strikeback will be the greatest news possible," Emilia said.

"For a while," Ainsley III observed. "It'll take a few years to dawn on the population that they're never going to leave. All we're doing, supplying them with food and power, is keeping them alive for the Olyix to cocoon."

"If we can destroy the Olyix enclave before they return to Earth . . ." Danuta trailed off. "Sorry. It's just . . . losing is too big to accept."

"Short-term loss," Yuri said. "Long-term gain. A cold equation, but ultimately everyone that the Olyix cocoon will return home."

"I sincerely hope so," Emilja said. "General, how long will it take you to launch Strikeback?"

"Three days to prepare; then it all depends on the position of Olyix transport ships."

"It only takes one to be in the right place," Eldlund said. "We'll find it."

"And the five of you?" Ainsley III said, in an unusually sober voice. "This is not a mission you can be asked or ordered to perform. Are you still willing to undertake it?"

"Fucking A," Kandara said.

"The greatest spy mission in the history of the universe." Alik chuckled. "Try to stop me."

"Exhortation, organization, and reprisals," Yuri said. "I will enjoy implementing that last."

Callum exaggerated a sigh. "Someone with a brain has to keep an eye on this lot."

Everyone turned to stare at Jessika.

"It will be an honor to fly with you," she said, then grinned at Kandara. "Who knows? It might finally qualify me as human."

INTERSTELLAR SPACE

YEAR 2 AA (AFTER ARRIVAL)

It took the massive fabrication station seven months to extrude the Sisaket habitat: a hollow cylinder thirty-five kilometers long, and eight in diameter, with a sunlight spindle stretched along the axis. When it was powered up, the spindle's radiance matched the spectrum of a G-class star, shining across an interior of sculpted hills and meandering valleys that idealized the rolling countryside of central Europe. Streams ran the length of the cylinder, slowly thickening as they wound between lakes of varying sizes, fed from twice-weekly night rains. Once germinated, the fledgling biosphere progressed fruitfully, greening the sandy soil and giving the atmosphere the warmth and humidity of late spring.

Dellian breathed it in as he stepped out of the portal just a couple of kilometers from the endcap. "Is this temperature correct?"

"Yes." Yirella chuckled. "You're just spoiled from living in tropical climates all the time."

He shivered and made a show of zipping up his jacket as he surveyed the view. They'd emerged near the top of a small grassy hill, crowned by a cluster of elegant houses. The newness of the habitat's biosphere was striking. There wasn't a single plant taller than a meter high, as if someone had given the green landscape a buzzcut. Different shades of green mottled the ground as far as he could see. Saplings of proto-forest on the slopes fashioned dark green wave lines undu-lating down into the emerald grasslands of the valley floors. Two kilometers away, the blank, near-vertical endcap rose upward like a cliff at the end of the universe.

They walked along the track to Alexandre's house: a building cut into the hill, with a broad shingle roof and walls that were mostly big windows separated by solid sections of wood plank. A long balcony ran across the front, giving a direct view of the domineering endcap.

"Nice?" he asked cautiously.

Yirella shrugged.

Plenty of people were gathering at the house, and Dellian knew most of them. All the binaries who'd grown up on the Immerle estate back on Juloss, or at least those who'd sur-vived the fateful Strike at Vayan two years ago; how many they'd lost still took some getting used to. Mingling with them were omnia who'd been on the *Calibar* when it was ambushed by the Olyix.

They found Alexandre on the terrace, a tall glass of spar-kling rosé in hir hand. Dellian couldn't remember ever see-ing hir drinking before and didn't quite know how to react. Disapproval would seem like disrespect, and that was some-thing he would never allow to happen. Alexandre's apparent youth didn't help his attitude, either. Sie now looked posi-tively adolescent thanks to hir rebuilt body. In fact, Dellian had a sneaking suspicion he might now look the older of the two.

If Alexandre was as perturbed by the age-switch, sie didn't show it. Sie gave them both a warm hug. "Thank you for coming. I need people who'll ground me."

"Happy housewarming," Yirella said.

"Sweet Saints, a housewarming." Sie shook hir head in bemusement. "I never imagined I'd have a housewarming. It seems so final, like: This is it. You're never going to move on from this, it's your peak in life."

"Nonsense," Dellian said. "This is the start of your new life. That's why we're celebrating it."

"Thank you, but I was quite happy with my old life."

"So was everyone on Earth before the Olyix came."

"Ouch! Who's the teacher now?"

"I didn't mean—"

But Alexandre was chortling, so Dellian grinned weakly and used his databud to call a server remote over—one loaded with plenty of alcohol.

"How are you coping?" Yirella asked. "Physically, I mean?"

"To be honest, I'm not sure," Alexandre admitted. "Most of this new body was grown inside a biologic initiator, which gives me a sense of . . . I don't know. Imposter syndrome?"

"But your brain is still a hundred percent original," she insisted.

"I know. One of the big original human fantasies, right? Having your time over. But there's got to be a lot of senescent cells left up here." Sie tapped hir head. "I guess wisdom and caution rule over impetuosity after all. I know I can run up mountains, but despite the urging of fizzing hormones, I just don't particularly want to."

"That's psychology, not physiology. We're all still in a state of shock and depression—you from when the Olyix intercepted the *Calibar* and cocooned the lot of you, us from being ambushed at Vayan when we thought we were the ones ambushing them. I can't conceive of a greater, more humiliating failure than that."

"Oh, my dear, no," sie protested. "That's so far from where we are. We have these splendid new habitats to live in safely, and all of us rescued from the *Calibar* have been rebodied. What could be better for morale than *that*?"

"That's just a short-term feeling," Yirella said. "In reality, the foundation for our whole Strike mission has been wrecked. The Olyix knew everything we planned to do, and they fooled us completely. They knew about our exodus habitats and worked out the limits of our expansion into the galaxy. They knew what to look for and where. They found us. I can't believe the effort they must have dedicated to pursuing us. It's almost impossible in a galaxy as vast as this one, but they did it. They are hubris to our arrogance. *Saints*, we built an entire fake civilization on Vayan as a lure. It was so real it even convinced the Neána. Yet it was all pointless. We wasted years—and took a terrible beating at the end of it. If it hadn't been for Ainsley turning up, we'd be in the cocoons next to you. There is no failure greater than that."

Dellian laughed.

"What?" Yirella asked.

"Ever wonder why we don't get invited to many parties?"

"Ever wonder why she puts up with you?" Alexandre taunted. "Because I haven't got a clue."

A server remote trundled up to them, and Yirella snagged a glass of wine. "Here's to a future relived—and relived properly."

They drank to that.

"Double celebration," Alexandre said. "This is also the day when the last of the *Calibar* personnel walked out of medical."

"Two hundred and seventy-three thousand, eight hundred and fifty-three successfully de-cocooned," Yirella said. "And only a hundred and three casualties."

"They were very old," Dellian said sadly.

"I know the feeling," Alexandre said. "This is a quite surreal experience I'm undergoing. I have a young body, and when I woke up, there you all were. Everyone who grew up in the Immerle estate, decades after I waved a final goodbye to you. What are the odds?"

Dellian groaned. "You had to ask."

"Not as long as everyone is presuming," Yirella said. "The Olyix sensor station was only twenty light-years from Vayan. It covered a bubble of space five hundred light-years in diameter. So actually, it's surprising the *Calibar* was the only generation ship they'd captured. There were several flying away from Juloss that must still be inside their operational range. But I'm glad it was you."

"How do you know where their sensor station is?" Alexandre asked.

"Ainsley told us. He extracted the coordinates out of the Olyix ship's onemind when he found the gateway location."

"I still can't get my head around that. Ainsley Zangari, an alien warship."

"A mostly human warship. And a huge bonus for us."

"Is he? Really?"

"We've already started retro-engineering some of his weapons technology."

"*Trying* to retro-engineer. Some of that mysterious Creator technology is beyond anything we know—or even understand."

"They're called the Katos," Yirella corrected primly. "And it's not just their technology; the Angelis and the Neána were part of the Factory, too."

"Allegedly. I mean, do we actually have any proof?"

"About the alien species, no—apart from the fact Ainsley must have been made somewhere. And he's definitely on our side. Thank the Saints." Her hand went out to rest on Dellian's shoulder. "He saved Del, too."

"You saved me," Dellian said, and lifted her hand up to kiss it.

"You two," Alexandre said thickly. "You'll get me all weepy. That's a curse of a young body. It's too emotional."

Yirella grinned. "Again: psychology, not physiology. You don't get to blame emotions on your body. They're all yours."

Alexandre put hir arms around both of them. "Saints bless you. Neither of you have changed. How strange; you've become my rock now."

"That might become a cyclic thing if we all wind up using biologic initiators to body-rebuild," Yirella said.

"You mean become immortal," Alexandre said.

"Yeah," Dellian said. "How come nobody did that on Juloss?"

"There are plenty of people who did that back on Juloss," sie replied. "Some who came on the founding generation ship were still alive to leave five hundred years later. However, given our life expectancy is around two hundred and fifty years, many citizens felt that was long enough for them. I don't know if it's a valid factor, but the majority of those who rejuve come from the early days of the exodus. I suspect it's a comment on the societies we build on the new worlds that they don't inspire as many to live even longer."

"I didn't know rejuvenation was common," Yirella said.

"It used to be common. Remember, you lived at the end of our time on Juloss; most of the population had flown away by the time you were born. You never got to experience our civilization in full swing."

"Did you get rejuvenated before?" Dellian asked.

"No. I thought about it a lot, but being a parent to all of you was satisfying in a way I knew would never happen again. And by then I was nearly two hundred. So I left to see a new planet begin, and I thought that would be a good place for my final days. It would have immersed me in optimism."

"That's so you," Yirella said happily.

Dellian looked up. Something had caught his attention, and he wasn't quite sure what.

"Ah, it's starting," Alexandre said.

Above them, the spindle light had begun to dim, sliding to a planet's rose-gold twilight. Shadows expanded out of the valleys of the cylindrical landscape, cloaking the interior. The lights of paths and houses glimmered all around. Dellian sipped his beer, then squinted at the endcap, which was . . . "Great Saints," he muttered incredulously.

The surface of the endcap was changing, its dark color draining away. Within a minute, the entire structure had turned transparent. He was staring out at the starfield, where each point of light was a steady burn, not the sparkle he was used to from a planet's atmospheric distortion.

"So many stars," Yirella said in an awed voice. "They're lovely like this."

"This is why I chose a house right up close to the endcap," Alexandre said. "There's something about seeing the stars at night that's fundamentally reassuring—to me, anyway."

Dellian forced a grin as he studied the panorama. It wasn't reassuring at all. The vertiginous way the stars rotated just intensified the knowledge he was standing inside an artificial habitat with a relatively thin shell. It emphasized how pitifully tiny and vulnerable they were.

He closed his eyes against the disorienting view, and once again the Saints' small ship exploded, enveloped by a dazzling nuclear plasmasphere. Glowing wreckage hurtled across the big structures orbiting an alien star. The loss of the *Avenging Heretic* electrocuted his soul.

Yirella's arm closed around him as he swayed, beer slopping out over his hand.

"Del!"

"I'm fine," he protested. "Just dizzy." He pointed an accusing finger at the stars as they tracked around the endcap. "I wasn't expecting that."

"Haven't you been in the habitats?" Alexandre asked in surprise.

"Not much. And not at night."

"Where are you two living?"

"We have quarters in the *Morgan*," Yirella said.

"I see."

"That sounds disapproving," Dellian said. "I'm a serving officer. We have to be ready."

Alexandre put hir hand on Dellian's shoulder. "I know. And believe me, we're all grateful for your service."

"Much use it does. We're alone, the exodus plan has failed, and the Saints are dead."

"My dear Dellian, you have to stop this. We're alive, the *Morgan* rescued a quarter of a million people, and we're going to start the real fight soon."

"Yeah, sorry." Dellian hung his head, ashamed not for what he'd said but for allowing the bleakness to creep up on him again. Since the Strike, he spent half the time thinking that the Olyix neurovirus was still in his brain—a depression worming its way insidiously through his thoughts, corrupting his outlook. Before, he looked at everything with optimism, knowing the Strike was going to work, that he'd live to see the inside of the Olyix enclave. Now he didn't even understand why he used to think like that.

"Look," Yirella said, a little too quickly. "In a couple of days, Kenelm's going to have the FinalStrike proposal council meeting. That's a huge statement of confidence in itself, of how we move on from here. Whatever we decide, this will mark the start of our resurgence."

"Damn Saints it does," Dellian confirmed. He tried to sound convincing. Supportive, even. But . . . Another meeting, more sitting around a table talking about things they might do. People supporting proposals, people arguing against, deals being made between factions. He truly hated this part of life after the Vayan ambush. There was no solid *goal* anymore—nothing he could grab hold of and dedicate

himself to. Nothing to keep his mind off what had happened.
So instead he was free to worry. Not a good thing in a squad
leader.

"An important moment for everyone," Alexandre said.

"I'm worried people will want to take the Neána option
and hide," Yirella said.

"Many will," sie agreed. "Among my *Calibar* compatri-
ots, anyway. But not all. Anger and fear make for an unpre-
dictable combination. Revenge isn't necessarily a good
motivator, but it certainly helps recruit waverers."

"Maybe. I think the meeting will be more symbolic than
anything else. But you'll come, won't you?"

"Try and stop me."

Yirella waited until Del fell asleep, then another half hour
beyond. He didn't sleep well these days—not that she was
much better. She knew he kept having nightmares of the
Avenging Heretic exploding, tormented by the question if he
was truly cured or if the Olyix neurovirus was simply hiding
in the caverns of his mind, biding its time. He no longer
trusted himself, which was savaging his self-confidence.

While she . . . The bleak despair was returning—the one
that had broken her before, a sense of the utter futility that
their lives had become. She'd never truly beaten it, but being
with Del had kept it in abeyance. Yet now that particular version of Del had vanished, claimed by the neurovirus, and the
darkness was threatening to close in on her once more.

Her optik displayed the white icon, and she opened it.

"Good party?" Ainsley asked.

"Okay, I guess."

"You're picking up my speech patterns."

"When in Rome . . ."

"Oh, sweetheart, Rome is so far away now—and not just
in space."

"We'll rebuild it when we return to Earth."

"Really? The Colosseum? You'll build a ruin?"

"Why are you always such a contrarian? Novus Rome
will be a memorial to the past. Obviously."

"Novus, huh? Smartass."

"I wish. I still hate the paradox."

"Not this again."

"This all the time."

"Look, it's just superficial logic."

"No, if we're right about what you found in the onemind's memory, *something* sent the Olyix a tachyon message from the future, and they built their whole insane crusade around it. If we win, if we exterminate the Olyix, then the God at the End of Time will know it, because the Olyix won't be there delivering all the elevated species as requested."

". . . so it won't bother sending the message to them from up there in the future in the first place. Or it sends them another message warning them about our attack plans. Yeah, I get that."

"We didn't know the message was real. We always assumed it was some kind of religious bullshit, just like we used to have back on Earth."

"Are you becoming a believer, Yirella?"

"Belief implies faith. That I don't have, not in mythology. But a tachyon message from the future? It makes you focus on what's real. The human race is now down to three tiny habitats adrift in a smallish galaxy that's lost in a vast universe. So vast that our animal brains can't even 'get' how big it is. The best I can do is know that I don't 'get' it."

"You guys really worship bleak, don't you? So what? The size of the universe is an abstract. It doesn't change the threat we're facing."

"Maybe not, but it undermines the threat. You realize how irrelevant everything is. So why fight? The Neána have a point; we should just slip into the dark and party away. Enjoy ourselves before the end comes crashing down."

"For fuck's sake, get a grip! You were supposed to be working through options for us. I'm depending on you."

"I know. I'm sorry. It's just the stress of responsibility. If we don't get *this* perfect . . . How did you call it? Game over."

"All right, if it helps, forget thinking the Olyix have a religious component. But you can't deny they're fanatics, controlled by whatever hellspawned entity is lurking up there in the future. No, not controlled: conned. The message gave them purpose, which makes them weak."

"Weak? How so?"

"They need a cause," Ainsley said. "An outside emperor to make them what they are. A tachyon beam message from a future god—that could so easily have been us. You know, when I was alive, there were cults and conspiracy theorists all over the world that predicted benign aliens would come and save us from ourselves."

"Do you think there were Neána on Earth back then, putting the theory out there?"

"No. That's not the point here. We don't need saving from ourselves; we never did. We've always had catastrophe preachers walking among us, profiting off the fear they create—either to sell something or to keep the population in line. But if you look at the progress we've made as a species, from clunkheads who chased antelopes across the savanna up to a society that settled distant stars— Hell, if I still had eyes I would weep with pride. Sure, whatever time you're born into, that progress was never fast enough, and fuck knows enough personal injustices were never redeemed. But overall, we have nothing to be ashamed of. So I don't care who sent that message to the Olyix or from when, because it doesn't give any fucker the right to intervene in our evolution. So my belief is very simple: The Olyix have to be stopped. By whatever means possible."

"Yeah." She looked over at Del, lying beside her. *Even when he's sleeping he looks troubled.* "That's kind of ingrained in me, too."

"So how's that grand strategy coming on?"

"Same as always. It's that Saints-damned sensor station that's the problem; it screws up every attack route scenario. We always thought the wormholes the Olyix arkships brought with them led right back to the enclave gateway. That way we could get there in one easy flight."

"Well that's not going to happen. The only place an Olyix arkship's wormhole connects to is a sensor station; I pulled that inconvenient fact right out of the onemind. Not that we shouldn't have figured it out before, given how much time we've had. There are thousands of those sensor stations scattered across the galaxy, so they're junctions. Hey, just like Roman staging posts. As soon as a station detects a sentient species emerging, they let the enclave know, and the enclave dispatches an arkship. Once it gets to the sensor station, it carries a wormhole on to the new species."

"Yes, but it means we have to hit the sensor station that's guarding our direct route to the enclave. Emphasis on: guarding. Which means a fast and overwhelming engagement. We have to get it absolutely right, or they'll shut down the wormhole to the enclave."

"Yeah. Well, on the plus side, we know the sensor station is thirty-seven light-years from our present location."

"And now they know we beat the ships they sent to our Vayan lure. The wormhole collapsed the moment you took out their welcome ship. That's going to stir them up."

"No shit, Sherlock."

"Look, I've been talking to Wim's physics team. We're never going to retro-engineer all of your weapons. The real optimists claim we might crack nucleonic molecule theory in a couple of years, but the Saints alone know how to handle ultradense matter, let alone create some for ourselves."

"So what do you want to do?"

Yirella drew a deep breath. "We have to hit them with the unexpected."

"Obviously."

"Not helpful. This is going to be risky enough."

"But, kid, we have nothing to lose."

"So we have nothing to fear. I remember the aphorism."

"Uh, I think it's more of a neologism, but carry on."

"Kenelm won't like the risk. Hir job is to protect all of us—and especially the *Calibar* survivors. I even agree with that. Which makes another lure a tough sell."

"This is as bad as convincing the Council to adopt the exodus habitat project and sacrifice Earth! I can just take control of your networks, you know. Remove Kenelm from the equation. That would make life a whole lot easier."

"Absolutely not! We steer, we don't force." She flinched. "To start with."

"Now you're talking."

———

Dellian let go of Yirella's hand as they walked into the *Morgan*'s bridge. She'd remind him of that later, he knew. Adults in a long-term relationship showing affection was hardly a social transgression; he just didn't think it was appropriate for something as official as a full session of the captain's expanded advisory council. She'd been silent when he put on a full dress uniform to attend, but he knew what she was thinking. Routine was important to him—especially now, providing the stability that enabled him to function at a level approximating his old self. If people knew that was a lie, they politely kept quiet about it.

The number of seats around the truncated table had been increased to thirty, allowing representatives from the *Calibar* to contribute. He smiled quickly at Alexandre, who was sitting almost opposite him.

Kenelm came in. Somehow the Strike mission's neat gray-and-blue uniform looked a lot better on hir than any of the squad leaders around the table. Wim accompanied the captain, stubble marring hir haggard face, divulging every one of hir hundred eighty-three years.

As they sat down, Ainsley appeared on the screen wall, an image of the ship that was currently drifting around the fringes of their little interstellar habitat cluster like an enigmatic guard dog.

"Thank you all for coming," Kenelm said formally. "We have several presentations from our developmental tactician groups to get through, which I hope will provide some clarity on our future policy."

Dellian didn't risk glancing at Yirella; he knew what her group had been formulating. People weren't going to like it. After the Strike and its fallout, everyone wanted to play it safe. Part of him wanted to agree with that, but he knew that his pre-Strike self would be contemptuous.

Two of the five proposals were for maintaining the habitats in interstellar isolation. "We know the Olyix now have dominion over the galaxy's star systems," Loneve, one of the *Calibar* survivors, submitted. "But the gulf between the stars is so much greater, and offers us true asylum. I understand that many have a sense of loss or disassociation about our situation, but we should not be afraid to prosper out here. As we grow and advance our technology—thanks to the principles we're learning from Ainsley—we'll see that the desire to cling to the traditional paradigm of planet-based existence is wrong. Out here we will be free in a way that has eluded us since we left Earth. And ultimately we may rise to heights that may finally enable us to challenge the Olyix directly."

Wim wanted almost the same thing but suggested splitting off the original *Morgan* Strike mission from the habitat population. "It solves the problem of different goals," sie said. "There are those in the *Morgan* crew and squads who have had enough of the Strike, and there are a great many from the *Calibar* who want to initiate a new Strike. Forcing both strands of opinion to live here together is untenable, not to mention immoral. We've already been through this division; we know it cannot be allowed to fester."

"And if the Strike fails again?" Loneve asked. "Then our position will become known to the Olyix. You would condemn us because of your actions."

"Then portal out as soon as the Strike mission leaves," Yirella said in a tone only just short of contempt. "And portal again and again until you feel safe."

The next proposal came from Ellici. "We use the next decade here to build the most powerful ships we can devise and arm them with the nucleonic weapons Wim's team is developing from Ainsley. That will give our new society time to settle down. When we're ready, people will be able to make an informed choice—who remains and who leaves. Look, right now the distance we have to travel seems daunting." She glanced at Ainsley's image. "Are you sure you got the enclave location right?"

"Oh, yeah," he replied. "Extracted straight out of the welcome ship's onemind, like pulling teeth the old-fashioned way. The enclave is forty thousand light-years from here, which puts it just past the galactic core."

"Okay. But actually that isn't so much of a problem, not with relativistic flight. And we can fit our Strike ships with the drive we developed for the *Actaeon* project, which will get us there in twenty years—ship's time. People can manage that. Ainsley can come with us, which is what you want, right?"

"Eliminating the Olyix is why I exist, sure," Ainsley replied.

Politician's answer, Dellian thought.

Then it was Yirella's turn. "We need to build another lure, and use that to invade the enclave directly—through their own wormhole," she said primly.

Everyone around the table disapproved, groaning in disappointment or simply saying no.

"Why would you even suggest that?" Tilliana asked. "The Olyix know we create lures. We'd be exposing ourselves."

Dellian almost winced at the pitying smile lifting Yirella's lips. "We create another lure precisely because they know that we know that they know about human lures. So obviously, from their point of view, we precious few—the *Morgan* and *Calibar* survivors—will never build another one, because we're busy with Ellici's proposal: hiding out here while we put together a new Strike armada to fly the long way around to the enclave."

"Risky," Ellici said. "You're trying to second-guess them second-guessing us."

"So to push the odds in our favor, we make it authentic."

"What do you mean, 'authentic'?" Kenelm asked, a hint of concern in hir voice.

"A human civilization."

"You can't," Wim declared. "That's . . ."

"What?" Yirella challenged. "Dangerous? Unethical? This is a war for our existence. There can be no restrictions, no line we will not cross. The Olyix hold our entire species captive. We are beyond desperate, here. Unless we get this absolutely perfect, we are living the last days of our species."

"What sort of human civilization do you want this lure to be?" Alexandre asked.

"The Olyix know of our Strike plan, so they know what we are supposed to do in the event we acquire the enclave location: rendezvous at the nearest neutron star. That course of action made sense back when Emilja and Ainsley put this whole exodus plan together. Neutron stars are distinctive, so much so that humans had mapped their locations back on pre-portal-era Earth. So any ship or settled world that receives a Signal revealing the enclave's stellar coordinates travels to the nearest one. All the ships that arrive join up and assemble a war armada."

"If we're not too busy arguing with each other," Dellian muttered.

"I'd like to see you come up with a better plan," Ainsley snapped. "You have no idea what it was like back then."

"That's not what I—"

"Let's keep it relevant, please," Kenelm said.

It took a lot of willpower for Dellian not to sigh in exasperation, but he managed to keep his cool. As always, he wondered why he was included in these meetings. *To help provide a full range of democratic views for the council to consider.* Which was, as Ainsley would say: bullshit.

"Firstly," Yirella said, "if the Olyix see us establish ourselves at a neutron star, they'll know it is for one reason— that we now know where their enclave is. It doesn't matter how we got it—a Strike mission snatched it out of a one-mind; the Neána finally told us. There're plenty of possible sources. But they also know that the neutron star civilization will be busy building an armada powerful enough to invade the enclave, which means they'll have no choice in their response. They'll have to come. The welcome ships they send through ordinary space will be carrying wormholes to deliver their fleet directly from the sensor station. That gives us our chance."

"No human civilization would broadcast radio signals," Kenelm said. "That's ingrained in us now—survival 101. And a human society at a neutron star certainly wouldn't."

"So our lure civilization does something else," she said dismissively. "We change the neutron star composition by dropping strangelets into it, or generate hyper-frequency gravity waves. We produce exotic matter with an abnormal signature. It doesn't matter *how* the Olyix sensor station notices them, just that they do."

"Then what?"

Yirella gestured theatrically at the image of Ainsley.

"I'm there to greet them," Ainsley said. "As are you,

equipped with some new seriously badass weapons hardware. This time, we don't have to worry about pulling our
punches to protect cocooned humans, so we can go in hot.
Capture a wormhole terminus and fly down it to the sensor
station. From there, it's just one long step to the enclave."

Dellian watched Kenelm glance around the table as sie
tried to judge the mood. Theoretically, sie had the authority
to issue any order on hir own, but the *Calibar* survivors
made it politically difficult to assert unconditional authority.

"So this would be a split?" sie asked. "Some of us would
remain here and some of us travel to the neutron star?"

"Yes," Yirella confirmed. "As before, we send out seeder
ships to found the lure civilization, then we follow in warships. The nearest neutron star is a hundred and thirty-seven
light-years from here. We time it so the seeder ships arrive
fifty years before us, which will give them plenty of time to
go exponential and initiate humans."

"Wait, you want to populate it with real humans? I
thought you were talking about cyborgs."

"Of course it has to be real humans. This is no time for
half measures."

"Absolutely not. You'd be putting actual people directly in
harm's way."

"I don't see that. The seedship gentens will have the same
level of technology we have. They'll be heavily armed. And
if we hothouse the neutron star humans, they might be able
to push their own technology development even further."

"What do you mean, 'hothouse'?" Tilliana asked.

"We do what the Neána did: grow fully formed adults in
biologic initiators; it's just an adaptation of the process we
used to rebuild the *Calibar* cocoons back into their proper
bodies. That way, they'll have fifty years straight to advance
their own society and develop new weapons."

"And what personality are you going to animate these instant adults with?" Ellici challenged.

"I've discussed this with the metavayans. They suggest
we give each of them basic human thought processes—
routines that take them up to genten operational self-
awareness, which we then individualize with personalities

compiled from volunteers in the habitats: memories, experiences, feelings, responses."

"So, basically, it'll be us living there? We're duplicating ourselves?"

"No. Their location alone means they'll have to live very different lives from us. That's a fantastic opportunity to expand the human experience."

"Absolutely not," Kenelm said. "I cannot agree to this aspect of your proposal. They would develop without any guidance from us. Who knows what views they will have? They might even be hostile to *us*."

"So?"

Kenelm gave her a shocked look. "People have to understand. We are fleeing for our lives. That has to be emphasized to every new generation so they understand the threat. You cannot seriously be proposing entrusting that sacred duty to gentens?"

"And to Ainsley."

Dellian thought Kenelm was going to let loose a contemptuous sneer at that, but sie managed to retain hir composure. "No," sie said firmly. "The risk inherent in this scheme is simply too great. We have to remain in control. It is our responsibility to ensure that any new humans are fully aware of their circumstances. However, the rest of your idea does have a degree of validity. A post-planetary human society at a neutron star would undoubtedly attract the Olyix."

"Yet if we designed that society, it would be terminally bland compared to what they could evolve for themselves," Yirella said. "Environment is always key to human development, and a neutron star's circumstellar disk will be a weird and harsh place to live. It should propagate something special—beyond anything we can conceive of sitting in a habitat."

"We went for absolute realism on Vayan," Wim said. "And for what? All any human in this galaxy has to do is shout *here we are*, and the Olyix will come. If you want a lure, you don't even need to send a seedship to the neutron star, just an initiator with a genten and have it build antimatter warheads so it can test them on the asteroids in the circumstellar disk and blow shit up on a huge scale. That way, they'll know for sure we're building planet-killers."

"It has to be completely convincing. Antimatter bombs are crude. We even made them back on Earth, for Saints' sake."

"I'm going to agree with Yirella, here," Ainsley said. "From what I managed to extract from the onemind, the Olyix are devoting a hell of an effort to detecting and ambushing humans along what's left of the exodus expansion wavefront. But there's one thing they won't be expecting at a neutron star civilization."

"What?" Kenelm asked.

"Me. Yirella was right. Logically, this hypothetical group of humans won't build another lure. We're delving into some pretty fucking audacious bluffs and outthinking maneuvers here, but that gives us an advantage."

"Are you saying this is the option you prefer?" Alexandre asked.

"Hey, pal, there are no absolutes here. All of these ideas could work. But there is a grade of probability, which you have to follow if you want to win—and win big. And remember, I cut my teeth in the crucible of Wall Street when it was at its vicious peak. So, yeah, for me Yirella's idea comes out on top. Gold standard for sheer audacity, if nothing else."

"And for any of these to work, we'd need your cooperation. Which effectively gives you a veto."

Dellian gave their old mentor a curious look. He knew hir well enough to recognize distrust in hir tone.

"We all want the same thing," Ainsley said, "but I'm not sure a straightforward assault on the sensor station is a good idea. That bastard is going to have a multitude of reinforcements by now—precisely because it's the logical place for whatever defeated the Olyix on Vayan to go next. They still don't know exactly what I am, because the welcome ship's wormhole died minutes after the onemind sent a ship down it to warn the sensor station. But they know the Vayan system had *something* that killed their ships, so they are going to beef up their defenses to a maximum and keep a serious watch. But if half of them fly to the neutron star, we'll have split their forces, which bumps up our odds of success. The only other option is the one Ellici suggested, that we travel directly to the enclave the long way around. For the ships, it only takes twenty years at relativistic velocity, but it gives the Olyix forty thousand years to improve their defenses."

"I thought time in the enclave went slowly," Dellian said.

"So it does, according to the Neána. But if you suspect a dangerous unknown is on the way to whup your ass, why wouldn't you put your biggest, smartest weapons division outside the slowtime bubble? Forty thousand years working on weapons R and D—who's *not* going to do that?"

"If you fly straight to the enclave, would you want us to come with you?" Alexandre asked.

This time, it was all Dellian could do not to frown. The distrust was palpable.

"Sure I'd like you to," Ainsley said. "And don't be coy; it's what the *Morgan* crew were expecting to do anyway. But forty thousand light-years is a Goddamn big ask, especially now we also have some workable options that don't put the same level of demands on you guys. And who knows what we might encounter on the way? Plus, there's the fifty-thousand light-year trip back to Earth if we succeed. So, yeah, Yirella's plan gets my first preference vote."

Kenelm took another look around the table. "I'd like an indicative vote at this point. With one stipulation—Yirella's plan does *not* include trying to establish a community of actual humans at the neutron star. That lure civilization is to be as artificial as Vayan was—which I'm sure will be equally excellent," sie added, with an appreciative smile at Yirella. "Those in favor?"

Every hand around the table went up, even Alexandre's eventually.

"Del?" Yirella asked.

Sheepishly, he realized he hadn't raised his own hand. It was just . . . *She and Ainsley outmaneuvered everyone so effortlessly. Why does that make me uneasy? It's like that time back on Juloss when she'd worked out what was really happening at the crash. She's not telling us everything. Oh Saints, is it because she doesn't trust us to do what we'll ultimately have to do?*

Slowly, he put his hand up, burning from the pitying grins Ellici and Tilliana were directing at him. But the light from the *Avenging Heretic* exploding eclipsed both of them.

"Well, that was conclusive," Kenelm said. "We will attempt to lure the Olyix to the neutron star."

What the fuck have we just said yes to?

LONDON

DECEMBER 10, 2206

There were parts of Connexion's Greenwich security operations center that were just accumulating dust now. It was another thing that told Kohei Yamada how bad things were. In the time before Blitz2, the circular chamber was conserved to operating room standards. Small cleanez would slide around, vacuuming and polishing every surface, and the air-con filters would remove any stray particle. But without regular servicing, the little machines became impaired, then inevitably failed. And Connexion's Greenwich Tower now operated on a skeleton staff with just two functions: those who supervised the vital interstellar portals that supplied London with electricity and food, and the security division who watched over them. Janitorial services and the maintenance department had been suspended for "the duration."

The wide arms of Kohei's chair were stained with rings from his teacups. He brought a thermos flask in with him every shift, along with a pack of biscuits or sandwiches. Crumbs were building up in the edges of the leather cushioning. However, none of the grime was affecting the systems yet, which made him suspect most of the hardware would last longer than Blitz2.

His team's job was to coordinate with London's Special Branch and Alpha Defense, monitoring the ongoing sabotage by Olyix operatives. Thanks to some amazingly good intel coming from Yuri, they'd managed to stop eleven attempts in the last two years, ranging from physical assaults on shield generator stations to darkware infiltration of the interstellar portals that brought electricity to London. The only downside was the restrictions Yuri put on rounding up the kingpins afterward. Kohei could see the logic behind it, not tipping the Olyix off to just how much they knew, but that didn't stop it from being as frustrating as hell. It also meant spreading their attention wide, tracking associates of associates to try to gain insights into whatever scheme was being planned next.

That morning he arrived at the center early as normal; what served as his apartment used to be a middle-management office on the tower's seventh floor. Kohei did a long shift every day; there was nothing else to do. He'd managed to get his (fifth) wife transferred to the safety of the Puppis system, where she'd been assigned to Bodard—the first of the exodus habitats completed by the industrial stations orbiting Malamalama. She was using her sixty-year-old botany degree to help stabilize the habitat's biosphere, which occupied her for long hours every day. They talked most days, him with the glum news of how London was coping with Blitz2 while she filled him in on the gossip from Nashua habitat, where all the branches of the Zangari family had fled to—which was like listening to the byzantine plot of some interactive soap opera with too many characters.

He settled into his chair and reviewed the log. Nothing outstanding. A small-time nethead crew from Balham was trying to access files from Connexion's Waterloo transstellar hub. They'd given up trying to use solnet a week ago and were now scouting the streets outside the cordoned-off station to see if they could physically splice into the data cables. It'd been sold to them as a power heist—which made a kind of sense, as Waterloo was where a power feed from 82 Eridani was coming in, and electricity was wealth in Blitz2 London. But in reality, it was a malware infiltration mission for the Paynors, put together and run through a convoluted route of lieutenants and in-the-dark underworld soldiers, giving the major family distance from the sharp end. Except it wasn't the family; Alpha Defense wasn't even sure if any of them were still alive. Nikolaj remained in their Kensington house, maintaining a front for the family's criminal activities while she organized an ongoing barrage of sabotage.

What Kohei didn't get was how Yuri always seemed to know about them before anyone in London did. But he just wrote that off as being part of the Yuri Alster legend. Who else would have some kind of spy in the Olyix arkship?

He sipped his tea slowly. Real loose-leaf tea from India, which he'd carefully scavenged from the kitchenettes on the tower's abandoned executive floors in the weeks after he'd moved in. There was enough left for maybe another seven months. In the meantime, he enjoyed the last taste of civilization as a self-awarded bonus for keeping London safe. He smiled as he drank, watching the Balham crew hanging around the barren Jubilee Gardens, trying to sneak their synth-mice into a sealed manhole cover. Special Branch had them completely surrounded with plainclothes officers, while five military ground drones waited in the utilities duct below the manhole.

A notification splashed across his tarsus lens. The department's G8Turing was registering an abnormal activity pattern in the Royal Victoria Docks area. Frowning, Kohei used his altme to call up supplementary files. Special Branch had set up a secondary observation there, centered on the Icona apartment block. Without the dedicated sensors and a secure hardline, that whole area would have been unobserved. Solnet coverage was poor and the civic sensors trashed. More associated files: The surveillance existed because Karno Larson lived there. When Kohei queried that, he saw the man was classed as *a person of interest*—a financier with ties to several of the major families, including the Paynors.

"Give me a visual," he ordered.

Sensors showed him a young white man with a longish nose cycling slowly eastward along Western Gateway's clear path. When he reached the low green zone barrier around the huge exhibition building, he wobbled off across a dirt square that used to be grass, then started back along the wide path down the side of the dock, steering around the ancient cranes preserved as monuments to the original port.

The Icona apartment block was one of the buildings he passed, overlooking the big dock.

There was almost no one else around. The exhibition center played a strong role deterring residents and visitors alike. A month into the siege, it had been designated an official green zone refuge for cocoons. To begin with, mobs had attacked and killed any cocoons they could find—those out in the open or unprotected by families. Then, when it slowly dawned that cocoons weren't contagious and that the victims were still alive, in a twisted, bizarre fashion—that the alien cells were preserving them—the government created green zones where they could be brought and kept safe. Kohei knew there were more than eighty thousand cocoons in the docklands exhibition hall; sensors were showing him the dark, glossy guard drones patrolling the perimeter. Thick blue plastic pipes pumped water out of the dock to supply the cocoons inside. After two years, they'd reduced the water level a couple of meters. And like the residue of the Thames outside, the surface had been smothered in a ragged mat of dark green algae—about the only vegetation that had survived in the whole city.

The cyclist avoided the few pedestrians who were heading toward the angular glass Crystal building at the west end of the dock, where the civic nutrition agency had set up a public kitchen. When he reached the end of the riverfront path, he turned back onto the Western Gateway and repeated the circuit. It was the third time he'd been around that morning. Kohei watched as he dismounted just before reaching the bulky Icona block again and wheeled his bike along. There were times when the man bent over—to pick something off the bicycle's tires, to lean against the wall for a moment to take in the sight, standing beside a crane, holding the thick iron struts. So casually, so naturally. The sensors watched him place a button-sized bug each time, all of them aligned on the Icona buildings.

"He's scouting for something," Kohei announced to the other three operatives sitting around the display bubble. The G8Turing had already run facial recognition, with no result. "Deep analysis," he ordered.

The observation sensors weren't quite top-of-the-line, but

with several of them focused simultaneously they began to work through a detailed investigation. The first anomaly was the difference in skin color between his dark hands and white face. The cyclist was wearing a fleshmask. Which was when Kohei started to take a serious interest.

The G8Turing captured every feature and movement of the fleshmask, then carefully started a virtual deconstruction. Kohei watched, fascinated as always by the process, as layers of lies were peeled away to leave a very different reality beneath.

"Ho boy," he muttered as Ollie Heslop's file splashed across his lens. He knew the name anyway—the one member of the Southwark Legion they suspected of escaping the Litchfield Road raid two years ago. "Where have you been hiding, Ollie, and what are you up to now?"

PUPPIS STAR SYSTEM

DECEMBER 10, 2206

Loi was overseeing Strikeback's warship portal deployment when the call from Eldlund came through. He sighed at his friend's timing, but couldn't help the short smile at what it meant.

"We're ready," Eldlund said. "The turtles have reached the end of the lake bed."

"I'm on my way." Loi cancelled his secure channel to the station's G8Turing, which was controlling the deployment, and the immersive display encircling his chair slid away like wind-torn mist. He was sitting on one of three couch-chairs in a small hexagonal chamber, its only illumination coming from a display bubble in the middle, projecting a million-kilometer-wide globe of space, with Earth nestled at the center. Tiny amber icons glided around the besieged planet like a cloud of fireflies—each one an Olyix ship, with the *Salvation of Life* a malign red blemish at L3, directly opposite the moon. The arkship had flown there after the invasion began, settling into a stable parking orbit where it received the transport ships bringing up the newly cocooned. Two hundred thousand kilometers farther out, green icons were slowly drifting into position, as yet undetected by the Olyix.

When its primary base on the moon was destroyed by Olyix Deliverance ships, Alpha Defense had dispersed to a series of secondary locations. The secure station in the Puppis system was designated as the operations center for the Strikeback operation's forward positioning office. It was logical; Puppis was where a great many industrial systems were based, originally in expectation of the planet's terraforming project. They'd all been taken over for the exodus habitat project—a major component of which were the new expansion portals that Connexion scientists had developed from the Olyix machines captured during an engagement in London. Unlike the old fixed-size portals that had to thread up, these could now enlarge themselves. There were limits, of course; a ten-centimeter-diameter portal couldn't be expanded up to a hundred meters. But a fifty-meter portal could certainly increase to half a kilometer. The latest generation currently under development were designed to expand out to six kilometers—large enough for a habitat to pass through.

As the rebuilding phase of the *Avenging Heretic* project had wound down, Loi had moved on to the deployment team, who supervised the covert positioning of Strikeback's expansion portals above Earth. This stage wasn't dangerous or difficult, just overseeing the G8Turing that handled the flight vectors. And as an added benefit, it was what his mother assumed he'd be doing during the Strikeback itself. Having her in the Puppis system working on the exodus had proved both a blessing and a bit of a nightmare. She got to see him regularly, which helped put her mind at rest—and it played into the story that he was still working as Yuri's assistant (which was partially true). Even though she was one of the leading figures in managing the exodus habitat manufacturing program, and had frequent Strikeback briefings, the *Avenging Heretic* was classified way above her pay grade. Loi was thankful about that—because if she ever discovered what his actual mission was during Strikeback, there would be hell to pay.

He stepped through the portal into the Knockdown team's ultra-secure office. Given it was the most critical aspect of Strikeback, only five people were allowed access. It was almost identical to the room he'd just left, except there was only Eldlund sitting in a chair in front of the display bubble. The projection here was bleak—a flat, desolate landscape smothered in grainy mist and illuminated from above by bright flickering light.

"Looking good," Eldlund said, smiling brightly at Loi.

"Uh, yes. Thank you. You, too," Loi replied. "Did you come here straight from a party?" His friend was wearing a flowing dress of crushed purple velvet with an exceptionally long split up the side of hir skirt. He wondered briefly who the lucky date was.

Eldlund laughed. "You're very sweet. So, ah, how's Gwendoline?"

"She's okay. Busy. Like all of us."

Eldlund's interest in his mother was something Loi couldn't quite get his head around. Sure, she was lovely, but she was his *mother*. He and Eldlund had become close over the last two years, which made what he assumed was a crush even harder to deal with.

"Not *quite* like us," Eldlund teased. "Given where we're heading . . ."

"Yeah, but she's not to know. She'd go into a massive panic, and I couldn't take that."

"Absolutely. The stress is getting to me, too."

"Hey, we'll be fine. Our suits are the best, and I've got your back. Always, okay?"

"I know. Reciprocated, by the way." Hir face became sober. "Our intruders are out of Gilbert Bay."

Loi scanned the bubble as his altme pulled data from the Knockdown network. At this stage of the mission, their task was to infiltrate portals into the area around Salt Lake City, where Olyix ships were landing in readiness for the city's shield collapsing. It wasn't easy to get physically close—not with the kind of sensor technology the Olyix boasted. The bioborgs Kandara had attempted to use as distractions on her failed mission to McDivitt habitat had shown they could detect fake creatures, so the Knockdown team had decided on a biological approach for their intruders.

With eight-letter DNA incorporated in the design, the Knockdown intruders resembled turtles. Measuring forty centimeters long, they'd been grown in vats over three months. But instead of the slow, stumpy legs that the genuine genus possessed, these had long, sinuous limbs that moved like snakes, making them relatively fast. The shell had a hide of chameleon cells, allowing them to blend into the landscape. Loi wasn't entirely sure that was going to be needed given the environment they operated in, but the biologists had been on a roll, so it passed review unchallenged. Their internal organs were more or less standard, although they could handle climates with a much higher temperature than ordinary animals, and instead of a brain they had a complex network of bioneural circuitry. A five centimeter expansion portal was held in a cavity just underneath the shell, providing secure communication.

"Show me," Loi instructed the G8Turing. The bubble display switched to a simple map of Salt Lake City, centered around Gilbert Bay. Sensor imagery was patchy; the Olyix had eliminated all the low-orbit spysats, but plenty of Alpha Defense's stealthed high-orbit systems were functional and provided a decent resolution. Visually, most of Utah was smothered under a Jovian-strength storm-swirl of cloud, with Salt Lake City a turgid violet glow fluorescing at the center. Lightning forks snapped outward constantly from the cirrocumulus peak, discharging into the clutter of secondary tornadoes that inundated the lakes and mountains around the city.

Eldlund flinched at the sight. "Damn, I'm glad we're not down there."

"We will be soon enough," Loi reminded him. He flipped the display to the features overlay, and zoomed in on the shoreline of Gilbert Bay at the southern end of the Great Salt Lake. It didn't exist anymore. Even in ordinary times, the massive body of water suffered heavy evaporation every summer, shrinking it down. Now with four Deliverance ships bombarding the city shield with intense energy beams, the surrounding superenergized atmosphere had boiled it empty in the first seven months of the siege.

Twenty-five intruder creatures had traveled in from the north, slithering across the warm granules of the lake bed. Now the three leaders were making their way over the buckled ribbon of asphalt that used to be I-80, with the rest following. Loi activated a direct link and looked through an intruder's eyes. The land was a jumble of fractured slabs of interstate and desiccated scrub. The image was so badly hazed that he thought the link was faulty before realizing the air was actually clotted with grains of dirt scoured from the land by hurricane-force winds. Low clouds scudded fast overhead, their darkness the shade of wounded flesh. He knew the Oquirrh Mountains began to rise up on the other side of I-80, with Kessler Peak in the distance. But even with the intruder's enhanced senses, he couldn't see more than twenty meters.

"Let's spread them out," Eldlund said, "then march them forward. Those mountains are tough in ordinary conditions, never mind wind like this."

"Okay." In his mind, Loi could see them as chess pieces advancing across the board—not that the squares were visible, nor the opponent. Somewhere in the maelstrom ahead, the Olyix transport ships were perched along the top of the Oquirrh range, waiting to pounce as soon as the shield fell. Loi directed the intruder forward, plotting a course to load into its inertial navigation routines. It began to move faster, sliding up onto jagged ridges of exposed rock that marked the start of the foothills. Intermittent streamers of mist streaked down from the slopes above, flowing around it as if it were being sprayed by a water cannon, then vanishing as fast as they came. The local air temperature had risen over twenty degrees Celsius.

"I hope our suits are going to be good enough," Loi muttered.

"Lim has done a great job. We're going to be pioneers; they were about the first things human-built initiators ever produced. How cool is that?"

"Scalding, if you must know."

"You're such a miserabilist. Concentrate on good news. There must be some."

"Right. Actually, we might have found a route in to Nikolaj."

"Yeah? What?"

"Kohei has tracked down some lowlife criminal that they're hoping to manipulate. If he's played right, they'll be able to shut down the Olyix sabotage operation in London without the *Salvation*'s onemind knowing we can read its

THE SAINTS OF SALVATION 75

thoughts. We need that. London's shield is close to break-ing."

"As close as Salt Lake City?"

"I think London is worse—just a few hours left now. Mum's really worried about it. Dad's still there on the ground, doing his good-guy charity thing."

"I feel for her."

Loi concentrated hard on the route up into the mountains.

LONDON

DECEMBER 10, 2206

Over a century ago, the front of the railway arch had been boarded up with a wall of corrugated iron, which left it dark and surprisingly cool inside. The thick brickwork even reduced the constant noise emitted by the stressed shield curving high overhead. Ollie's flashlight threw a bright beam across the rough floor as he walked in, carrying the hefty watercooler bottle. Twenty paces in, past the protective line of active-shot rat traps, the cocoons of his brother Bik and their grandmother lay on the ground. He and Lolo had moved them into the archway a couple of weeks after Blitz2 began. There was nowhere else. If he'd taken them to one of the official green zone refuges that were being set up, the security agencies and police would have spotted him. So he made it his duty to look after them, keeping them clean and safe.

He shone his flashlight down on the horrible mass of transformed flesh that used to be their torsos. It was difficult now to tell them apart. They were both about the same size, and the myriad features that used to make their faces so individual had slowly sunk away, just like their eyes and ears and mouth, rendering the skulls as blank masks of flesh. Roots like strings of white wax had wormed their way out of each torso, sinking their tendrils into the raw soil in search of basic nutrients.

There was a small table between the two cocoons, with a nearly empty watercooler bottle on it. Ollie shoved it aside and put the new one down in its place, slightly overhanging the edge. Once he was sure it was aligned properly, he turned on the tap at the bottom. Water dripped slowly onto the ground, where the roots had grown into a small crater shape. He'd checked on solnet how to care for a cocoon, like so many who couldn't part from a loved family member, and learned it was important to give them a regular supply of water.

He smiled weakly at his brother's eroded face. "I'm close, Bik," he promised. "Really close now, yeah? I'm going to find out where Nikolaj is hiding, and when I do you'll be sorted. Trust me, whatever it takes. I'll make that bitch grow you back to what you was, see? Then you can go do parkour again, as much as you want."

Every time, he hoped to see something, some tiny twitch of flesh, just a sign that Bik had heard him. *People in comas know what's going on around them, right?* But now, as always, what was left of Bik remained motionless.

"See you soon, bro."

Lolo was waiting back in the curtained-off section of the industrial shed, switching on the lanterns. Sie gave him a contented smile. "Are they okay?"

"Sure, yeah." He jerked his thumb back toward the kilns. "Did you smell anything back there?"

"No. Why?"

"Thought I could smell smoke. One of the doors must be out of alignment."

"More likely the ducts."

"I'll check it over tomorrow."

"I can do that. I'm not freeloading here, you know."

"Thanks." He watched appreciatively as Lolo stood on the bed and stretched up to close the skylight blind above it. Sie was wearing a t-shirt that rode up to show off plenty of toned abdomen. "Nice."

Lolo gave him a cheeky grin and stepped down. "Thank you."

A kiss, with their arms around each other. Easy and undemanding, a promise of intimacy later. Knowing he was going to be having sex lifted Ollie's mood out of the melancholia elicited by visiting the cocoons.

"I have to knead my dough first," Lolo said, and walked over to the marble-topped table sie used for cooking.

"Is that what you call it?"

"You can be so basic. I'm experimenting with flake pastry. It's difficult to do properly by hand."

The disapproving tone didn't fool Ollie for an instant. He started taking off his clothes, and *yes*, put them in the laundry basket like they were fucking married or something. At least the kilns meant they had enough electricity to power the washing machine; hand cleaning stuff would've been just unbearable.

With the sound of Lolo pounding and rolling the dough, Ollie settled back on the bed and accessed the files that had been streamed from the surveillance gear he'd planted around the Icona that morning. He told Tye to pull an image of every person who went in or out of the building. There weren't many. It didn't surprise him. Despite everything, London these days had a decent vibe about it, a sense of pulling together that even a cynic like him couldn't escape. Neighborhoods had cohesion. People looked out for one another. Everyone was level. But not Docklands. It was probably the lurking presence of the green zone, with its multitude of cocoons, that made it subtly disaffecting. If you lived there, it was because you had no choice.

In the fourteen hours since his visit, eight people had gone through the Icona's doors. Ollie started reviewing them. National files still existed; it was just getting to them that was the problem. The lownet had gone, blown away by security agency G8Turings in a vicious darkware war as the Olyix sabotage began. What was left of solnet was a much simplified version, which made monitoring straightforward for the authorities. So he had to set up convoluted routes using every trick Gareth had ever taught him.

He was disappointed that Larson himself hadn't used the Icona's doors, but then Brandon Schumder had said the man never left his apartment. However, Tye did identify Cestus Odgers, who had gone in at twelve-thirty carrying a hessian tote bag and then out again at one twenty-five, sans bag. The files Tye extracted from London's business register showed Odgers was a memorabilia trader, with several commercial ventures down the years. He even co-owned a trade convention that had put on a couple of shows back in 2195.

"Got one," Ollie cried.

Lolo looked around. "One what?"

"A way in to Larson. Bloke called Cestus Odgers. He deals in all that crap Larson likes. He's still dealing by the look of it, and I've got an address on him."

"Oh."

"Come on, we've spent two years pursuing Nikolaj. This is the best shot yet."

"I know." Lolo put the dough down with a sigh and came over to the bed. Sie slipped through a gap in the white veils and lay beside him. "It's just . . . Nikolaj is different. If you're right, she's working for the Olyix."

"*If* I'm right?"

"Ollie." Sie cuddled up and kissed him urgently. "I need you to be careful. Promise me."

"Hey, I'm not going to blow this now. I've got too much riding on it. Bik and Gran are depending on me."

"Yes."

"Wow, the enthusiasm."

"I'm sorry, it's just . . ." Sie stroked Ollie's cheek, then slid a finger down to the slim black insurance collar. "Why do you need this?"

"You know why, because you just said it. Nikolaj works for the Olyix, so there's no telling what she's got protecting her. I need to get physically close."

"I'm frightened. For you. It's not just Bik and your grandmother that need you. I do, too—especially now. There's got to be someone else who can do this. Can't you just . . . *grass* them?"

Ollie chuckled at how foreign Lolo sounded right then. "If I thought it would do any good, I would send every file I have to Special Branch. But you've met them, remember? Was that a happy time?"

"No."

"So, that's settled then."

LONDON

DECEMBER 11, 2206

Cestus Odgers was easier than expected. Ollie turned up at his house, playing the desperate innocent routine, saying how eager he was to sell the *Nightstar* model for a cryptoken full of watts. Odgers wouldn't buy it for himself. "It's a small piss-poor market these days, fella. And I don't have that kind of money anymore. But I know someone that does."

The finder's fee was a half-charged quantum battery. Ollie didn't try to haggle. *An easy mark.* So the call was made to Larson, who agreed to meet. But Ollie had to have the model for inspection, to prove he wasn't a time waster.

So once again he found himself cycling into Docklands, this time with the *Nightstar* rattling along in the trailer behind him. He'd never had weapons peripherals, like some in the Legion. Instead he put on the jacket with the systems from his stealth suit, ran diagnostics on the darkware Tye was loaded with, and finally stashed the nerve-block pistol and synth slugs into the *Nightstar*'s hangar deck. A twenty-centimeter ceramic blade was strapped to his forearm, under the jacket.

The Icona entrance had an old-style intercom, with an actual physical button for every apartment. When Ollie pressed for the third-floor penthouse, Tye used the passive sensors stitched into his jacket to see if he was being scanned. But the only electrical activity it could detect was a small current in the intercom panel, powering a camera.

Larson's voice came out of the intercom. "Come on up, and bring the model." The door lock buzzed.

Ollie hadn't anticipated having to carry the model, and definitely not up three flights of stairs. It wasn't excessively heavy, but getting it up the twisting stairwell without knocking it against the wall was a bastard of a trip.

He was sweating heavily by the time he reached the third floor and came out onto a long corridor with a half-dozen doors. There were no windows, but one of the doors was open, providing some light. As he passed it, he saw the apartment had been ransacked. Tye detected an active local network using sensors lining the corridor to scan him, so it infiltrated the node and launched a series of darkware packages into the system.

The door at the end of the corridor didn't have a handle; instead there was a single red LED glowing in the center. Ollie stood in front of it, looking twitchy, as any chancer would.

There was a soft click, and the door swung inward a couple of centimeters.

"Come in," a voice said from inside. "The power hinges don't work, so you'll have to push."

The door was as heavy as a bank vault's. Hard to get moving, but once he'd applied enough pressure it swung back as smoothly as if it were floating on oil. Ollie staggered in with the *Nightstar* clutched in front of him. Tye splashed the progress of the darkware as it slipped undetected through the penthouse systems. Larson clearly took his security a lot more seriously than Schumder did. There were five concealed guns in the walls and ceiling, as well as a panic room. Tye disabled the weapons.

Ollie peered around the purple-and-black mosaic that was the *Nightstar*'s curving wings. The penthouse was open plan, presenting a single split-level reception room with a high ceiling, and a window wall looking out across the Royal Dock outside. Once upon a time it must have been a swish place to live, but now . . . Tall glass display cabinets cluttered the floor, the only furniture left—esoteric tombstones turning the big space into a mausoleum of extinct trash-culture. Every centimeter of their shelf space was full of figurines and toys and show-branded games and badges, but that still wasn't enough space for the collection. Ollie managed to walk six paces into the room and then couldn't go any farther. Plastic crates were piled up in the aisles, over-flowing with more junk. Models of vehicles combined with furry alien creatures to form long, unruly dunes, onto which tides of actual paper books had fallen, their bizarre, colorful covers slowly fading as entropy brittled them. Signed post-ers of ancient blockbuster movies in fanciful gothic frames covered two walls, while the final wall was made up of screens stacked like oversize glass bricks. Most of them were dead, leaving the few live rectangles playing drama shows that had peaked over a century ago. To Ollie, they were windows into odd alternative pasts that—given Blitz2—actually now seemed quite enticing. The central screen was playing a *Nightstar* episode.

He looked down at his feet in puzzlement. There really was no way farther into the room without wading through and over this hoard of valueless treasure. "Hello?"

"Welcome, welcome," said a voice overhead.

Ollie assumed it was a speaker, but glanced up anyway just as a peculiar motion caught his eye. The room's ceiling had exposed metal beams, painted as black as the concrete they supported. They now served as rails for an industrial hoist mechanism. Ollie's jaw dropped. Karno Larson was hanging from the hoist on metal cables. He was obscenely large, his torso a flaccid globe covered in a shiny green toga that was more like a wrap of bandages, ensuring no skin was visible. Limbs were equally gross—thick appendages that were so bloated they seemed incapable of movement. His corpulent head rose out of the toga without any sign of a neck, rolls of skin glistening under a film of perspiration. Straggly gray hair was tied back in a ponytail, woven with strips of orange leather.

The harness that held him also sported various modules that Tye was telling Ollie were medical support machines. Tubes snaked out of them, disappearing into the toga between the bands of cloth, swaying about as fluids pumped through.

Staring up as Larson slid toward him like a dirigible Peter Pan, Ollie could easily believe the man was the victim of a cocooning gone horribly wrong. The hoist came to a halt, and motors made a loud whirring sound, lowering Larson down toward the jumble of ancient merchandise. Globular feet touched a batch of coffee-table books featuring science fiction artwork, and they started to bend beneath him.

"What an excellent—" Larson paused and his head bowed forward, allowing him to suck air from a tube, "—specimen."

"Are you all right?" Ollie blurted, which was probably dumber than anything even Lars had ever said.

"Absolutely fine, my dear fellow. You don't get to live this long without making a few compromises."

Yes, you fucking do. "Right."

"In these sorry times, I feel quite privileged. I am the last person alive who appreciates the culture of ephemeral modernity." Motors whirred again, and slim wires Ollie hadn't noticed before lifted Larson's arms into a benediction posture, as if he were the puppet of an unseen deity. "So every relic I desire now flows to me, as your presence proves. I am become the ultimate steward of this glorious genre of human creativity. As such, I have determined that when we fall to the Olyix, I will welcome them here into my temple of unparalleled artistic wealth. And together, we will carry this unique trove to the end of time. Their God will rejoice in what I bring."

"Uh—" Ollie let out a long breath of dismay, as he realized that Larson was utterly crazy. But the information about Nikolaj's location was in that deranged head of his. "Isolate the penthouse," he told Tye.

"Done."

"Please hold the *Nightstar* up," Larson said. "It looks truly magnificent. You say it is handmade?"

A smiling Ollie proffered the *Nightstar* as if it were a religious artifact. "Tye, disengage the hoist."

Larson's shiny forehead crinkled into a frown. "Something is wrong." He sucked on the air tube again, then let out a wild mewling sound as the cables that held him started to unwind off the winch drums. He toppled backward in a curious slow motion, as if gravity hadn't quite established a decent grip on him. The toys and books he landed on bent and crumpled in a grinding dissonance.

Ollie pushed his hand into the *Nightstar*'s hangar deck and tugged out his nerve-block pistol. It occurred to him that using it on Larson might not be the smartest idea. Who knew what would happen to a body like that if the nervous system suffered a failure? Tye was busy splashing up the medical data from the man's modules. Ollie wasn't much good at reading the details, but the number of amber icons was unnerving. He fished the synth slugs from the *Nightstar* and clambered over the ridiculous memorabilia to stand where Larson could see him.

"Take—take—" Larson gasped. He sucked frantically at his air tube.

"Take what? No, listen, I don't care about this junk. I'm here to find out where Nikolaj is. That's it, that's all I need, understand? So, where is the Paynor family house where she's holed up? Tell me that and I'll let you up again."

Larson's frightened eyes stared up at him.

"Tell me." He held up his ace, the synth slugs, remembering the speech he'd given Schumder. Though to be honest, he wasn't sure he could even find a bone on Larson without some kind of hospital scanner.

"I—I—Help!"

Ollie set his jaw as several of the medical icons turned red. He had to do this. And quick, because—"These are synth slugs, and they've got this sparkle. Okay, forget that. They're like a diamond—they *are* diamonds. Girl's best friend right, cos they're fucking hard, like me. And I'm going to let them eat you—er, no, eat through you. Yeah. That's going to be agony, see. If you don . . ." A whole series of Larson's medical icons turned scarlet. One of the modules on the harness started screeching out an alarm.

"Fuck!" Ollie shouted.

Larson's mouth was opening and closing feebly. Obese fingers wiggled like electrocuted worms.

"Air?" Ollie cried. "Do you need air?" He knelt down fast and tried to lift Larson's head. The pile of crap he was poised on shifted alarmingly, jolting the pair of them. For one horrific moment Ollie thought the massive body might roll on top of him. Larson's tongue was protruding between his lips.

"What's wrong?" Ollie yelled. "Oh, fuck, fuck!" The medical modules were trying to send an emergency call to a specialist cardiac hospital in Chelsea, but his own darkware was blocking it perfectly. "No! No, please. Tell me where Nikolaj is. Please! I'll call the paramedics. I swear. They'll save you. Just tell me."

"He has gone into cardiac arrest," Tye announced.

"No, no, no! He can't do that."

"Life signs are flatlining."

Ollie looked pleadingly at Larson's vacant face. "Where are the Paynors?"

"Multiple organ failure. Support machines unable to sustain basic body functions."

Larson stopped breathing.

"You piece of shit," Ollie screamed, and hit him, fist slamming directly into that wretched pudgy face. Hit him again. A third time. Nothing. "You bastard! You stupid, stupid bastard! Why did you let yourself get like this? Why?" Ollie sagged back, gazing in disbelief at the one chance he'd had to find Nikolaj, to save Gran and Bik. *Two years. Two fucking years to find him. And he fucking DIES?*

Ollie had no real awareness of walking downstairs and back out of the Icona building. It was only when the light and sound of London's devil-sky engulfed him with a greater vehemence than usual that he started to notice the external world again. Buildings and docks were just smears of drab color. Even the abrupt change of the data splashed across his tarsus lens didn't really grab his attention. It was only Tye saying, "Eight targeting lasers have now acquired you," that jolted him alert again. His surroundings crunched into extreme focus.

Paramilitaries in black armor were crouched at the corners of nearby buildings. Overhead, three ugly urban counter-insurgency drones hovered just above the Icona's roofline. Various barrels pointed down at him.

Ollie let out a wordless scream of hatred, clenched fists rising.

"Ollie Heslop, you are under arrest," a voice boomed out. "Deactivate any peripherals and get down on your knees. Put your hands behind your head and lock your fingers together."

"Fuck you!" Ollie bellowed back. There were tears streaming down his cheeks. He couldn't believe this was happening. He'd walked through the Icona's entrance ready to get Nikolaj's location, to start saving Gran and Bik. Now he had nothing, and Special Branch had found him. Bik and Gran were lost, doomed to be taken by the Olyix when London's shield finally broke.

"You will not be told again. Deactivate your peri—"

"No!" He took a step forward, jabbing a finger at his black collar. "Scan that, you shits! Go on. Scan it. See that? See what it is? I'll use it, I fucking swear I will! Just piss off and leave me alone." The tears were flowing faster now, and with them came miserable sobs making his chest judder. "Leave me alone," he wailed. "You've won. Do you understand? Whoop bloody whoop. What more do you want? You can't send me to Zagreus, not anymore. We're all going to be cocooned anyway, so what's the fucking point?" He slumped back against the wall and slowly slid down it. His head bowed low so he didn't have to see anything, and he carried on sobbing. When he had no tears left—when every thought was numb—he'd do it. The collar really was insurance. Packed with explosives, it would decapitate him instantly, and the blast would shatter his skull, pulping his brain. The Olyix wouldn't be able to cocoon that.

It was the only victory he had left.

Twenty minutes later, he still hadn't moved. The tears had stopped a while back. In his head, he was living in the past, replaying the memories of the time before. Of Bik larking about. Gran, always so stressed and tired as she struggled to bring up two boys, to get them to go to school, to stop them hanging with the wrong crowd. *No. Not them. Me. I was the one who let her down. I should have stayed at university. I*

*shouldn't have got myself thrown out. I shouldn't have gone
back to the Legion.*

*It's why I've finished up here. It's why we're all here. I
was so dumb, I helped the Olyix. I did this to London, to the
world.*

The sound of approaching footsteps registered through
the black grief. He took a breath and focused on the collar
icon. The last thing he'd ever see. *Here we go—*

"Ollie, darling."

Un. Be. Fucking. Leavable! Ollie started to laugh hysteri-
cally. He was at absolute rock bottom, the worst state it was
possible for a human to be in—but no, there was still a single way he could be brought lower. And who was the one and
only person who could do that . . . ? "What are you doing
here?"

"Ollie, please don't do this."

He glanced up. Lolo was standing ten meters in front of
him, wearing a scarlet summer dress with big white polka
dots that glimmered an unwholesome lilac under the devil-
sky. Despite that, sie looked amazing. Beautiful face so full
of sorrow and worry and love.

"I'm pregnant, Ollie."

Ollie's entire body shut down. Not a muscle moved—
certainly not his lungs, probably not even his heart.

*I must have triggered the necklace. More than once. And
this is what Hell is—the same world, but progressively
worse each time you die.*

"I'm sorry," Lolo said. "I should have told you. I've
wanted to tell you. But there's never been a right time, has
there? Please, this is Kohei Yamada. Listen to him. None of
this is as bad as you think, Ollie. Really, it's not."

A man was standing next to hir, face stiff from anti-aging
treatments, wearing a windbreaker with a Connexion logo.
Ollie drew down a punishing breath.

"Hello, Ollie," Kohei said. "We want Nikolaj, too. And
we know where she is. Interested?"

INTERSTELLAR SPACE

YEAR 5 AA

Six hours before the *Morgan* departed, Yirella sat on the edge of her bed, looking straight ahead at the cabin's inactive texture wall. Once again, the file played in her optik. She'd viewed it at least once a day since she'd recorded it, and still she felt a mild pang of guilt.

I had no choice. I hope they understand.

"You cannot keep on consulting people and putting off decisions until some mythical consensus deal appears," the recording of her said. "That's not true leadership, and its lack is what we have been guilty of for thousands of years. Sometimes you just have to make the choice—because if you're in the position to make that choice, you have the right to make it. Our circumstance means we have no choice but to do this, to create you. This civilization we are starting has a similarity with my generation. Like you, we were born unasked. We had no choice over the course of our lives because of the circumstances we found ourselves in. But unlike us, you *will* have freedom of choice. That is the most precious gift I can provide you. By the act of being born alone and empowered in this unique place, you have been granted freedom. You may choose to help a struggle that is now ten thousand years old . . . or not. That ability is the one thing that cannot be taken from you. When you exercise it, obviously I hope you choose to join me. But if not, I wish you well on your journey to whatever goal you have found for your-selves."

The recording ended. The same soft sigh as always es-caped her lips. *Too late to worry now.* She never did quite understand why regret burned her this way every time she played the recording. *I did the right thing.* Although it would be history that made that judgment. *That's if there's anyone left to review human history.*

Maybe it wasn't guilt that caused all the angst but appre-ciation of the responsibility she'd undertaken, the arrogance. The scale of what she'd done was so momentous, and only one other person shared it—which didn't lift any of the re-sponsibility off her shoulders.

The cabin door opened, and Dellian came in, trailed by a remote loaded with all their possessions—a couple of cases that carried everything they'd accumulated. It didn't seem much for two lives. People long back in history had acquired whole houses full of material memories.

But the way he smiled at the sight of her made the uni-verse a better place. Not even an Olyix superweapon could kill his love, and that was worth more than any treasure. "Hello, you," she said.

He gave the blank walls a befuddled look. "Doesn't the texture work? Saints' sake! The *Morgan*'s refit took three months. They must have checked stuff like this."

She got up and gave him a hug. "Calm down. I was wait-ing for you, that's all."

"Oh. Thanks. So what have you got?"

She told her databud to switch the environment on. The walls turned to bare metal bulkheads, with thick oblong windows riveted into place. They looked out from a giant space station of spires and disks that hung high above the nightside of a planet whose continents were single cities. Their glittering lights shone as though all the stars in the sky had descended to populate the ground, while above it all, hundreds of planets shared the same orbit around the sun in a stippled ring, each of them shining with the rich sapphires, whites, and jades of an Earthlike world. Weird and wondrous spaceships cruised gracefully around the station, departing and arriving in constant streams.

"That is quite something," Dellian admitted.

"It could be ours," she said wistfully. "The way we live, what we build. After FinalStrike."

His arm tightened around her so his head was pressed into her chest. "We'll get there. You'll see."

"Yeah."

"You ready?"

"Sure."

He broke away to stare up at her—a gaze that was unnervingly intense. "We can still stay here, with the habitats. It'll be a good life."

"For us. What about our descendants if the FinalStrike doesn't work?"

"Like Loneve says, they'll develop new weapons here, something that can defeat the Olyix. Besides, I thought you wanted that: a society that's broken the exodus cycle."

"I certainly do. But I've invested too much in this FinalStrike mission now, and you'd hate it here. Don't pretend you wouldn't."

"I guess we know each other pretty well."

She bent down and kissed the top of his head. "I guess we do."

It was nothing like the time the *Morgan* had departed from Juloss. Then, they'd gathered to celebrate the other Strike ships departing, with everyone making their own way out across the galaxy. It had been a ceremony of hope and anticipation, their commitment to the goal unbreakable. This time there were barely a hundred people in the starship's main auditorium, out of the thousand who were on board. More than seven hundred were already in suspension chambers to hibernate throughout the twelve-year voyage to the neutron star. Even then, they'd be arriving fifty years after the seedships, which were traveling at an even higher relativistic velocity.

"Where's everyone else?" Dellian asked. He was wearing his squad leader dress uniform for the occasion, which put him in a minority.

"Busy," Yirella said. "There are a lot of new systems to monitor."

Dellian was skeptical about that; monitoring systems was what gentens were for. He glanced up at the screen at the back of the auditorium's stage, which showed the space directly outside the *Morgan*. Thirty newly completed Final-Strike warships were holding station in a loosely spherical formation five hundred kilometers in diameter. They were all modeled on the original *Morgan* design—seven grid spheres stacked in a line, wrapped with thermo-dump spikes. But there had been changes. The rear section now contained the drive developed for the *Actaeon* project—five ribbed ovoids glowing an eerie aquamarine—while the fifth deck housed nucleonic weapons developed by Wim's team: long slivers of solidified light that pulsed in the rhythm of a human heartbeat. Beyond the fleet were the three habitats, their shells visible only as shadows against the ridge of stars that cut across the profound darkness of deep space.

"You okay?" Yirella asked.

"Sure."

People were starting to sit down. He gestured at a row of seats near the stage. "We're so small, aren't we?" he said. It felt like a confession.

"Did you talk to Ainsley before he left with the seed-ships?"

"Not much. Why?"

"We used to talk about how little impact life actually has on the universe."

"I don't think I'm up to that level of philosophy."

She put her arm through his, then waved at Alexandre, who'd just come in. "Don't be so self-deprecating."

"Do you miss him?"

"Yes. Because we're a little less safe without him. But it made sense for him to go on ahead with the seedships. He can protect them until they propagate a neutron star civilization that can build its own defenses."

"Right." Again he felt a mild unease. Despite all the advisory council meetings and debates and committees producing strategies for discussion, FinalStrike was still Yirella's concept. It was logical, smart, and had the best chance of success. And yet . . . *Maybe I am paranoid*. At some fundamental level, he knew Yirella wouldn't betray them. So maybe the doubts were a relic of the Olyix neurovirus?

I hope so.

Which was about the craziest thought he'd ever had.

Alexandre joined them, sitting next to Yirella; then the rest of the squad arrived and spread out along the row.

"You've got about a minute left before they shut the portals back to Sisaket," Dellian told their old mentor with a grin.

"Not a chance," Alexandre said. "Look what happened last time I let you go off by yourselves."

"You shouldn't use us as an excuse to leave the habitats behind," Yirella said. "We're going to confront the Olyix directly. The odds of success are unknown."

Dellian gave her an exasperated frown. "Saints! This is all your idea."

"I know. But you have to be following the plan for the right reasons."

"Hey, you two, stop fighting," an amused Janc said. "Captain's here."

Kenelm strode onto the stage. Dellian was pleased to see sie was wearing hir uniform, too. He found familiarity and tradition reassuring at this point, even though he wasn't half as confident as he had been when the *Morgan* had left Juloss. The fight was so much bigger than they'd realized back then. More desperate, too.

Loneve's face appeared on the screen, blocking out half of the FinalStrike fleet.

"I would've liked to use my old departure speech," Kenelm said, "but we all know it is no longer applicable. This time, as we venture forth, we are facing a threat greater than we could have imagined. The Vayan lure may not have had the result we expected, but we have emerged stronger and more knowledgeable. And more—we saved a quarter of a million humans from enslavement, which is an achievement we can take enormous pride in. Now those lives we liberated will go on in safety out here amid the stars, free to choose their own destiny."

Dellian felt Yirella stiffen at Kenelm's words.

"It is unlikely we will ever see each other again," the captain continued, facing Loneve's image, "but I would suggest that our descendants will meet your descendants back on a reclaimed Earth."

"A prophecy we will strive to fulfill," Loneve said formally. "On behalf of all of us who have chosen this life, I thank you for your service and wish you the best of luck."

"Gonna need a hell of a lot more than luck to win this," Falar muttered. Tilliana jabbed him with an elbow.

Kenelm gave Loneve's image a dignified bow. "This is a bittersweet parting. We advance once more to confront the ancient enemy. The Saints are no longer with us, but their spirit infuses every one of us. The FinalStrike mission will honor their memory with the same selfless determination they showed us. Know this, Saints: We will not let you down."

"We will not let you down," Dellian promised solemnly. *Or we'll die trying.*

Kenelm gestured, and everyone stood. "We depart not in sorrow, but with hope," sie said.

Dellian's optik display showed him all the portal connections with the habitats shut down. The *Morgan*'s drive powered up, and they started to accelerate. Around them, the rest of the thirty-strong fleet was moving, spreading wide as they left the three habitats behind, assuming the broad circular formation that they would maintain for the next hundred thirty-seven light-years.

He watched the screen in silence as the dim habitats began to shrink away behind them. Then three expansion portals grew rapidly, their slender blue rims glowing in welcome as the habitats slid into them. Before long, even that sight faded from view. *That's it; we're committed now.* He turned and kissed Yirella. "Whatever happens, I'm glad we'll face it together."

She gave him an uncertain grin. "Thank you."

Dellian faced the squad. "Okay, one last training session tomorrow, then it's straight into the suspension chambers. I seriously do not want to spend twelve years stuck on this ship staring at you guys."

LONDON

DECEMBER 11, 2206

The holding cell was all concrete—walls, floor, and ceiling. Its door was metal and half a meter thick, blast proof.

Ollie still hadn't taken his insurance collar off. He sat on the carbon-frame cot, next to Lolo. They didn't hold hands. Didn't talk. Both of them staring ahead.

Finally, Ollie couldn't stand it anymore. "WHAT THE FUCK?" he screamed.

Lolo started crying.

"Oh, for Christ's sake." Ollie tentatively put an arm around hir.

"I'm sorry. I'm sorry. I'm sorry."

"Why, though?" Ollie asked, genuinely perplexed. "This is a shit time to be alive, and getting worse. I was probably about to die squaring off to Nikolaj. The London shield will fall just like Berlin. How could you get *pregnant*?"

"It just sort of happened. My gender cycle is off. I think it was the stress. It was an accident. But it's a beautiful accident, Ollie. We're going to have a baby!"

"The kid . . . We're not going to get out of this, you know that, right? It's going to be the shortest, most miserable life ever. My kid . . ."

"Ollie, where there's life, there's hope. Always."

"You are so fucking stupid."

"I'm sorry."

He leaned in closer. "Stop saying that." One hand strayed to Lolo's stomach, pressing against the red fabric. "How far on are you?"

"Two and a half months."

"You don't show. Are you sure?"

"Pregnancy tests are infallible. I took four."

"Why didn't you tell me?"

"I was afraid. I mean, this isn't the best day in the world, is it?"

"This day wouldn't have happened if you'd told me."

"It's not my fault!" sie blubbed.

"I know. All right. I'm the one who's sorry, okay? I shouldn't be shouting at you. It's just . . . timing, Lolo. Timing is really not your thing."

"They're going to offer you a deal."

"I know."

"Don't do anything crazy, okay? I love you. I can't do this without you." Hir hand went to hir belly.

He nodded brokenly. "Got it."

"Do you really think London will fall?"

"Not now. Not for you. I'll make sure of that. If nothing else, you're a Utopial. You're entitled to repatriation back to Akitha." He lifted his head up, hunting around for the sensors that must be there but remained invisible. "Hear that? And that's before you make me an offer!"

"I can't go without you," Lolo said.

"Let's just see where this takes us, okay? They must need me pretty badly, else I'd be facedown at the bottom of the docks by now." Ollie gave the blank walls an expectant look.

The door swung open less than a minute later. Kohei Yamada walked in, still wearing the same jacket. Two armored paramilitary guards stood outside.

"Right, then," Kohei said. "Lolo, time for you to say goodbye to your boyfriend. Ollie and I are going to have a little chat."

"I'm not going anywhere," Lolo insisted.

Ollie knew that tone well enough. He sighed and put his arms around hir, kissing hir gently. "It's okay. This is our ticket out, so don't blow it for me."

Lolo scowled at Kohei, then made a show of standing up reluctantly. "Be careful. I don't trust them."

"Me neither."

"You know they took Bik and your grandmother when they brought me in? They loaded their cocoons on a truckez."

Ollie gave Kohei a sharp look. "No shit?"

"So," Lolo said portentously. "What you said."

"Uh, what was that?"

"You're not paranoid if they are actually out to get you." Sie gestured around the cell.

"Take care," Ollie said, and gave hir a kiss, resting his face on hirs. "And . . . eat properly, all that crap. And no nark, either."

"I'd stopped over a month ago. You never noticed."

"Oh. Sorry. Do you know what it is?"

Lolo frowned for a moment, then shook hir head in mild exasperation. "My genes are dominant, Ollie. Our child is omnia, of course."

"Good. That's good."

A last kiss, and Lolo walked out of the cell, looking back urgently as the door swung shut again.

"I love yo—"

Ollie took a breath. "I meant what I said," he said firmly. "Sie's back on Akitha before we even discuss any terms."

"Tough guy, huh?"

"I know my rights."

"Fair enough. Zero isn't a hard number to remember."

"Sie's a Utopial citizen."

"Which entitles hir to exactly shit."

"Fuck you!"

"But as a gesture of goodwill, I agree. Lolo Maude will be permitted to return to Akitha."

"Oh. Right. Thank you."

"Ollie, it's a one-way trip. Sie won't be coming back. And you're a known criminal with a record file bigger than a Sumiko interactive file. You like Sumiko, right?"

Oh, fuck. "Yeah." If they knew that, they knew everything. He sank back onto the cot. "What do you want?"

"Same as you: Nikolaj."

"You said you know where she is. What do you need me for?"

"Ah, this is where it gets complicated. We can't let her know we know about her."

"So just take her out. Snipers. Drone shot. You were going to do that to me, and I'm nobody."

"Far from it, Ollie. You're a very important somebody. Today, anyway."

"Fuck you again."

"It's like this. Nikolaj works for the Olyix—"

"Why?" he blurted. "I don't get that. I never did. Her and Jade both. They both betrayed us."

"So did you, Ollie. You tried to take down the Croydon power relay station. Without that—without the power it supplies to the London shield generators—we'd all be cocoons stored inside the *Salvation of Life* right now."

"We didn't know, okay? We were stupid, yes, but the Legion didn't betray nobody. We done it for the money. We thought we were working for a London major, that's all. Not fucking aliens! But Nikolaj and Jade, they *knew*. And they still did it. They had to have some deal going with the Olyix, right?"

"Is that what you think?"

"There's nothing else, no other reason. I've thought about this for two years. That's why I was going for her."

"I understand that. Revenge is hardwired into all of us, right back there behind all our civilized behavior. It's primal. And when we lose everything else, that's what we have left."

"No, you don't get it. Nikolaj was going to be my leverage."

Kohei gave him a curious look. "You wanted to make a deal with her?"

"I was going to force her to deal, yeah. I didn't have anything to lose. Then all this shit happened." He flapped his hands at the cell. "And Lolo—I mean . . . fuck!"

"What deal?"

"She knows the Olyix. The Olyix know how to reverse cocooning. They must do. They can give me Gran and Bik back."

"Ah." Kohei smiled.

Ollie didn't like that smile. It wasn't in any way sympathetic.

"I get it now," Kohei said. "That was a smart move."

"Yeah? Then how come I'm here?"

"Fate. And poor old Karno Larson. What did you do to him?"

"Nothing! I swear. He just died. You can't blame me for that."

"No. But we still have the raid against the Croydon station, and the house on Lichfield Road. Those charges are still pending."

"Yeah? So? What you going to do? Lock me up? How long's that going to last?"

"About ten hours."

"Huh?"

"The London shield will fail in maybe ten hours at the most, unless we stop Nikolaj's sabotage operations. They're chewing away at the generators, one bite at a time."

"But . . . if you know about that, stop them."

"There's a bigger picture here, Ollie. Even I don't get to see all of it."

"Wait. You're going to *let* London fall? You can't mean that."

"To stop London from falling, we need to eliminate Nikolaj first—and in a way that doesn't cause any suspicion. That's you, Ollie. A gang kid with a grudge hunting for vengeance—nothing suspicious about that. You're not smart enough to be anything else."

"Shit. You want me to kill her?"

"I'm not a politician, so I'm not going to use crap like 'threat cancellation' or 'conflict resolution.' Yes, we want her dead. But when you do it, she has to know it's you, and you're doing it out of revenge for the Legion."

"I don't get it. If she's dead, what does it matter if she's suspicious—and anyway, suspicious about what?"

"That we know about her. That we sent you. Okay? So just do what we ask. It doesn't make any difference to you."

"It does. You're asking me to kill someone. I'm not even sure I can."

"You killed Karno Larson."

"I didn't! He . . . It wasn't my fault!"

"Sure. And what about Nikolaj?"

"What about her?"

"You've been trying to find her for two years. What were you planning on doing when you did catch up? Go out for a romantic meal, maybe a club after?"

"Fuck you."

"Ollie, we're running out of time here, okay? I need to know your answer."

"Tell me why she can't know about you," he said stubbornly. It was all he had left now, making sense of the shitstorm that had become his life.

"Think about it. She works for the Olyix, right? They're in communication with her, so if she gets suspicious, then so will they. And we cannot allow that under any circumstances."

"But if she's dead, she . . . Oh!" Ollie wanted to curl up into a ball. Some zero-nark would be good, too. "If she's suspicious I'm working for you and kills me—riiight. Fuck. You don't trust me to do this."

"Actually, I do. The problem is, you'll be walking into an exceptionally hostile environment. There are no certainties. So we have to plan accordingly."

"Yeah. I suppose."

"Let me add a sweetener," Kohei said.

"What? You're already sending Lolo home." He glanced up sharply. "You are, aren't you?"

"Yes, but I need you committed to this—and I mean truly committed. We have one shot, and it has got to work."

The cell door swung open again, and Ollie stared at the woman who came in. She was wearing a plain white shirt and dark trousers, so not someone who cared about appearance, then. And her face was pretty plain, too. Maybe some Asian ancestry, light-hazel eyes, black hair trimmed neatly— the kind low-level corporates would have to demonstrate style and individualism. A person you'd struggle to remember, the perfect everywoman.

"This is Lim Tianyu," Kohei said.

"Pleased to meet you," Lim said.

"Sure."

"Lim is part of Alpha Defense's medical team, right, Lim?"

"I have that privilege."

"Medical?" Ollie said. "For defense?" This wasn't making a whole lot of sense, which wasn't good.

"Lim has been researching cocoons."

"Research?"

"My team has been looking into reversing the process," she said. "And we have had some very promising results."

"You're fucking kidding me!"

"No. The process is at an experimental stage, but in order to advance it, we need to move up to full human testing."

"Oh, bloody hell. You're talking about Gran and Bik, aren't you?"

Kohei shrugged. "Somebody's got to be first. This is their chance, Ollie. Otherwise, they're going to be sent off to a green zone refuge, along with all the millions of others we're holding on to. So you tell me. Even if London survives into tomorrow, how confident are you that the government population recovery program will get around to them before we defeat the Olyix and send them packing?"

"You bastards. What if it doesn't work?"

"Truthfully," Lim said, "I give the process a seventy-five percent chance of providing them a full recovery into a re-grown body."

"And what odds did you have of forcing Nikolaj to make that happen?" Kohei asked mildly.

Ollie knew what his answer was going to be. Of course he did. It was just that saying it out loud—admitting it—was another defeat. But then he'd lost the game of life the day the Legion took their first payment from Jade. "You take them off Earth to do this," he said weakly.

"My laboratory is in the Delta Pavonis system," Lim said.

"So Lolo can confirm we're playing straight with you," Kohei said. "Ollie, I need an answer. Time is not our friend today."

"Okay. I'll do it."

Leipzig fell as Kohei walked Ollie up to the deployment room they'd set up on the Greenwich Tower's third floor. The news splashed into his tarsus lens while he was still on the stairs. A single shield generator was brought down by dark-ware, simultaneous with a power shortage from physical sabotage against a cable. In ordinary times, the secondary power supply would have responded instantaneously. But components overstressed by two years of abuse were too de-graded, the darkware threw sand in the eyes of the management G8Turing, and the rerouted power dropped out for too many milliseconds. The generator blew, kicking off a cascade as the remaining generators were unable to compensate.

Orbital spysats watched the protective wall of artificially solid air burst apart. Seconds later, the Deliverance ships switched off their energy beams. It made little difference. The ravaged air outside crashed down like a deluge of elec-trified magma. It was as if the city were struck by an earth-quake. Millions of windows shattered, roofs collapsed, walls fissured. The taller buildings swayed alarmingly. Some began to topple, falling amid a thunder of dust clouds that spun into ferocious whirlwinds as storm air roared in to scour every road.

Civic sensors revealed people staggering along the streets, barely able to stand in the hurricane-force squalls, their screams lost in the cataclysm's howl. Airborne debris became shrapnel, slicing into skin. Desiccated grass and barren trees started to smolder.

Every network link into Leipzig went out at once as the remaining portals into the city were switched off. Kohei was obscurely pleased about that. He'd seen what happened after a city shield collapsed—the humans hunted, subdued, and collected. He didn't need to see it again.

Yuri's icon splashed across Kohei's lens. "Did you see Leipzig?"

"Yeah," Kohei said. He gave Ollie an uncertain glance; it wasn't as if they could motivate him any harder by allowing him to access the feed.

"According to our latest intelligence, there's a new type of Olyix warship on its way. They'll be here in another five days," Yuri said. "We don't want to leave it that long before we launch Strikeback, but it'll be another day before everything we need is in position. If you're going to shut down the sabotage against London, it'll have to be soon."

"I've got all my teams in position. We just need Ollie to do his stuff. Another thirty minutes max."

"Okay. Well, good luck. I'm really sorry to put these restrictions on you."

"I get it. Don't worry."

"Look, if Ollie screws up, get yourself back here to Delta Pavonis."

"Thanks for the offer, chief, but there're a lot of people down here who deserve to get out. Not just me."

"Don't be a martyr, Kohei. There've been so many over the last two years that nobody will ever notice another. Besides, your wife is expecting you."

"Yeah."

"One thing. Whenever you do come out here, I'm not going to be around, so I just wanted to say how much I appreciate what you've done. You're an excellent security operative, Kohei."

"What do you mean, 'not around'?"

"We all have a part to play."

"Didn't someone just say something about being a martyr?"

"I'm not. You'll find out eventually. But we won't ever see each other again."

"Chief," he implored.

"You're a good man, Kohei. I trust you to save London. Now goodbye." And Yuri's icon vanished.

"Shit!"

Ollie gave him a worried look. "What?"

Kohei paused, realizing his arms were trembling. Then he looked at the stupid young man's face. Ollie had been given several new peripherals Lim had brought, created by some fancy new technology developed by Alpha Defense. The units were supposed to be undetectable, but they'd had to rush the implantation. As a result, Ollie was clearly in pain, his face hot and sweaty, grimacing constantly.

"Nothing," Kohei replied as cheerfully as he could.

"Didn't sound like it," Ollie said sullenly.

"You're not the only operation I'm running, sonny. Don't flatter yourself."

The deployment room had a three-meter portal set up. A five-strong squad of paramilitaries was waiting; Kohei's lens data showed him fifteen had already deployed. Eight counter-insurgency drones were already flying high over the city, heading for Chelsea.

"Let's go," Kohei said. He wanted to keep Ollie moving, not give him time to stop and think. There was something about him, a vulnerability, that Kohei found unsettling. It had taken ten minutes just to coax him out of his fleshmask and bomb collar. Ten minutes they couldn't afford.

Ollie glanced uneasily at the portal and its guard of para-militaries. "Where does it go?"

"I told you. Nikolaj is in Chelsea, the Paynor family's house on Pelham Crescent. This portal goes to a house on Onslow Square, just around the corner."

"Pelham Crescent?"

"Yes, it's on the Fulham Road. Let's go." He gestured impatiently.

Ollie looked around without much interest at the room they emerged into. Typical old posh London: a sitting room with high ceilings, big sash windows, and expensive furnishings—which had all been pushed against one wall. Made Claudette Beaumant's place look cheap. The paramilitaries followed him and Kohei through. Another squad of them was already in the house, making it seem cramped.

Kohei walked him through into the hall with its classic black-and-white marble floor. "Right. Lolo is online. You have one minute to confirm sie's okay and that we've kept our side of the deal."

It took Ollie a moment to understand what he'd been told. The pain from the peripherals they'd just inserted was puls-ing into his brain despite the local anesthetics. His thoughts were foggy, numb, as if everything around him were on some kind of time delay before it registered. Lolo's icon splashed across his tarsus lens.

"Hey, you," Ollie said. "So where are you?"

"Back on Akitha. I'm really here, Ollie! I'm somewhere in the capital; I recognize the skyline."

"What about Gran and Bik?"

"They came through the portal with me, but then Lim Tianyu went with them somewhere else. I'm not allowed to go there, apparently."

Ollie scowled at Kohei.

"It's an ultra-secure facility," Kohei said in a jaded voice. "Sie's not got anything like the clearance to visit. But sie'll have full observation access to the procedure. Right now, the escort team is waiting for hir family to arrive. As you can imagine, they're in quite a state."

"Oh. Yeah," Ollie grunted. He'd never thought about Lolo's family. Sie'd rarely mentioned them, other than telling him how an expanded Utopials family was superior to any other arrangement.

"Wrap it up," Kohei said.

"Love you, Lolo," Ollie said. "You're the best."

"Ollie, darling, *please* be careful."

"Middle name."

"No it's not. It's not. It never is."

"Listen, this will all be over in half an hour. They've given me some really fancy peripherals, best ever. I'll join you right afterward, okay?"

"Promise me!"

There was no way of telling over a comm connection, but Ollie just knew sie was crying. *Again.* "I promise. You think I want to leave our kid without a dad?"

"Ollie!"

"Gotta go. Be seeing you."

The paramilitaries abandoned the hall, stepping back through the doorways. Kohei opened the front door.

"You won't see us," he told Ollie, "but we'll be with you. There's a lot of synth-bugs in that house. We'll watch every second."

Ollie stepped outside. "Got it," he said, trying to sound nonchalant.

"Hey, Ollie . . ."

"What?"

"Good luck," Kohei said solemnly. "I mean it."

"Sure."

The glossy black door closed, leaving Ollie alone under

the stone portico. London's dry air gusted around the stark dead trees in the square to stroke his face. He wasn't used to that; it was the first time in too long he'd ventured outside without his fleshmask. The medics who'd inserted the peripherals had given him some cream for his cheeks and nose, but it still felt weird. His bare skin was so sensitive.

He walked out onto the main clear path along Sydney Place, just a few meters to Fulham Road. Turn left, and Pelham Crescent was directly ahead. The white Georgian building glowed malevolently under the devil-sky, curving around a small park that was like every other open space in the city in Blitz2—a forlorn cemetery of trees and bushes.

Ollie's thoughts were still numb as he walked up to the front door. A man was standing outside. He broke the spell. Ollie grinned at him. Expensive suit, dark—always dark. It was the uniform for a low-level family soldier. A warning frown was growing on his face as he stared down; his hands made a *move on* gesture.

Ollie knew there was only one way to handle this—the way Piotr would have done it: with overwhelming confidence.

"You," Ollie snapped. "I'm here to see Nikolaj. Open up."

"Piss off."

"Not a chance. She owes me. You either let me in now, or I come back with a missile drone and I blow the door open while you're still standing in front of it. So you make your little secure call to her. You tell her Ollie from *the Legion* is here, and then you open the fucking door."

Ollie watched uncertainty shade the man's face. A pause, then hatred was crowding out the doubt. The door swung open. Ollie smirked mockingly as he stepped inside.

There was no sign of any member of the Paynor family inside. There hadn't been for months, Kohei had told him, since they infiltrated the place with synth-bugs. They didn't know what Nikolaj had done to them—killed them or held them hostage somewhere else. Either way, she was now running the family's operations, such as they were, during Blitz2.

The house was like a five-star boutique hotel, the current guests untouched by the events of the last two years. The family's senior lieutenants had their own rooms. They ate together in the dining room, which certainly had no rationing. They partied every night with young boys and girls, fueled by zero-nark (mild cut only; Nikolaj still expected them to perform their duties outside). They wore Savile Row suits and played with any trinket they wanted.

Walking amid the decadence, Ollie felt sick. This was going to be the Legion, the life they'd desired—richer, more successful. *Do these people know they're helping the Olyix? How could they not? So they don't care. Bastards!*

A teenage boy was waiting for him at the bottom of the stairs, completely naked apart from a silver necklace with a ruby-encrusted pendant that was a nest for nark pads. He was a golden youth whose striking features were even more eye-catching than Lolo's. Following him up the stairs, all Ollie could think was how this kid was barely older than Bik.

"Nikolaj has a suite on the second floor," Kohei had said. "We've never seen her leave it. So if they try taking you somewhere else, it's a trap."

They reached the landing. A couple of the family's soldiers stood at the top of the stairs. One was even bulkier than Lars, though the musculature looked a lot sleeker—the difference between a gorilla and a panther. Trying to ignore the silent intimidation as they fell in on either side of him, Ollie walked along with head held high. The kid knocked on a dark oak-paneled door at the far end of the landing, then waited.

Tye told him he was being deep scanned, which would expose all the systems left over from his Legion days that he'd shifted into his jacket. Nikolaj would expect something like that. But this was where he'd find out just how good Lim's new peripherals were.

The door opened. Ollie went inside while Tye assessed the door. It was what it seemed to be—ordinary oak without any modern reinforcement mesh. Even the locks were basic. That was a worry. After he killed Nikolaj, he'd need to hold off the family soldiers until Kohei's paramilitaries stormed in to rescue him. And he wasn't sure that door would last against the weapons and muscles he'd already seen.

It was a pleasant enough lounge: a big antique desk, leather couches, a high-quality stage, the curtains drawn shut, and a chandelier blazing bright as if it was still drawing power from a solarwell. Nikolaj was standing in front of the desk, head tilted to one side as she appraised him. Icons splashed across his tarsus lens. Her altme was connected to the house's network, but the encryption was high-level. Tye couldn't break it.

Planning, always planning, even now. *If I use the desk to barricade the door, it might hold them a little longer.* All he needed to do was work out how the hell to shift the monstrosity across five meters of thick pile carpet.

Tye scanned the room, searching for hidden weaponry. If there was any, his passive sensors couldn't locate it. Ollie tried to think where he would emplace it while Tye continued to scan; it wouldn't hurt to verify the synth-bugs were watching over him.

"You've got some balls, showing up here," Nikolaj said.

Ollie faced her, target graphics locking onto her head. She was taller than Jade—leaner, too, as the blouse and red trousers revealed. Hair cut short, styled badly in Ollie's opinion, making her head seem oddly long, especially with that thin nose and rounded chin.

Do it. Just do it now. Come on.

But there was a score to settle first. He owed the Legion that much. She had to *know.* And it was what Kohci demanded for his flesh. So he said: "The Paynor family owes me. It owes me a lot for Croydon."

"Oh, Ollie, I'm very disappointed."

"I don't give a fuck. I don't even care about the money."

"Then what do you care about?"

"Do you know what Jade said to me, just before the police raided Lichfield Road? Before the last of my friends died in the fight?"

"Does it matter?"

"Yeah, it matters. It's the only thing in the world that matters."

"Somehow I doubt that, but tell me anyway. I can see how it's eating you up."

Ollie's tarsus lens remained focused unerringly on Nikolaj, with Tye analyzing her skin's infrared emissions, searching for a temperature fluctuation—any anomaly that would show a peripheral going active. But there was nothing. That wasn't right. "She said: Olyix forever."

He waited, watching for the alarm in her eyes—the realization that he knew she was a traitor. But instead she pursed her lips. "No."

"What?"

"That is not what the Kou-Jade said to you. You're lying. Why?"

"Who the fuck is Kou—" It was very strange. Ollie heard the loud bang at the same time the world seemed to freeze and he went completely numb. Then his view shifted as he toppled over.

Every sense returned, shrieking into his brain. He hit the floor amid an agony so intense he thought it would burst his brain apart. Eyes looked along his body, past his waist to . . . Ollie screamed in terror. His legs were gone, shredded into a puddle of gore that glistened across the carpet. Behind him, there was a five-centimeter hole in the door.

"Analysis indicates you have been hit by a wyst bullet," Tye said; its voice seemed to throb in time to the red medical alerts splashed across his vision. The world was retreating, cold seeping along his spine and making him shudder.

Then Jade was there in front of him, kneeling down to frown gently at him. "You're bleeding out," she said. "But I can save you." She beckoned.

The door opened, and the naked boy came in. He was holding a large pistol in one hand and a medical case in the other.

"I'm going to apply Kcell patches on your wounds, Ollie. No one has to die, not anymore. We will save all of you. We love you."

Ollie tried to talk, but annoyingly his mouth had trouble working.

Jade leaned in closer. "What?"

"Everybody dies," Ollie told her happily. "So let's you

and me go meet the Legion together." And he ordered Tye to fire the new weapons peripherals. All of them.

Kohei ran up the stairs, close behind the paramilitaries and just ahead of the paramedics. Gunfire resonated through the house as the last of the Paynor family lieutenants were taken out. They weren't being given the chance to surrender.

Into the lounge.

"Shit!"

Three bodies on the floor. One: a naked boy, his left pectoral muscle in tatters, forming a crater around the hole the micro-missile had torn on its way to his heart. Two: Ollie, on his back, legs missing below his hips, a wide smear of pulped meat across the carpet where the wyst bullet had unleashed its deadly fibers, pureeing his bone and muscle from the inside. Blood was still pulsing weakly out of the broken femoral arteries. Beyond Ollie, Nikolaj was body number three. There was a neat hole in her temple where the organ-buster kinetic had penetrated her skull, leaving a soup of mashed alien brain to leak out from ears, nostrils, and mouth. Micro-missiles had detonated in her hips and elbows, severing her limbs from her torso.

Kohei's helmet visor slid up as he kneeled beside Ollie. He struggled for something to say. "You got the bitch." Cursing himself for such inanity. "You saved London, Ollie."

The paramedics started shoving emergency modules on Ollie's ragged leg stumps. Kohei had seen enough injuries in his time to know their efforts were all useless.

Ollie's jaw moved laboriously, releasing a gurgled whisper.

"What?" Kohei leaned down, straining to hear.

"Fuck you." A last grimaced smile.

The medical kit started emitting shrill warning tones. Kohei sat back, letting out an abject sigh as he closed his eyes. "Chief, whatever you've planned, it better be Goddamn spectacular." He gave the order for his tactical teams to intercept the sabotage operations Nikolaj was running against London's shields. "With extreme prejudice, every motherfucking one of them."

GOX-NIKOLAJ QUINT

SALVATION OF LIFE DECEMBER 11, 2206

Fuuuuck! As always, the pain of violent body death was excruciating. Our human Nikolaj body was struck by so many weapons; Ollie Heslop had five peripherals secreted in his flesh. They must have been of Neána design, for the house's sensors had missed them completely. That doesn't surprise me. Neána treachery is a constant in this universe. I'm sure the God at the End of Time will deal with them severely for their defiance.

I knew something was wrong with the encounter. Ollie Heslop was tense with worry when he entered my office. I acknowledge that was to be expected. Like so many humans, he was badly traumatized by the impending kindness of our purpose in elevating his species. However, his mind was also tainted by the events of Lichfield Road and Kou-Jade's last fight. We would all be very interested to know what happened to the Kou-Jade's human body. The human team that assaulted the house was clearly trying to capture her.

Ollie Heslop had many tells. After all my time spent among humans, especially those of disrepute, I knew something was wrong. Emotional association is an alien trait that I'll have to purge after the elevation is complete, but until then it allows me to operate efficiently on Earth.

Then Ollie Heslop spoke his lie. Those were not Kou-Jade's last words. I assumed he was nerving himself up to enact some pitiful act of vengeance, as so many humans do. Naturally, I instructed Joel to shoot. The shot would maim Ollie Heslop to a near fatal degree. He could then be subdued, and we would embrace him lovingly.

Then the *little shit* went and—

No, that is badthought. That is human thought, contamination from the emulation we use to mask our identity in Nikolaj's body. It is expelled now. I am Gox. I am Quint. Not human.

Ollie Heslop used his hidden peripherals. I felt agony in my shoulders and hips. Horror flooded my unified mind at seeing our human limbs being blown off my torso by micromissiles. Human bodyshock overwhelmed all my bodies. Damn, I hate such weakness.

Ollie Heslop was lying on the floor, looking at me as I wailed helplessly. His lips parted in a vicious sneer. A peripheral in his right wrist tracked around until I was staring directly into its narrow muzzle. There was a flash—

It took too long to recover equanimity. Every time it is longer than before. All my bodies feel discomfort at this, as if letting go of a human emulation is somehow a bad thing.

My remaining bodies were still for a moment. Taking a breath—if we were human.

Desist. There are no emotion-triggering floods of neurochemicals in my four remaining quint brains. They are perfect. I am not subject to random, animal bursts of chaos. Quint superiority is paramount.

The *Salvation of Life*'s onemind became aware of my disquiet. "Explain what has occurred," it required.

"I have reverted to four Gox. My human Nikolaj body was eliminated."

"How?"

"It was shot by a human: Ollie Heslop. The only surviving member of the Southwark Legion street gang."

"Identity correlated. He was used to attack the London power supply grid at Croydon."

"I confirm. Humans of his low status are easy to mislead. They are greed-susceptible."

"Why did he kill your Gox-Nikolaj body?"

I paused, considering my response. Ollie Heslop's fervor

provided testimony to his mental state, the driven fury of vengeance lust. A so-human trait. And yet—there was something wrong about the act. Something intangible. "His given motive was that he sought retribution on Nikolaj. He considered himself betrayed by Kou-Jade, his ostensible colleague in the crime family contracting the Legion. Such a reaction is common with humans. With the eradication of their society's strictures, similar altercations are becoming common."

"Explain your doubt."

"I. Have . . . Definition in this instance is complicated and tenuous. It is my instinct. I have experienced more time in association with humans than any other quint. I have witnessed them in extremis. I have a large familiarity with them. Something about this encounter does not play right."

"In what way?" the onemind asked.

"There are behavioral indicators that indicate excessive stress."

"Ollie Heslop managed to intimidate and protest his way inside your heavily protected building. He went there with the express purpose of killing Gox-Nikolaj, knowing he was placing himself in considerable danger. That would cause any human to be stressed."

"The London shields are about to be eliminated. I find the timing an uncomfortable coincidence."

"You feel you are right?" the onemind inquired critically. "Do you suffer neurological distort? Have you been subject to a Neána neurovirus?"

"No! I remain pure now and always. Such a minor discourse fail is due to residual human emulation routines. I am the best infiltration asset on Earth. This has been proved to you over the multiple assignments I undertook on Earth and the other human star systems."

"I concede your efficiency claim, despite Verby."

"We now know our sabotage mission against the Delta Pavonis astroengineering facilities was exposed by the Neána metahuman, Jessika Mye. That was an external factor."

"Agreed. However, such infiltration assignments are drawing to a close. Earth's city shields are falling at an accelerated rate. Our final success draws close. You will be reallocated to shipboard duties. Together we will maintain the gift of humans in sanctified equilibrium until we present them to the God at the End of Time."

"I am grateful for this chance to serve the God at the End of Time."

"I will authorize a convener to form a replacement quint body for you. You will be whole again."

"That will be welcome."

"Ongoing: Ensure there are no further residual human emulation thoughts within your mindfunction."

"There will be none."

FINALSTRIKE MISSION

FLIGHT YEAR 7

When he woke, Dellian's body was sluggish, his thoughts slow. He wanted to go back to the comfort of sleep with all its agreeable dreams—dreams that were now scudding away like clouds over the horizon. But no, that wasn't allowed. His blood was speeding up as various umbilical tubes retracted from their abdominal sockets. Sensation of pressure draining from his skin. Individual muscles began to register their aches, tingling ferociously. And as for the taste in his mouth . . .

He grimaced and tried to sit up. The suspension chamber's ribbed cushioning obediently rose to support his back. Nothing it could do about the churning sensation in his stomach—a churning that was rapidly growing in potency. Even now, with all their society's knowledge of genetics and human biology, the body still remained obstinately idiosyncratic. You just couldn't switch it on and off for convenience when you were on massive interstellar voyages.

"Saints!"

He vomited weakly, the liquid mixing with the slops of clear gel that still clung to his skin. A flock of beetle-sized remotes skittered over his chest and arms, cleaning him up. The sickness triggered a headache, which his boost glands responded to by releasing a mild sedative. That just turned his head fluffy.

The light on the outside of the transparent casing grew brighter. He saw Ovan looking down at him, a sympathetic expression on his face as the casing slid down. "Take it easy, remember?"

"Right," he moaned and held up an arm. The beetle-things retreated from his skin.

Ovan grabbed his hand and helped ease him out.

The motion set his inner ears spinning. He sat on the edge of the chamber until his senses settled.

"Shower first?" Ovan asked.

"Pee!" He knew that was psychological; the waste tubes would have taken care of his bladder. But, still, when you've gotta go, you've gotta go. Leaning on Ovan, he made his way across the compartment to the washrooms. He saw Yirella was still in her suspension chamber. All the monitor displays were in the green. That made him feel a whole lot better.

The shower finished his transformation into something living. He had to sit down for it, letting the soapy water soothe away imagined cold from his bones along with the last of the gel. He managed to walk over to the dryer hoop without help. The warm air jetted over him as the hoop tracked around, and he brought his databud out of standby mode. Reading the optik display made him slap the hoop's off button. "What's happened? We're only seven years out. Our watch was scheduled for year nine."

"The *Mian*'s drive efficiency was falling. Cinrea was watch captain when the problem started, so she made the decision to decelerate the fleet. That was a year ago."

"Decelerate? You mean we're not relativistic?"

"No. We're at effective rest velocity in interstellar space. Have been for five weeks."

Dellian started the hoop again, taking his time. Ovan brought him a pack with newly printed clothes in it.

"So what are we doing, waiting for the repairs?"

"That's almost finished now. The physicists traced the fault to a manufacturing problem in a component batch. Cinrea's ordered every ship to run a complete check on their drive units."

Dellian pulled his trousers up, disheartened to find the waist was too big.

"Sorry," Ovan said. "I didn't think; I just used your file. We all lost weight in suspension."

"I probably needed to."

"None of us did. At least I've put it back on now. It took me a few weeks, mind. And the suspension systems don't completely halt muscle atrophy, either, so you need to watch for that. You're not as strong as you were."

"So how long have you been out?"

"Nearly two years. I was on the same watch detail as Cinrea. As you and I know each other, I was designated your recovery buddy."

"Thanks."

"So you can do the same for Yirella. Cinrea's ordered Kenelm to be woken, too, along with all the advisory council."

"Why? I thought you said the drive was repaired."

"Because we detected a Signal."

"No, you didn't. You can't have. The Saints are dead. And anyway, we're too far from the enclave to pick up a Signal even if they broadcast it before the Olyix caught them."

"Dellian, it didn't come from the Olyix enclave."

There was something about the *Morgan* simply hanging stationary between stars that unnerved Dellian at a fundamental level. Flying at close to light speed was the ship's own protection, making it phenomenally difficult for the Olyix to even detect—let alone intercept—them. But this—floating inert in the near-absolute darkness of space with no emergency evacuation portal connecting them anywhere—was creepy. He felt extremely vulnerable.

Unsurprisingly, Yirella wasn't terribly sympathetic.

"That makes no sense at all," she told him their first night together, after she'd come out of suspension. "This location is completely random. Even if an Olyix sensor station was within five light-years and could detect us—and that's close to impossible—it would be ten years until they could get here."

"I know," he said miserably. "It's just . . . We're really alone out here. I feel that."

"Del! We are a thirty-strong fleet of warships, the most formidable humans have ever built. Come on, pull yourself together."

He grinned weakly as he slipped out of his robe and lay on the bed, trying to ignore how skinny he'd become. "Yes, ma'am."

She gave him a judgmental moue and got onto the bed with him. Her long t-shirt did nothing to disguise how thin her legs and arms had become in suspension. That just made them look even longer.

"And you needn't think about that tonight," she said smartly as she caught his blatant stare. "We both need to recuperate properly. That includes no unnecessary physical exertion."

"Unnecessary?"

"Yes."

He put his arms around her, enjoying the way she pressed against him. "I'm allowed a cuddle, though?"

"You are allowed precisely one cuddle."

"Ah, who said romance was dead."

Yirella giggled and snuggled up closer. "I'm glad they woke you up first. It was nice seeing your face when I opened my eyes. Reassuring."

"Ha, all I got was Ovan."

They lay in comfortable silence for a while.

"What do you think we'll do about the Signal?" Dellian asked.

"I know what we need to do: nothing."

"Really?"

"Yes. It's intriguing, but ultimately not relevant to our mission. My problem is what Kenelm will do."

"I'm sure you'll steer hir right. You usually do."

Yirella shifted around to put her face centimeters from his. "Del, I was thinking about something before we started this flight. Thinking about it a lot, actually. I really hope it's not relevant."

"Okay. What?"

"We know about Sanctuary, right?"

"Yes," he agreed cautiously. "You more than anyone."

"Right. And no one was more delighted than me when Ainsley told me it's not just a myth. It's real. Or at least it could be. Some rogue humans joined the Katos mothership and set out to establish a refuge the Olyix would never find. He even said one of his family went with them. A granddaughter, I think."

"You think they didn't make it?"

"Not the point. Ainsley said that when the Factory that made him finally broke up, all the factions went their separate ways—the Katos and some humans to build Sanctuary; the Neána back into hiding; the Angelis war fleet to another galaxy; and the human generation ship to found a new planet. And there is never any communication between worlds that humans settle, which means . . ." She gave him an expectant glance.

"The Factory is in our past! The generation ship that was part of the alliance went on to establish Juloss!"

"Maybe. Certainly not directly. In our lineage, we live on a generation world for five hundred years, then abandon it and move on. Ainsley said he was created about two thousand years ago, in a linear timeframe. That suggests the Factory probably existed three generation worlds ago, in our lineage."

"Juloss was founded by a generation ship from Quiller, which in turn was founded by Sergiu," he recited. "And before that, Falkon."

"Yeah. So my guess is the Factory probably happened between Falkon and Sergiu."

"Okay, makes sense." He tried to see where she was going with this, but failed as usual. "So?"

"So if Sanctuary is in our lineage, how come we didn't know about the Factory? And worse, why don't we know about the Ainsley ship—or ships?"

"Oh. Saints. Yeah, why?"

"The answer has to be security. Kenelm has access to all sorts of classified protocols."

"Yes! Like the order sie was given: If the Olyix didn't respond to our Vayan lure, we should go full-on Neána and build a hidden interstellar society."

Yirella nodded.

"So you're saying sie knew about Ainsley-type ships?" he asked.

"Somebody had to know. And Kenelm was very quick to hand me command authority over Bennu's network when Ainsley appeared. Think about that—an unknown threat emerging in the middle of a battle that's going badly wrong, and you give the problem to me. Me! I'm smart, but I'm the first to admit I can't handle stress well."

"Saints, sie knew Ainsley wasn't a threat!"

"There's one other thing. We—you and me, the squads—didn't know people on Juloss could life-extend with biologic initiator body-rebuild techniques. We were led to believe that technology existed to restore the cocooned into a new body, so recovering the *Salvation of Life* wouldn't be fruitless. And it worked so well on the *Calibar* people it's obviously a very mature technology."

"They're still with us!" Dellian exclaimed, glad to be keeping up. "The people from the Factory. Saints, they're in control. They always have been. They're immortal."

She shrugged. "Possibly. We know nothing about the omnia who made up the *Morgan* 'crew' outside their official files and what they chose to tell us, same as we don't really know much about Juloss society, because we lived there in its final days. We were brought up to fight, not to question. Our reward for living the life planned for us is freedom after we've won. That's the deal we accepted."

"I did," he said quietly. "I'm not sure you ever have."

"I'm living with it because I choose to. I chose you."

"So you're not infallible after all."

She kissed him. "Oh, I think I made some good choices there."

"I wasn't complaining. So if these immortals exist, and knew about Ainsley, do you think they kept the technology to build more of him?"

"I don't know, but I doubt it. If they had the ability to build more, then they'd build them. The Factory came about by a unique combination of alien technologies. It was a one-off. We don't know how many Ainsley-type ships they built two thousand years ago, but we don't have access to those technologies anymore. We can't build new ones."

"All right, so what do you want to do about this?" Somehow, he couldn't envisage a mutiny. Though he was fairly sure the other squad leaders would stand with him if they found out about Kenelm. *Or would they? Is this why Yi was so worried and guarded for all those months before we left?*

"I don't know," she said. "I despise the lack of honesty. And if we do ask Kenelm what's going on—why the secrecy—we'll get the usual answers: for your protection, denying information to the Olyix in case of capture. All that politician crap. I doubt we'll get a genuine explanation about their agenda."

"Have you got any idea what that is?"

"It has to be connected to the original Strike operation. Occam's razor says it's something simple like not revealing how expendable they consider us binaries, or just ensuring each generation world does its duty at the end and produces a bunch of warships to send on Strike missions."

"So they're, like, orthodoxy enforcers?"

"Something along those lines, sure. I always did think it was extraordinary how our lineage stuck to a single political-cultural ideology so rigidly across every iteration at a generation world."

"But the generation world model has failed, hasn't it?" he said bitterly. "There's never been a Signal from any Strike. By the time the generation ship from Quiller met the aliens and built the Factory, they must have been seriously concerned about that. So why did they stick with a failed strategy?"

"I'm not sure they did. The Factory built the Ainsley ship or ships. But you're right, Ainsley is incredibly powerful, so why bother carrying on with the Strike missions?" She shook her head, as if there were too many thoughts cluttering her brain. "Consider what happened. Ainsley was in some kind of condensed mode while he lurked in the Vayan system. All he did was wait and watch. We were the ones who built the lure. And the Olyix knew nothing about Ainsley, which suggests Vayan was the first time they'd encountered a warship from the Factory."

"So there *is* only the one?"

"I can't believe that. But there probably aren't many. And we're now finally picking up a Signal, but not the Saints' Signal. Someone else has defeated an Olyix ship. That can't be a coincidence. After thousands of years, they're defeated twice within eighty light-years. That's close in galactic terms—practically neighbors. The Factory must have sent them here, to this section of space—a long way from where they originated, which gives everyone involved in the Factory a massive head start if it turns out the Olyix can defeat an Ainsley-class ship."

"Sanctuary," he said. "Even if the Olyix find out where the Factory was, they'll never be able to find where the Katos mothership went. Not now."

"So it is all about security, after all. That's a hell of a secret to keep for two thousand years."

"But . . . the whole Strike mission—ships like *Morgan* and all the squads—we're just a cover so the Katos mothership could get away clean?"

"We always knew we were expendable," she said slowly. "If this is all true, then we're dealing with entities that we don't really understand. Certainly I can't imagine how superior an immortal human would consider themselves compared to us short-lived binaries. We're probably just muncs to them."

Delhan felt his fists clenching in anger. "We need to confront Kenelm. Force hir to tell us what's going on. The squad leaders will back me, I know they would."

"No, Del, absolutely not."

"Why not?"

"Firstly, this is all conjecture—a tower of hypotheticals. Secondly, the fleet is taking us to where I want us to be: the neutron star. If we expose an immortal clique that's been maneuvering our mission to conform to their own agenda, the political fallout inside the fleet will be enormous. Saints knows what people will do! I can't have that, not now that we're so close. I'm happy for this delay to push our arrival date back even further. It's *fortuitous*. But I can't risk Final-Strike being compromised. And so far, I don't believe Kenelm—with all hir secrets—has done that."

Dellian wanted to punch the pillow in frustration. She was right, of course. That never changed. But that didn't mean the situation was fair. Being used so insolently was totally humiliating. Needing to hit back was instinctive, not to mention justified. "All right," he said. "But if I think Kenelm is manipulating us away from the FinalStrike, I will—"

"I know. And thank you for having faith in me." She kissed him—a longer, warmer kiss than before. The cabin lights dimmed to a rose-pink glimmer.

"Is this a bribe?" he asked, smirking in the dusk. "We're not supposed to, remember?"

Yirella chuckled. "Think of this as our first act of rebellion against Kenelm's authority."

The advisory council was smaller now. Back to a manageable number, Yirella thought as she and Dellian sat down next to each other. He was wearing his uniform as he always did, but that was Dellian for you: He possessed an old-fashioned dignity that didn't really have a place in this era. But she loved him for it.

Kenelm took hir place at the table. "My gratitude to Cinrea for managing this incident so capably. I'd say thank you all for coming, but as none of us had a choice . . . We'll start with the *Mian*'s drive, please."

"The problem has been resolved," Wim said. "We've manufactured replacement components, and they are functioning normally."

"That's it?" Kenelm's tone was surprised.

"I hate the phrase," Wim admitted, "but it looks like this situation was a one-off. We've run a complete review on every propulsion system in the fleet. All the units were fabricated to the correct specification."

"I don't understand how a batch of bad components got past our performance and quality examination routines," Tilliana said. "Were you running those same procedures when you checked the fleet?"

Yirella managed to keep a straight face, which was more than Wim did. Sie directed a furious glare at Tilliana. "Give me some credit. The analyses we've spent the last six weeks running were completely new. Even the hardware we used was different than before. The fleet can accelerate back up to relativistic velocity without having to worry about any more component failure."

"So now we have to decide our destination," Kenelm said. "Do we—"

"I'm sorry, captain," Tilliana persisted. "But if it happened for one component, it can happen for others."

"You're not seriously suggesting we run analysis on every component in the fleet?"

"No," Tilliana said. "But it's the coincidence that bothers me. Here we are at rest velocity, and—Saints!—we pick up a Signal. How about that for amazing?"

"What do you mean, coincidence?" Cinrea asked. "Are you saying the component failure was deliberate? That somebody wanted us to be stationary to receive the Signal?"

Yirella gave Tilliana a surprised glance. *And I thought I was the queen of conspiracies!* She couldn't decide how strongly she should intervene to refute her friend's suggestion. *Because I certainly didn't know about the Signal.*

"We only received it because we're stationary," Tilliana said. "Our sensors would have trouble picking up a Signal when we're traveling just under light speed, but it wasn't an issue when we began this flight because we're no longer even looking for a Signal anymore. We know the location of the Olyix enclave now, and if the Saints did send their Signal, it won't reach us for tens of thousands of years. So, coincidence?"

"Yes," Kenelm said. "Because to sabotage our flight at the right time and place, you'd have to know there was going to be a Signal to intercept."

"More than that," Yirella said, looking directly at Tilliana and hoping there was no guilt showing. "The Signal is irrelevant—especially to us."

"What?" Tilliana spluttered.

"It contains the Olyix enclave coordinates, right?"

"Yes," Cinrea said.

"Well, we already know the location, so we don't need to investigate the Signal's origin. QED, it's irrelevant."

"All right," Kenelm said. "I'll reserve judgment on that for now. What else do we know about the Signal?"

"The K-class star it originates from is seventeen light-years away," Cinrea said. "As soon as we detected it, I sent the *Urquy* and *Konvo* an AU out from the main fleet to give us a decent baseline measurement. Analysis revealed the transmitter is a massive spherical array; we estimate its diameter at ten thousand kilometers. So its broadcast is omni-directional. They're beaming it out across the whole galaxy. Its strength is phenomenal—strong enough to reach the fringe of the galactic core from here."

"How are they powering that?"

Cinrea smiled. The screen at the end of the table came on, showing a fuzzy image of a star with a halo of smaller stars. "That's the best visual image we could manage with our current sensor array. We estimate there are at least four thousand solarwell MDH chambers in operation."

"Human technology," Wim said happily.

"Pre-invasion human technology," Cinrea corrected. "We haven't used solarwells since the exodus started."

"They're quick and easy," Yirella said. "Exactly what you'd need to power a continuous Signal. You don't need elegance here. The Olyix know their ambush ships were beaten at that star, and what we'd do when we find their enclave location. They'll be heading back there right now from their sensor station, probably with a whole fleet of Resolution ships. Which means you need to get the Signal out *fast*. It's how I'd do it."

"What about the Signal itself?" Kenelm asked.

"Short, but broadcast in one hundred human languages. Its message is very simple. The location of the Olyix enclave, triangulated by pulsar, and a warning."

"Which is?" Dellian asked quickly.

Cinrea flicked a finger at the screen, and text rolled down.

This is the warship Lolo Maude, with a message for all surviving humans still fleeing our stolen Earth. A lure was established at this star system to attract the Olyix here. When they arrived, I assisted the Strike mission to defeat them. Be aware that the Olyix know about

THE SAINTS OF SALVATION   125

our generation worlds, and they have plotted the
course of our expansion into the galaxy. They know
our Strike ships create lures. Their weapons technology
has now advanced past anything our original Neána
allies gave us. They have ambushed countless human
ships and societies during the last two thousand years.
Please consider this stage of our exodus to be over. Do
not engage their ships; it has become too dangerous.
Find a new strategy. I wish anyone who receives this
message well in your endeavor, and trust that one day
we will join together again on all the worlds we have
lost. Go in peace, and remember that our love is always
stronger than their hatred.

"That's it," Cinrea said. "Constant repeat, no variation."
Tilliana closed her eyes. "It's an Olyix lure," she said.
"How so?" Kenelm said.
"They know everything about us: the generation worlds,
Strikes, lures. All of it. They know what we're supposed to
do after we receive a Signal."
"Oh, Saints," Dellian said in alarm. "Once we receive a
Signal, we're expected to travel direct to the nearest neutron
star."
"You think they're waiting there for us?" Cinrea asked.
"High probability," Tilliana said.
"No," Yirella said as she recovered from the shock of the
message. "It's genuine."
"Okay," Kenelm said wearily. "How so?"
"Two reasons. The logical one: This is a high-power signal, and becoming stronger, right?"
"Yes," Cinrea confirmed.
"There is no conceivable scenario in which the Olyix
would broadcast their enclave location—not in a transmis-
sion that will ultimately be detectable clean across the galaxy. Any aliens who pick it up won't be able to translate our
written languages because they have no linguistic or sym-
bology references. However, the pulsar map is math-based,
so it's relatively easy to determine. The Neána will understand that. The Katos, too. Maybe it will even make the Angelis war fleet turn around and head for the enclave. If you're

a species that's suffered and fled from an Olyix invasion, the one thing you don't have is the enclave location. Because once you have that, defeating the Olyix becomes theoretically possible. So no, that Signal is not an Olyix lure. It's real."

"Okay," Tilliana said cautiously. "And the second reason?"

"Lolo Maude is sort of my ancestor."

"What?"

She would have laughed at everyone's reaction if it hadn't been so damn tragic. "I traced my genetic ancestry when I was undergoing . . . treatment back on Juloss." She glanced at Alexandre, who gave a discreet nod. "It goes all the way back to someone called Bik Heslop. His claim to fame—the only reason he was in our records—was because he was the first human ever to successfully undergo de-cocooning."

"So who is Lolo?" Dellian asked.

"Sie was the partner of Bik's brother, Ollie Heslop, who— Well, he died in London to help the Saints get on board the *Salvation of Life*. Both Lolo and Bik left Earth for Akitha."

"How does that prove Lolo's message is real?"

"Proof is an absolute we can never establish in this case, but it's another byte of data that adds to the authenticity. Lolo and Bik's extended family was on the Pasobla; that's the same exodus habitat that took Emilja and Ainsley from Akitha when the Olyix finally returned to the human worlds. So Lolo must have been on the same generation ship as Ainsley when it left Falkon. Sie was at the Factory. Sie became one of their warships, just like Ainsley."

"We never knew before if there were more Factory ships than just Ainsley," Alexandre said. "So now we do. You're right, it does add to the authenticity."

Yirella gave him a small nod of gratitude. "You also need to consider how close the Lolo and Ainsley ships were located on a galactic scale," Yirella said. "It can't be coincidence. This whole part of space is the front of the human expansion wavefront. Everything is concentrated here."

"All right," Tilliana said. "So the Lolo Maude is a genuine Factory warship, and it took out an Olyix ambush. The Olyix response to that is still going to be automatic; while we sit here, they're on their way back to that star in considerable force. When they get there, they'll destroy that transmitter globe as fast as they can. And once they realize what's been broadcast, they'll set up an ambush at every neutron star along the expansion wavefront. Like you said, this is where human activity is concentrated—if anyone else is left. The Olyix will be waiting for all the remaining Strike missions."

"Exactly," Yirella said. "But they haven't gotten the message yet. It's too early. So we have to continue our flight to the neutron star. We have the advantage now."

Kenelm glanced at Wim, then Cinrea. "Are we ready to resume our flight?"

Wim nodded. "Yes, captain. A year decelerating to here, then another year accelerating back up to relativistic velocity means that we'll arrive later than we were supposed to, but I'm confident there should be no more problems with our drive systems."

"But where's the other Strike mission now?" Ovan blurted.

"Excuse me?" Cinrea asked.

"Lolo Maude didn't build a lure. We know Factory ships just wait in some kind of reduced state for the Olyix. It was a Strike mission, just like the *Morgan*. Whatever humans were at that star bioformed its planet. So, right now, if they're following protocol—"

"Saints, yes!" Dellian said in excitement. "They'll be heading straight for the same neutron star as us."

"All the surviving Strike ships will be," Tilliana said. "As soon as they detect the Signal, they'll fly there—and every Factory ship as well. Hell, if there are any left, we might even get some generation ships changing course and joining us."

"We won't be alone anymore!"

Yirella hadn't seen Del as jazzed up as this since they detected the Olyix ship approaching Vayan. This was almost the old Dellian. She reached out and squeezed his hand. "Not necessarily," she said apologetically. "Lolo's Signal was very clear; humans have to develop a new strategy now that the Olyix know everything. That implies the neutron star will be the last place any human will be going."

"Oh. Right."

"We can't speculate on how others will interpret the warning," Kenelm said. "Perhaps they will all stay away, or perhaps they will send an exploratory mission. However, I'm in agreement with Yirella that—although it is admittedly momentous news—Lolo's Signal does not alter our objective. Therefore, we will resume our flight to the neutron star. Tilliana?"

"Yes, captain?"

"Liaise with Wim, please. I want a tactical scenario drawn up for our deceleration phase at the neutron star. We will not be caught out and ambushed again."

KRUSE STATION

S-DAY, DECEMBER 11, 2206

There were eight principal coordinator seats in the Kruse Station's Strikeback Command Center, their solid frames almost lost amid the bright geode stalactite holograms that spiked out from the chamber's smooth walls and ceiling to fill the air. Adjutant-General David Johnstone acknowledged his staff as he came in, then sat in his own seat at the back, giving him a perfect view of more data than any human could absorb. Another sheet of holographic displays curved around him as he took off his wire-rimmed glasses and tucked them into his jacket pocket.

"Are we ready?" he asked.

The eight coordinators he'd brought with him from Alpha Defense, immersed in their own digitized nest of laserlight, acknowledged him one by one.

"Once more unto the breach, dear friends," Johnstone said softly. "But when the blast of war blows in our ears, then imitate the action of the tiger." He paused for a moment, eyes shut as he drew a breath, then told his altme to open a feed to the G8Turing that would be directing the Strike. Immediately the graphic dendrites in his displays burst into digital leaf as data surged in. Training allowed him to keep calm when what he wanted was to be anywhere else. Besides, who else could he entrust this job to? But the flood of fresh real-time information did reinforce the suspicion that it was too much. The reality was that he'd be playing a very small part in the attack, a janitor shuffling around the feet of the G8Turings.

A tiny purple icon flashed somewhere above him and interfaced with his tarsus lenses, allowing him to access the symbol. "Let them in," he told the command center, with only a small hint of resentment.

The door behind him opened. Emilja Jurich and Ainsley Zangari walked in. For once, neither of them had their aides with them. As always, Emilja looked imperious and dignified in a high-collared black silk dress, while Ainsley had shrugged into a navy-and-burgundy college varsity jacket as if he were on his way to a frat party. Johnstone managed not to frown at the sight of him; Ainsley had been absent from Council meetings for months. There were rumors . . .

"Don't worry, general." Ainsley chuckled. "We're not going to interfere. We're here to observe. This is history."

"And provide you with some moral support," Emilja added. "Some of the decisions that led to today are ethically questionable—and that's just from Ainsley's point of view."

"Fuck you! I was right about those Olyix shits all along."

"I believe you may have mentioned that occasionally."

"I appreciate the political support you've given me over the last couple of years," Johnstone said neutrally. "The Sol Senate doesn't exactly share your opinion."

"Bunch of fucking politicians," Ainsley growled. "They're the ones who didn't give you the weapons we needed to defend Earth, then they blame you. Assholes. We should have dumped the lot of them in Leipzig. Show them how hard reality can bite."

Emilja smiled coldly. "Are we ready, general?"

"Yes. If it doesn't work today, then it never would have." He ran a fast gestalt review, checking the positions of the Olyix ships in the Sol system; the stealthed expansion portals around Earth; the status of the massed warships at Delta Pavonis, Puppis, Eta Cassiopeiae, 82 Eridani, and Trappist 1; the Knockdown team— "How's it going?"

"We're ready, sir," Loi replied. "Everything is in position, and sensor coverage is excellent."

"Good. Stand by." And finally: "*Avenging Heretic*, we are go for Strikeback."

"Roger that, general," Yuri replied. "We're ready."

"Godspeed, *Avenging Heretic*. See you on the far side of eternity." Johnstone consulted the dense panorama of data. The G8Turing splashed up suitable opening moves. He studied them for a long moment. A squadron of three hundred Olyix midlevel transport ships was curving down out of their thousand-kilometer orbit, the lead vessel heading for the glowing blemish that was London—still defiantly existing. He gave them a vindictive smile. "Not that easy, motherfuckers." A series of stealthed portals splashed across his vision, eager amber stars high above the Atlantic Ocean. "Initiate phase one."

Three thousand kilometers above Earth, in the center of the inner Van Allen radiation belt where the concentration of hazardous electrons and protons was at their greatest, forty expansion portals opened to their full eighty-meter diameter. The ships that came through had been built in the vast industrial facilities orbiting Nanjing, the third Trappist 1 world to be settled by China. As soon as the invasion began, all those facilities that had been involved in the terraforming venture were reconfigured to build habitats for the exodus, and the new Yi Xian class of attack cruisers.

Designed mainly as weapons platforms, the cruisers were basic dodecahedrons sixty meters in diameter, accelerated by a trio of fusion rockets. Their protection came from close defense shields that wrapped the carbotanium fuselage in a five-meter-deep cloak of nitrogen, locked into a density gradient by bonding generators, like a cross section of a gas giant's atmosphere—with a gaseous outer layer that quickly thickened into a shell of unnatural solidity and toughness. The simplicity and modularity of the design allowed for mass production. By the time S-Day arrived, Trappist 1 had produced more than eight and a half thousand.

Two thousand of them deployed out of the expansion portals at the rate of one every five seconds. Each one came out on a vector slightly different from the previous ship's, and ignited its fusion rockets, accelerating away at four gees. They didn't have quite the maneuverability of the Olyix transports, but they made up for that in sheer numbers.

The Olyix ships above Earth immediately began evasive maneuvers, streaking away from their orbital track at seven gees. High above them, the Yi Xian cruisers kept coming, spreading out like a falling storm cloud. The first forty to emerge fired an octet of conventional fusion rocket missiles that accelerated down at fifty gees. They ignored the Olyix ships above the mesosphere and plunged on down into the stratosphere, where the transports were powering up through the ozone layer in their bid to escape.

Earth's damaged atmosphere was hit by multiple hypersonic shock waves rippling out from the missiles as they tore the beleaguered air apart. All of them ejected a barrage of tiny sensor spheres that spread out in mimicry of a meteorite shower to provide unparalleled observation data to Strikeback command's G8Turing. With the lead Olyix transport ship still a hundred kilometers west of the Azores, and traveling at Mach eighteen, the missiles began to explode their twenty-five-megaton warheads in a carefully calculated sequence.

The sensor spheres observed the intense atmospheric devastation, tracking energized blast waves and radiation surges, scrutinizing their effect on the exposed Olyix craft. Alpha Defense had designed the nukes with an enhanced gamma emission effect. The transports seemed to have very little resistance to the radiation. As soon as the bombs started to explode, they began to lose acceleration. Those closest to the blasts lost power altogether and began to tumble out of the sky. Then the colossal blast wave struck the remaining ships. Several disintegrated, and the remainder were slammed about helplessly, spinning out of control toward the glaring breakers far below. The sensors tracked every aspect of their decay and death for the G8Turing to analyze.

A second batch of missiles was fired from the Yi Xian cruisers. These had smaller warheads and detonated to the west of the first barrage, close to Bermuda, where the desperate Olyix were racing for the top of the mesosphere. Their fate provided another tranche of detailed performance data to the Strikeback G8Turing, refining the operational parameters of the Olyix ships. Johnstone watched the information build.

Soćko's icon splashed into his display. "You've rattled them," he said. "The *Salvation* onemind is deeply shocked by the attack. They didn't expect us to use nukes on Earth. It's redeploying Deliverance ships to protect the transports."

"But not recalling them?" Johnstone asked.

"No. Not yet."

"Very well, let's get it to take us more seriously. Move to phase two."

Eight hundred portals opened above Earth, completely encircling the globe. Cruisers poured through. The majority started to head down to the planet, while others formed up into fifty-strong attack formations and accelerated along interception courses toward incoming Deliverance ships. Space was drenched with slender fusion plumes, fashioning a crosshatch of incandescent light above the upper atmosphere, caging the whole planet.

Eight thousand miles above the Indian Ocean, a Deliverance ship performed an eleven-gee parabolic maneuver to align itself on one of the attack formations. Incredibly powerful energy beams stabbed out from it, slicing straight through the cruisers' defense shields, killing the ships in a blaze of energized vapor. The formation's survivors responded with a synchronized barrage of Calmissiles. They were small—two meters in diameter—but they used the same principle as human sublight starships, making the teardrop-shaped casing a single portal. Holes accelerating through space at twenty-five gees.

The Deliverance ships only knew they were there because of their exhaust plumes. They shot energy beams at them; they fired kinetic harpoons; they detonated thirty-five-megaton warheads, whose plasma spheres saturated local space with high-energy particles. None of them had the slightest effect. Every assault simply passed through the hole, ejecting from the portal's inert twin thousands of kilometers away.

The first Deliverance ship was struck by seventeen Calmissiles within a one and a half second period. Traveling at over seventy kilometers a second, each of them cored out a perfect tunnel through the ship, slicing through whatever solid structure they encountered. Milliseconds later, each of those gaps was flooded with their fusion plasma exhaust. The Deliverance ship started to disintegrate, only to have the ruptured fragments instantly turn into a sleet of raw atoms.

"Okay," Soćko said. "That frightened the onemind."

"Start the clearance," Johnstone ordered. "Every Olyix ship below geostationary orbit." He focused on the display section locked on northern Utah. "Loi, stand by."

KNOCKDOWN MISSION

S-DAY, DECEMBER 11, 2206

There were three of them in the transit chamber when its blast doors rumbled shut and locked with a loud series of clunks. In front of Loi, the rims of seven expansion portals glowed a vivid turquoise, surrounding a center of insubstantial gray, as if they were being lit from behind by weak moonlight.

His suit closed around him in readiness. It was a brute of a thing, adding more than half a meter to his height. Beside him, in hir own suit, Eldlund stood three meters tall. Lim Tianyu was a mere two meters sixty centimeters.

For a brief moment, as the light vanished, Loi was gripped by a pang of claustrophobia. The helmet was solid, like the rest of the suit, its thick carapace the same dull pewter sheen as medieval suits of armor. Loi knew those old knights used to ride on horses specially bred to carry the enormous weight—something else he shared with those long-ago nobles. Right now, he weighed in at more than half a ton. Unlike the armor that modern mercenaries and corporate security wore on their combat missions, very little of that weight was weaponry. This was all about protection. His armor's primary purpose was to defend the wearer from radiation. Not even a tactical nuke's gamma pulse could get through it. Nearly a third of the mass was artificial muscle, without which he wouldn't even be able to stand, let alone move. The weight and toughness made it apposite for endur-ing Earth's wrecked climate. No, this suit didn't have knights of old in its heritage; its grandparents were more likely to be army tanks.

His tarsus lens splashed the armor's external sensor image, and his breathing became calmer. Tactical displays showed him the titanic battle going on in space above Salt Lake City. As well as the armada of human warships, the newly enlarged portals above Earth were also shooting out a swarm of sensor satellites to enhance Strikeback's intelligence-gathering. The G8Turing plotted the byzantine weave of ship vectors. In orbit, Olyix transport ships were being massacred in their hundreds. Deliverance ships were fighting a furious rearguard action against the deluge of cruisers, but there was nothing they could do to stop the Calmissiles.

"You smashed it, boss," Eldlund exclaimed. "We're kill-ing them!"

"Damn right," Loi agreed. "Here comes the ground wave."

Thousands of cruisers were descending into the Earth's upper atmosphere, unleashing a deluge of Calmissiles to-ward the Olyix ships that ringed every surviving city. Loi bit on his lip. They couldn't afford to use nukes close to the overstressed shields, but neither could they avoid using them. This phase had to be convincing.

"Loi, stand by," Johnstone ordered.

The tactical splash gave Loi the three best portal options for deployment. "Three and five," he decided.

"I concur," Eldlund said.

"Brace yourselves."

"Got it," Lim said.

All three suits leaned forward.

In front of them, the gray pseudo-center of portals three and five melted backward, allowing a different, more vacant, texture of gray to resolve. Air howled in, bringing a flurry of dirt and dust that churned vigorously around the walls. The suits swayed fractionally from the impact, but held position.

Loi consulted the tactical display again. Down in South America and over in China, five-megaton warheads were detonating twenty to thirty kilometers above the ground, close to the convoys of Olyix transport ships lifting off. When the shock waves slammed down, ships lurched around violently before beginning their fatal nosedives. Those that hadn't yet launched juddered about on the ground, their hulls thudding into rocks and slopes, crumpling on impact. In response, the Deliverance ships bombarding the city shields diverted their energy beams upward, targeting the incoming missiles, which relieved some of the pressure on the city shields. More Olyix transport ships used the respite to take off, seeking a precarious sanctuary in the sky.

In reply, the black loci of Calmissiles descended in silence, consuming air and X-ray lasers with equal serenity, until they punched through the Deliverance ships, eviscerating the wreckage.

Even though Loi had been at most of the Knockdown meetings and knew the plan by heart, watching the numbers wind up was unnerving. The cruisers were expending munitions at a phenomenal rate, and he was keenly aware of the reserves. They'd pushed manufacturing stations to the maximum in order to be ready for today, but even so it was going to be tight.

The Knockdown tactical display splashed the cruisers above Utah, closing to their optimal attack points. Deliverance ships around Salt Lake City responded to their approach by firing at the gathering above. Missiles began to streak down in retaliation, slicing incandescent lines through the crud-clotted air.

Three command icons splashed green.

"Go," Johnstone said.

Loi started moving toward portal five. It took time to get up to a run, even with all the artificial muscle the suit was packing; that much inertia couldn't be overcome easily. When he and Eldlund had been practicing in the suits, they'd found the best way to stop when you were sprinting was just to drop to the ground, then dig your knees and elbows in to bulldoze through dirt until you halted.

He'd reached a reasonable jogging speed when he passed through portal five's blue rim. His balance shifted, which the suit's network corrected. There was an intruder synth-turtle just behind his heels, squatting on the side of Mount Kessler's steep slope in the heart of the Oquirrh range. Eldlund emerged from portal three, twenty meters to the west, with Lim following him out.

The gale pummelling the mountains was so thick with a hail of soil and stone flakes that Loi's visual sensors couldn't see them at all. The stones pinged off his armor, making it sound like he was being shot with old-fashioned bullets. He kept moving forward, sustaining his momentum despite the unstable ground. The tactical splash exposed the Olyix ships ranged across the nearby mountains. They'd emerged a kilometer from a transport ship—while two and a half kilometers beyond that, along a precarious ridge, a Deliverance ship had pulverized the top of Farnsworth Peak, creating a flattish plateau on which it had sat for the last two and a half years while it assaulted Salt Lake City's shield.

The transports were starting to take off while the Deliverance ships were shooting upward at the swarm of missiles hurtling down. This time it was the Calmissiles that arrived first. Their exhaust plumes were bright enough to shine through the murky atmosphere, turning the slope into a stark monochrome wasteland. Loi could even glimpse the hulking shapes of the other two armor suits lumbering along.

Five Calmissiles punctured the Deliverance ship at Farnsworth Peak, cutting clean through and boring vertically down into the mountain until their spacial entanglement casings were switched off seconds later. By then the incandescent exhausts had already devastated the interior of the Deliverance ship. It burst apart in a cascade of molten slivers and jagged structural segments.

The glare faded, replaced by intense flashes from somewhere overhead as a fusillade of nuclear warheads detonated. Loi could just make out the shadow shape of the transport ship lifting off—a truncated-cone profile with its nose angling up as it started to accelerate. More explosions bloomed, their shock waves crashing down in massive pressure surges. The transport ship was more than three hundred meters high when the full force of the blast wave struck. It was flung down, twisting sharply as if trying to regain its correct flight vector. Then it smashed *hard* into the ground. Splits multiplied along the fuselage, but it remained intact.

Loi designated the fusion chamber exhaust ports at the rear, and the suit fired a tactical missile. The warhead was only a two-decaton nuke, and it exploded twenty meters away from the ship. Still, it was powerful enough to lift half of the transport off the ground as it shunted the whole mass along. The nose crunched into a rock clump, and the fissures in the fuselage ripped wide open. The aft quarter crumpled badly, blackening as the nuke's small mushroom cloud was immediately torn apart by the wind.

Loi crouched down. Even so, he wound up sprawling on his back as the blast wave flipped him over. Three high-velocity drones streaked forward from Eldlund's dispensers, hitting the transport ship's mangled fuselage and sticking fast.

"Entanglement suppression active," Eldlund exclaimed. "The *Salvation* onemind doesn't know what's happening to the ship."

Loi had righted himself and was plowing forward as fast as he could go. The flashes from nukes overhead were coming less frequently. All part of the Knockdown strategy, allowing the remaining ships to escape to orbit.

The transport was in bad shape. Its somber-red fuselage had so many cracks and gashes it was clearly never going to fly again. Internal tanks had been torn open. Fluids were gurgling out to splurge over structural spurs and the curving decking before splattering on the baked ground. Some of the liquid bleeding from the ship's vitals was cryogenic, bubbling away from exposure to the hot winds, producing vigorous clouds of white vapor that veiled the deeper mysteries of the interior.

Loi switched his suit sensor array to active, and it probed clean through the clouds, exposing the layout ahead. The ship was one he was painstakingly familiar with, identical to the original design of the *Avenging Heretic*. Directly under the fuselage skin was a thick seam of systems to manipulate exotic matter, allowing the ship to fly through a wormhole. Gravitonic drive units and fusion generators occupied the aft quarter, now mostly mangled slag thanks to the tactical nuke he'd fired. The bulk of the ship was composed of cylindrical compartments linked by overlapping circular corridors that resembled wide pipes.

He reached the ship and gripped both edges of a wide fissure. Artificial muscle cranked up to full strength, and he actually heard the grinding sound through the suit insulation as the gap was pried farther apart. Then he was inside, battling to keep a decent footing on the oily fluid coating the corridor walls, while icy white vapor from the broken cryogenic tank gushed around him, blocking the visual sensors. Millimeter-wave radar delineated something moving up ahead. The splash showed him an odd profile—an octopus whose tentacles projected radially out of its body in two equidistant rings, top and bottom, with whip cables sprouting from the midsection. It was clambering toward him fast. His shoulder-mounted mag-miniguns deployed, swiveling forward. They fired a couple of half-second bursts, producing a ferocious jackhammer vibration that made his teeth rattle. The body of the Olyix construct was immediately reduced to tattered shreds—almost the same consistency as the bubbling fluid Loi was slewing through.

Three more of the things came flailing along the corridor. He blasted each of them, then he, Eldlund, and Lim arrived at the central compartment. It was a basic cylinder that ran the height of the ship, separated into three sections by simple walkway grids. Halfway up, in the center of the walkway, was a two-meter-diameter sphere, held in place by ten radial poles. There must have been more than twenty of the Olyix creatures in there, of different sizes and with varying lengths of tentacles. They were moving sluggishly as though they were drunk, and sensors didn't see them carrying anything that resembled weapons. Loi and Eldlund opened fire. Ten seconds later, their armor suits were covered in ribbons of gore, the creatures were all dead, and the compartment's walls had hundreds of fist-sized holes where the armor-piercing micro-harpoons had struck.

"That makes it easy," Lim said. She began to scale the wall with the ease of a jazzed-up freefall climber, using the holes to jam feet and hands in. If they weren't big enough, she punched or kicked them until they were.

Loi used his suit sensors to watch the two corridors at the bottom of the compartment while Eldlund covered the three entrances at the top. The gale of cryogenic vapor had withered away, leaving everything in stark relief.

Lim reached the midsection walkway and swung onto it. If the transport ship's onemind was alarmed at her presence, there was no physical sign of it. But Loi kept vigilant as the blood fizzing around his body turned to pure adrenaline. *So great-grandfather Ainsley's paranoia is hereditary, after all.*

The tactical splash showed him that the nearly two dozen Olyix transport ships around Salt Lake City were now airborne. The surviving pair of Deliverance ships was lifting with them, their energy beams cutting apart the last barrage of missiles. Two hundred kilometers above them, a formation of cruisers swept eastward, with a second formation following fifteen hundred kilometers behind. The gap between them was the one that the Olyix ships were aiming for. After two years analyzing the flight capabilities of the transport ships, Strikeback had determined that over fifty percent should be able to make it through that gap and continue to climb.

"Starting extraction now," Lim announced.

Loi's suit sensors zoomed in. Lim had placed a glossy black package on the surface of the sphere, next to one of the radial spokes. Its surface rippled as if it were composed of a particularly viscous liquid.

This was the part they were completely dependent on the Neána for. The aliens were the ones with the neurovirus, which they claimed couldn't be used by humans. They had to rely on Lim and Jessika. Loi wanted to believe they'd pull through, but Kandara's suspicions kept playing in his mind. So much had to be taken on trust. *Our survival.*

Lim's gauntlet split open, and she pushed her right hand into the black surface and kept on going up to her wrist. "I'm in," she announced.

Loi scanned the corridors again. Nothing moved along them. He began to wonder what was in the other compartments. They'd never explored, never dispatched mobile sensors. This was a single-target mission—the most important one on Earth. Everything else was set up to facilitate this.

All Lim had to do was interface with the organic neural processor housed inside the sphere and load the neurovirus into it. Loi couldn't help it; he began to draw up size comparisons. Even if the mass of the neural processor only took up half of the sphere, it would still be seven or eight times larger than Lim's brain. So they didn't just have to trust that the Neána were true allies; the neurovirus had to work perfectly as well—something that had been assembled in a Neána abode cluster unknown centuries ago, and probably longer than that. Which made him wonder how they knew so much about Olyix thought routines. *Did they have captives they'd experimented on? That goes right against their supposed philosophy of hiding between the stars.*

Soćko had promised them it would work. "I took out a transport ship's onemind with it, remember?"

"Got it!" Lim exclaimed. She withdrew her hand carefully, and the gauntlet sealed up again. The surface of the package bowed inward, then it flowed into the sphere as if it was being sucked in.

This part had always seemed the weirdest to Loi. The neurovirus had allowed Lim to copy the onemind's identity patterns. But for the *Avenging Heretic*'s flight to succeed, they needed the specialist nodule of cells deep inside the transport ship's neural processor, which was entangled with the *Salvation of Life*'s neural strata. If the armor suit weren't so heavy, he'd be tapping his feet with nervous impatience.

The black package emerged back out from the hole, and Lim plucked it off the sphere. Thirty seconds later she'd half clambered, half jumped back to the floor of the compartment.

"Let's go."

"Hallelujah!" Eldlund exclaimed.

They hurried out, Eldlund taking point. Loi dropped a ten-decaton nuke on the compartment's floor as he stepped into the corridor, set the timer for ten minutes, and didn't look back.

It took them seven minutes to lope back to the portals. They were back on Kruse Station when the nuke detonated, obliterating what remained of the transport ship and any evidence of the Knockdown mission.

THE *AVENGING HERETIC*

S-DAY, DECEMBER 11, 2206

The five of them sat at their consoles in the white oval bridge, watching the image suspended between them. The *Avenging Heretic*'s internal sensors showed them an engineering drone holding the black extraction package Lim had brought back from the Knockdown mission, lowering it carefully into an open white cylinder.

Callum tried to stay focused on the drone, but his mind kept visualizing pure data—not in columns or graphics, but swirling masses of symbols he had vague recollections of. The intrusive specters flowed straight into his brain from the *Avenging Heretic*'s network via the neural interface—a distraction he couldn't ignore, because trying to ignore it made him concentrate harder.

He sort-of knew the data concerned the status of the Olyix nodule's cells—how the support cylinder was meshing its own capillary tendrils with them, establishing nutrient feed and extraction, and finally a direct neurological connection. Verifying functionality.

"The nodule is alive," Jessika pronounced.

Her voice allowed Callum to focus, reducing the errant data to a sparkle.

"And the support unit?" Kandara questioned.

"It's sustaining the cells for the moment. Long term, we'll just have to wait and see."

"If the nodule lasts for today, we go," Yuri said. "Strike-back, we're green."

"It's been an honor to know you," Johnstone's voice declared. "All of you. There is no precedent in human history for what you are undertaking. Future generations will thank you in person. I can only wish you good fortune."

"Be seeing you." Alik chuckled.

Callum's thought/wish/order switched his attention back to the image ringed by their consoles in the digital sensorium that was now his skin over the real world. The *Avenging Heretic* hung in space, ten AUs out from the glare of Delta Pavonis, alone except for a small blue-edged disk a hundred meters beyond its squat nose. A tactical splash of North America showed a flotilla of Olyix transport ships racing upward from Utah like a flock of terrified birds, with one surviving Deliverance ship at their apex. They were already three hundred kilometers above the planet and accelerating hard.

"Deploying interception squadron," Johnstone said calmly. "Stand by."

Twenty expansion portals opened two hundred kilometers above the fleeing transports. Cruisers streamed out. Missiles launched, their fusion plumes a lacework of flaring light, twisting restlessly then attenuating into a glowing shroud as if a borealis storm had thundered up out of the atmosphere. Five Calmissiles sought out the Deliverance ship, destroying it within seconds. The nuclear missiles started to explode in and around the transports, turning a vast section of space into an anarchic nebula.

"Go," Johnstone ordered.

The expansion portal in front of the *Avenging Heretic* grew rapidly; white light shone through. The *Avenging Heretic* surged forward, emerging in the middle of the nuclear holocaust above Utah. Ultra-hard radiation saturated the fuselage, and the disintegrating wreckage of Olyix ships shot past at catastrophic speed.

"Disengaging suppression," Jessika said. "Entangling with the *Salvation* onemind."

Callum held his breath, knowing he wasn't—not with his body in the suspension unit in the middle of the ship. He wasn't even breathing air. But the simulacrum obliged. He counted seconds away as pounding blood grew louder in his ears.

All his goodbyes had been made two days ago. Savi, of course; they'd remained relatively civil to each other for decades. She'd wanted to know why he was calling her and making such maudlin small talk. *Always was smarter than me.* His deflection was risible, and he guessed she knew that.

"I have an assignment when S-Day comes," he'd said. "It's a tough one. It might take a while."

"And if I ask you what it is, would you tell me?"

"I can't. Security. You understand that, don't you?" It wasn't meant as a taunt, a reminder of Zagreus, but he was worrying needlessly. She didn't take offense. They were long past that stage.

Then the really tough calls—the kids and their families. For the great-great-grandkids he made recordings; they were twins, only seven months old, so in the future they'd hear his love spoken from the past like some historical artifact. *I hope they're bored by the messages. That'll mean they're living for real.*

"It's accepted us," Jessika said. Her face betrayed considerable elation. "The pattern fooled it into recognizing us as the ship the Knockdown team took out."

"What's it saying?" Yuri asked.

"It doesn't so much say things as provide autonomic impulses, like we're an extension of it. I'll try and show you. Look inward."

Callum reluctantly closed his eyes, seeking out . . . sounds? Colors? Heat? Cold? Instead, the faint sensation was like a balance response to shifting ground. He wanted his body to sway, then bend, pivot. Something unseen beckoned him forward, to safety. Concern enveloped him like a physical constriction—the urge to get free of the shocking danger that had erupted without warning around the planet of the newly beloved. More concern over those already sleeping at their start of the great voyage to the God at the End of Time. Batwing rustling of a billion calculations a second echoed in a black cavern the size of mountains, reluctantly determining the safest route away.

He opened his eyes—a demand to see their current situation. Space had darkened around the *Avenging Heretic*'s fuselage as the plasma residue from the missile nukes evaporated. Below lay the huge crescent of Earth, smeared in dirty white storm clouds. He couldn't tell if they were over land or sea; nothing was visible beneath the blanket of rucked cirrocumulus peaks. Wreckage was still flashing past them, the husks of broken transport ships dwindling as they fell, whirling helplessly toward the grinding hurricane swirls.

His reaction to the tumultuous vista was complex: so many emotions. Delight at the rout of the Olyix even though he knew it was irrelevant, a move in the most complex chess game ever devised. Then there was the doubt and insecurity about their mission, which made him want to shout: "No, turn around; I don't want this. I can't do it. I want to join the exodus. The Neána are right: We should hide between the stars and live quietly with our friends and families." Instead, his father's face seemed to have ghosted its way into the bridge, looking at him expectantly.

Oh, bloody hell. We must be fucking crazy.

That might have been spoken out loud, judging from the way the others were grinning at him.

Acceleration began as Jessika activated their gravitonic drive. They rose amid the Olyix survivors from the siege of Salt Lake City, reaching for the relative safety of altitude. The tarnished white globe of Earth now had dozens of flotillas striving for the haven of the arkship at its Lagrange 3 point orbit, three hundred eighty thousand kilometers above the surface, directly opposite the moon.

When they were four thousand kilometers out from Earth, the various Olyix flotillas began to merge into larger groups. Callum kept watch through the fuselage sensors while experiencing the urges to congregate from the *Salvation*'s one-mind. The impulses gradually began to make sense as the G8Turing refined its interpretation, enhancing the basic impulse into a multi-themed complexity; picking the individual strands apart was even more difficult, like trying to isolate a specific instrument from an orchestral symphony.

He was amazed and impressed that Jessika could make any sense of it.

"Alpha Defense is consolidating its cruiser fleets," Yuri observed.

"Chasing us," Alik said. "And, oh, look, strategically never quite catching up. Bummer, huh?"

"The cruisers were specifically built to have a lower acceleration than the transports," Kandara said. "Some of the transports have to be allowed to escape."

"That's got to be suspicious," Callum told her.

"The onemind isn't thinking in those terms," Jessika said. "Its entire attention is focused on a strategic withdrawal, safeguarding the cocoons it has on board. Its main worry is what to do with all the ships retreating to it—including this one. There's not enough hangar capacity on board. We're being instructed to fly directly into the wormhole."

"Can we do that?" Yuri asked.

"The negative energy regulators are fully functional, so that won't be a problem. But our mission is to stay with the *Salvation of Life*."

"What do you suggest?"

"The Olyix retreat is still taking a lot of punishment. Plenty of ships are damaged. I can mimic impairment to our regulators. That might get us assigned to a hangar."

"Do it," Yuri said.

Callum kept watching their flight to the arkship. Cruisers were still firing barrage after barrage of missiles at the fleeing Olyix transport ships. The rate of dispatch was lower now, giving the wholly true impression that human munition stocks were depleting. There were almost no Calmissiles being fired at all, allowing the few surviving Deliverance ships to defend the transport flotillas more effectively.

Jessika's request to the *Salvation* onemind was a whispered tune on the edge of Callum's subconscious, a feeble little plea. He didn't think the arkship would pay anything so diminutive the slightest attention. It was completely absorbed by the Strikeback attack.

"Do you think it'll conform to our strategy?" he asked.

"The son of a bitch Goddamn should conform," Alik said. "We need that. We need it to do what we want. Strikeback is all about backing it into a corner. That's why this whole attack exists. The only reason—"

"It will," Kandara said. "The onemind has showed considerable tactical aptitude. It must know we could have launched our surprise attack directly against it. A thousand Calmissiles would have turned it into the universe's biggest lump of Swiss cheese, and rotational inertia would have finished the job."

"Ah, Lord bless the mighty Calmissiles." Alik laughed. "Just look at those mothers go."

"We're lucky to live in an age where such wonders exist," Kandara said levelly.

"Oh, go fuck yourselves," Callum grumbled. "Using portal fuselages as a weapon was a good idea, and you know it."

"Don't we just." Yuri smirked.

"It was, Cal," Jessika agreed. "The onemind is genuinely disconcerted by them. It knows it's incredibly vulnerable to a mass strike."

"It also knows we wouldn't risk that," Yuri said. "We're desperate, but not so much that we'd slaughter every cocoon on board, which is what would happen if it disintegrates. It knows we're working on saving them, on reversing the cocooning process."

"Trust Johnstone," Kandara said. "The strike against *Salvation* will be precise. The onemind will know we're trying to cripple it by killing the wormhole now that we've eliminated the bulk of the Deliverance ships. That's a logical move on our part. That leaves it with only one option."

Callum felt the impulse from the *Salvation* onemind come—a multifarious incitement to all the Olyix transport ships in their flotilla. He was pleased he didn't have to query Jessika what it meant.

Time for the *Avenging Heretic* to flip over and decelerate toward the *Salvation of Life*. The maneuver would leave all the approaching transports vulnerable to the cruisers who had no such need. They weren't going to rendezvous with the arkship; they were going to flash past at high velocity and launch a final massive barrage of missiles. He could even sense how disconcerting that was to the Olyix.

Deliverance ships clustered protectively around the *Sal-*

vation of Life were dispatched to intercept the cruisers, as were the ones escorting the transports. The timing was going to have to be perfect.

Trust Johnstone.

Fortunately it was more than just the adjutant-general. Strikeback was two years of effort and planning, millions of people involved manufacturing warships, thousands of people managing the effort. Hundreds of tacticians crafting and analyzing the plan, building in multiple contingencies. Six supervising, in conjunction with the most powerful G8Turing hypercube ever built. This was not simply throwing the dice and hoping.

Knowing that still didn't stop him from fretting.

The *Avenging Heretic* was eight minutes out from the *Salvation of Life*, and decelerating at three gees, when four stealthed portals opened a thousand kilometers from the arkship's aft end. Twenty Calmissiles streaked out, followed by a flock of sensor satellites. The remaining five Deliverance ships guarding the arkship immediately fired salvos of high-velocity missiles. As before, it was no use. Fifty-megaton explosions had no effect. The Calmissiles simply swallowed anything that crossed their vacant boundary: radiation, particles, plasma . . . Seconds later all twenty holes struck the *Salvation of Life*, cutting clean through the rock at thirty-two kilometers a second. High-resolution sensors revealed the damage. The narrow tunnels seethed with rapidly cooling fusion flame from the Calmissile drives. Where they intersected machinery, the damage was severe, but structurally the arkship remained unbroken. The new tunnels were insignificant on something that size.

Callum felt the onemind's concern deepening. It was analyzing the attack vectors the Calmissiles had flown, seeing how humans were targeting the arkship's engineering systems—and, more important, the wormhole terminus mechanism. Amid it all was a faint reply to Jessika's request, an acknowledgment that was one of utter insignificance, simply an inclusion to the general orchestration of hundreds of Olyix transports that were damaged but still flightworthy.

"We have a hangar assignment," Jessika confirmed.

The first wave of retreating transport ships was arriving at the *Salvation of Life*. As they closed in, each ship activated its negative energy regulators—hundreds of small fin-like protrusions bristling up out of the smooth fuselage like porcupine spikes reacting to a threat. In the center of the *Salvation*'s aft section, the open throat of the wormhole glimmered with the signature violet sparkle of Cherenkov radiation. It was only just smaller than the diameter of the arkship. Looking down it, there was no funnel-like perspective, no distant vanishing point at the end of a tunnel through space-time. The wormhole's throat was simply a place where the real universe ended.

Callum shivered as he accessed the sensor image. *What if the nothingness escapes?*

The transport ships dived into the glowing emptiness, their maneuvers as elegant and agile as a shoal of fish, instantly vanishing from view. Then the *Avenging Heretic* was only a hundred kilometers away, soaring along amid its own kind. No longer decelerating, but aligning themselves on the scintillating target. Seventy kilometers. Forty.

"Er—" Callum managed.

Behind her console, the unreal Jessika had her eyes closed, her face composed in perfect concentration. She even had perspiration glinting on her brow. The *Avenging Heretic* glided smartly out of the flow of transport ships, elevating itself away from the wormhole. Then they were skimming over the surface of the arkship, its dreary rock a blur of mottled gray, fluctuating wildly in brightness as the nuclear-tipped missiles chasing the transports continued to detonate behind them. A surface far too close as Jessika flew them in a tight, twisting trajectory. Even in this state, Callum perceived the shadow impulses of hard gravity variabilities tugging at his suspended physical body, as if they were riding an out-of-control roller coaster. Sensors revealed the *Avenging Heretic*'s own shadow flowing over the rock like a fluid ghost, flickering in and out of existence with every flash of light from the explosions.

Blackness eclipsed them so fast he yelled in shock. They'd streaked straight into a hangar entrance in a perfectly measured deceleration burst. Jessika's piloting ability was phenomenal. He couldn't imagine a transport's onemind being so agile and precise.

Did the Salvation *onemind notice we're too good?*

He took a breath, wondering if he should conjure up some tranquilizers from the suspension tank's support modules, because that kind of thinking was where healthy paranoia bubbled over into outright crazy.

"Holy shit!" Alik exclaimed. "Damn, that was a ride."

Sensors focused on their new surroundings. They were in a vast cavern whose rock walls were threaded with crinkled black roots, as if they'd dropped into the underground grotto of Nordic elementals. The floor was already home to more than twenty transport ships in various conditions, from little visible damage to those with fuselages warped and split from close proximity to nuclear blasts. The *Avenging Heretic* slipped smoothly among them, searching for a space to land. Jessika steered them toward the rear of the hangar where several badly damaged ships were parked, and slowly settled the *Avenging Heretic* amid them.

"Oh, sweet mother Mary," Kandara said. "I don't believe this. We made it."

"They're in," Johnstone exclaimed as the density of tactical data expanded toward solidity in the air around him. A single frozen image hung poised to his left— the tail end of the *Avenging Heretic* disappearing into the darkness of a hangar entrance at the middle of the arkship. Other icons splashed, confirming the entanglement communication channel with the ship had gone, deactivated in case the *Salvation of Life* was able to detect it.

He focused on the ring formation of twenty stealthed portals surrounding the *Salvation of Life* six hundred kilometers out. "Initiate phase five," he ordered.

The portals expanded. Calmissiles flew out of them, volley after volley curving sharply to hurtle in toward the arkship, lining up on the aft section where the wormhole glimmered. Long lines of Olyix transport ships were still racing into it.

Johnstone wanted to start praying. This was the moment—

the greatest gamble of all time. The Neána had assured them that the arkship was capable of traveling down the wormhole, even though it carried the terminus generator on board. If it didn't—if they were wrong, or the onemind refused to retreat—the combined punctures of eight hundred Calmissiles would obliterate the *Salvation of Life*.

Alpha Defense estimated there were now more than a billion human cocoons on board.

"Come on," he implored. The lead Calmissiles were twenty seconds out. Fifteen. "Run away, curse you." Ten.

The strange wavering lilac light of Cherenkov radiation flooded out past the arkship's rim. Somehow, the vast cylinder of rock was sinking into it. The light vanished, and with it the *Salvation of Life*.

Johnstone searched every data splash for information, but there was none. Hundreds of Calmissiles were crisscrossing the zone of space where their target had been moments earlier. The command center coordinators began directing them to intercept the abandoned transports and Deliverance ships.

His chair swiveled so he was facing Emilja and Ainsley. They were staring at the chamber's central display, watching the patch of empty space where the massive arkship had been.

Ainsley raised a fist in victory. "That's it, then. We dickpunched the bastards." He started laughing.

"Heaven preserve us," Emilja said. "What have we done?"

"The only thing we could," Johnstone assured her.

"They will come back."

"Oh, yes. And when they do, there is only one thing left for us to do: run. We need to be ready."

"Christ's sake, you two," Ainsley said. "Lighten up. We won. In a couple of centuries, we can fight them on our own terms. You'll see."

Emilja gave him a pitying smile. "Thankfully, I won't. That is our children's fight. And they are not going to thank us for it."

NASHUA HABITAT, DELTA PAVONIS

S-DAY, DECEMBER 11, 2206

Gwendoline Seymore-Qing-Zangari was in the department of exodus habitat construction's main lounge—a huge communal area where the staff could go and chill. The design subroutine that had produced it had aimed for European stately home but had landed at corporate employee informal function zone. However, the sofas were deep and comfy, the holographic projector top quality, the software in the servez delivering drinks reasonably semi-sentient, and the printed snacks surprisingly good. She could have gone to her apartment with its spectacular view along Nashua's cylindrical landscape, but being alone when such a decisive—*the decisive*—battle for the future of the human race was being fought would have been too depressing. No way was she going to observe with her family. And since she'd arrived two years ago, there'd been precious little time to make any friends. So she'd chosen to settle down and watch Strikeback with her team; they'd all grown close enough over the last twenty months, even though they weren't Zangaris. She'd brought in a few colleagues from her London office—ones she'd worked with in the past and knew were super-competent. Others had been assigned to her by Delta Pavonis: some from Alpha Defense—which in reality meant the Sol Senate, checking up that the Zangaris and Utopials were upholding their part of the arrangement to build the exodus fleet—and the rest from various astroengineering consortia, weighted in favor of the Eta Cassiopeiae Billionaire Belt.

The display hanging in the air was heavy on data tags, with plenty of long-distance sensor imagery of explosions above Earth and, more disturbingly, in the atmosphere.

"We really are never going back, are we?" Matilde d'Gorro said bitterly. "Not with that radioactive shit piled on top of the Olyix toxicology." She'd been one of Gwendoline's executive administrators back in London, partying as hard as she worked—which was with total dedication. Now she was a paid-up miserabilist, but still kept her impressive focus, which was why Gwendoline continued to use her.

"They're single-phase fusion bombs," Bettine Abbey, one of the Billionaire Belt science directors, responded. "Clean ignition, so they don't pump out much contamination."

"Ten thousand of them?" Josquain sneered. "Those gamma emissions will—"

"We've terraformed worse. Look at Ulysses."

"Delta Eridani was different. It didn't have the kind of particle decay Earth's going to suffer. And anyway—"

"Enough," Gwendoline said. "None of us will ever be returning to Earth."

"But it's our homeworld," Matilde exclaimed, almost in tears. "There are still whole areas of the biosphere we know nothing about. How are we going to catalogue them now?"

"Save it for the people who are never going to join the exodus," Bettine snapped.

"Earth is more than just humans!"

"Oh, fuck, you're not seriously going speciesist on us? Today?"

"Time out, both of you," Gwendoline ordered. She knew she should be kinder, more sympathetic, but everyone was exhausted, everyone was frightened, and everyone had family who were affected. The arguments about drawing up lists of those who'd get to embark on the exodus habitats were fractious at best. She'd heard there'd been physical fights break out over them.

We just don't have the psychology to deal with Armageddon. Though judging by the confidential medical reports the

Zangari council had allowed her to see, humans certainly had the mood drugs for it.

She watched the clusters of Olyix transport ships fleeing Earth. They were flocking together in huge squadrons and accelerating hard for the *Salvation of Life* up at Lagrange 3. That puzzled her. A surprise first strike against the alien arkship would have been better tactics, surely? They could have disabled the wormhole and gravitonic drive, leaving the arkship stranded. The cocoons could have been rescued. But now the Olyix onemind knew the Strikeback cruisers and missiles were approaching and was undoubtedly preparing to flee.

"Call Loi," she told Theano, her altme.

"Network unable to connect."

"What? Try again."

"Unable to connect. He is offline."

She grimaced. He was heavily involved in Strikeback, possibly even in the command center along with Yuri, so he'd be incredibly busy right now. And definitely wouldn't appreciate a call from his mother. But . . . "What's his location?"

"Classified."

"Well, what was his last non-classified location?"

"The Delta Pavonis star system."

"Okay. Well, leave a message for him. I want to—" She stopped in surprise as Ainsley Zangari III's icon splashed into her tarsus lens. "Yes?" she asked.

"Stop trying to call Loi," Ainsley III said.

"I just wanted to—"

"You're tripping all sorts of security alerts. He's involved in Strikeback; you know that. Which, if you hadn't noticed, is rather critical to our survival right now. Stop being his mother, for fuck's sake. He's old enough to take care of himself and make his own decisions."

"But—"

Ainsley III's icon vanished.

What the actual hell? She glanced surreptitiously around the lounge to see if anyone was looking at her. No. *Now you're getting paranoid.* But the reaction from Ainsley III was disturbing. So Loi was in the command center helping.

That wasn't a reason to snap at her. Unless he wasn't in the . . . *Oh, shit!*

Horatio, at least, responded straight away to her call. "Hey, you. Did you know this was going to happen?" he asked breezily.

"What?"

"The fight back, silly. What did you think I meant?"

Very conscious a G8Turing security routine would be monitoring her closely now, she said: "It is what we've been working toward."

"It's magnificent, Gwendoline! The Deliverance ships have all gone. The London shield isn't under attack anymore. There's no sound, no devil-sky light—not anymore. I've got people here in the community center crying their eyes out. We knew the settled worlds would help us. I've always kept telling everyone that, but it's been such a long two years. You should see the party that's kicking off down here."

"I'm so glad," she said. For some reason her eyes were tearing up.

"The government's opened some visual feeds from orbit. We can see the Olyix ships retreating. Are your forces going to invade the *Salvation of Life*?"

"I have no idea what's going to happen next. And if I did . . ."

"You wouldn't tell me."

"Damn right."

"Good for you. God, I am so happy right now. I wish you were here, just for today. You have no idea what it was like seeing those bastard Deliverance ships turn tail and run."

"I miss you," she said. "Really badly."

"Yeah, so much likewise. But this helps, right?"

"Helps?"

"You and me," he said. "I know it isn't the victory people here think it is right now. I'm guessing we can't even switch off the shield, the Olyix have ruined the climate so badly. Which means everyone has to leave."

Gwendoline couldn't do it, couldn't tell him. There was no ice left anywhere on land, not anymore—no glaciers, not a single mountain left that was crowned in stately white. What was left of the Arctic ice cap was shrinking rapidly, while the massive Antarctic ice shelves that had so slowly thickened again after the twenty-first century's anthrochange had finally fractured, breaking off so the remaining country-sized bergs were melting fast. Rising sea levels would soon add to the misery of the surviving cities, as dangerous as the overheated atmosphere tormented with its single world-throttling storm. "They do, yes," she said softly. "We think the Olyix will be back. And you don't want to be around when that happens; nobody does."

"I want to be with you when that happens, to go . . . wherever. The two of us together."

"You can be here inside of a minute, you know that. You have the portal."

"Yeah, but in the meantime I have to be here. I can't abandon my people, not now. I'm doing so much good here, Gwendoline. I'm helping."

And it'll all be for nothing. "I know. I'm so proud of you."

"You're keeping your end of the bargain, as well, aren't you?"

"I am. Of course I am. We're going to build hundreds of exodus habitats—thousands if we get the time."

"Thank you. Love you."

"Love you."

FINALSTRIKE MISSION

FLIGHT YEAR 9

Yirella was already yawning when she and Dellian walked into the hibernation compartment. There was something about the place that was simply restful: its size, the quiet efficiency of all the sarcophagi-like suspension chambers, the reduced lighting, and a temperature several degrees below the rest of the *Morgan*. She suspected this was the way temples and churches had felt on old Earth.

They went into the washroom together and undressed, smirking like they were back in the senior year on the Immerle estate.

"We had last night," she said coyly.

"I know."

Being together for the last fourteen months had been good. Everyone who'd been revived for the Captain's Council had been active while the fleet accelerated up to relativistic velocity.

Yirella had relished contributing to all the review-group meetings about the Signal from Lolo Maude, speculating on what had happened and where the original Strike mission had gone—if it had. The *Morgan* had constructed new sensor arrays to study the K-class star, but that had added nothing to their knowledge. All they had were assumptions and guesswork, which put her in her element.

Outside of the meetings and official watch duties, she and

Dellian had treated the time like the holiday they'd never had on Juloss. So much so that, during the last month, she'd found herself resenting the approaching day when they'd be back at point-nine light speed. The interlude had given her a chance to relax in a way she never had before. From their perspective, the goal they were heading for was so remote it could be comfortably ignored, giving her a degree of freedom that was unique in her experience. Limited freedom, maybe, but the *Morgan* had centuries' worth of music and drama and literature on file that she could dip into whenever she wanted, and it had Dellian, who for once wasn't stuck in an eternal cycle of fitness routines and combat training sessions. It was like finding out what being human was actually like—a year of living what they'd always been promised.

By the time they stood beside his suspension chamber and she kissed him goodbye, she was struggling with a tangle of emotions.

"See you in a heartbeat and three years," he said tenderly.

"That's a date."

Yirella refused to look back as she walked over to her own chamber. A medical technician was waiting for her. "I can manage," she said, slightly irritable, as sie offered her an arm.

There was the inevitable moment of coffin fever as the transparent lid slid shut. On the other side of the glass, the med tech gave her a thumbs-up, and she nodded, taking an apprehensive breath. Slim robot arms slid out of the padded sides of the chamber and carefully plugged umbilical tubes into her abdominal sockets. She closed her eyes and activated her neural interface.

The little biotech unit hadn't been removed after she'd helped with Dellian's treatment. She'd told Alimyne it would help her work, designing the neutron star civilization, allowing her to access and direct the G8Turing formatting routines a lot faster than through a standard databud. Alimyne had reluctantly agreed.

And she'd been right; it had proved incredibly useful in crafting the directives that the seedships would use as a foundation for the neutron star civilization they were to birth. But it also gave her a much greater access to the *Mor-*

gan's network than a databud. Combined with the override routines Ainsley had provided her, she had a level of control over the ship that would have alarmed Dellian had he known.

Yirella used her direct link to load a simple instruction into the suspension chamber management routines and closed her eyes, smiling faintly as the umbilicals fed the preliminary sedative into her body.

Consciousness arrived easily. Yirella's body recognized it as if she were waking up in the morning rather than recovering from hibernation, but then it had only been three days. She felt refreshed and roguishly thrilled by what she was about to do. First she checked that the compartment's monitoring routines were ignoring her; the overrides she'd loaded had created a blind spot around her chamber. No alerts had been triggered.

The umbilicals unplugged, and the lid slid back. While she showered she reviewed the ship's status—particularly the location of the active-duty crew—then finally reviewed the other illicit procedure she'd begun. Two decks down, a biologic initiator had spent three weeks producing a human body. The cyborg didn't have a full range of organs, just basic modules that could sustain the biologic muscles that overlaid a carbon skeleton, which in turn had been dressed in very realistic skin.

And it was ready.

Her routines scouted the route up to the suspension compartment, creating a safe passage. Yirella walked the cyborg up carefully.

She was dressed and ready when it entered the washroom, carrying a case of additional remotes the initiator had produced for her. Looking at the perfect replica of herself was the strangest sensation. She didn't know if she should run or smile in admiration.

This part of the plan was always going to be the most ambiguous, because she and Ainsley didn't know quite what they were dealing with. One version—the original idea— had the initiators producing a batch of insect-sized remotes packed with sensors that she could control while resting in the chamber. It certainly had the least risk. Then the *Morgan* had detected Lolo's Signal—a random factor that could never have been anticipated. Her year off everything—worrying, plotting—made her reluctant to hand everything over to remotes. She wanted to be more involved, telling herself she could do a better job than any sensor, that she needed to be in the room. So she'd designed the cyborg.

Her doppelgänger lay back down in her suspension chamber, and the lid slid back up. That way, any of the duty crew performing a routine visual check—which was a mandatory once-a-day inspection—would just see her resting in there as normal.

It was a long way around the *Morgan*'s life support section from the hibernation compartment to the captain's private quarters, and several decks higher. Yirella took it carefully, deactivating the monitors section by section, constantly checking the position of any crew in the corridors so they didn't come across her. Three and a half hours later she was outside the door. She ran one final review of the quarters to make sure Kenelm wasn't inside. It seemed to be clear—unless of course Kenelm was using routines every bit as sophisticated as hers. After all, if she was right, sie had been on the Factory when Ainsley was made.

Yirella hesitated just for a second, then sent an override code into the door mechanism. It unlocked silently, and she walked in. Kenelm's private quarters were made up of eight rooms: a formal reception room, a lounge, an entertainment room wrapped around an interactive stage, a dining room, a spa, a bedroom, a washroom, and a study. Lights came on as she stood on the threshold. The small sensor remotes clinging to her clothes extended their insect legs and clambered down onto the floor. They spread out, and she closed her eyes, riding them, multiple images flowing into her brain through the neural interface. It allowed her to pervade every room of the quarters at once, examining the structure and fittings simultaneously.

There were no independent sensors active, and no Kenelm sleeping on hir bed. Sie really had gone back into hibernation a day after Yirella, as scheduled. Yirella allowed herself to exhale and got to work. The remotes carefully recorded the layout of each room: the way everything had been left when Kenelm went for suspension, the position of all the loose items, even the way the chairs were oriented. It might have been excessive caution, but she didn't want Kenelm to know someone had been snooping.

When everything was mapped, the obvious place to start a forensic-level analysis was the study. She dispatched the majority of the remotes there while she sat down in the dining room. Kenelm certainly had some of the best food extruders in the fleet, and after three days on fluid nutrients oozing into her via the umbilicals, she was ravenous.

Five hours later the remotes had examined and explored every square millimeter of the study and everything in it, even scanning for hidden alcoves or passages. Yirella stood in the middle of the room, looking around with the results splashed inside her head. Network cables seemed to be woven everywhere beneath the decking and walls. Power cables were bright fizzing lines; the ephemeral outlines of systems and sensors glimmered like fading holograms. She was here in person because she knew intuition was something that couldn't be enacted through remotes. But now, it turned out that staring suspiciously around the study wasn't the mystery-busting breakthrough in real life that it was in all the books she'd accessed.

She wasn't sure what she was going to find, but the study certainly didn't contain it. Her principal fear was that anything that might verify Kenelm had a hidden agenda would be contained in deeply encrypted files buried somewhere in the *Morgan*'s network. Given how much data was stored in the ship's memory cores, they would be almost impossible to find unless a genten ran a full content analysis through each individual file—a task that would likely take centuries.

The remotes were directed into the formal reception room. After all, wasn't it Saint Yuri who said the best way to hide something was in plain sight? She frowned. *Or was that Saint Callum?*

The bedroom was next. When the remotes finished that, she lay down for a short rest . . .

Lounge.

Dining room.

Spa.

By the time the remotes scampered en masse into the entertainment room, Yirella had been in the captain's quarters for nearly two days—eating, sleeping, fretting. The antique book she was flicking through almost dropped through her fingers when the remotes told her they'd completed their scan. Everything was normal. Nothing was out of place, nothing was hidden behind false panels, there were no concealed alien gadgets.

"Shit."

She got up and slid the book back onto the shelf with all the others after a quick check of the images she'd taken to confirm it was in the right place. Kenelm had twenty volumes detailing the complete history of Falkon's terraforming process. They'd been printed on that planet, according to the title page. Her hand rested on the spine. She didn't move it away.

Kenelm clearly valued the books. And why not? They were important, a part of their heritage.

But why these?

Her brief flick through a few pages showed her they were spectacularly dull scientific papers. Even the illustrations were boring: bacteria, genetic sequences, three-D graphs, a clone tank, laboratory equipment, assessment team expeditions, skyscraper-sized biologic initiators, orbital geological surveys.

She remembered Saint Yuri's story, how he doggedly followed Saint Callum's desperate hunt for his wife, Savi. How every good detective understood that people could be defined by what they considered important.

"What am I not seeing?" she asked, and pulled out volume one.

THE *AVENGING HERETIC*

WEEK FOUR

"Gotta admit," Alik said. "This is my idea of exercise."

Kandara just rolled her eyes in derision at male hormones as she pulled on her ubiquitous black singlet. There was barely enough elbow room for that in the tiny cabin. "Very flattering. You need to use the gym more. We don't know how long we're going to be doing this." She started hunting around for her sneakers. She saw them under the cot, beneath a tangle of his clothes.

"I was hoping for quite a while."

"Idiot." She shoved his legs out of the way and sat on the edge of the cot to get her shoes on. "I mean the whole mission."

"Oh. Yeah." Alik's stiff features compressed into a sulky frown.

"Seriously? Second thoughts already?"

"No. Just waking up to the sharp end of reality. Time is an abstract, you know. People don't really grasp it properly. I think it's because we're all in denial about growing old."

She gave his solid face with all its reprofiled muscle and plastic-sheen skin a weary glance. "Well . . ."

"Yeah, yeah, I know. Don't rub it in. Someone in my position has to go with the flow. Everyone on the Hill has more clone parts than original these days."

She patted his legs. "Not anymore."

"Hey, DC survived. Well . . . its shield was intact when S-Day started."

"I bet Rio's a mess." For a moment she was back there, running along Copacabana's hot sands with the young and exuberant, strutting their stuff under the sun. The smell of street-stall food and sun cream in the breeze, the bands playing along Avenida Atlantica, living the daydream, a viz-u producer would stop and beckon them over. Nightlife: the football supporters going crazy in bars, sirens of emergency bikes bulldozing revelers off the clear routes. Marches of pride, marches of protest, lovers alone in their world, families thronging the parks, everybody living good under the sun. The Carnaval—a beautiful, wild, joyous party of laughing maniacs winding its way along the streets like an earthbound rainbow.

No more.

And now this sterile, modified alien spaceship was the rest of her life. *Probably coffin, too.*

"Sweetheart," Alik snorted, "the whole fucking world's a filthy mess now."

"Yes." Sweetheart! Oh, Mary.

"Hey, on the bright side, we'll get to see it made new when this is over."

She grinned in bemusement. "That is so not you."

"What?"

"Optimism. That we'll get to complete any stage of this insane mission, let alone finish it."

"So why are you here?"

"Somebody has to be. What use am I back there? Now that the *Salvation of Life* is retreating, there won't be another one-on-one fight on Earth until the Olyix reinforcements turn up—in twenty, maybe thirty, years' time. I'll be too old by then."

"Never!"

"Now you're just trying to get inside my pants."

"Can't blame a guy for trying."

"You can stop. Both of us are practical adults."

"Okay. Tonight?"

"Sure."

His narrow smile tightened as his gaze slid across the

shallow bulges on her forearms. "Hey, I thought you'd got rid of your peripherals . . ."

"I did. The originals." She winked. "Then I got myself some new ones."

"Jez-us. But Lim said they might be dangerous when we're in the tank. No one knows what long-term immersion will do to them."

"Yeah. Which is why Lim made these tank-proof ones for me in an initiator."

"Why the hell wasn't I told they were available?"

"Did you ask?"

"Fuck's sake!"

A grinning Kandara stepped out of his cabin into the main lounge. It was the lower third of the ship's main cylindrical chamber, ringed by the tiny personal sleep cabins they used when they weren't in their suspension tanks. That didn't leave much floorspace, and the table occupied most of it. At least the mid-deck had room for the exercise machines, along with the washroom and a G8Turing-run medical bay, which she prayed she'd never need. Prejudice—but she preferred human doctors. Top deck housed the suspension tanks and their support systems. Her initial hope that they'd each get one of the other chambers for personal quarters was quickly dashed when the engineers started filling them with drones and printers and a batch of Neána-technology initiators. The old Olyix bio-gunk tanks were now full of raw materials the human machinery used. Everyone on their mission strategy team swore the trove of equipment would cover most contingencies. Kandara didn't believe that for a second; they were corporate denizens who just didn't grasp the maxim that no battle plan survives contact with the enemy.

Callum was sitting at the central table, eating scrambled eggs and salmon, with a mug of tea steaming beside his plate. "Morning," he said, waving a fork in her direction.

She gave him a mildly awkward smile and went over to the food printer. Her altme, Zapata, splashed a reassuring green medical icon; her gland was working fine, keeping her neurochemistry stable. *Not that there's been any trauma to trigger schizophrenia. And if the gland packs up, I'll just use*

Alik for stress relief. It was all she could do not to laugh out loud. *Ah, the romance.*

"I'm going to stay out another twenty-four hours," she announced as the printer squirted out her smoothie. "One more aerobics session."

"I haven't got a clue why you think you need that," Callum said. "It's us truly old crocks that should be hitting the treadmills."

"Treadmi—? Am I the only one who uses the exercise apparatus?"

"I used one of them a couple of days ago. My legs are still on fire with DOMS."

"Sweet Mary, I thought the docs fixed us all up. What kind of state were you in before? We were only in the tanks for three weeks. That was just a kindergarten trial run. The real slog doesn't start until we reach the sensor outpost, or whatever it is."

"Tell me about it."

She collected her smoothie and sat down beside him. The gloom in his tone was one she shared. It had been a huge blow to discover the *Salvation of Life* wasn't flying directly back to the enclave. Instead, as they came to comprehend more of the onemind's thoughts, they realized the wormhole ended at some kind of local observation base. The Olyix had built thousands of them scattered across the galaxy, each one watching for the emergence of sentient species in their own particular sector. That was where the wormhole back to the enclave star system waited.

It was a perfectly logical setup. Just one they hadn't anticipated. She almost wanted to break cover so they could send Alpha Defense a message: *You smartasses didn't think of everything after all.*

"You know what bothers me about it?" she said.

"Tell me."

"The Neána didn't know."

"About the outpost?"

"Yeah. We are completely dependent on their knowledge and their technology. And the first time we use it . . . Pow! Instant problem."

"Pessimist. I'd say *issue*, not problem. So the Olyix enclave is farther away than we expected. It doesn't change the mission profile, or what we're dealing with. And to be fair, when they arrived on Earth, Jessika and Soćko weren't expecting us to do anything as fucking stupid as this mission. Deliberately abandoning every planet we have so our descendants can have a crack at the enclave? When you look at it the morning after, it's really not a good idea."

"I know. But really, this ship: It's just a tiny part of the whole exodus plan. Whether we live between stars like the Neána or go for Emilja's migratory option and hop between planets while we build up an armory of the universe's most dangerous weapons, there will be a time when we have to face the Olyix. All you and I are doing really is giving our species a fractionally better chance to succeed. If we fail, then they'll find the enclave by themselves eventually."

Callum raised his mug of tea. "Great pep talk. Thanks."

"Sorry." She chuckled. "What can I say? I'm a pragmatist."

"I'll take that. At least it means we have a slightly better chance of pulling this off."

Kandara raised her glass of smoothie. "And in the meantime, enjoy the view." She sipped the green slush and wrinkled her nose at the taste. It wasn't quite right, not like the one she used to blend at home, with real fruit and horrifically expensive organic yogurt. Did knowing it wasn't real emphasize the taste difference? *If there is one.*

Alik came out a couple of minutes later. He wore a white t-shirt and shorts. It didn't look right. Kandara had become so used to seeing him in a suit that having him walking around in his underwear unsettled her world almost as much as knowing they were inside an alien arkship, which itself was inside a wormhole.

"Gonna get a shower," he announced and headed up the ladder to the mid-deck.

Kandara watched Callum struggle to keep his face composed. "Just don't." She sighed wearily.

"I'm not judging. But you kids make sure you use protection, okay?"

"Oh, fuck off!"

He started laughing. Despite herself, Kandara found she

was grinning happily. "It's a long flight," she said defensively.

"And getting longer."

"Oh, Mary, forgive me." She walked over to the food printer and ordered up a bacon sandwich with mashed avocado and a tiny dash of spiced tomato sauce, plus a warm pain au chocolat. Add black coffee and an orange juice, and she was truly the child of international resort cuisine. *One way of keeping the lost Earth alive.*

Yuri came out of his cabin as she was sitting down again. He was wearing an FC Dynamo midfield shirt and black shorts. Somehow the choice suited him. "Morning," he said. "I thought I'd get back into the tank today."

"Impatient for action?" she asked.

"Bored."

"The creeperdrone fake is making progress," Callum said. "We'll soon have something to see."

During the first week of the *Avenging Heretic* sitting in the hangar, all they did was observe, and absorb as many of the arkship onemind's thoughts as they could. Once they established that the onemind had essentially zero interest in individual ships, Jessika set about infiltrating the local neural strata and gently deflecting its scrutiny. The perception cells on the thick trunk-like pipes that webbed the hangar surfaces still saw everything; it was just that the interpretation routines that received those images didn't care.

With a zone of out in the open concealment established, they watched the biological creatures that tended to the *Salvation of Life*'s basic maintenance tasks. She'd seen recordings of the arkship's three caverns—not dissimilar to a human habitat's interior. The variance came from the way the environment was sustained. Humans used machines in their space habitats; the Olyix chose a menagerie of creatures instructed by the onemind.

Very few Olyix quint ventured into the hangar. Some had appeared in the first days, performing inspections on the transports that showed the worst damage. Other than that, there had been very little activity. Things like giant slugs slid slowly across the gently curving floor and up the black bark of the pipes in a routine that seemed completely unaffected by the arrival of the transport ships. Smaller spidery organisms skipped about on five legs, tending to specialist cell patches. It was one of those that Jessika constructed in the *Avenging Heretic*'s biologic initiator, like the creeperdrones black-ops teams used to use to spy on their targets. They had detailed files on all the creature types humans had encountered during their visits to the arkship before the invasion—size, weight, coloring, speed and maneuverability, even a guess at the autonomous intelligence level.

The fake spider creature had been released into the hangar three days ago. Jessika had directed it, slowly taking it around the base of the walls, avoiding the genuine Olyix service creatures. As it went, it spooled out a single long-molecule fiber that conducted data. She stopped the creature every few hundred meters and emplaced a sensor clump the size of a pinhead, opening up their view of the hangar.

Kandara approved of that. Nothing could sneak up on them now. Not that there was ever going to be much they could do if the Olyix did spot them.

Now the remote had reached the big entrance to the hangar. An invisible force membrane covered it, holding the air in—similar to Earth's shields, although this one had permitted the transport ships to pass through. Jessika walked the creeperdrone fake forward. The force opposing the remote was similar to walking directly into a hurricane. It edged forward, exerting itself at the top end of its power. When it broke through, it was in vacuum. The downward curving passage beyond was devoid of the pipe trunks that covered the hangar; naked rock walls continued all the way to the hole that broached the arkship's surface. The creeperdrone stood on the edge and looked out.

"Has it glitched?" Alik asked.

They were back in their tanks, which put them back on the simulation bridge. It had changed since their initial flights back in the Delta Pavonis system. Now there were split levels and curving rails. Walls had unoccupied crew stations, with chairs; consoles had rows of switches and keyboards between small screens filled with slim, colorful graphics. Instead of the original display that had hung between their consoles, they now had a panoramic wall screen ahead of them. Kandara suspected either Yuri or Callum was oozing memories of old sci-fi shows into the simulation template. But she did have to admit, the bridge *felt* a lot more like a real spaceship now.

Everyone stared at the main screen. It showed nothing. When she reviewed the direct feed from the remote to confirm its location, the lip of rock slipped into her vision. It was in the right place. "What's happening?" she asked. "Why can't we see the wormhole?"

"Technically, you can," Callum said. "It's the part of the image that doesn't exist. At a guess, I'd say the interior of the wormhole is a continuum that doesn't permit photon propagation."

Kandara had forgotten Callum had a physics degree. Sure, it was a century out of date, but still it was the only one on board. "You mean it's dark?"

"No. There is no visuality. It's a structure composed entirely of exotic matter, so it probably doesn't even qualify as an open space. It's not surprising the creeperdrone's sensors see nothing. I'm guessing our poor old animal brains interpret that as black."

"What about Cherenkov radiation?"

"Not in here. Though now you bring it up, there should be somewhere the arkship's physical structure intersects the exotic matter. Maybe. I don't know."

"So what you're saying is we're not going to see the end of the tunnel approaching?" Yuri said.

"That's about it."

"The *Salvation of Life* will certainly be aware of it," Jessika said. "From what I can make out, there're only a couple of days' travel remaining until we're at the sensor base."

"We need to finalize our actions," Yuri said. "Do we try and release a Signal transmitter there?"

"It's not the enclave," Alik said quickly.

"Yeah, but we both know now the enclave is a lot farther away than anyone was thinking. The pulse those Signal transmitters are going to put out have a limited range."

"I thought detection was limited by the size of the radio telescope humans use to find it."

"You're right," Callum said. "But the farther away we are, the longer the Signal will take to reach this part of the galaxy. If the exodus habitats haven't picked it up after a couple of thousand years, then they'll probably assume we didn't make it. Nobody will look for it. And if they do, catching the pulses becomes progressively more difficult over distance."

"The Olyix aren't going to abandon this sensor station we're heading for just because we broadcast its location," Kandara said. "They have to use it to send their next wave of ships to Sol and the settled worlds. That's going to take them a century or more, depending on how far away we are. If anything, they'll reinforce it with ships from the enclave star system, wherever that is."

"It might not take a century," Jessika said. "I've been examining what I can in the *Salvation of Life*'s onemind. The Olyix were surprised when they arrived at Earth; they didn't expect humans to have accomplished interstellar travel so quickly. We know they were trying to establish their own portals between Sol and the settled worlds, but it looks like they had a backup in case that didn't work."

"What fucking backup?" Yuri demanded.

"There are nine ships on their way from the sensor station to the settled worlds. As far as I can make out, they left decades ago."

"Sweet fucking Mary," Kandara snarled. "How long until they get there?"

"I don't know. Maybe a few decades, still. But you can be sure one or more will be diverted to Earth now. It's the key to their crusade—capturing as many humans as they can to make pilgrimage to their God at the End of Time. There are billions of people still on Earth, and once the Resolution ships arrive, there's only going to be one outcome."

"So you're saying don't try and Signal Sol when we get to the observation base?" Alik asked.

"We can't," she said regretfully. "It will expose us. If that happens, the chances of us getting to the enclave are going to be nonexistent."

"Makes sense to me," Callum said.

"I'm for trying to reach the enclave," Kandara said. It would have been nice to fire off a Signal transmitter, sure in the knowledge that people would receive it, but ultimately it was an empty gesture. That wasn't why she was here. Besides, so much effort and sacrifice had gone into placing them on board the *Salvation of Life*; sending the Signal from here would be a betrayal.

"This ain't a half-measures mission," Alik said. "We aim for the enclave and burn these motherfuckers."

"Question," Callum said. "What about the Neána? Jessika?"

"What about them?"

"If they detect our Signal coming from the sensor station, would they be able to use it?"

"To do what?" she asked.

"To fight. To fly here and force their way down the wormhole to the enclave. Surely that's your ultimate goal?"

"I'm not Neána. I'm human, or try to be. I don't know what the Neána endgame is."

"Sorry. I thought you might be able to guess."

"As much and as little as you."

Kandara squashed a smile. She could see Callum's cheeks were flushed. *We're really melding with the simulation—or it with us.*

"The Neána aren't going to help us," Alik said. "They've done all they were ever going to do by sending you to warn us."

"How do you figure that?" Jessika asked.

"Because if they'd wanted to attack Olyix installations with warship versions of the insertion ship that brought you, they would have sent them to Sol and ambushed the *Salvation of Life*."

"Good point," Yuri said.

"Face it," Alik said. "We've had entire teams of strategists, psychologists, and scientists trying to work out the Neána ever since you put that axe through Feriton's skull. Hell, there was one think tank that even drafted some science fiction writers in to give a fresh perspective. And all they came up with was jack shit."

"All right then," Yuri said. "When we arrive at this sensor

station, we stay quiet and hope the *Salvation of Life* flies straight into the wormhole that goes back to the enclave."

The *Salvation of Life* emerged from the wormhole terminus into real space five weeks and one day after leaving the Sol star system. Finally, Alik had something to see. He hadn't told the others, not even Kandara, but the anti-existence of the wormhole had started to get to him. Not claustrophobia exactly, but a sense of being nowhere, the ultimate lost child. After all he'd seen in his time with the FBI, after all he'd been through—the horrors and deaths—*this* was what got to him? Literally a nothing? Life really could be a complete bastard sometimes.

But now there was something real to see outside again. Over the last two days Jessika had walked the remote creature along the precarious edge of the hangar entrance, the top of a cliff with a fall to infinity, emplacing minute sensor clumps before withdrawing it back into the *Avenging Heretic*. The clumps revealed an ordinary-looking starscape surrounding them, a heliocentric panorama anchored by a red dwarf star. Alik was so deeply immersed in the visualization he was sure he could feel its radiance on his cheeks. He was no expert on constellations, but it didn't look too alien.

"Star correlation places us approximately a hundred and seven light-years from Sol."

"Soćko got lucky," Callum said. "He must have just escaped the wormhole in time. Any longer and the ship would have fallen out of the wormhole here."

The visualization showed them they were leaving a vast open hoop behind. Its silver-white surface had a violet aurora that was fading rapidly. Alik guessed that was the wormhole terminus.

"*Salvation* is accelerating," Jessika said. "Here we go."

"Accelerating where?" Callum asked.

"Another wormhole terminus," Jessika said. "It's dominating the onemind's thoughts. Its only goal now is to return to the enclave star system."

"What about us?" Kandara asked. "Is it going to take the transport ships with it?"

"I think so. It certainly isn't ordering any ships to disembark here."

The visualization was expanding as the *Salvation of Life* rotated slowly, allowing the sensor clumps to gather a full three-hundred-sixty-degree image. The terminus hoop was in an orbit seventy million kilometers out from the surface of the red dwarf. The sensors were showing several other objects sharing the orbit, all of them massive.

Given the minute size of the sensor clusters and the extreme distances, resolution was sub-optimal. But it still revealed that the majority of the closest objects were pentagonal dodecahedrons, with each flat surface measuring two thousand kilometers across.

"They have to be radio telescopes," Callum said. "This is an Olyix sensor station, after all, so I can't see what else they could be. Bloody hell, the scale of them! No wonder they picked up Earth's radio broadcasts."

"This is where we're heading," Jessika said.

The visualization refocused. Looking along their vector wasn't a good angle, with the arkship's rocky surface becoming a Mars-red crescent filling three quarters of the image. Three million kilometers ahead of them was a nest of seven broad hoops, with the outermost an easy two hundred kilometers in diameter. Inside it, the other hoops were progressively smaller, with the innermost a mere thirty kilometers wide. They were all aligned at an angle to one another, with the central one finishing at ninety degrees to the first. The surface of each seemed to be a shiny purple chrome, without any visible markings. Thermally, they were a steady twenty-seven degrees Celsius.

"What do you think?" Yuri asked. "An Olyix habitat?"

"Most likely," Jessika said. "There are several wormhole terminus hoops close to it. We're heading for the nearest."

"No space traffic visible," Kandara said. "This place is like a ghost star."

"I haven't seen any planets, either," Jessika said. "In fact, the ecliptic plane is remarkably clear of any solid matter; no asteroids, comets . . . They cleared it all out."

"Hellfire," Callum exclaimed. "I was wondering how they

powered their wormholes, given the energy they require to stay open is huge. Take a look at that star's equator."

Alik waited while the visualization refocused again, following everyone's whim. He'd said nothing about all the wonders of this alien star, because frankly it was way outside his comfort zone. The nesting ring thing was so much bigger than the habitats humans built—if that was what it actually was—and the radio telescopes were the size of fucking moons. He'd always known this flight was a long shot, but they were now getting seriously out of their depth—and still sinking. Reluctantly he looked at the gleaming red disk that was the small star. The equator was clearly visible, marked by a slim dark band. Magnification expanded until it became blurred.

"Is that solid?" Yuri asked incredulously.

"Seems to be," Callum said. "It's rotating faster than the star, but it's on the top of the chromosphere."

"The star's got a radius approximately a third of Sol," Jessika said. "Which gives a circumference of . . . Shit! One point three million kilometers."

"They built a ring of solid matter one point three million klicks?" Yuri said. "What the hell from?"

"Out of something tough enough to sit in a star," Callum added wickedly. "And function as a generator. My God, if that's what they've built to power wormholes, what do they need to power something that slows down time inside the enclave? How big? What does it do, eat stars whole?"

Kandara chuckled. "Ever get the feeling you've bitten off more than you can chew?"

"Not Goddamn funny!" Alik told her.

"Relax. We're not here to go *mano a mano* with these fuckers. We're a bacterium on an elephant. Utterly insignificant. But if a bacterium gets into its bloodstream . . ."

Alik closed his eyes and exhaled as he slumped back into the seat. He knew the gesture wasn't real, yet it still helped calm him. "I think reality is finally biting me on the ass."

"Lucky you," Callum said. "Me? I'm still in complete denial about all of this. Yuri?"

"I wish cloning was not illegal. I would grow one and send him instead. Maybe I should have done that anyway."

"Good call."

"You guys are wusses," Kandara said. "I wouldn't miss this for anything."

"Yeah, but you're—" Alik closed his mouth.

"Pure psycho? Face it, there's only me and Jessika functioning normally here. And she's—" She made a mock gasp of horror and put her hand over her mouth.

"Wasn't born human," Jessika goaded.

"We must be one of the biggest concentrations of fuck-ups in history."

"Hope never dies," Callum said solemnly. "But it sure as hell gets overlooked a lot."

"Stuff that guru shit," Alik sneered. "I never said I was giving up hope. I'm a practical guy. We just carry on and get the job done."

"Very profound," Kandara said.

"I've got the *Salvation of Life*'s course vector," Jessika said. "We're on track to fly into the wormhole terminus next to the habitation rings—the biggest one there is. Twenty klicks across. You could fit two arkships in that side by side easy."

"How long?" Yuri asked.

"Eighteen hours."

They spent the rest of the time on the tiresome bridge. Alik started to think about livening it up a little, maybe make it a bit more luxurious like some of the penthouses he'd visited. And how come there was only this? You were either on the bridge or oblivious in the tank. They hadn't even simulated the utilitarian compartments on the real *Avenging Heretic*.

Several times during the hours that crawled by, Deliverance ships soared around the *Salvation of Life* in long curves like eagles guarding their nest.

"Why?" Yuri asked after the eighth one performed a graceful spin as it looped around the arkship. "This is their star system. There can't be any threat here. What are they looking for?"

Jessika frowned. "I think it's some kind of ritual. They're celebrating a successful mission. Or a returning mission;

I'm not quite sure which. There's emotional content in the onemind's thoughts that I've not experienced before."

Callum grinned. "Dance like nobody's watching."

"A happy Olyix!" Alik murmured. "The universe is not only stranger than we imagine, but stranger than we can imagine."

"Mary save me!" Kandara declared. "I'm locked up in a ship full of philosophers."

"The Olyix can't always have been miserable fascist bastards," Yuri said. "Something changed them."

"The God at the End of Time happened," Kandara said. "Simple."

"And none of them ever questioned it?" Callum said. "I find that hard to believe."

"Some of them did," Kandara said. "Once. That's why they're not around anymore."

"I wonder," Yuri said. "If Olyix mainstream culture is fascistic, allowing no dissenters, there must be a resistance, a group of non-believers."

"Unlikely now," Jessika said. "Individual Olyix don't die; they just incorporate a new body into their quint whenever an old one starts to fail. They're not born anymore. They've become a truly artificial species. Any of their number who don't conform were probably eliminated millennia ago like Kandara said. The Olyix transformed themselves into a monoculture. There is no opportunity for change now."

Kandara sat up abruptly. In the relative calm of the bridge it was almost startling, a real show of emotion. "Unless . . ." She stared intently at Jessika.

"Yeah?" Alik pressed, interested by her reaction.

"The unbelievers saw what was happening and made a run for it before the Olyix version of the Night of the Long Knives. Now they're hiding among the stars, doing what they can to warn other species without getting caught themselves."

For once Jessika's composure deserted her. "I . . . don't have any information on that."

"Neána biotechnology is remarkably similar to Olyix biotechnology," Callum said. "And how did the Neána know about the enclave and its properties? They either visited before they dispersed into their abodes, or just maybe they were there when it was under construction."

Everyone looked at Jessika.

"I have no answer," she said meekly.

"I'm calling bullshit," Alik said and grinned at Kandara. "If the Neána had ever been to the enclave, they'd know where it is. Equally possible the neurovirus extracted some information from a quint or onemind about it being a slow-time zone."

"And the biology?" Callum asked.

"Terrestrial-style planets will probably follow the same evolutionary route at a biochemical level," Yuri said. "That's the theory the Connexion exobiologists always favored. Sure, the farther along the evolutionary timescale you got, the more fantastical and divergent the animal life would look to us. But if a planet has the same elements available, the basic cell chemistry would be similar. Occam's razor."

"Damn," Kandara said in frustration. "I really like my conspiracy theory."

"Keep at it," Jessika said, her humor bouncing back. "Time on this trip is going to need filling."

"I disagree," Callum said directly to Yuri. "Our composition is due to a million acts of chance and random mutation. That's why we have our distinct biochemistry. We have no idea what natural Neána biochemistry is like."

"Of course you disagree," Yuri grunted.

"That's the spirit, boys," Kandara said. "I can see our time in here is going to pass so quickly."

Alik groaned in dismay *I wonder if I can simulate some artificial humans in here for proper company?*

FINALSTRIKE MISSION

FLIGHT YEAR 15

At first Yirella didn't even have the strength to moan in dismay. Waking from suspension was always a struggle, but at least it meant she was alive. Every time before she opened her eyes, she always had the same thought. *Who's there?* Would it be Del, one of her other friends, or an Olyix quint waiting for the chamber lid to open?

She felt the umbilical tubes withdraw from her abdomen and forced herself to open her eyes. A face was slightly out of focus on the other side of the transparent casing. Human. That was a good start. With nausea strumming away at her stomach, she squinted up. Protocol was always to have a good friend greet you when you were coming out of suspension. She recognized the face—Matías, one of the other squad leaders. Nice enough guy, but hardly in the "good friend" category.

The lid slid down, and she slowly sat up, the cushioning rising in tandem to support her.

"You okay?" Matías asked.

Yirella just remembered in time not to nod her head. She held up a finger and croaked: "Getting there."

Matías waited patiently until she was ready to climb out. She gritted her teeth and managed to raise a leg. He offered an arm as she finally swung both legs over the edge of the chamber. That's when she saw Rafa, one of Matías's squad members, standing a couple of meters away. For the first time in years, she felt self-conscious about being naked. Then she noticed the sidearms they both wore and did her best not to smile.

She stood on the decking, gripping the rim of the chamber to prevent herself falling. An embarrassed Matías handed her a robe.

"What's happening?" she asked. Data in her optik was telling her the *Morgan* was at half light speed already and still just under a light-year out from the neutron star.

"You're needed at the Captain's Council."

"Okay. I'll have a shower and get along there." It was malicious, but she couldn't resist.

Rafa coughed.

"It's urgent," a miserable Matías said. "We're to escort you straight there as soon as you're dressed."

"Really? Why?"

"Look, I'm sorry, Yirella. All I know is that they need to consult you. It's very urgent."

"Seems about right." She gestured at the oily fluid still beading her skin. "But first, the shower."

Rafa was about to say something, but Matías said: "Of course."

She took her time in the washroom and used her databud to order chicken soup from the food printer. As the water sluiced the oil off her skin, she used her interface to check on her cyborg. It was sitting in standby mode where she'd left it seven years ago, in one of the many empty compartments on a lower deck, not far from where the squads used to have their idiot bare-knuckle fights. According to the log, none of the crew had noticed it—not that they patrolled the *Morgan* looking for intruders. For a moment she was tempted to bring it up out of standby mode, just in case. But that was silly, because there was no physical threat. Having it accompany her to the council would be the equivalent of comfort food. And as soon as she stepped out of the shower, a remote rolled up carrying her chicken soup. So . . .

The cup the soup came in seemed inordinately heavy as she carried it with her on the interminable walk around to the captain's quarters. They had to stop five times for her to sit and rest. She obstinately refused Matías's offer to summon a remote medical chair for her.

Kenelm was sitting at the head of the table in hir reception room. The stern expression sie wore would have been intimidating at any other time. Today, Yirella found it hard not to smirk right back at hir. Alexandre was sitting halfway along the table, and hir gesture invited Yirella to sit. She accepted gratefully and drank some more of the soup. Every limb was shaking from the exertion of the walk. Directly opposite her, Tilliana gave her an anxious glance.

Cinrea and Wim occupied the seats on either side of Kenelm. Then there was Napar, captain of the *Collesia*; and Illathan, who commanded the *Kinzalor*. They directed troubled expressions her way.

"I apologize for bringing you here right out of suspension," Kenelm said, "but we've encountered an unexpected development."

Yirella turned her head to look at Matías and Rafa, who were standing behind her. "Is this to be an expanded council, captain? If so, shouldn't squad leader Matías be sitting with the rest of us?"

"Matías is here to ensure order," Kenelm said levelly.

"Order?"

"Yirella, we've detected something odd at the neutron star," Alexandre said in a weary voice. "Actually, disturbing is more like it. We're hoping you can help us understand what's going on."

"I'll do my best."

"I came out of suspension nine months ago to assist Wim's approach protocol team," Tilliana said. "Five fleet ships assembled remote sensor satellites to perform the observation."

"I remember the specifications," Yirella said. "The sensors were good, taken from the original *Actaeon* array design."

"Yeah. The sats decelerated at fifty gees, until they matched velocity with the neutron star. Then they stuck out their probes and sent the data back to us through portals."

"And?"

"The neutron star's rotation speed has changed."

Yirella took a moment to absorb that monumental fact. "Well, that's good. It should help call the attention of the Olyix."

"Good?" Wim said frostily. "That's your take? Good? We have absolutely no idea how to do that."

"We do," Yirella countered. "There are several theories on how to accomplish it." She drank some more soup.

"Yes, but we don't have the technology to actually do it."

"Ainsley probably has. He was carrying some amazing systems."

"Ainsley didn't know how they worked."

"No, but the team you led back at the habitats made astonishing progress on Ainsley's neutronic functions, didn't you? That was impressive. Put enough effort into a retro-engineering project, and you should ultimately be successful."

Wim shot Kenelm an agitated glance.

"You're suggesting that Ainsley analyzed his own composition?" sie asked.

"I don't know. What are you asking me?"

"We're asking you about this," Kenelm said.

The screen at the end of the table came on, showing a starfield. Right at the center was a small ring of faint red speckles.

"And that is?" Yirella asked, but she knew. She knew because it was beautiful and perfect. Everything she hoped it would be. Yet she still wanted —needed—confirmation.

"The neutron star civilization," Wim said tightly. "The infrared emission of close on a quarter of a million individual objects orbiting three hundred and eighty-four thousand four hundred kilometers from the star. Best our sensors can measure from here is that they vary from one kilometer to twenty-five in diameter. There are a small number that are even larger, though their infrared signature is lower."

"Wow!"

"Three hundred and eighty-four thousand four hundred kilometers is a very specific distance."

"The distance the moon orbited our lost Earth," Yirella said. "So Ainsley has a sense of humor, after all. Who knew?"

"You're saying Ainsley did this?" Wim challenged.

"I'm saying he enabled it." She sipped some more soup, keeping her gaze on Kenelm over the rim of the cup.

"How did that happen?" Kenelm asked. "The lure civilization you designed was supposed to consist of ten habitats and some neutronic weapon platforms. They were going to announce their existence to the Olyix by targeting the neutron star with chunks of mass to create an artificial pattern of super-high-energy X-ray emissions. Now we see this. How? How could this possibly happen?"

Yirella put the cup down. "It happened because I gave the humans full control of the seedship initiators."

"You did *what*?"

"What humans?" Wim asked. "The lure population was androids."

"No, that was the original idea. I changed it."

"On whose authority?" Alexandre asked.

"Mine. What you're seeing around the neutron star is a natural space-based human civilization—one that has developed without limits or restrictions so that it can advance a long way beyond us."

Kenelm closed hir eyes, hir body frozen. "Oh, sweet Saints; you didn't."

"Oh, but I did—with Ainsley's help. I did what I know we have to do to *end this*. I gave humans the most sophisticated technology we had, and set them free to build whatever they wanted."

"Those are real humans?" sie demanded. "Do you even understand the danger you've exposed them to?"

"Don't be so melodramatic. They're not in any danger, precisely because I took away your restrictions. All those over-cautious, play-by-the-rules Utopial orthodoxy limits your kind have been imposing on us for millennia. The limits that have stunted us, and reduced us to helpless victims; limits that have condemned billions to imprisonment by the Olyix. The blind subservience that means I wouldn't be far wrong to call you a traitor to our species."

"Enough!" Kenelm shouted, hir fist slamming down on the table. "Matías, she is to be placed under cabin arrest until we can convene a full council."

"No," Yirella shouted, equally loud. "You don't have that authority. Your captaincy is a lie."

"Yi," Tilliana said desperately. "What are you doing?"

"I have a question for our captain," Yirella said. "One question, that's all. You're not afraid of that, captain, are you?"

"Get her out of here," Kenelm ordered Matías.

Yirella smiled viciously. "How old are you?"

"What?"

Her neural interface ordered the screen to display a single image, one she'd copied from volume five of the Falkon terraforming books. Five tall omnia smiling at the camera as they stood on a large expanse of windswept marshland, with a gray sea in the background. Equipment cases were open around their feet.

"Oh, shit," Kenelm whispered.

"What is this?" a confused Alexandre asked.

"That," Yirella said, "is expedition team eighteen B-three of the Falkon Terraforming Office biosphere establishment division. They're taking samples in a coastal marsh to measure the propagule density in the sediment. Important work, given Falkon was only just ending phase three of its terraforming process at the time, *two thousand and twenty-eight years ago*."

Tilliana looked at the image, turned to look at Kenelm, turned back to the screen. "Fuck the Saints! It's you."

LONDON

"I saw the sky yesterday afternoon," Horatio said wistfully. "We had a break in the clouds for about five minutes. I'd forgotten how strange that blue is—so light but with a depth to it, as if it's not really there. It was quite a revelation looking at it, even if it was only for a short time."

Gwendoline's image on the screen gave him a mournful smile. "I'm glad you enjoyed it."

"They say that's the third time the clouds have parted this year. I missed the first two. They were only for a few seconds." He sat back on his flat's settee, enjoying the memory. Outside, the sky above the shield was darkening to twilight. But inside, the ceiling lights shone brightly. He was still mildly surprised every time he switched them on and they actually worked. In the twenty-five years since Blitz2 had ended, London had only been without a public supply of power for four years while the settled worlds gradually improved their support to Earth. He suspected he shared the same impressed perplexity Londoners of the 1920s experienced when they changed from gas lighting to electric bulbs. *Will such a marvel last?* Those early years had been a profound lesson in how so many privileges had been taken for granted.

With the power back on, printers worked again (after a

great deal of maintenance); and eventually they even got community recycling systems organized. The only real production issue was food. Organic base fluids were rationed for another five years until a host of new offworld factories were completed. Now you could print most dishes again, though some flavorings were still hard to come by. In the last ten years, London had undergone a re-greening, with the long dead gardens being revived and vegetables planted. Parks that had irrigation systems had even seen grass shoots rising again—all because water was now available in quantity. The Thames was flushed clean every fortnight when they opened a section of the shield and allowed the ominously warm river water to flow through the city once more. He'd even seen some banana trees flourishing along the banks recently.

Heat under the curving shield remained tropical. Even without the Deliverance ships firing their energy beams at every city shield, pumping terawatts of raw energy into the atmosphere every day, global temperatures hadn't dropped by more than a couple of degrees since the *Salvation of Life* had been forced to retreat. There was nothing anyone could do about that except turn up the air-con, pumping their home's thermal load out into the city's humid atmosphere. When the environmental technicians expanded a high-altitude aperture in the shield to let in some fresh air, it was as if a portal was opening into a pre-invasion desert.

"Small steps," Gwendoline said.

She seemed oddly anxious—a strange mood for her. He didn't quite understand it.

The last surprise she'd given him was three years ago, when she moved from Nashua to Pasobla in the Delta Pavonis system. But that at least was understandable; Loi had just announced that Eldlund was pregnant, and Gwendoline wasn't going to miss out on being a part of her grandchild's life. Besides, as she'd pointed out, "I can do the same job in Pasobla as I can here; their industrial systems have the same screwups as ours. I've already spoken to the Utopial exodus project committee, and they'll accept me as a level two citizen."

"Level two, huh?" he'd teased. "That low?"

"Shouldn't take me more than a month to work my way up to level one. And they'll accept you, too."

That had soured the mood. "I'll think about it," he'd said, as he always did. Keep kicking the can down the road long enough . . .

"I've already got authorization to bring the portal with me."

"Dear God, how did you work that?"

Her lips had twitched in a taunting grin. "Level two, remember. It's part of my golden handshake package."

"There are no corporate executives anymore."

"Yeah, keep telling yourself that."

He'd never been so tempted to join her and Loi and Eldlund. That night, he'd even packed a suitcase. A pathetically small one. But then he got a call from one of the community centers. *Sorry to call late, but we've got some scheduling problems that need sorting. You always handle this kind of thing so well, Horatio.* People depended on him.

The suitcase remained packed. It sat right there in the cupboard next to the case with the portal. Ready. Because one day he would join his family in their safe haven. One day soon . . .

"Not so much steps as wading," he now countered. "The sea level has risen another ten centimeters since November. It came over the Thurrock rampart last week. Even if the air ever does stabilize enough for us to turn the shield off, half the city would vanish underwater."

"Yes," Gwendoline said. "I saw the projections. They're worried about New York—enough that they've increased the city's evacuation rate to New Washington."

"I'm sure they're loving that in the Billionaire Belt." Again, he was picking up on how distracted she was. *I don't get this. What isn't she saying?*

Her smile chided him gently. "The last of the Belt's original habitants portalled out seven years ago."

"How many have you dispatched now?"

"Classified. But all the settled systems are building exodus habitats at a phenomenal rate."

"Really?"

"Relatively, yes. Consider the size of a habitat, and the ancillary systems we have to send with them. And they have got to work, Horatio. At heart, they're starships—beyond help if anything goes wrong."

"I don't doubt you."

Gwendoline leaned in closer to the camera, giving him a better view of her face. It was remarkably unchanged, but then she'd never looked her age even back when the invasion happened. Zangari money had seen to that. And her anti-aging regimen had continued without a break when she went to live on Nashua, which was set up to allow Zangaris to carry on their sumptuous lifestyle with very little change. Then after that, Pasobla had excellent medical facilities, especially for *level two* citizens. Just looking at those fine mid-twenties features made him so aware of how many decades he was showing now. Thinning, graying hair, the gradually expanding waistline, the old-man grunt every time he heaved himself up from a chair. His memory not as sharp as it used to be, and now he was having his altme monitor his diet carefully, keeping the carb intake down to avoid full-blown type one diabetes and the insulin gland that would entail—assuming he could even get on the implant list. If it wasn't for his bicycle trips keeping him relatively fit, he knew he would have piled on weight and related problems. Visits to the gym had become more and more of an effort, and he didn't know when he'd last been for a jog along London's streets; he kept telling himself it was too difficult now everyone was on boardez and bikes and resurrected taxez and modified trollez. It was like the roads of the early twenty-first century out there, for heaven's sake. No portals, of course; there never would be again. There wasn't that much power to spare from the settled worlds. The hubs, loops, and radials of Connexion's London transport network were a legend of time past that they told the children about.

"Utopials are good people," Gwendoline said. "I like it here. You will, too."

"Gwen—"

"Horatio," she said firmly, "it really is time for you to leave London now."

"I can't just abandon people. They depend on me."

"*I* depend on you."

"No. We have the memory of us. A beautiful memory—and a memory I'm so profoundly grateful I possess."

"Lacasta needs you."

It was a blow so low, Horatio couldn't speak for a moment. "Don't."

"Sie's nearly three now, and sie wants to meet hir grandfather, not just see him on a screen. Sie needs your arms around hir, for you to hug hir and love hir. Don't deny hir that."

"Why are you doing this?" he asked, aghast. "I can't leave. It wouldn't be fair."

"You 'checking your birth benefit' isn't fair to us, your family. All it's going to do is get you cocooned."

"I'm not virtue-sacrificing. I can see what's happening."

"You can't, Horatio. Trust me, you don't know anything."

"Yeah? The Londoners who are leaving? They're chosen carefully."

"It's random. A lottery."

"A lottery by area. It's always evenly distributed, sure—always someone from the next street, someone either you know or a friend's friend knows and talks about. It's deliberate, tunneling down into the personal, to give the illusion that you're going to be leaving real soon now. To keep the hope alive."

"Without hope, Earth would have fallen into anarchy. You can't afford that, not living under shields."

"I know. But you can't save us all."

"I can save *you*."

"And if everyone like me leaves?"

"Sorry, Horatio, my darling, but you're not that unique."

He hunched forward, hating that their talks had come to this. At the start of Blitz2 he'd felt so empowered, staying and helping those who needed it—which was just about everyone. He had a purpose that would never exist if he'd followed Gwendoline to Nashua. But that had faded as first years, then eventually decades, flowed past. People were coping now; the city was working again. It was a very different type of economics from what had come before—the ultimate closed-cycle manufacturing. If a printer needed raw material, it had to come from disassembling something—especially if you needed specialist compounds. That took organization and cooperation at a local level, which was the area Horatio excelled in. It had kept him busy for years.

"I know," he said miserably.

"Then here's something you don't know." She glanced around as if there were people in her home and drew a determined breath. "The G8 monitors might cut the link on me, but . . . Trappist One has gone."

"Gone? You mean the Chinese evacuated everyone, from every planet? That's incredible."

"No, Horatio. Gone, as in fallen. The portal links failed last night, just after they detected wormholes opening. Resolution ships came through in force. The Olyix are back. It won't be long now. Every settled world will go. Earth! Earth will fall. Probably in a few hours."

"Oh, shit."

"So tell me now what you can accomplish by staying. You have family here. Does that mean nothing to you?"

"It means everything!"

"Good. Then open the portal. I know it's still working; the G8 Turing runs checks on it every hour. Come through now. Right now."

"Every hour?" he asked dumbly. *Every hour for twenty-five years? Longer even than we were married.*

"Yes, Horatio," she said in a voice that finally gave her age away. "I've never given up hope."

"God, I don't know what to say."

"Yes, you do."

"All right," he said. And after two and a half decades it was so surprisingly easy. There wasn't even any guilt.

"You'll come?"

"Yeah. I've just got a couple of people I have to say goodbye to."

Gwendoline's lips lifted slyly. "You can bring her, if you

want. Let's face it, I haven't been living in a nunnery for twenty-five years."

"Not that kind of goodbye," he said, just a little too quickly. "Give me a couple of hours."

"I'm going to call Loi. He'll be here to welcome you."

"And Lacasta?"

"Try and stop hir."

FINALSTRIKE MISSION

FLIGHT YEAR 15

It was Ellici who was standing over Dellian's suspension chamber when his eyes opened. Her smile was indecently cheeky as her gaze lingered on fluid-beaded skin. He ignored it, and the arm she proffered, as he slowly clambered out. The spin gravity didn't do his sensitive stomach any favors when he tried to stand. *Spin gravity?*

Icons and data tables expanded in his optik. "We're not under deceleration?" he asked in confusion. The last time he'd been awake was three years ago — the final duty tour before they were due to reach the neutron star. The data showed him they were point-nine of a light-year out, which theoretically meant the fleet should have completed their survey of the neutron star.

Ellici offered him her arm again. "Wow, she really didn't tell you, did she?"

"Huh?" Instinctively, he looked over at Yirella's chamber. It was empty.

"They used to call it plausible deniability back on old Earth," Ellici said.

He didn't like repeating *what* the whole time; it made him sound totally dumb. But— "What?"

"Yirella has caused quite a stir. Surprise! There's going to be a big council about it tomorrow. Everyone wanted you to be part of it. Alexandre authorized getting you out of suspension."

"Oh, Saints, is she in trouble?"

"Depends on your point of view."

"What's she done?"

"How long have you got?"

He made it to their quarters to find Yirella holding court with about twenty people, eight of them squad leaders. The remainder were omnia, wearing ship uniforms from across the fleet. Everyone looked grim.

She got to her feet and hugged him for a long time. It was only when he started swaying, about to fall, that she let go. He sat down fast on a couch, and everyone else filed out.

"It's all true," she said bleakly. "Every paranoid theory I ever had, and then some. It's not just us backward binaries that are puppets; the whole omnia exodus was manipulated. I never thought this—being right, *winning*—would make me feel like crap."

"Saints. What did you find out? Wait: I just realized. *Alexandre* authorized me coming out of hibernation?"

"Yeah. Sie's acting captain at the moment, and has been for two days. A lot of people—crew and squads—are seriously pissed with Kenelm right now."

"So sie has been steering us politically?"

"Yes, it looks like it."

"But you don't know for sure?"

"Sie hasn't been terribly forthcoming. Yet." She handed him a tall mug of beef broth and a plate of warm, thick-cut bread. "Eat that and listen, you have to be ready for tomorrow."

The council was held in the *Morgan*'s sports arena, which was packed with seats. Dellian suspected that having people attend in person added to the feeling of involvement and therefore legitimacy. It wasn't nearly big enough for everyone on the fleet, so ninety percent of the participants had a virtual presence, with texture walls transforming the open space into an old-style amphitheater with grass banks. Everyone on the fleet who wasn't currently in a suspension chamber was accessing the gathering.

When they walked in, Dellian hardly noticed the churn of people hunting for vacant chairs. All he could focus on was Kenelm sitting at one side of the dais that had been set up at the far end of the arena. "So how old is sie?" he asked Yirella.

"I'm not sure. Maybe three thousand years?"

"Saints alive!"

They eased past people and stepped up onto the dais. Yirella was given a seat between Napar and Illathan. The two captains greeted her amicably. The remaining fleet captains made up the front row of the virtual attendees, some obviously fresh out of hibernation.

Dellian went and sat close to Cinrea, who had chosen the other side of the dais from Kenelm. It was strange seeing hir in a uniform that no longer had the captain's insignia. As he settled in, Dellian noticed just how much animosity was being directed Kenelm's way by the audience in the arena. *At least no one is upset about what Yirella did.* It still hurt that she'd not confided in him about her plan for the neutron star. He just couldn't let go of the notion that it was because of the neurovirus that she no longer entirely trusted him.

Alexandre rose from hir chair in the middle of the dais and motioned for silence. "We've a lot to get through, and plenty to decide. I'd ask you not to make fast decisions. We can afford to take our time; it will be another year before we can match velocity with the neutron star. So . . . Kenelm, I think it's appropriate for you to start. Would you like to tell us where you came from originally?"

Kenelm inclined hir head. "Thank you for the opportunity—"

"Traitor," someone in the audience yelled.

Dellian thought it sounded a lot like Ovan's voice.

"No," Alexandre said, raising hir hand in warning. "I will not permit that kind of abuse. We have moved on past such intolerance. This council will listen respectfully to Kenelm and Yirella before deciding what our options are."

"I apologize for the impression my existence must be

generating," Kenelm said. "But I assure you the purpose my colleagues and I uphold is purely to advance the human interest and help us survive the Olyix. I have never abdicated that responsibility. It is all I exist for."

"Can you tell us where you came from, please?" Alexandre asked.

"I was born on Kanima, two thousand six hundred years ago. I left on the generation starship *Byessel*, which founded Falkon. That was where our group was formed at the behest of Soćko and Emilja. They were already concerned by the drift away from original Utopial ideals and the ongoing lack of success of any Strike mission. We were all level one citizens tasked with keeping the whole exodus project on track. I am proud of the part I have played in that."

"You manipulated us?"

"We guided—admittedly with a disproportionate degree of influence due to our status. Because of that, our society has remained Utopial, which I believe to be a positive achievement. The Utopial ideal is the height of human culture, demonstrating compassion and inclusion for every individual."

"How many of you are in this group?"

"I believe there were about a thousand of us on Falkon," Kenelm said. "After that, we divided at each generation world. Some would go on Strike missions; the rest would continue our undertaking through generation ships. By the time we reached Juloss, there were less than fifty of us. We did, of course, retain our level one citizenship, which allowed us considerable influence."

"And on this mission?" Cinrea asked.

"Loneve and I were the last."

"So we are free of manipulation?" Yirella said. "This council can make an independent choice?"

"Of course. That has always been the way. If someone had put up a compelling suggestion to alter the Utopial exodus policies, then a vote in council would have been respected. Out of everyone agitating for change, I always suspected you could be the most effective, Yirella. I do admit, however, I never envisaged just how much you were prepared to risk to achieve your ambitions."

"Thank you. I think."

"Before any decision is made by this council, I would like to emphasize how concerned Emilja, Soćko, and even Ainsley had become by the lack of any Signal. That is why all of us in the group agreed that, after the Factory, we would press our respective worlds to consider ending expansion by generation ship and instead follow the Neána option of establishing a secluded interstellar society—built on a Utopial foundation, of course."

"So you believe we should do nothing about the Olyix but hide from them?" Alexandre asked.

"No. It is more than that. Humans can *live* between stars; we can thrive there in a way we never do on a generation world. And, thanks to the Vayan ambush, we now understand just how powerful the Olyix are, how widespread. They are overwhelming, and they are hunting us."

"I thought that was the point of our exodus, to give humans time and resources until we are strong enough to challenge the Olyix."

Kenelm shrugged. "The Strike concept was put together in a time of extreme crisis, when humans didn't properly understand what we were facing. I don't think even the Neána did; certainly Soćko was troubled by our failures. Ainsley and Emilja managed to get what passed for the human polity of those days to support the idea of postponed vengeance and rescue, then throw in a triumphant return to Earth as the grande finale. But with no Signal ever detected, Emilja came to the realization that using lures to send our finest directly into an unknown enemy stronghold was a supreme folly. However, by then, the concept had built a colossal psychological and political momentum, which kept growing with every millennium. One person—even someone as powerful as her—could not stop it with a single proposal. Politics at that time were volatile—especially after contact with the Katos, Angelis, and Neána. So instead it was decided we should adopt a double aspect approach. The warships built by the Factory, like Ainsley, were our last attempt to secure an advantage against the Olyix. They were intended to fight them here in this section of the galaxy and establish a safe zone for humans. It is far easier to destroy a wormhole terminus carried into our territory by an Olyix ship than to challenge the enclave itself."

"The Saints sacrificed themselves for us!" Dellian yelled. It was out before he really knew he'd said it. He flushed hot from all the looks directed at him—and a few smirks, too—but he didn't repent.

"Four humans and a Neána," Kenelm said smoothly. "Their loss is regrettable, but utterly insignificant compared to the number of humans lost to the Olyix. Billions from Earth alone—and probably quadruple that number by now as the Olyix caught up with the expansion wavefront."

"So you were going to abandon the Strike?"

"That was the second aspect. Our group members would point out to councils on planets and generation ships that the Strike concept was making no progress; we were no nearer to invading the enclave than we were when we abandoned Earth. There was no Saints' Signal detected; the lures didn't work; we had no idea where the enclave was. So the Neána option was to be presented as an idea whose time had finally come. The pressure we could maintain—for centuries, if necessary—would eventually result in a vote for its adoption. In cases like the *Morgan*, I could simply say that it had been included as an order if our lure was taking an unexpectedly long time to attract the Olyix."

"But we beat the Olyix at Vayan," Ovan said.

"Ainsley beat the Olyix at Vayan," Kenelm replied. "I'm sorry, but the Strike mission is no longer valid. Nor, with all respect to Yirella, is FinalStrike. The enclave is *forty thousand* light-years away. We now have a golden opportunity to establish ourselves safely between the stars. Let the Factory ships harass the Olyix forces and raid their sensor stations; a guerrilla-style campaign will deny them an effective presence here for millennia. And who knows what we may ultimately create if we end our migration, if we can consolidate everything we build?"

"That's what I've done," Yirella said forcefully.

"No," Kenelm said. "You gave humans the ability to expand without any appreciation of the consequences. That is the precise opposite of everything I stand for. Are they even Utopial?"

"Who knows?" she replied with mock nonchalance. "If it really is the pinnacle of human cultural evolution, I'm sure they chose it."

"I propose to this council that the fleet should now commit to following the Neána option," Kenelm said. "The neutron star civilization has revealed themselves to every Olyix sensor station in the galaxy! It is a recklessness that will have catastrophic consequences unless they understand that they have to evacuate immediately. I would suggest we dispatch a single ship of volunteers from this fleet to the neutron star to warn them and *fully* explain the circumstances."

Alexandre gave Yirella an almost comical look of expectation. "I cannot agree with the methods this clandestine group of level one citizens has used, but Kenelm does make a valid point about how dangerous it would be to try and invade the enclave."

"Agreed," Yirella said sweetly.

Kenelm gave her a curious look.

"Yirella," Alexandre said, "you have the floor."

Dellian smiled encouragingly as she got to her feet, but she never saw it; she was facing the audience completely unfazed by them. He knew where that confidence came from: She was right. She was always right.

"We were going to lose," she said simply. "That much was obvious to me after our disastrous Vayan lure was ambushed. Ainsley only just managed to take out the upgraded Resolution ships. He said some of their weapons were a surprise even to him. Which, given he was made two thousand years ago, isn't actually that much of a revelation. So consider what we were going to do next: lure the Olyix yet again, with almost the same level of weapons technology plus Ainsley. That was crazy stupid. Kenelm is quite right; we have no idea what waits for us at the enclave. But their numbers must be phenomenal. It would also be logical to assume their strongest weapons are reserved to defend it. If we are going to fly into this extreme danger, we need to be the best we can be."

"That did not give you the right to unilaterally remove the seedship limits," Kenelm said. "And I know you know that, because you did not even try to gain council approval. You simply went ahead and acted alone. You have endangered the whole human population that you illegally seeded at the neutron star."

"Don't be ridiculous," Yirella said. "If you're in a position to make the decision, then it's your decision to make."

Kenelm was so surprised by her blatant contempt that sie swayed back in hir seat.

"And I wasn't acting alone," she continued. "Ainsley agreed with me that we have to try and end this abhorrent deadlock. Our Strike mission was almost at the breaking point before the Olyix arrived at Vayan. Our ancestors were asking too much of us, and we were asking too much of ourselves. Now it's different. The initial batch of humans that the seedships grew in biologic initiators were given basic thought routines, enabling them to function until they began to think for themselves and develop their own personality with all the awkward opinions and stubbornness that makes us what we are. They were supplied with all the information about the expansion and the Strike mission. They know the Olyix are poised to ambush us at every lure and that they're watching for generation starships at every star system with a planet we can terraform. The neutron star society is not at risk. They're waiting for us. Ainsley has told them we are coming. They could have left, but the star's rotational change is a huge indicator they haven't. It's been sixty years in real-time since the seedships reached it. That's long enough for them to determine their own destiny and build whatever they wanted."

"What did Ainsley tell them to do?" Alexandre asked.

"He gave them no advice," she said, then paused to smile shrewdly. "At least, that's what he told me he was going to do. We planned to give them the facts—all the knowledge humans have amassed; dispassionate accounts of our history and the societies we've evolved for ourselves; everything we know about the Olyix. That way, they can choose for themselves how they will live. For that is what real freedom is. And we still don't know what they decided, but it must be a high-functioning civilization. Certainly people who are in conflict and turmoil couldn't maintain the kind of sustained effort it must have taken to change the rotation of the neu-tron star. That is no small undertaking—and is one that I believe vindicates my decision. I realized the neutron star was the greatest potential for advancement we had, and probably ever would have, because a neutron star is the one place humans have never been before; it is different from anywhere humans have tried to settle. Those circumstances were not a combination I could ignore. If anything excep-tional was ever going to emerge, if we could change the way we think, it would be here. And if it worked, the inhabitants would decide where they would go—without our lingering ideology or the expectations of past generations weighing them down. It boils down to two options: They can wait for us to arrive and join us on the FinalStrike mission to the enclave, or they can withdraw into the gulf between stars to live as they wish."

"If you go to the enclave now and lose, the humans who are safe here will be hunted down," Kenelm said. "This is not your decision."

"Of course not. That is why I propose that the entire fleet should finish this voyage and go to the neutron star. Only then will we have all the facts. I have opened a route to the last opportunity we will have for at least a millennium. This is it, our peak. If the neutron star humans have gone away to is their own version of Sanctuary, our choice is simple: We must follow the Neána option and leave the Olyix for future generations—once again. If there are people at the neutron star, however, and they wish to confront the enclave with whatever weapons they have created, then our choice opens up again. Those who want to join with them can do so; those who no longer have an appetite for conflict—for the FinalStrike—can fly into the night and be safe."

Dellian heard Cinrea mutter, "Smart," under hir breath.

Alexandre conferred briefly with Napar and Illathan, then stood and faced the audience. "The captains are not in favor of dispatching a single ship to the neutron star," sie said. "After all we have gone through, this fleet should face our destination together. Therefore, we have a clear choice. Ei-ther this fleet diverts from our current vector and settles for a quiet life between the stars, or we travel on to the neutron star and see what awaits us there. Please consider these points, discuss it with your friends; Yirella and Kenelm will both be available if you wish to ask them more questions, as am I and the other captains. We will hold an advisory vote in five days. And may the Saints grant us wisdom."

LONDON

FEBRUARY 12, 2231

The bicycle was a compromise for Horatio. He had to physically visit the various community exchange centers he helped manage, and without the old portal hubs, distance was a problem. His flat was in Bermondsey, which put three of them close enough for him to walk to, but another was in Kennington, and he was currently helping out at two in Lambeth. He refused to use a cabez—not that he could afford one. So bike it was.

His flat was on the second floor in a block on the corner of Grange Road, giving him a view out over Bermondsey Spar Gardens. Over the last four years, a group of volunteers had progressively reseeded the park with grass. It didn't have an irrigation system when they began, so they'd installed tanks and slowly laid out a network of old drainpipes scavenged from nearby buildings. Dead and desiccated London plane trees and sycamores still stood silent sentry duty around the perimeter, but now the grass provided a welcome emerald blanket in the midst of the urban desert. It was a popular venue at all times of the day.

As soon as the call with Gwendoline ended, he got two cases out of the cupboard. The first contained all the essentials he'd packed three years ago—which on reflection were now either utterly worthless or embarrassingly stupid, and too many were both. The second contained the portal, a simple twenty-centimeter circle with a gray pseudosurface. His altme confirmed it was still operational—not that he doubted Gwendoline, but it was becoming critical now. He set it up vertically, ready to thread up as soon as he got back. *Probably the last portal left that you have to thread up; the settled worlds all use expansion rim models now.*

When he started pedaling along Bacon Grove, a jazz band was playing to an appreciative audience on the old basketball court; they'd settled in for the evening with picnics and wine. Even now, London had few working streetlights, and none at all down Bacon Grove, which was so narrow it didn't even have a clear path. He had to rely on the bike's dynamo-powered headlight and his own memory. Bacon Grove narrowed to a short bollarded path that quickly opened out onto Curtis Street. A couple of hundred meters later he was at the back of the old business park.

The big brick and carbon-panel warehouses had been an ideal place to site the community exchange center. Horatio looked up at the walls with their brown cladding of dead ivy, so old now the leaves were brittle and crumbling from entropy. He felt both elated and depressed. Exchanges like this had achieved so much, helped so many. Now he was going to abandon it all, fleeing to the safety of the settled worlds and exodus. *So what was the point?*

For a long moment he stood there immersed in self-pity. Then, angry at himself for such weakness, he pushed the small rear door open. As soon as he was inside, embraced by the noise and smell of the recycling systems, those treacherous doubts vanished. He knew it had all been worthwhile.

Once power had returned to the city's grid and domestic printers came on line again, people were left with the problem of finding supplies of processed compounds needed for fabrication—of anything. London's economy now was so very different from the one he'd grown up with. That had been the one outcome of Blitz2 that delighted him. The Universal culture's hyper-capitalist consumerism that worshiped *product* and *status* was gone, replaced by a kinder, more thoughtful system—and best of all, one completely community oriented.

Horatio had been one of the pioneers in setting up an exchange. His time with the Benjamin Agency meant he knew kids who recycled stuff a long way outside any corporate licensing or monitoring by the Dangerous Substance Inspectorate. They built their semi-legal products for untraceable cryptoken payments—mainly for London's major crime families or local flea stalls. It was an underground market that he knew he could bring out into the open and adapt to help people regain a reasonable standard of living.

Over the years he'd helped expand the concept, and now it was fundamental to London's post-Blitz2 way of life. Nothing was imported anymore, outside of essential organic fluids and pellets for food. So people would bring their old and defunct printed items to the exchange, receiving local recrypt-tokens in payment. The exchange would recycle the products in huge Clemson vats or metal-eating geobactor silos, which the community teams had built and maintained. Then the various raw sludges would be processed in more conventional refineries to produce valuable compounds that could be bought for recrypt-tokens and used in the printers again.

At first, the newly refurbished printers turned out simple household components that had failed due to long disuse—primarily water pumps and filters. Horatio was always amazed what a difference restoring drinking water had made to everyone's standard of living. Then, with fundamentals available again, new clothes started to appear, along with a plethora of solar cells coating walls and roofs.

Most districts had exchanges, each with their own tokens. That was one of the hardest parts of the enterprise to ratify, so these days Horatio had become a kind of local treasury official, overseeing the various recrypt-tokens and making sure they were regulated sensibly, setting costs and making sure those same innovative kids didn't forge or abuse the system. He knew he'd been reasonably successful by how much he was in demand.

"A proper corporate financier," Gwendoline would tease him during their calls. But she advised how the trade could be structured and secured against mishandling. Good advice, he admitted, as she explained how it was derived from her original designs for Corbyzan's economy—her project to build a society that mirrored Utopial post-scarcity society but one based on Universal policy. It remained a source of mild shame that he'd never quite realized just how knowledgeable his wife was in her field.

He wheeled the bike past the tall cylindrical vats that churned with genetically modified microbes, nesting amid a chaotic jumble of mismatched pipes. Everything was scavenged, everything was repurposed. But it worked. He waved at the duty crew who clambered amid the valves and regulators, armed with signal tracers and pliers and hammers, making sure the whole thing ran smoothly. Even at this hour, the exchange still had a few customers. The vats and silos ran twenty-four seven, and people kept odd hours under the shield.

Horatio had insisted on setting up a café in the warehouse's old management offices, maintaining its importance as a social center for the community as well as a vital resource. The staff was finally starting to close the counter down when he arrived. Maria O'Rourke was there, as he'd known she would be, putting the day's unsold cupcakes into a fridge. His altme didn't even have to splash the shift schedules; he knew them by heart. He and Maria had been together for three years now. She used to manage a pub in Walworth before Blitz2, then drifted through various volunteer jobs until she wound up helping in the exchange café. They'd argued a lot at first, because she had her own way of doing things and wasn't his type at all. But love under the shield was a strange thing, and oh so welcome in such an abnormal existence.

Maria caught sight of him and smiled, a smile that soon faded as she puzzled what he was doing here now, when she was due to walk back to his flat in another twenty minutes. Then she saw his drawn expression, the worry he knew he couldn't hide.

"What's happened?" she asked.

That was when he caught sight of Niastus and Jazmin sitting at one of the tables, where Jaz was nursing their four-month-old baby. Horatio wanted to close his eyes and weep. Along with Martin, it was Niastus who managed the recycling machinery in the exchange; he and Jaz had contributed so much to the community. Horatio looked up at the heavens in dismay.

"Horatio?" Maria asked, more insistent now.

Horatio made a decision. She'll kill me, but what else can I do . . .

"Come with me," he told the three of them. "No questions. I won't ask again." He leaned the bike against a table and turned around, walking for the door he'd just come in through. This way it was all down to them.

All he could see was Gwendoline's face, lips shrinking toward disapproval. "The universe is a neutral canvas," she'd told him once. "It has no intrinsic good, only that which you paint onto it."

Surely this counts as doing something good?

Maria caught up with him as he opened the door, grabbing his arm. "What is going on?"

"We're leaving. Please, don't ask questions. Just trust me, okay."

"Leaving?" Jaz said. "Leaving where?"

Niastus took her arm, his gaze never leaving Horatio. "Just go with it," he told her.

"But . . ."

"Come on," Horatio said insistently.

They made it to the old warehouse's rear door. Horatio waved to the crew busy with a leaking manifold, feeling like shit. The one thing he couldn't work out would be Gwendoline's reaction to him bringing these people with him. The kids and their baby, okay, she'd deride him for being a sentimental old fool. *True enough.* But Maria? What would happen after they got offplanet? Would he have to shake hands and wish her well on her way? *More likely Gwendoline will throw me out of the nearest airlock. But she said I could bring somebody. Was she kidding? Fuck!* It was done now.

The door shut behind them, leaving them by themselves on the crumbling tarmac of a neglected street, without any lights. Horatio realized he'd relied on the bike headlight to get here. And he'd left the bike because it wasn't practical, and— "Shit." He was normally so good at thinking things through. His altme activated the light amplifier function in his tarsus lenses, and the road became a little clearer, its surfaces speckled with indigo static.

"Hey," Maria said calmly. She slid her arm around him. "Want to tell us what's going on?"

"We have to go," he said. "To my flat. First."

"Why?" Jaz asked.

"There's a way out. And I think we're going to—" Gwendoline's icon splashed into his tarsus lens, emergency coded. Horatio's skin chilled down at the sight of it. "Yes?" he asked.

"Oh, God, Horatio," Gwendoline said. "They're in orbit!"

"What?"

"The Olyix. Their wormholes just opened above Earth; they're only five thousand kilometers up. The orbital sensors didn't even detect the carrier ships coming through the Sol system. Resolution ships are flying out like a bloody locust plague. The first ones are already in the upper atmosphere."

"No fucking way!" he gasped, and looked up in shock. The murky shield curved above the city, as mundane and eternal as always. Its unnaturally solid air made the crescent moon an insubstantial shimmer in the east, above Dartford.

"They're coming for all of us," Gwendoline said, her voice weak with fright. "Wormholes have opened at Delta Pavonis and 82 Eridani, the shield over the capital on Eta Cassiopeiae has already failed. And—oh Christ—Rangvlad has gone."

"Gone?"

"Yes, we've lost all the interstellar portal links to Beta Hydri. We have to go, Horatio. Now. Pasobla is starting its countdown. I can't stop it. Not even Ainsley can."

"Ainsley?"

"Yes, he was here for some ultra-level security conference with Emilja. Now he's going to have to come with us; there's no way back to Nashua. For the love of God, Horatio, open the portal!"

"I'm coming. I'll be there in five minutes."

"Shit, 82 Eridani just went. Hurry!"

He looked at the others. "The Olyix are here. I have a way offworld. I can take the four of you, but it's now or never. You coming?"

"Yes." Niastus took the baby from a trembling Jaz. "Do we run?"

"Fuck, yeah," Horatio said. As he said it, the city's sparse aurora of light died. Streetlights went off, along with all the house lights that didn't have battery reserves. Behind them, the community exchange fell silent apart from a loud metallic buzzing of unbalanced pumps spinning erratically into shutdown.

"Christ on a crutch," Maria exclaimed. "You're not joking, are you?"

"No. Come on." He started jogging toward Curtis Street. The others kept up with him, so he increased the pace. Voices emerged up ahead, questions shouted between rooms in the terraced houses. Curtains were opened, revealing lights that still had battery power; people pressed themselves against the glass to see what was happening.

Then London's always-precarious network crashed.

It was stupid, but Horatio responded by looking upward again, as if appealing to ancient gods. Vast lightning webs seethed far overhead, cracking the sky open. He squinted into the frenzied glare. Something was moving at its heart—a dark-gray elongated oval shape that just kept growing. The lightning forks stabbing out of it were permanent now, clawing at the shield and expanding to create a single jagged sheet. It was as if daylight had returned; the whole gleamed under the terrible forces emitted by the huge alien ship.

"Is that—" Maria gasped.

"Yeah." He'd slowed to take in the shocking manifestation; now he surged forward again, crossing into Curtis Street. *It's only a few hundred meters. Please!*

The light changed abruptly, shading to a disturbingly intense violet. Horatio had hoped he'd never see that light ever again: devil-sky. Huge patches of the shield were fluorescing from whatever beams the ship was firing down. It was much brighter than during Blitz2, and getting brighter.

The shield would never hold against that, he knew.

Jaz was whimpering as she and Niastus stumbled along together, shielding their eyes from the lightstorm above. She was young, only nineteen, Horatio remembered; Blitz2 had ended before she was even born. So she would've listened to her parents' stories with healthy teenage skepticism and boredom; *it was tough when we were young, you kids today have it so easy*. Now reality was crashing against her senses with a brutality she'd never known.

He veered over toward her. "It's okay. Five minutes and we'll be out of here. Just hang on, yes?"

She nodded frantically, clutching at Niastus—her only dependable rock in the storm erupting around her.

The devil-sky light vanished. Horatio felt a stab of pure panic, like boiling adrenaline flooding his brain. There was only one reason for that. He almost didn't dare look upward yet again, but . . .

The air provided a foretaste of what was about to come. There was still no wind, not even a breeze, but it seemed to squeeze him. Then he saw it, something moving in the sky—a dark column like a twister, but broken into segments. And moving fast, like airplanes used to, already several kilometers high. He stared in amazement. The apex of it was a crumpled building, bigger than the community exchange behind him, spinning its way upward, shedding hunks of wall, its panel roof twisting and disintegrating. Below it was a tail of debris: smaller buildings, inverted cascades of earth, even tree trunks. Something had reached down from the sky and pulled them up.

Instinctively he knew what that building had been: *shield generator*. The Resolution ship had somehow reversed gravity and pulled the city's only defense out by its roots. He spun around, seeing a couple of similar columns already peaking, the debris starting to curve groundward.

"The wind's going to hit," Horatio shouted. "Find something to hold onto." He looked along the street. There wasn't much. A few dead trees, some iron bollards at the far end, where the road narrowed to feed into Bacon Grove. "Those!" He sprinted off toward the bollards. Above him the furious barrage of sheet lightning began to calm. With the glare reducing he could see there were two Resolution ships hovering over London. *Crap, they're huge*. Clouds began to boil around their edges, slamming down toward the city.

Wind was already blowing fast down Bacon Grove when they reached the bollards. Horatio and Maria clung to each other around one of the posts, while Niastus and Jaz hugged tight, with their baby between them. Horatio braced himself as the noise of the storm's leading edge impacting the ground struck. It was bone-shaking, riding a pressure wave that was almost strong enough to pull them apart. The heat was something else he hadn't anticipated, making it hard to inhale.

Windows all along the street shattered, the shards joining the thick airborne streams of roof slates. There was so much debris in the air that even the gigantic lightning halos around the Resolution ships were eclipsed, plunging the street back into a gray twilight. His clothes were flapping against his limbs, as if they were trying to pull free of him and take flight.

With Maria's face centimeters from his own, Horatio could see the frightened grimace sculpted into her features as she dug her fingers into his arms. He knew that she'd be seeing exactly the same expression on his face.

"What do we do?" she yelled. It was barely audible above the howling wind.

He winced as a denuded pine tree crashed to the ground fifty meters away and tumbled along until it was pinned against a wall; smaller branches vibrated until they snapped off, to be sucked back up into the churn of rubble above the rooftops. "This isn't going to get any better," he bellowed back. "We need to try and move."

Jaz looked at him in pure terror, but Niastus nodded.

"Everyone hold on to each other," Horatio said. "We crawl." It was the best he could think of—present the smallest slimline profile to the wind. To stand up was to be snatched into the air.

He estimated it wasn't quite two hundred meters to the front door of his block. After the first few meters pushing hard against the gale, he wasn't sure if he had the strength to make it. A frightening number of lethal shards were hurtling along Bacon Grove—slates, tree limbs, glass, cans, bags of rubbish splitting open to shed their contents like oversize artillery rounds. He didn't even know how many times the ground trembled from seismic shock as some nearby building collapsed. Once, a two-seat cabez came rolling toward them like an oversize metallic football, crashing from side to side in sprays of shattered glass and ripped bodywork. They all had to scrabble aside to avoid it. The battered chassis missed Maria by less than a meter.

Some eternity later, they reached the end of Bacon Grove. Horatio's block was on the other side of the broad intersection. He couldn't tell if the wind streaking along Grange Road was slightly slower. There was plenty of rubbish tumbling along; taxez bounced and gyrated past them. They watched as an unconscious woman rolled along the tarmac, her skirt acting as a sail, broken limbs flopping about, skin flayed raw, her face painted in blood. Horatio was pretty sure she was dead.

"What the fuck is that?" Niastus cried.

Horatio followed his frantic gaze upward, just knowing it was going to be *bad*. The nearest Resolution ship hanging low above London was spilling a dark waterfall from an open slot in its aft fuselage—a cybernetic pterodactyl shitting on the city. His tarsus lenses zoomed in as best he could, and the outflow resolved into a dense stream of globes.

It had been twenty-five years since he'd last seen those shapes, and the sight of them made him whimper like a frightened child trapped in a looped nightmare. "Olyix hunting spheres," he yelled as another taxez crashed past, twirling off into the Spar Gardens. "Move!" It was insanity—there were so many lethal fragments scything through the air along Grange Road—but he preferred to take his chances with them. They crouched low and scuttled forward, stopping once for a shop awning to cartwheel past. They ducked for a round table that spun and pogoed. Small particles were slamming into him constantly, impossible to see and dodge before they hit, but each one was like a kick from a pro cagefighter.

Less than a minute and they made it to the other side, and clung to the shelter of the wall, where the wind had eased a fraction. Horatio's knee was in agony where a chunk of masonry had hit him. Blood was running down Maria's face from a nasty gash on her forehead. A weeping Jaz was supporting Niastus as he tried to stand upright, the baby clutched to her torso.

The door's glass panels were cracked, but not yet shattered. It wouldn't open. Horatio could see the frame was warped. "Together," he told Niastus. They put their shoulders down and thumped against it. It held. They hit it again, finally shifting the obdurate frame. There was a terrific roar, and the air swirled violently. Horatio fell hard into the hallway, not understanding what had happened. Then he caught sight of the Olyix sphere streaking away along Grange Road—with things falling out of it. He looked down at the tarmac. Dozens of capturesnakes were lying there, starting to twitch. Of course they were the one thing the wind didn't blow away.

"Go!" he screamed and grabbed Jaz, pulling her inside. "Go, go. Upstairs."

The tips of the capturesnakes rose up like armored cobra heads, tracking around. Horatio pushed Niastus toward the stairs. "Help him," he told Maria.

"But you—"

"Go. I'm right behind you." Several capturesnakes started wriggling their way toward the open door. It would be useless trying to shut it, he knew. Jaz and Niastus had made it up the first few stairs. Maria gave him a desperate look, then turned fast and started heading up. "Come on," she urged the others, half pushing, half lifting Niastus. "Second floor, number twenty-four. Move!"

Horatio backed into the stairwell. It was reasonably narrow, brick walls and concrete stairs with metal rails. Obsolete ducts ran along the edge of the ceiling. He'd made it to the first turn when his altme finally got a signal from the portal. Gwendoline's icon splashed into his tarsus lens display.

"Horatio!"

"I'm here. Almost at the flat. Thread up, for God's sake. Now!"

"Horatio . . . are you secure?"

"There are capturesnakes. They're chasing us. Don't worry, I've got them."

"Horatio!"

"Hurry!"

"I . . . I'll try."

"Try what?"

"We can't let any Olyix through, not even a capturesnake. It's security."

"Fuck! I said I've got this. No capturesnake is coming through."

"Oh, Christ."

"Thread up!" He saw movement down in the hallway and pulled out his voltstick. It telescoped out to its full meter length. The bulbous end fizzed with purple static. He'd never been proud to carry it. After all, it was his job to reason and persuade the wilder kids—those who'd lost their way, who just needed some sympathy and guidance. Force was never the answer. But he knew those lost kids well enough to acknowledge some were beyond even his negotiating skills, and London was balanced so finely on the edge of anarchy. So . . . always the voltstick when he left the flat. A practical precaution.

Two capturesnakes darted forward, undulating rapidly as they came up the stairs. His altme's self-defense routine told him to strike the one on his left first. He jabbed down, catching it just behind the tip. The voltstick discharged in a brutal flash, and he was already swiping right. Another flash. Thin smoke puffed upward, drenching him with the smell of burnt plastic and oil fumes.

"What the fuck was that?" Maria demanded.

"I told you I've got this."

"I got clearance," Gwendoline said. "We're threading up."

"You're a Zangari," he told her. "I expected nothing less." His altme highlighted another capturesnake squirming up the stairs. More were slithering into the hallway.

Horatio waited until the next one was a single step below him, then swung the voltstick down. The capturesnake flipped to one side, then lunged forward at the same time the voltstick struck the concrete. It coiled around his ankle, grating against his skin. *Bollocks, this is going to hurt!* He brought the voltstick back, scrunching it into the rear of the capturesnake. Where it was wrapped around his ankle became a tight ring of searing hot lava. Horatio screamed at the vile burst of pain, instinctively jerking the voltstick away. The smoldering capturesnake twitched as he shook his leg, dislodging it. The next three were already on the stairs.

Eyes watering from the pain, he started up the next flight of stairs. There was no light on the second floor, so his tarsus lenses had to switch to full infrared. He could see the scarlet and peach profile of the others stumbling onward to his flat. Behind him, glowing amber auroras lurked below the top stair, like small suns ready to begin the day.

"One meter portal's threaded," Gwendoline said. "How much longer?"

Maria was fumbling with the door lock.

"Almost with you." He stood square in the corridor, an immovable barrier between the stairs and his flat. Behind him, Maria finally got the door open. A wan emerald glow oozed out into the corridor.

"Who the hell are they?" Gwendoline demanded.

The tips of three capturesnakes rose up above the top stair. Horatio struck a pose, holding the voltstick ready to thrust and parry as if he were channeling some buccaneer ancestor. They launched themselves at him—two writhing across the floor, one somehow scooting along the wall. The tactical routine gave him the best attack strategy, the angles to thrust and stab, optimum time between the strokes. Perfect had he still owned those glorious long-ago adolescent football field reflexes.

He hit the one on the wall easily. The tarsus lens dimmed automatically to protect his optical nerve from the flash, but he saw the capturesnake drop and shudder in eerie death throes. He missed the next, but the swipe carried on in a powerful arc and caught the third straight on. Vision dimmed again for the flash, at the same time something hit his left knee with bewildering force. He crashed to the ground, the air knocked from his lungs.

"Horatio?" Maria cried.

"Fucking go!" he yelled back at her. "Gwendoline, they're my friends." Even he could hear the raw pleading in his voice.

"I can't," Gwendoline said.

"They've got a baby!"

"Oh, motherfucker."

Horatio didn't hear anything else; her voice vanished behind a wave of pain from his leg. Adrenaline coupled with raw panic overrode his body's muscle lock, and he stared down his trembling torso. The capturesnake had wound around both knees like a sinuous manacle, its tip puncturing the skin, allowing it to tunnel up through the quadricep muscle. He could see it pushing its way deeper into him and screamed in shock. Once again he brought the voltstick down, thrashing at the obscene alien device in frenzied horror. The pain of the discharge was excruciating, forcing him to stop in tears after the third or fourth strike. Panting on the ground, he saw the capturesnake was dead, or at least inert. His leg was numb, which he knew wouldn't last. He reached down and gripped the awful thing, pulling . . . It took an age to yank it free amid unbelievable pain. A frightening amount of blood gushed out of the wound. But far worse than that was the sensation of something moving inside him, pushing along his femur toward his groin. The capturesnake had performed its function, injecting him with a blob of Kcells, the start of cocooning. His stomach heaved, and he grew faint.

Hands gripped his shoulders and started to drag him back, out of the corridor and into the flat. When he looked up, he saw Maria's manic grin as she tugged him along. Beyond her, at the far end of his lounge, an innocuous circular portal was standing vertically on spindly mechanical legs, showing a bright green room on the other side. He gazed numbly at the apparition from a lost past.

Jaz was on all fours before it, passing her baby through the circular portal.

"I'm coming," Horatio told Gwendoline.

"We've got the baby," she replied.

Niastus pushed Jaz, and she started to crawl through the portal. Horatio clenched his teeth at another wave of pain firing up from his leg. The clump of Kcells the capturesnake had violated him with was moving again. "I'm going to need a medical team," he said.

"On their way."

Niastus started to clamber through the portal. A capturesnake dropped onto Maria's head. She screamed, shuddering about as if she'd been electrocuted. It fell off her, and Horatio swatted it with the voltstick. Four more were rushing into the flat. The corridor floor outside was swarming with a whole pack of them, dark shells glistening in the jade light.

"Horatio!" Gwendoline called.

"Go," he begged Maria. The lead capturesnake leaped forward. He struck it perfectly with the voltstick, surprised and disappointed at how weak he seemed to have become. Something bit his foot. He saw a capturesnake had penetrated his boot leather to jab into his ankle. More capturesnakes were slinking forward quickly, as if they could sense his growing vulnerability. He slashed about wildly with the voltstick. "Go. Please."

She stared at the approaching pack of capturesnakes in horror. "No."

"Live for me."

"Horatio!"

A capturesnake speared his abdomen. He brought the voltstick down on it in a classic hara-kiri stab. His back arched up, muscles rigid as he received the full blast of the voltstick. The universe was growing fainter, somehow receding in every direction. "Go."

"I love you," Gwendoline said.

"Every day forever." His final smile was ruptured by the tip of a capturesnake forcing its way into his mouth; it started to worm its way down his esophagus. Biting it was useless; the flexing skin was hard as rock. He started to choke as the green light dimmed. Maria's body was filling the portal. A final swipe at two capturesnakes surging after her, the satisfying flash of incandescence as their alien guts fried. The green light grew brighter as Maria's legs quickly slid across the rim, then vanished completely.

I'll be waiting there for you after the end of time.

THE *AVENGING HERETIC*

YEAR TWO

It was Callum's second extended period out of the tank's oblivion, and he was surprised at how quickly it had gone. The crew's schedule was simple enough: Two people were on duty for three months, then everyone would be brought out of suspension for a month together, and after that a different pair would begin their duty watch.

He'd thought his first watch would be difficult; he'd shared it with Jessika. There were doubts still lingering in his mind, not simply because she was alien—or should that be: her origin was alien?—but because he'd never known. All that time spent working together on Akitha, even going out for drinks a few times in the evening after work, a couple of binaries laughing gently at the foibles of their newly adopted Utopial home. There'd been no hint, not a clue, that she wasn't fully human. After all life had thrown at him by that time, he'd always considered himself able to read people. So the failure was all his own, and that inevitably kindled a spark of inward-focused anger.

Logically, of course, he had no reason to be suspicious of her. She had been created to help humans—a real-universe version of an angel dispatched to Earth. The final proof being that she was here, supporting this crazy-stupid mission. Which left him looking like the petty one for harboring doubts. He probably overreacted, trying to compensate with excessive politeness, and laughing a little too hard at her jokes. To the extent that after ten days together she asked: "Are you okay?"

Shamefaced, he'd diverted by replying: "It was just Kandara's crack about the Neána being a splinter group of the Olyix."

"It got to me, too," she admitted. "But there is the counter argument: How come we didn't know the enclave location?"

"There's a lot of things your group of Neána humans weren't told. What your species actually is, where the abode cluster is. Security."

"Fair enough. But if I were you, I'd be more worried about Kandara's other belief."

"What's that?"

"That I'm not in charge of my destiny. That I have subconscious orders to betray you, or something worse."

"Thanks. Way to reassure me."

"But on the bright side, what could I actually do at this point to make it worse?"

"Uh . . ."

"Quite."

Callum admitted she'd won that one. It made the rest of their watch go smoothly.

Then six months later when he and Yuri began their watch together, he was prepared for weeks of grumpy avoidance and barely civil grunts when they did encounter each other. But it turned out Yuri was actually far too professional for that. Not that he was a big talker.

"I was thinking about something Jessika said," Callum confided to Yuri at breakfast during their second week.

"Which is?"

"If she was a Neána, some kind of double agent, how could she damage the mission?"

"Yes. And?"

"Well, I don't think she has a hidden agenda."

Yuri rolled his eyes as he ate some syrniki. "Glad we got that sorted out."

"But it did make me think about what might happen. You know, worst case scenarios and such."

"Ah. So?"

"We know more about the *Salvation of Life* now; even I can understand some of its thought routines. The basic ones, anyway." It had taken a long time, and plenty of coaxing from Jessika, but these days he could make a degree of sense out of the impulses flowing into his brain from their entangled cell nodule. The *Salvation of Life*'s onemind was surprisingly sedate. He'd always had the belief that any entity fanatical enough to embark on forceful conquest would be deranged—an opinion enforced by the human viewpoint. Earth's history was crammed with examples, from individuals like Hitler and Pol Pot to the popularism that had damaged so much in the so-called democratic nations from the end of the nineteenth century onward. The realization that the onemind was methodical and composed in its beliefs and purpose had proved unnerving. Basically, that cold intent frightened him more than he'd expected.

"It can't see us, Callum," Yuri said in a reassuring tone. "Jessika made sure of that. The visual routines for the hangar simply edit our creeperdrones out of its perception."

The fact that Yuri knew exactly what to say suggested to Callum that the old security chief had been thinking along similar lines.

"No, it doesn't see anything amiss," Callum agreed, "because right now its observation is autonomic. There is no problem; therefore it isn't looking for a problem. But if it really starts to look, do you think the glitch we've introduced into its local routines will hold?"

"And it will start to look *hard*," Yuri concluded.

"Bloody right, pal. Once we trigger the Signal transmitters, the whole Olyix star system is going to know humans somehow piggybacked a ride to the enclave. They will tear the *Salvation of Life* apart to find us."

"Remaining here with the *Salvation*, and maybe calling to any future human attack force, was only a secondary aspect of the mission. Our absolute priority is to broadcast the Signal, to let humans know where the enclave is. You knew that when we began. We have to accept the inevitable. Once broadcast, the Signal cannot be cancelled."

"I do accept it, man. But it doesn't mean we can't take some precautions."

Yuri sipped some tea from his oversize mug. "Such as?"

They spent the next ten weeks cheerfully shooting down each other's wilder ideas, developing the concepts that did survive until they had something to bring to the others at the next watch changeover month.

Jessika's revival was always immaculate; she awoke from the tank as if she'd been dozing for a couple of hours. Alik and Kandara took a lot longer, and Callum identified with their crabby resentment as they were helped out of the tanks. His own body still took way too long to recover every time his period in suspension ended.

In what was becoming tradition, twenty-four hours after they were out of the tank, everybody gathered around the table for a big Chinese meal. Callum even got the printers to provide therm-foil containers, so it looked like they'd ordered out.

"A bunker?" Alik asked as he tried to use his chopsticks to hook a prawn out of his fried rice.

"A fallback refuge," Callum said. "They're going to come hunting us after we trigger the Signal. There're not many places we can be. They'll figure it out eventually."

"Figure it out, or search the entire arkship," Yuri said. "Callum's right. We need to be ready to abandon ship."

"And do what?" Kandara asked. "The *Avenging Heretic* gives us options."

"Limited options," Yuri said. "After we pop out of this wormhole, our absolute priority is to trigger the Signal; only then can we think about getting inside the enclave. And triggering the Signal is going to create an instant shitstorm. They'll know we're here right away, so they'll release the hounds. If we try and escape by flying off in real space, we have nowhere to go; we'll be thousands of light-years from Sol."

"If we try flying away, the Deliverance ships would catch us anyway," Jessika said. "Their acceleration is a lot higher than ours, and I'm guessing they're not the most powerful warships at the gateway. Not by a long shot."

"I expect you're right," Yuri agreed glumly.

"We originally assumed that if we could get to the enclave star undetected, we could stay invisible to the onemind after we sent the Signal," Callum said. "Now that we understand a little more about how the *Salvation of Life* works, I don't think we can. At the very least we need a decoy."

Jessika picked up some stir-fry noodles with her chopsticks and gave him a thoughtful look. "We could hijack another transport ship. There are twenty-seven in this hangar alone, in varying conditions; most of them are flightworthy. It could make a valiant fight for freedom and get tragically nuked."

"That sounds risky," Yuri said. "You'd have to neurovirus its onemind."

"Which Soćko proved we can do."

"Yeah, right," Alik said. "But here's the thing. He was inside the transport ship, and had a direct physical connection to its neural fibers. How you gonna get inside one of them here?"

"It's a plan that needs work," she admitted. "But I'm still putting it out there."

"Okay," Yuri said. "That's fallback number two. But I think we should start by exploring Callum's option."

"We either do it or we don't," Kandara said. "What's to explore?"

"Location," Callum told her. "I've been riding the onemind's local perception routines for a few weeks now."

She grinned at him. "Everyone should have a hobby."

"There are twelve passages out of this hangar. Some are just tunnels, their version of utility channels; some are proper access corridors. And there are chambers off both of them, it seems. I'd like to send our creeperdrone spies down them to see if there's anything suitable."

"And if there is?" Jessika asked.

"Start building up a reserve of equipment."

"You mean transfer the contents of the *Avenging Heretic* into a cave?"

"No," Yuri said. "We won't need that much. We can breathe the *Salvation*'s air, remember? So we need basic equipment, and enough food to last us a couple of months. Maybe a year."

"Months?" Alik said. "You're shitting me!"

"No. Inside the enclave, time flows slowly."

"Says who?" Kandara said harshly. She jabbed a chop-stick toward Jessika. "The Neána? How do they know? If your kind weren't here, how did they find out? And if they were here, when was it? What does that make them?"

"It makes them a species who can neurovirus an Olyix onemind," Yuri said. "Who can extract such knowledge from an arkship's memory. And even if they are cousins to the Olyix, or rebels, what the fuck difference does it make now? It's not like we can turn around and head for home. So far, all the information Jessika and her colleagues have provided is correct. We're committed to this mission, and that means assuming the enclave is a bubble of slowtime."

"From what I've determined from the *Salvation*'s one-mind, there is an enclave," Jessika said earnestly. "Just like my original information."

"Yuri and I talked about this," Callum said. "The enclave was built to take the Olyix to the end of time, so time has got to be flowing slow in there. Really slow. A year inside will cover centuries out here, if not longer. It has to; there's no other way. Even if you go forward to when this galaxy be-comes quiescent and stops producing new stars, you're look-ing at billions of years."

"What are you saying?"

"If a human armada doesn't come knocking within a year or two of enclave time, they never will," Yuri said. "That will be thousands of years passing outside."

"So what do we do then?" Alik demanded. "If they never come?"

"Please, you knew that was always possible. But we do not consider this, yes? We do not let it distract us. We con-tinue our mission, we survive as long as we can. Then . . ." Yuri shrugged and ate a chunk of sweet and sour chicken.

"Join the rest of the human race in a cocoon and find out what this alien god has in mind for us," Callum said.

"Or go out in a fantastic blaze of gunfire," Kandara said wickedly.

Yuri grinned at Alik. "See? So many choices. And you were worried this flight would be boring."

Alik closed his eyes. "Jezus H. Christ."

Callum piloted one of the creeperdrone spy creatures. He was confident in the operation now, even though it was painstakingly slow. The little spiderlike thing provided a slightly weird view from its bulbous eye clusters. He didn't understand why Jessika hadn't incorporated a more ordinary lens, but she'd muttered something about authenticity and avoiding variance the one time he'd asked.

It was making its cautious way down a wide passageway. The floor was cut clean through the rock—a perfectly smooth surface that had dulled down the years. Walls and ceiling were a tousled weave of woody tubes—some as thick as oak trees—which were tangled by finger-wide stems, forming an enigmatic tapestry of alien browns and grays. There were fewer leaves in here, and the bioluminescent strips threaded along the bark were spaced widely, creating long stretches of shadow. Pools of liquids with sticky rims had coagulated on the floor under the fractured tubes, which Callum assiduously steered the spy creature around.

Half a kilometer from the hangar, the floor started to rise up. There were vents in a couple of the big tubes—fat, bulbous shapes that he first mistook for knots in the bark. When he paused the creature close to one, he could see it was slowly dilating and contracting, breathing out damp air. The nearby bark was all covered in a furry blue-green growth, like a mold that was transforming into a fern.

A couple of hundred meters up the slope there was a fork in the passage. He steered the creature into the smaller passage. It branched again, then came out into a junction with five tunnels, one going vertical, which was almost completely jammed with tubes in a faintly obscene twining contortion. Onward, again down the narrowest tunnel. There was a gap in the web of arboreal tubes just big enough for a human to wriggle through. It was lightless inside.

Callum paused the creature and focused his consciousness on the chaotic tumble of the onemind's thoughts. Filtering and interpretation was far more art than science. But eventually he believed he was perceiving the narrow tunnel where the creature was waiting. Whatever lay in the gap

seemed to be a natural cessation in the onemind's percep
tion.

"What do you think?" he asked Jessika. "Trap or genuine
perception break?"

"Let me review," she replied.

It was nearly an hour before she spoke again. "There is
some kind of activity in there. The tubes go in, and I can
sense pressure in the fluids. But there's very little flow. The
impulses are all part of the autonomic process. I'm guessing
some kind of fluid reserve."

"A tank?"

"Tank, bladder, reservoir—whatever. A place to store reserves."

"No armored quint inside waiting for us?"

"Ninety-eight percent: no. I think it's clear."

Callum took a breath and refocused on the spy creature.
He eased it into the gap. At first guess, it was an original fissure in the asteroid before the Olyix started converting it into
an arkship. The walls were irregular, creating a cleft that extended over fifty meters, varying in width from twenty meters down to paper thin at the extremities. A cluster of silky
spheres five meters in diameter was affixed to the walls close
to the entrance with tough strings of fiber encasing them like
nets. The tubes plaited around them, slowly pushing fluids in
and out. Callum thought they looked like eggs laid by some
beast twice the size of a T. rex, and ten times uglier.

Beyond the egg tanks, the cavern was empty.

"This place goes against everything we know of asteroid
composition," Kandara said. "I've been on enough of them
to know they're either S-type— the solids—or a congealed
pile of rubble. They don't have caves and caverns. That's
strictly part of planetary geology: Cavities in rock form
from water eroding limestone. And the one thing you don't
get in space rock is limestone, because it's sedimentary. The
other thing you don't get on an asteroid is water, let alone
free flowing water."

"The obelisks Feriton reported seeing in the fourth chamber were made from sedimentary rock," Alik said.

"A fourth chamber which didn't exist," Yuri countered. "It
was a simulation."

"And yet, here we have a bona fide cave. Somehow I don't think the Olyix produced it for aesthetic satisfaction. It could be significant."

"I really don't care about asteroid formation processes," Callum said. "We have a cavern that has minimal perception inside. End of story."

"But why is it there?"

"I dunno. Bring it up at the next philosophy-of-geology lecture. We have our refuge."

"We have the first possible site for our refuge," Yuri said. "Although I agree it is favorable. Let's keep reviewing the locale."

After another three days, they agreed Callum's cave was the one they were going to use. There were other cavities within a kilometer of the hangar, but they were either smaller or packed full of the arkship's biological structures.

"So how do we get to it?" Alik asked.

"The visual glitches in the hangar perception routines should cover us in here," Jessika said. "It'll take time, but I should be able to extend them up the passageway to the cave."

"And physically?" Yuri asked. "How do we get our supplies there?"

"Trojan horse. We'll use an initiator to assemble a creeperdrone in the shape of one of the medium-size creatures, and use its internal cavity as a cargo hold. That way we can move stuff there slowly."

"I'd like to establish our own sensors in the passageway first," Kandara said. "The same type we've installed around the hangar; they can keep watch for any of the *Salvation*'s own creatures or a quint moving about. The last thing we want is your cargo creature unexpectedly bumbling into anything too analytical. We only make a delivery run when the passage is completely clear, agreed?"

"Yes, ma'am," Callum said.

"Okay then," Yuri said. "We go ahead with this. Let's start with a wish list. And, Kandara—personal defense weapons only."

"Mary, but you really know how to kill a party."

NEUTRON STAR

MORGAN'S ARRIVAL

The fleet was still two AUs out from the neutron star when Ainsley appeared, velocity matching perfectly so that the elegant white ship held position a thousand kilometers from the *Morgan*. The duty crew on the bridge had no warning; there wasn't a single sensor on any ship in the fleet that had detected the giveaway gravitational waves that theoretically should have been coming from Ainsley's drive as the ship approached.

"A stealthed gravitonic drive," Yirella muttered as she clambered out of bed. "Who knew?" The alerts zipping into her databud had woken her after only a couple of hours' sleep. She'd gone to bed expecting to be well awake and refreshed when they finished their deceleration maneuver an estimated million kilometers outside the neutron star's unnatural ring. So far, contact had been limited: a few messages from the fleet when they were a light-month out, announcing they were coming—in peace. A brief: *We know, you are welcome,* in reply. And details—what orbit to go into, contact protocols; the neutron star inhabitants were organizing a reception congress to discuss "unified intent." All reasonably predictable, if a little stark. There were no images of them or their habitats, no explanations of what the thermally active ring particles were.

Then right at the end came the only question the neutron star inhabitants asked: Is Yirella with you?

That was embarrassing.

In a pleasing way.

Dellian was sitting up beside her, a befuddled expression on his face as he scratched his neck, then his arm. Yawned.

"Your other boyfriend's back, then," he mumbled as he considered the data rolling through his optik.

Yirella resisted a sigh of exasperation. He was never going to let that go. She'd tried to explain to him that giving the seedships independence and freedom was her idea, her gamble, her responsibility. And she was only too aware, had she confided in him what she'd done, that burden of knowing would've chewed him up. Yes, it should have been a formal proposition to the council, duly debated and voted on. Except it would have been voted down. Kenelm's reaction alone proved that, and he wasn't the only one with that view on her utter irresponsibility. So every time she tried to mollify Del it came across as petulant and self-serving, which had to stop. She was confident he would ultimately forgive her, or at least stop snarking, given enough time—say, a couple of centuries.

"So it would seem," she replied.

"What now?"

"Nothing. I expect Ainsley is just confirming we're not a disguised Olyix attack."

"What about us making sure this isn't an Olyix ambush?"

She pressed her teeth together, refusing to show him how that riled her. "Good call. Cinrea is on watch. I'll tell hir."

"Don't suppose I'm needed."

"Did the bridge call for you?"

"No."

"That's good, then; they don't think we're about to be shot at." She quickly put a tunic on and left the cabin. When the door shut, Dellian had rolled over to face the wall, his eyes closed.

"Saints," she hissed quietly.

A white icon slipped into her optik. "Trouble in paradise?" Ainsley asked.

"And you can go to hell, too," she snapped at him.

His chortle was immensely annoying. "It's good to see you. Genuinely. How was the flight?"

"Eventful." She told him about Kenelm, and the group of Utopial devotees Emilja and Soćko had gathered to steer exodus generations.

"Well, we did think it would be something like that, didn't we?" Ainsley said. "Two thousand years of political fraudulence, though; gotta admit, that's impressive. My father used to tell me that when he was a kid, change—in culture and technology—was so endemic that people were complaining no one had a job for life anymore. I wonder if Dad would approve of this particular reincarnation of sinecure."

Yirella smiled. "I thought politics was a calling, not a job."

"You're young. You'll learn."

"So what in the sweet Saints have people built here? They changed the star's rotation rate!"

"Yeah. How better to announce to the whole galaxy: Here we are. This civilization got very smart, and . . . libertarian isn't the word, and post-scarcity communism doesn't fit, either; I'm not quite sure how to describe their politics. Put it this way: They were very argumentative once they started to think properly for themselves. But they did agree to majority consensus. It brought a tear to my eye."

"So are they going to fight the Olyix?"

"You'll see. It's quite a congress they're putting together for you."

"They, uh, asked about me."

"Ah, yeah, about that; I may have pushed your role in our little conspiracy to facilitate their society."

"Oh, Saints."

"Don't go all morose on me. It'll work in your favor."

"You think?"

"I predict. But then, predicting is how I made my fortune when I was human."

"I checked. You inherited a fortune."

"I inherited a small fortune, and turned it into the greatest accumulation of wealth in history."

"Yeah, almost as big as your ego. So what next?"

"You finish decelerating, they send a portal over to the *Morgan*. You all go through to the congress. Simple."

"Nah, nothing ever is. Not in these times."

As the fleet approached its negotiated parking orbit a million kilometers out from the ring, the *Morgan*'s sensors started to capture the warm particles in high resolution. Yirella, Ellici, and Wim formed one analysis team, gathering in a small conference room to pore over the images and data tables compiled by the genten. The room's walls were all but invisible behind the thick hologram projections—a perspective that seemed to place them at the heart of the little system, sitting on the surface of the neutron star itself.

"There's some standardization," Wim observed. "There are thousands of particles that have a similar size and mass; we've given them a preliminary type classification. Not that it matters, because they all have exactly the same external skin—that copper color. So we don't know what any of them actually are."

"And there's nothing under a kilometer," Yirella said. "But their thermal emission ratio is fairly constant across the types." She studied close-up images of what looked like asteroids but seemed sculpted from polished copper. Their surfaces moved, though—slowly, the bulges and dints undulating with a lethargic arrythmia. As she watched the time-lapse images she had a disturbing flashback to a biology lecture featuring a fetal sac with a teratological embryo shifting around inside.

The thought was deeply uncomfortable, so she gave up and called Ainsley. "What the hell are those things?"

"Habitats, ships, factories, stores of processed materials, labs, experiments, sensors; everything you'd expect from an advanced civilization."

"But they all have the same surface."

"It's a development on the mirrorfabrik shielding you use," Ainsley said. "The cloak protects them from the neutron star radiation. It's useful for defense, too."

"That's odd," Ellici said as she pulled up more detailed

sensor data. "Really odd. The neutron star has an unsymmetrical gravity field."

"How can that be?" Wim mused. "There's no theory that can account for uneven mass distribution inside a star, let alone a neutron star."

"It's got to be those inner stations," Ellici said. "The hundred and fifty big ones. Their gravitational emissions are off the scale. They must be affecting it."

"We saw what the Resolution ships could do at the Vayan ambush," Yirella said. "This could be a similar emission. Some kind of directional gravity beam?"

"If enough of them pull at the neutron star's surface, they might create a wave in the outer crust; it's only ions and electrons down to about four hundred meters."

"Love the way you call it 'only,'" Wim said.

"But susceptible to external forces," Yirella countered. "I wonder if we can get an accurate surface map? See if there are physical waves splashing around down there."

"They wouldn't be big," Wim said. "The neutron star's only twenty-one kilometers in diameter, so a wave would be maybe a couple of millimeters high. Probably less."

"We're missing the main point," Ellici said. "Why?"

"Because they can?"

"Because they're weaponizing neutronium would be my guess. Remember, Ainsley has some kind of super-dense weapons we haven't seen in action yet."

"And here we are in orbit around two point three solar masses of neutronium," Yirella said. "Matter that's just as dense as you can get. Weaponize that, and the Olyix will be in serious trouble."

"Anyone would be," Wim said. "That's a take-over-the-galaxy weapon."

"I disagree," Yirella said. "It's a terrify-the-galaxy weapon, yes, but you can only destroy one thing with it. That doesn't compel people to submit, just to run away."

"Or die."

"Good job they're on our side, then," Ellici said.

Yirella grinned over at her friend. "There's one thing missing from this ring—from the whole system, actually."

"Which is?"

"The seedships."

"Then where are they?" Wim said, frowning.

"Inside the museum particle?" Ellici suggested.

"Surplus to requirements," Wim said. "Plus the ring orbit is uncomfortably close to the neutron star. The radiation down there is dangerous. If we didn't have mirrorfabrik shells, the fleet wouldn't be in this parking orbit. We'd be a lot farther out."

"The seedships were obsolete," Yirella said. "They didn't bother maintaining them. Simplest solution applies."

"Interesting insight into their psychology, then," Ellici said. "Human cultures normally display a reverence for the past. You know there was a protective dome built over the Apollo Lunar Module at Tranquility to preserve Armstrong and Aldrin's footprints from overeager tourists."

"That probably died the day the Olyix super-nuked Theophilus crater. It was a miracle they didn't crack the whole moon open with that one."

"Most likely," Wim said testily. "Your point?"

"This is the first human civilization we know about that has no past, no heritage," Yirella said. "I deliberately chose not to burden them with expectations and traditions. Their value system is going to be different from ours. And Ainsley told me they were . . . argumentative at first.

"That indicated they took time establishing the boundaries and behavior profiles that parents normally instill in children. But of course they had to determine those for themselves. So yeah, they'll probably look at things differently. From a strictly logical point of view, the past is really dead to them, an irrelevance."

"Sentimentality is an inbuilt human trait," Wim said.

"Is it?"

"Don't start bringing up nature versus nurture, not here. Please."

"Their society, particularly the individuals themselves, aren't old enough to experience death from old age, not yet," Yirella said. "They have never known that kind of loss. That must impact their outlook."

"Saints, what have you created?"

"I have no idea," she said, and grinned. "Wonderful, isn't it."

A small spherical craft with the ubiquitous copper skin flew out of the ring to the *Morgan*, accelerating and decelerating at twenty gees. When it had maneuvered into the starship's largest airlock, it opened up to present a single portal, three meters in diameter. Alexandre was standing in front of it, at the head of a delegation of senior officers and fleet captains. They could glimpse a verdant green landscape framed by the glowing blue rim—one that seemed to be mostly rainforest. A human figure walked through.

Yirella couldn't stop her lips twitching as she regarded the neutron star human in fascination. The visitor was an easy three meters tall, and she thought probably omnia; something about the sharp facial features elicited the instinctual assumption. Gender—if there was one—was hard to determine, what with the colorful ribbons of cloth that were wound spiral-style around its body—and which seemed to be moving as if still being wound. It was a perception issue, as if her eyes couldn't quite resolve the subtle motion. The bands of color were also traveling along the fabric in the opposite direction to the—apparent—physical motion. Then there were the visitor's eyes, which were pale golden orbs, not at all biological. Also unusual was their skin, which was black but not as dark as her own, and had a kind of indigo mottling as if some reptilian DNA had somehow seeped in. The whole reptile theory was enhanced by the tail, over a meter long and sinuous, with strong muscle bands swishing it from side to side in a controlled pendulum motion that suggested it was anything but vestigial.

Dellian leaned in toward her and whispered: "Is that how you designed them?"

"No. The initiators were set to produce standard binary humans. There's been plenty of body modification going on here."

"Free to do what they like, huh?"

Yirella was about to give him a *really* glance when the

exotic visitor turned to face Alexandre, who was beginning hir official welcome speech. The cloth strips on its back parted to flow around five metallic sockets protruding from the spine. Yirella couldn't figure those out at all; they were quite brutalist, given the technology level on show in the ring.

"I am Immanueel," the visitor said in a high voice that hinted at amusement. "I thank you for your greeting. This is a momentous occasion for us." Immanueel began to look around at the people lined up behind Alexandre, searching— then drew a breath and walked straight to Yirella. Everyone parted to give them a clear path.

Yirella wasn't used to looking up at people. Of all Immanueel's modified aspects, she found their height the most unsettling.

"The genesis human," Immanueel said reverentially, and bowed. "I am honored. You created us unbound—the greatest gift sentience can be given. We thank you for our lives and freedom."

Yirella opened Ainsley's white icon. "What in the Saints have you done?"

A mocking chortle came back at her. "Everyone needs a creation myth. Don't blow it. Messiah."

"Oh, crap." She composed a gracious smile for Immanueel. "It is I who am flattered by this encounter. This ring and what you have done to the neutron star is extraordinarily impressive. You must be rightly proud of your accomplishments."

"Thank you. We have built a habitat suitable for you. The congress of determination can be held as soon as you are ready."

Yirella glanced over at Alexandre, who seemed more entertained than upset that Immanueel was treating her as if she were in charge. "I believe we are ready now," she said politely.

Immanueel turned and gestured at the portal—a pose Yirella associated with a medieval courtier ushering their royal charge. "Then I would be delighted if you would accompany me."

"Of course." There was the tiniest specter of doubt itching

away in her mind that this might be some luxurious trap—
which made her annoyed with herself. *This is what happens
when you're brought up to believe everything outside the
fence is your enemy.*

The habitat that the portal led to might have had a terrestrial
environment, but visually Yirella found it disorienting. She'd
been expecting to come out in one of the many larger cylindrical particles that the fleet's sensors had found in the ring.
But Immanueel had said: We built a habitat for you.

Should've paid attention.

The portal opened onto a wide plaza of stone slabs. Their
surface was infused with lichen blooms, while moss was
packed tight in the cracks. They looked old, as if they'd been
laid many decades ago, if not longer. But then, ordinarily,
she would have thought the thick woodland of bald cypress
and oak trees surrounding the plaza must have been well
over a century old, given their size. Whatever fast-grow genetic tweaks that'd been made to their seeds had produced an
authentically ancient-looking biosphere. *We could have
done with that on Vayan.*

On the other side of the plaza from the portal was a disk-
shaped building, suspended thirty meters off the ground on
fluted columns. The supports were twirled by wisteria trunks
almost as thick as the nearby trees. They swamped the building, decorating it in deep violet flower clusters so that only
the disk's window band rim was visible. It left her with the
impression of something sacred that had been abandoned to
nature, like one of old Earth's pre-industrial temples.

Finally, her subconscious hauled her gaze up beyond the
tree canopy so she was looking along the bulk of the habitat.
A frown crept onto her face. The cylinder bent along its
length—a long curve that put the endcaps out of direct sight.
So . . . considerably longer than any of those cylinders the
fleet had categorized orbiting the neutron star. It took a moment for her to work out what was wrong with what she was
seeing. She was standing on the floor of a cylinder with a
landscape curving above her in defiance of any planetary
geography, its apex hidden behind an axial strand of glaring

light. It was the typical layout of big human habitats like Sisaket, which they'd left behind at the start of the Final-Strike flight. Such habitats rotated around their long axis to provide Coriolis gravity on the floor of the shell—except this wasn't a simple cylindrical geometry. Instead she was standing inside a tube that circled around on itself to form a toroid, so it couldn't be rotating around the axial sun tube.

"Saints alive," she muttered. *This is an artificial gravity field.* "You can manipulate gravity," she said to Immanueel.

"Yes."

"Again: impressive."

"I would say thank you, but it is you we should be thanking."

"How do you see that?"

"We exist because of you. If we have built something that impresses you, I am pleased. You are the root from which all we are has grown."

Yirella just knew she'd be blushing. "Ah, right."

She searched around for other neutron star inhabitants, but the only people on the plaza were ones from the fleet still coming through the portal. "Where is your delegation?" she asked.

Immanueel tipped their head to one side in a distinctly avian motion. "I'm sorry. This physical aspect of mine will be present for the congress. Further attendance of my faction colleagues will be through their direct data aspect involvement. Apart from Ainsley; he has manifested as an android."

"He has?"

"Yes." Immanueel performed another elaborate gesture, indicating the elevated disk building. "If you would join us?"

Together, they walked across the plaza toward the lofty braids of wisteria trunks, and Yirella realized she'd misjudged the size. The disk was a lot bigger than she'd thought: a hundred fifty meters in diameter at least.

"What is this place?"

"It is your Hospitality House."

"I love the flowers."

"Thank you. We timed the blossom season for this moment."

She saw the blue glow of a portal rim just behind the pillar. They stepped through together, coming out in the center of the building. It was a single big hall, twenty meters high, walled by the curving rim of windows. Right at the center was a thick multifaceted crystalline pillar, flared at the base and ceiling. She wouldn't have been surprised if it was a real diamond; the pristine gleam certainly laid a claim to authenticity. Each of the facets shone with a prismatic luster that was slowly fluctuating, as if tiny things were moving inside, distorting the light.

"My colleagues' aspects," Immanueel said formally. "Most of them are at analytic."

Yirella inclined her head to the pillar. "I'm delighted to meet you."

As one, every point of light swung to rose-gold, flooding the spacious hall with a glorious twilight haze. Yirella smiled politely. She was sure she was misinterpreting some of Immanueel's conversation. When she glanced around, she registered the vaguely puzzled expressions marring Dellian and Alexandre's faces. "And by analytic, you mean?"

"Ah. The mode my colleagues utilize to encompass this congress will scrutinize and deliberate. When we elevated ourselves out of our birthform, we redistributed our mentality across several physical repositories. Today, each individual currently resident in the ring is a unified corpus. This biophysical body is only one part of me."

To her mind it sounded like heresy, but she asked it anyway. "Like an Olyix quint?"

The pillar flickered excitedly with opalescent light.

"A not dissimilar analogy," Immanueel conceded. "Except that once we matured, we chose to amplify our minds; our corpus are a great deal more than simple backup, which is the basis behind the quint model. My mind, for example, is perfectly interfaced with a quantum processing network as well as biological components that are subject to neurochemical and hormonal distortions. This way, I retain a complete human emotional response to my environment as well as uplifting my intellectual capacity and thoughtspeed. A different set of neurological segments amplifies intuition, or whimsy. I consider that aspect to be the most connected with the birthform mind. I still dream, Yirella."

The smile she gave Immanueel was tainted by sadness. "And which corpus component holds your soul?"

Immanueel clapped in admiration. "An excellent question. You are truly the genesis human Ainsley spoke of. It is a question that would no doubt delight the ancient Greek philosophers."

"And you?"

"The soul is an abstract. It is everywhere and nowhere within the corpus. It is nothing and everything."

"The one flaw in rationality, yet also the path to greatness."

"Exactly. Our humanity, the same as yours."

"Completely different."

"I confess I was worried about meeting you, Yirella. There is a saying from old Earth: Never meet your idol. But you are everything I envisaged you would be."

"You haven't had to argue with her yet," Dellian said in a low voice. "Let me know how much admiration you have left after that happens."

Yirella gave his grinning face the finger.

"Ah, the genesis human's boyfriend," Immanueel said.

"Has a name," Yirella admonished.

"Never could be assed to learn it," a familiar voice announced loudly.

She turned to see a pearl-white human male striding across the floor. She knew he was male because he was naked—and anatomically correct. His facial features were easily identifiable. "Hello, Ainsley."

"Hey there, kid. Good to see you, in the flesh."

"The initiator couldn't do clothes?"

"Never had you down as a prude."

"Okay: The initiator couldn't do color?" The android's whiteness was absolute—eyes, hair strands, the inside of his mouth. Everything was just the same plastic material.

"I'm being economical. Just because we're post-scarcity doesn't mean we should be profligate."

"Couldn't be assed, then?"

"Fucking A."

Yirella didn't know if she should be laughing or sneering at Ainsley's android avatar, yet somehow she wasn't surprised by it. "So what now?"

"Congress!" He winked, a disturbing pucker on his perfectly smooth face.

Dellian smirked.

"Oh, Saints save us," Yirella groaned. She saw there were eighteen captains in the big hall. "Shall we begin?" she asked Alexandre.

"I think so, yes." Sie bowed slightly to Immanueel. "I hope you will be patient with us. Not everyone here is as fast as Yirella."

"Of course."

"Then I'd like to start by thanking you for this reception. You said you built this habitat for us?"

"Yes. I'm pleased you like it. It took us six weeks to mature it."

Alexandre drew a breath ready for his next question, but Yirella held a hand up.

"We're not at your level, are we?" she said.

"Excuse me?"

She closed her eyes, focusing on what she'd seen and heard. "Natural gravity is a product of space-time curvature."

"Yes?"

"But you have full mastery of it. This habitat is proof of that."

"We do."

"So you can create wormholes, for which you'd have to manipulate negative energy?"

"Yes."

"The same technology as the Olyix. So, you have a phenomenal amount of control over the fabric of space-time." She clicked her fingers. "Seasons. You said you timed the seasons so the wisteria would be in flower for today. That means this is an enclave, but the opposite of the Olyix one."

"Huh?" Dellian grunted.

"Now I am the one impressed," Immanueel said.

She turned to Del. "This is and is not a new habitat, depending on your observer viewpoint. It was built a short while ago, then Immanueel's people changed the internal time flow. Inside the Olyix enclave, time flows slowly relative to an external observer, allowing them to travel to the end of the universe without suffering too much aging and entropy. In here, time flows quickly relative to that same observer. So those trees in the forest are genuinely hundreds of years old."

"Fuck the Saints," Dellian muttered.

"Which must take a phenomenal amount of power?" Yirella looked expectantly at Immanueel.

"We derive it directly from the neutron star."

"Wow."

"If we are to successfully negate the Olyix enclave, we knew we had to understand the mechanism that creates and maintains it. It was one of our first accomplishments after we extended our minds."

Dellian looked around at the crews from the fleet. "Anyone still think Yirella did the wrong thing?"

Ainsley's white hand slapped him on the shoulders. "My man!"

"All right, Dellian," Alexandre said. "Let's try and be constructive here, shall we?"

There were tiers of heavy wooden chairs arranged in a semicircle, all facing the crystal pillar. Yirella got the impression they were all handmade—and if not, someone had made a big effort to design tiny differences into the carved oak.

Immanueel sat in front of the twinkling pillar on the largest chair; its bifurcated backrest was obviously intended to accommodate a tail. The captains and crew from the fleet found themselves spaces in the rows of chairs facing their host. Yirella wound up in the front, sitting between Ainsley and Alexandre, with Dellian on the seat behind her. She knew from his buttoned-down expression that he was stifling a laugh.

"What?" she asked from the side of her mouth.

"We're in the court of the elven king now," he replied.

When she glanced forward again, she had to agree. Immanueel's size made for an imposing figure, and their chair could easily be a throne. Looked at without modern filters, the baroque rustic hall with its weight of new ages bestowed the setting a convincingly regal appearance: the benign monarch granting loyal courtiers an audience.

Some of them with regicide and revolution on their minds. She saw Kenelm three rows back, hir disapproval unconstrained as sie scrutinized the hall's gently domed ceiling.

"If I may, I will start with a brief history," Immanueel said. "We initiated our transition up from baseline human form five years after we were birthed out of the seedship biologic initiators, some fifty-five years ago in Earth standard years—normal space-time existence. Yet we are not a monoculture. Many of us chose neural expansion in tandem with corpus elaboration; others did not. Some, like myself, decided to wait here and meet you for the sole purpose of traveling together to the Olyix enclave and instigating Final-Strike."

Yirella shot Alexandre a surprised glance, which seemed to be mirrored on hir expression.

"As such," Immanueel continued, "we have devoted ourselves to developing what Ainsley insists on calling weapons hardware."

"So you are going to help take on the Olyix enclave?" Alexandre asked.

"Indeed, yes. I hold the view that the Olyix cannot go unchallenged—especially in view of their impact on human history." Behind Immanueel, the pillar underwent a burst of shimmering colors.

"Can I ask how many of you hold that view?" Wim queried. "In fact, how many of you are there?"

"That last question is now unanswerable," Immanueel said. "Many of us have already left; they have already begun to expand and populate their own domains."

"Who left?"

"They are called the egress faction; they refute the notion of inter-species conflict. They rightly regarded it as immature and irrelevant to high-scale evolutionites such as ourselves. We do not need to fight; we are able to simply rise above such animal-origin situations. It is our belief the Olyix do not have the ability to capture and cocoon us. However, since we began to change this star's rotation speed, the Olyix will inevitably arrive here at some point. Therefore the egress faction departed, traveling to other stars where they will establish themselves in new space-time-extrinsic domains."

"You mean enclaves?" Yirella said.

"I expect some egressor domains will incorporate alternative time-speeds relative to universal space-time, yes."

"Sanctuary," Dellian exclaimed.

"New sanctuaries," Immanueel corrected. "We have no knowledge of the Sanctuary that Factory humans and the Katos went on to establish."

"How many of this egress faction left?" Yirella asked.

"Fifty-seven thousand eight hundred and thirty-two," Immanueel replied. "Each of them established a squadron of powerful battle cruisers in case they encountered a Resolution ship before they could inaugurate their domain."

"I'm sorry? Each of them?" Yirella's question kicked off a lot of murmuring in the audience behind her.

"Yes."

"You mean they all went their individual way?" she asked incredulously.

"Of course. We are all individuals. That is the freedom you gave us. Everybody here is independent, and nobody is answerable to another. It is the final liberation. Thanks to you, genesis human."

She could well imagine the expression on Kenelm's face.

"Wait," Tilliana said. "You told us all these egress people are now expanding their population?"

"Correct. Although individual, we retain our social nature. Everyone who left here has or will found their own society."

"At *fifty-seven thousand* different stars?"

"Yes. To begin with, anyway. Stars are needed as a power source for space-time-extrinsic domains. I expect they will simply take gas giants out of orbit and convert their mass to energy once they have constructed the appropriate structures."

Like everyone in the hall, Yirella was silent for a moment

as she tried to appreciate the implication of what Immanueel had just told them. "So who remained?" she finally asked. "Apart from yourself."

"We call ourselves the history faction."

"Okay. So how many of you are there in this history faction?"

"Three thousand five hundred and seventeen." Their hand waved leisurely at the crystal pillar, which briefly flared a twilight amber.

The hall was silent again. "Three and a half thousand?"

"Yes. That number troubles you? You consider it to be low? Do not worry, I assure you we have the ability to destroy the Olyix enclave."

Yirella couldn't make herself look at the Ainsley android. Her body had chilled too much to do anything but stare at Immanueel on their not-throne. Very carefully, she said: "The seedships were tasked with growing a base population of a hundred thousand humans in biologic initiators. You have been here for sixty years now. I'd like to know what happened to everyone who isn't egress or history."

"I see you are concerned," Immanueel said. "Not all of the original hundred thousand elected to a corpus elaboration. Call them naturalists. They remained in their original bodyform. Many even refused neurological enhancement."

"People like us, then?" Dellian said.

"Indeed."

"So where are they now?" Yirella asked.

"Those who were birthed here are now dead."

"What?"

"Do not be alarmed. They all died from old age. Many underwent multiple cellular replacement treatments—rejuvenation, if you like—during their life. The eldest was just short of four thousand years old when she finally passed. It was a moving ceremony. Every corpus who was here at the time attended in a biophysical body to honor her."

Yirella let the air out of her body in a long breath. *I need time to adapt to the possibilities that are open here, to make them part of my instincts.*

"The naturalists must have had children," Wim said.

"They did," Immanueel said enthusiastically. "There were

eighteen separate domains built to house them, each with a slightly different social structure. Some more . . . *successful* than others." For once, Immanueel's serene composure flickered. "George Santayana was correct: Those who do not know history are doomed to repeat it. But all who were birthed here eventually adapted and prospered. The domains containing their societies were taken away by the egress faction, where they will be protected and nurtured once time is restarted within them."

"Four thousand years," Wim mused. "What were their populations when they left?"

"Uncertain. Those of us who are corpus don't like to interfere with naturalists. But it would be several million in each domain. Some had started to develop sub-domains."

"What sort of lives did they have? What did they do?"

"There are recordings of their existence available for you to review should you wish to indulge your curiosity."

"Thank you. I would be interested."

"So now you must start to decide," Immanueel said. "I will be traveling to the Olyix enclave along with the rest of the history faction to launch our FinalStrike. Are you going to accompany us?"

"Is there any point?" Dellian asked. He shrugged. "I mean, it sounds like each of you is at least as powerful as Ainsley. What the hell can we contribute? Saints, I don't even get why you even bothered waiting for us."

"In terms of warships and weapons, we believe we have the resources to tackle the Olyix directly, thus completing the goal that Ainsley and Emilja set all those years ago. Once the enclave is breached, we need to locate the *Salvation of Life* and all the other arkships that store human cocoons—a not inconsiderable task, which by necessity will be conducted in an active war zone. Which leaves us with the question of your participation. You have committed yourselves to liberating natural humans from the Olyix, and those in the original *Morgan* squads have combat experience inside an Olyix vessel. We wished to honor your commitment by inviting you to join us. After all you have endured, we sincerely believed you deserved the chance to contribute to FinalStrike should you so choose. And, of course, we desired to meet the genesis human."

Yirella was conscious that everyone was glancing at her again. Her cheeks grew warm from the blood rising in them.

As if sie'd sensed her discomfort, Alexandre said: "Immanueel, thank you for explaining everything to us. We do have a lot to talk about."

"Of course. Please feel free to use this domain to relax in. The facilities are the best we can produce, and, I expect, a welcome change from the life support sections of your ships. If you require anything, simply use your databud to order it."

Everyone rose to their feet like a young Immerle estate class dismissed from a lecture. Chairs scraped along the floor; everyone was speaking at once.

Yirella walked over to Immanueel as they stood up. "We need to talk," she said.

In her mind, Yirella envisaged the two of them strolling along one of the gravel paths that wound between the torus domain's old bald cypress trees, with startled birds flying between the high branches, chirping indignantly at the intrusion. Instead, Immanueel led her to a portal across the floor of the hall.

She walked through into a weird hemispherical chamber twenty meters across, with metallic imperial-purple walls that could have been components of a machine—that, or they were inside a nest burrowed into a scrapheap. The strange geometrical protuberances had deep cracks between them—an effect that arched right overhead to the apex. Light came from a multitude of small sparks that slid slowly along the bottom of the cracks in an eternal progression, going nowhere.

"What is this place?" she asked. The floor was so smooth she was worried she'd skid across it if she started walking. There was no color beneath her feet, as if a hologram were stuck in neutral, giving the impression she was standing on the glass lid of an exceptionally deep well shaft.

"My centrex," Immanueel replied.

"Uh?"

"Home. I wish us to be friends, or at least form a strong alliance. I believe inviting someone to your residence has a strong significance in your culture?"

"It does. Did. An invitation to share was a large social force on old Earth, but those were different times. Post-scarcity changed the social implication. However, the custom remains—which is rather sweet. But you know this. I gave you all the records you access."

"Indeed."

"So if you are corpus, physically distributed across many elements"—she gestured around extravagantly at the machine rilievo that made up the wall—"is this them?"

"Some, yes."

"Okay, I have to ask: Why genesis human?"

"It offends you?"

"No. It spikes my curiosity, although I know Ainsley is responsible. I regard him as somewhat eccentric, especially for an AI—or whatever he actually is. He's more than a genten, but less than human, despite how fast and smart he is."

"He described himself thusly to us, too. Smart, but without imagination. That seems to be an intrinsic part of the human soul, if not its very heart."

"Don't go all romantic on me now. Intuition, imagination, impulse; they're all part of random biochemical interactions in our neural structure."

"Indeed. But never really imitated outside a biological brain. However many random factors an artificial mind can generate, it cannot be truly imaginative. The idea for us came from you, not him, did it not?"

"Yes."

"So simply calling you originator, or first mother, or similar, didn't seem to convey the grandeur of what you did. In a very real sense, Yirella, you created us."

"Okay. I guess I can live with it."

"It pains us that your value is not fully recognized among your peers. You should be leading the fleet."

"Us? Is the whole history faction listening in?"

"Not so much that as they are attuned to my conversation with you."

"But only with a small part of their consciousness, right? An aspect?"

"Correct."

"Do you *really* need us to come with you to the enclave?"

"Our FinalStrike can be conducted without you. Of course it can. However, your squads are ideally suited for the task. They will make a genuine contribution."

"Closure," she said wonderingly. "You're offering us closure."

"Indeed."

"I'm concerned about throwing the squads into combat inside the enclave. No matter how advanced you are, and how many aspects you bring, the Olyix are equally formidable."

"You are correct. Even we cannot offer certainty."

"You must have some idea what's in there. You build your domains on the same principle."

"The principles of quantum temporal mechanics that create and sustain the Olyix enclave, yes, we know them. Its internal nature, no. This is what humans have always dreaded—"

"The *other*."

"Indeed. Olyix thought processes are genuinely alien. We can produce guesses at how the inside of the enclave is structured—logical guesses. But we can't actually know."

"And once you do, you have to immediately formulate a plan."

"It gets worse."

"No plan of battle survives contact with the enemy."

"Exactly. An active combat environment is perpetually fluid. It needs a commander who can make choices. You, perhaps, could contribute." Immanueel bent forward, spine curving so their tail stood up in a fashion that Yirella found oddly disturbing. They leaned against the wall, pressing hard against the asymmetric contours. The shiny purple components began to move around their body, creating an alcove that fitted like a glove. Nozzles clicked smoothly into the sockets down Immanueel's spine, incorporating them into the wall's constitution.

"No thank you," she said. "Tilliana, Ellici, and the other

tactical teams might provide you with an alternative view-point if we come across something unexpected, but I really don't do well in high-stress situations."

"I understand, and even sympathize. We will not call upon you for instant opinions, but we would welcome your participation in overall strategy preparation." With their motionless body embraced by the centrex, Immanueel's voice became omnidirectional.

"Well, at least you didn't say you'd be honored."

"Nonetheless, you know we would be. It would be fitting for you to accompany us; that way you may witness your triumph. You are the architect of the true FinalStrike, Yirella. Forgive the presumption, but given that the enclave is forty thousand light-years away, if you don't come with us, you will never know the outcome. That is not what you want."

"Oh, Saints!"

"May they rest in peace."

"You're right, of course. All the original *Morgan* squads are hungry for payback. After all, it's what us poor binaries were born for. Even I have trouble shaking my conditioning."

"Life is to be rejoiced. The reason for birth, good or bad, should not be part of its consideration."

"You really are different." Yirella started to walk around the centrex, hunting for a pattern in the shapes and flow of lights that made up its curving sides. "But I'm glad you and the other history faction corpus members think we should make the effort to liberate our species."

"Not just ours. If the Neána are correct, the Olyix hold many races hostage for their God."

"Ah. Now there we have the puzzle at the heart of this problem."

"The God at the End of Time."

"Yes." She turned from examining a silhouette that was like an elongated combustion chamber ribbed with slim heat fins. It took a moment for her eyes to find Immanueel's body on the wall. The mottled black-and-blue of their skin was changing color, deepening toward the imperial-purple sported by the rest of the shapes. "Before he left to escort the seedships, I asked Ainsley to make a request of whatever society arose here." She cocked her head to one side, regarding the chameleon body with detached interest. "Did you build it?"

"Yes. We built your tachyon detector."

"And? Does it work?"

"Theoretically, yes."

"Theoretically?"

"It has not detected any tachyons."

"I'm seriously hoping that's because there are none directed at this star."

"So are we. The proof will come, of course, when we deploy it at the reception point."

"Yes."

"I feel obliged to point out there are problems with this path you wish to take."

"Such as?"

"We believe we understand why you want it. We cannot concur your idea will work."

"I heard that message when I was inside Dellian's brain; the Olyix neurovirus implanted it deep and hard. In fact, it was close to being the core of the neurovirus, because it justifies what they have done. *Bring me all of your life, bring me all of your light. Together we will see the universe reborn out of us.* It really did come from somewhere in the future. So if the tachyon beam is traveling back from that point to where and whenever in history the Olyix picked it up, it should also exist in this time. In fact, it should exist in every time before the moment it was sent."

"And as it travels faster than light, it creates a constant shock wave of Cherenkov radiation as it cuts through spacetime."

"Yes," she said. "Which I'm hoping will allow the detector to track where it will come from."

"We understand your reasoning, but first we have to confirm the location of the reception point—information that is presumably available to whatever onemind rules the Olyix enclave. Yet even if we manage to extract that data, we are then left with the task of determining the spatial location of the receiver point when the message first reached it. If the Olyix received it a million years ago, that reception point will have moved a phenomenal distance over the intervening time. Everything in the universe is in motion relative to everything else. This neutron star is currently orbiting at two hundred kilometers per second in its orbit around the galactic core. On top of that you have this galaxy's relative speed to the local supercluster, and then the great attractor mass on top of that—and those are only two factors to be taken into account. Frankly, the farther in the past the message was received, the less chance we have of finding the course of the message in our current time."

"I know," she said. "But with the proper knowledge, it will be possible to intercept it, right?"

"Theoretically what you want to achieve is possible, but there are considerable practical problems."

"Ten thousand years ago the Olyix invaded Earth, and our ancestors set out to find them and bring our people home. And now here we are, you and me, finally getting close to achieving that goal. So surmounting *considerable problems* seems to be what humans are getting really quite good at."

"And what happens—what is your endgame—if you find the message tachyon stream?"

"Go to the source—in this time."

"Again, we anticipated this would be your strategy. You think that by eliminating the source—a planet, a star system, a species—in the present, the message will never be sent from the future. The Olyix will not become religious fanatics, and Earth and all the other worlds will not be invaded."

"Yeah."

"And what of paradox?"

"That level of quantum temporal cosmology is beyond me," Yirella admitted. "All I can focus on is that Saints-damned tachyon message that is changing the past—our present—by setting the Olyix crusade loose on the galaxy. Therefore if we can eliminate, here in our present, whatever civilization, species, or young god that sends it, then it will not be sent."

"Your logic is impeccable. But what about causality? Everything we know about causality dictates that time travel should not be possible."

"You are speaking of linear time."

"Of course. Our perceptions only enable us to see time as linear. But the very nature of linear time implies that—from an external observer viewpoint—the history of the entire universe from creation to heat death exists in a static form, allowing us—consciousness—to perceive time moving in only one direction. Ergo, the universe's entirety—both space and time—was created as a complete whole. Which argues that change is not possible."

"Except that our perceptions must be wrong, because time travel *has* occurred," she countered. "The God at the End of Time sent a message from the future. And you have to concede that this timeline must be different from the one that existed before the message changed the behavior of the Olyix."

"Ah. Well, the very concept of timelines implies a multiverse. One theory—and one that we corpus favor—has it that instituting a causality violation such as time travel is an anomaly that *creates* a new universe. Meaning if you go back in time and kill your grandfather, that death happens in a new universe—one where your future self does not yet exist and now never will. A universe in which you are now an interloper—but also one in which you will never have a double. However, if you were able to somehow travel back to your original universe, your grandfather would still be alive there."

Yirella pursed her lips. "Time travelers are Gods? Interesting."

"More like the builders of time machines are Gods. On every occasion the time machine is used—for every tachyon message that is sent through time, or every time someone goes back to kill their grandfather or a tyrant—that act creates a new copy of the universe that branches off from the original."

"Meaning every alternate universe is the product of a time machine. But they're still a perfect copy of the 'original' universe up until that point just before the split?"

"Yes."

"So the tachyon message the Olyix detected didn't actually come from this universe?"

"In the anomaly-creation theory, yes."

"So the God at the End of Time exists only in certain universes, whose history played out in specific ways?"

"Possibly. But if we take as our assumption that the message was sent from the time of the heat death of the original universe—when the God perceived a condition it needed to address—then this makes our present the desired outcome of this new reality."

"Meaning that the God at the End of Time likewise exists—or will come to exist—in this reality, because this is its desired outcome. So the physical conditions for the God at the End of Time to come into existence are present in this universe, right here, right now. Its birth star is real. If we destroy the place it comes from here in the present, then it will never be born, and won't send a message—which creates another copy universe. The cycle ends, and the paradox loop is broken."

"That is our reasoning, which is why we built the detector for you. We do not necessarily think your strategy will work, but we cannot ignore the possibility that it might."

"Thank you. I guess that makes the whole universe Schrödinger's cat. We don't know the outcome until we open the box, and even then we won't know because opening the box from the inside means we cease to be the observer."

"Correct. Clearly some form of time travel or manipulation is possible; the message proves that. But have you considered the implication of classic temporal theory being correct? That there is only one universe and it is possible to alter the timeline? If so, there will be a considerable price for your strategy of resetting the timeline."

"Yes. I cease to exist. As do you, and everyone else alive here and now. In a multiverse, there will still be some universe in which we all exist, but if not, generations blink out as if they never existed."

"Not quite."

Yirella's eyes narrowed as she studied the imprecise profile of Immanueel's body, which was almost indistinguishable from any other section of wall now. "What do you mean?" she asked.

"To negate the evolution of the God at the End of Time will mean the message will never be sent, and subsequently the Olyix will not commence their abominable crusade. They will not invade Earth. The history of the last ten thousand years will be very different."

"Yes, it'll save us from this whole disaster. That's the whole point. And if I can't do that—if your time-travel-is-creationism theory is right—it'll mean ending the cycle of new universes created by the God's tachyon message, in which every one contains the same Olyix threat. That alone makes the effort worthwhile."

"But my dear genesis human, although the Olyix invasion was an unmitigated disaster for us here and now, the vast majority of Earth's population is still alive in cocoon form, and our FinalStrike mission will hopefully result in us reinstating them in their bodies. Not only that, but with the technology available now, a high percentage of them will never have to endure the low socioeconomic index lives they were living up to the point of the invasion. Records indicate that out of the nine billion living on Earth at the time the *Salvation of Life* arrived, four billion were significantly disadvantaged by the Universal culture's economic structure that was prominent in that era. They would never have risen out of that. Now, our initiators and gentens can provide a post-scarcity environment for everyone, and medical science can prolong the life of baseline human bodies indefinitely, as well as opening the opportunity to elaborate up to corpus level."

"Are you seriously suggesting to me that the Olyix invasion was a good thing for us?"

"It depends on your perspective. For those who fled Earth and the settled worlds in their exodus habitats, it was a catastrophic time when their lives were disrupted forever. Subsequently they spent the rest of their days fleeing in dread across the galaxy—an era of such profound experience that it has shaped the psychology of every generation world since, producing a tainted legacy, with yourself and the squads as the ultimate outcome. But now the era of the exodus flights is over, one way or another. Some of the exodus, whom we should honor for their incredible commitment, strove to provide future generations with a chance at freedom. Some—billions more—fell to subsequent Olyix capture along the expansion wavefront. Were you to consider this whole epoch from the perspective of a low-income, low-satisfaction Earth resident in 2204, then if FinalStrike is ultimately successful, their view would be very different from yours. Imagine: There was a frightening disconnect in their life, and then they wake up thousands of years later in what equates to a billionaire's paradise where they can do or be anything. Now ask yourself: Does the human race have a net gain from you changing the timeline to one where the Olyix invasion does not happen? And in doing so, becoming unborn yourself, along with everybody born from the day the *Salvation of Life* arrived at Sol onward? Others will be born instead, of course, but all those lives will not only no longer exist, they never will have existed."

"Fuck the Saints," Yirella exclaimed.

"That is a true paradox," Immanueel said in a sympathetic voice.

"But you think causality precludes a classic-theory reset of the timeline, and that by eliminating the possibility of the God at the End of Time, all I'll be doing is preventing this current cycle from repeating?"

"It is a complete unknown. And will probably remain so. The observer—you—cannot observe what will happen to themselves within a paradox. And all time travel is a paradox of one kind or another."

"I really need to think about this."

"Of course. And there is a third option. Some of our more—shall we say—unconventional theorists posit that temporal loops can only be triggered by an extrinsic factor."

"Extrinsic?"

"The trigger originates from *outside* this universe."

"You mean, when a time machine creates a new branch?"

"No. Completely outside space-time, no matter if our existence is within a universe or multiverse."

"Fuck the Saints!"

"It is a theory that permits any and every causality violation you may want to consider."

"Are you seriously saying the God at the End of Time doesn't come from this reality?"

"It is a theory—unprovable until tested. If correct, it

would mean destroying the message's origin world in the present is impossible, for that origin world is not even a part of our reality."

"So what do I do?" Yirella asked, despairing.

"Nothing. If it is an extrinsic factor, nothing we do will have any effect. If we live in a multiverse where any attempt to modify our timeline simply creates a new different timeline, nothing in our past will change. And if we do live in a pre-ordained simultaneous totality-existence universe, your decision, whatever it is, will make no difference, because it has already been made and taken effect; there is no such thing as change. In each case, all you can do is simply enjoy the life you currently experience."

"Saints, I'm not enjoying this experience, trust me."

"Yes. And yet from what Ainsley has told us, and what I myself have observed, you have and enjoy Dellian, do you not?"

She didn't trust herself to answer. Instead she nodded ruefully. "Some kind of time travel is possible. The message proves that, right? I don't think worrying about the possibility of resetting myself out of existence is a reason for inaction. After all, I have lived here and now; that cannot be taken away. It's only the universe that will forget me, not me myself. So if I consider the enormity of what's in play . . . I think that the God's decision to send the message to the Olyix was the original decision, and our actions are determined by it. In that I have no choice. Therefore—" She took a breath. "I want us to bring the tachyon detector to the enclave. If we can work out where the Olyix were when the message was received, that's when we make the ultimate decision: Do we go after the God at the End of Time?"

"Your first decision—and the one we were fully expecting you to make. Very well, genesis human, we will bring the tachyon detector with us."

THE *AVENGING HERETIC*

YEAR FOUR

When he thought back to what the *Avenging Heretic*'s bridge used to be like during S-Day, all Alik could remember was basically a blank room with a big holographic projection in the middle. Now, it was the kind of chamber that belonged in a drama series—which he guessed was where a lot of it had been bootlegged from. The chief suspect was Callum, with Kandara as his accomplice—though she just laughed when he asked her. The alterations had been slow to materialize. One day the shape of the chairs had changed. They were bigger and bulkier, something that belonged in early-twenty-first-century war vehicles, but they were comfier, so no one said anything. Consoles increased in increments throughout the second year, their surfaces becoming army-green metal, acquiring black trim, which then developed glowing blue edging as the overall light was reduced. Control functions became more intuitive. The tactical display graphics grew into hemispherical bubbles around everyone's head, with added neon-ziz. Chrome toggle switches popped up like cautious mushrooms—a few at first, then they were complemented by U-shaped guards, and eventually lined up in long rows. The chairs expanded again, with added protection, and straps, and crash webs. Red strobes and battle-station Klaxons protruded from the ceiling.

"For fuck's sake, people!" Alik bellowed the first time Jessika tested them. His virtual avatar ears were ringing, while he blinked simulated blotches from his vision. "This is turning into a gamer fetish bunker. We're neurovirtual in here."

"Ambiance helps instill the right attitude," Yuri said.

Alik's teeth ground together at the mockery in that voice.

"Yeah," Kandara chipped in. "Live the experience, man."

He glowered at her and saw Callum trying to suppress laughter. Despite being on a ship with people who could be *really fucking annoying* when they wanted to be, he did admit the new formation was a considerable improvement. It made it somehow easier for his mind to mesh with the *Avenging Heretic*'s network. The simulation was, after all, window dressing, but it was customized to accelerate response time during the drills. So he supposed—grudgingly— that it did generate the right level of alert tension. Their mission was tactical at heart; they needed clear commands and unrestricted target and threat intelligence. But still, *edging that glowed . . .*

In addition to all the precise information coming at him through the console displays, Alik had the *Salvation* onemind's more prosaic thoughts at the back of his mind. He could understand them better now; years of the spectral presence lurking like a malign secondary subconscious every time he opened the neural interface had given him the practice to focus on individual routines. That and Jessika's invaluable intuition meant it was easier for him to sort through the cascade of alien impulses, teasing out the relevant aspects without the onemind realizing.

Right now he was experiencing something that the onemind had never projected before: eagerness. The end of the wormhole was close. They would arrive at the enclave, where it would be welcomed and become accepted. *That's wrong*, he thought. *Embraced? Supported? Favored?* The sentiment didn't really have a human equivalent.

"I don't get it," Alik said. "What kind of reception is it expecting?" He looked over at Jessika, whose chair's puffy safety cushioning had practically absorbed her, leaving only her head and arms visible.

"It's content about becoming established within the enclave. Its purpose will have been achieved; it has returned with over a billion people to deliver to the God at the End of Time. So now it's going into—I think—a storage orbit or resting place of some kind inside the enclave, along with all the other arkships that have returned in success. It can take up its rightful place."

"It thinks this is a success?" Alik asked. "It got its ass kicked on S-Day."

"Depends on perspective," Callum said. "Earth is uninhabitable now. There'll be tens of millions evacuated, which is basically a token when you consider the global population is still probably around the six billion mark. That means the next wave of Olyix will scoop up everyone left. They won, the bastards. This round. Because us being here is a success, as well, isn't it?"

"Jez-us, you are getting fucking bleak, man."

"I felt it, too," Yuri said. "*Salvation* is not . . . happy, exactly, but content. Its active part in the Olyix crusade is over, and it's anticipating the next phase of its existence."

"Until our descendants come knocking." Kandara smirked from behind a display that was mostly sculpted in blood-red graphics.

"See," Callum said, grinning. "Optimism."

"Yeah, right," Alik muttered.

"I wonder how many arkships are inside the enclave," Callum mused. "How many other species."

"We'll know soon enough," Jessika said. "It's going to be interesting. I don't know how long the Olyix crusade has been going. We weren't told."

"Why the hell did your abode cluster think that's classified?" Kandara asked.

"I don't know. My best guess would be that information will expose something about the Neána that increases their vulnerability to the Olyix."

"How long they've been around, that they were close enough to the Olyix to observe them?"

Jessika's hands rose through her display icons in an elaborate shrug.

"Is it even worth guessing how many species they've done this to?" Callum asked.

"Utterly pointless," Jessika said. "We have no idea of how many sentient species rise up to a technological level in the galaxy in—say—a five-thousand-year period."

"And how many fall of their own accord," Yuri said.

"And those that are sentient but don't go along the technology route," Callum added.

"Jez-us, can we focus on some positives here, people?" Alik said. "Please. This day deserves that, at least." He focused his attention on the sensor data.

As always, the sensor clusters that their creeperdrones had installed around the hangar entrance showed nothing. Alik couldn't stand looking at the non-space of the wormhole fabric. So for actual flight progress, he had to rely on the onemind's strange perception of the wormhole—a dull gray tunnel whose wavering walls were threaded with golden strands. Now at some implausible distance ahead, those glowing lines had knotted together, creating a dawn light glow.

The *Salvation of Life* was fixated on the end of the wormhole.

"Not long," Jessika said. "Stand by."

Alik wasn't sure what he was expecting. After all, they'd exited a wormhole before, back when they reached the Olyix sensor station. He didn't remember the onemind being tense about that.

He waited in silence as the arkship continued its stoic flight through nothingness. He was having trouble accepting that they were finally arriving at the enclave. Four years of flight—plenty of which had been spent in suspension—should have prepared him. Although, to be honest, he hadn't really expected to get this far.

The end of the wormhole flight, when it came, was an instantaneous transition. Alik's visual display flipped from the emptiness he was trying to ignore to images of normal space. The impact was bewildering. At first, half of space seemed to be a glaring white nebula.

Data blossomed across the basic displays surrounding his seat like leaves surging into life along a tree's branches after a long winter. The information deluge was as bad as the visual one. He ignored the factual summary the ship's genten was assembling as a smile of wonder grew across his face. His eyes were slowly making sense of the sensor feed, revealing a large star in the foreground. Behind it, the galactic core was a vast jewel blazing white-gold across space. He couldn't believe that many stars actually existed, never mind in a single congregation. "Jez-us wept. Where the fuck are we?"

"A long, long way from home," Yuri said quietly.

Despite the grandeur of the galactic core, Alik was startled by the star they had arrived at. Tables of numbers multiplying around him confirmed how exceptional it was. "That is one big-ass star," he said.

"Yes," Jessika agreed. "About twice the size of Sirius. The sensors haven't found any planets—not on this side, anyway."

"Not even a gas giant?" Alik asked, running through the information.

"No. But that ring is something else," she said.

Alik focused on the thin band orbiting one point five AUs out from the star. Unlike the usual mucky gray of asteroidal regolith, this ring gleamed with refracted light from the brilliant star, as if quartz dust had settled like frost to coat every particle.

"The particle density is crazy," Callum said. "That can't be natural."

"It's definitely not an accretion disk," Jessika said. "So I guess we know what happened to the planets."

"Why the hell would you *do* that?" Yuri asked.

"Because you can?" she replied.

"No," Callum said. "Check out those knots in the ring. They're alive with activity."

Alik directed his sensor feed to expand the area Callum had mentioned. The resolution wasn't great—there was only so much you could do with sensor clumps the size of a pinhead—but each of the knot particles was slowly rotating around a vast artifact in a slow-motion hurricane whorl. "Olyix industrial stations?" he wondered out loud. The main bulk of the things were spherical, with dozens of tapering spires radiating out. On the surface below them, a web of precise lines of purple and amber light cast multicolored shadows up on the summits. Spaceships—a lot bigger than the Deliverance ships—were holding formation nearby. As he watched, another ship rose up from the station to join them.

Alik shifted focus to the next knot, where a similar station was surrounded by a flotilla of Deliverance ships. As he pulled the focus back, he could see a series of similar knots stretching right around the ring; there must have been thousands of them. *Which means tens of thousands of spaceships—more like hundreds of thousands. Jez-us.* One of the stations farther along seemed to be clamped to a big rock particle, shaping it into a cylinder. *An arkship! So that's why* Salvation *has caves like you get on a planet: It used to be a part of a solid world.*

"They must have broken the planets down into digestible chunks," Jessika said. "Now they have the entire mass of the solar system as raw material to manufacture warships and arkships."

"Found the radio telescopes," Kandara announced.

Alik switched to the zone her icon was indicating. Three AUs outside the ring, glowing bright in the glaring starlight, were pentagonal dodecahedrons, big brothers to the ones they'd seen orbiting the star of the Olyix sensor outpost. If their positioning was constant all the way around the star, there would be a hundred fifteen of them. "That's good. We can use them to help boost the signal from our transmitters," he said. "We just need the ones aligned on the section of space where Sol is."

"The genten's nearly finished star mapping," Jessika told him. "But judging from the apparent size of the core, we're about fifty thousand light-years from home."

The number didn't really resonate with Alik. At some point in the last four years, he'd resigned himself that he'd never return to Earth. In reality, he probably wouldn't even last more than a few hours after they reached the enclave star system. Setting up their fallback refuge had driven that point home. Even so—fifty thousand light-years!

"How the hell is any human armada ever going to get

here?" he asked. "If they pick up our Signal, which is going to be unlikely verging on fucking never, they'll have to fly *fifty thousand light-years*. Which—and correct me if I've screwed up the math—will take them *fifty thousand years*."

"For a neutral observer it'll take that long," Callum said. "But relativistic travel will make it a lot shorter for anyone on board the armada ships."

"Yeah? Well, we're going to be those neutral observers, so we're looking at a hundred and twenty thousand years before anyone turns up. Goddamn! This is insane!"

"Are you saying we don't send the Signal?" Yuri asked.

"I don't fucking know. This whole mission was one giant mistake."

"We send the Signal," Kandara said. "The *Avenging Heretic* is going to get ordered to fly to some kind of dock for repair, or maybe they'll want to scrap it and recycle the mass."

"Oh, yeah, sure," Alik sneered. "The Olyix are known the galaxy over for their environmental credentials. Recycling, my ass."

"It doesn't matter," she said with icy patience. "The *Avenging Heretic* will leave this hangar soon. That's why we put the refuge together. One way or another, the Olyix will know we are here. So we send the Signal, and if it isn't humans who detect it, maybe someone will. The Neána perhaps. Someone who can do something other than run and hide. We will have accomplished *something*. I did not come all this way just to walk up to the onemind and surrender like a fucking coward."

"I'm not talking about surrendering," Alik said angrily.

"Then why don't you tell us exactly what the hell you do want to do?" Yuri asked.

"I don't know, man. Send the Signal, I guess. It's just . . . This place. They've broken up planets so they can use them! I feel so Goddamn small. And don't any of you try telling me you don't feel that, either."

"I'm with Alik," Jessika said. "I've just found the power ring. Check out the star's equator."

Surprise at having her agree with him battled with Alik's dismay. "They built one for *this* star? The circumference is over thirteen million kilometers!" But the display showed him she was telling the truth. A dark band was spinning above the corona, whipping up million-kilometer twisters of incandescent plasma that spun off huge, arching prominences.

"It would have to be," Callum said. "I've been checking the number of wormhole termini in this orbit. Over a thousand so far. They are going to need the mother lode of energy to sustain them."

The sensor clusters were showing faint purple glimmers following their own orbit ten million kilometers outside the ring. Some were brighter than others; those were open, with ships moving in and out of them.

"Fucking hell," Yuri said. "Do all of them lead to sensor stations?"

"I hope so, because as sure as it rains in Glasgow, I don't want there to be other enclaves."

"Son of a bitch, what have we walked into?" Alik murmured.

"Exactly what we knew would be here," Kandara said. "Come on, get a grip."

He wanted to scowl at her, but she was right, of course. That didn't help, either.

"Okay," Callum said. "So we can see the wormholes. Where's the gateway into the enclave?"

Alik checked the displays, seeing the indigo shimmer of the wormhole terminus shrinking behind the *Salvation of Life*. A stream of big pyramidal ships was flowing in a wide spiral around the arkship. The onemind was greeting them all, returning to that strange state of satisfaction it had displayed when they arrived at the sensor station. In return, the ships were sending their welcome and congratulations that mingled with a thirst for information. The response to their curiosity was a flood of memories so vast that Alik couldn't begin to absorb it. Instead he caught flashes of Earth and humans and city shields glowing like half-buried suns and MHD asteroids shattering in nuclear fire, the gargantuan explosions leveling Theophilus crater.

"Motherfuckers," Alik said, his mood darkening.

"The gateway has to be different, doesn't it?" Kandara

said. "The wormholes lead away from here. We want something that goes . . . inside space?"

"I'm going to see if I can find the location in the onemind's thoughts," Jessika said. "Hang on."

Alik watched the flock of pyramid ships that had greeted them shoot away skittishly. Despite their rigid geometry, there was something unnerving about such avian behavior, as if they weren't quite in control of their actions and were simply letting instinct guide them. Then he saw why they were departing. A whole flotilla of Resolution ships was approaching. Their size should have made them stately, moving with a ponderous surety, but instead they were fast and agile, an effortless show of power and precision that was intimidating all by itself. They twisted around the *Salvation of Life*—a salute to all it had achieved—then plunged on past, heading toward the wormhole's intense Cherenkov gleam.

"They're heading for Sol, aren't they?" Kandara said.

"Yes," Yuri agreed.

"It will take them a while, though," Alik said. "Decades, you said."

"Yeah," Kandara agreed reluctantly. "So people will have some time to get ready. Exodus habitats will be built. They've probably already launched a dozen more by now."

"And in a hundred and twenty thousand years, they'll be here to liberate us."

Kandara gave him the finger, backed up by an exasperated glare. He knew he'd be on the receiving end of more grief when they came off duty.

"I've found the gateway," Jessika announced. "It's a million kilometers inside the ring, about one and a quarter AUs from us."

Alik watched the display as the sensors zoomed in on the area of space she'd designated. In the back of his head, he could feel the onemind determining the course it had to take to reach the gateway, the vectors it needed to fly. It was preparing to increase power from the main generators and feed it into the gravitonic drive, which had been idle while they were inside the wormhole.

There were other thoughts he caught, too. A small subsection of the onemind started to orchestrate the ships it was carrying, designating their destination. None of them would be required once they were through the gateway and began the long hiatus until they arrived at the era of the God at the End of Time. Damage assessments were being reviewed, discovering if the ships had deteriorated further during the voyage home. Those that could no longer fly would be removed, their oneminds transferred into the empty bioneural core of new ships, while the ships themselves would be released into the ring, where they would vacuum ablate to dust and gas over the next million years—dust that would ultimately merge with other particles that would go on to feed the industrial constructors.

Okay, now that's what I call sustainable recycling, Alik thought in dark amusement. A kind of long-term planning that put the exodus habitats to shame.

"We need to deploy the Signal transmitters," Yuri said. "If the ships in this hangar start to wake up, they might notice our activity. And from what I can understand out of the one-mind's thoughts, we haven't got long now."

Jessika increased the level of distortion infecting the neural strata that covered the hangar as much as she dared to shield their exit from the *Avenging Heretic*. Alik and Callum steered more than a dozen creeperdrone spiders along the passageways and corridors leading to their refuge cave, alert for any quint or larger creatures who might be coming their way. With a perimeter watch established, they got ready to leave.

The bridge simulation faded from Alik's mind, and he opened his eyes to see the others sitting around the table in the main life support section. For some reason, they'd seated themselves in the same order they always used on the bridge. When he glanced around the cramped compartment with its little nests of dirt in acute corners and long-dried smears of food trodden into the floor, he was surprised to find how he'd grown accustomed to having just a few square meters of personal space.

"Okay then," Yuri said dispassionately. "Let's go."

The environment suit the initiator had extruded was similar to the kind of gear Alik had worn on tactical raids back in his early days with the Bureau—a one-piece made from a gray fabric that had a weird blurred sheen, very hard for an eye to focus on. Presumably it would be equally difficult for the optically sensitive cells on the biological lattice of pipe trunks and leaves stretched across the hangar. The helmet was a lot more than the old tactical team gas masks, too. This was a simple hemisphere, with the same gray covering and no visor, so the optical fuzz was complete. He put it on, locking the collar, and his tarsus lens fed him the image from the helmet cameras, providing him with a sharp resolution and excellent zoom function. It had air recycler filters built in, so there was no breath exhaled for an infrared giveaway. Not quite a full space suit, but if they did suffer a depressurization event, it could protect them from the vacuum while they got to safety.

The one thing it lacked was armor reinforcement. That made him uneasy at some deep level; his instinct was to fight back if they were cornered by the Olyix. Intellectually, he agreed with Yuri that a firefight would accomplish nothing, but that didn't make it easy.

As he pulled the suit's front seal up, he saw Kandara—her back to Yuri—shoving a bulky pistol into her waistband before closing her suit up. They exchanged a knowing glance, smirking like kids putting one over on their parents.

The *Avenging Heretic*'s hatch opened. Alik saw Jessika pause for a second on the rim of the hatch before she sealed her helmet and stepped down onto the hangar floor. Yuri followed, carrying the small biological life support module that contained the nodule of Olyix neural cells entangled with the *Salvation of Life*'s onemind. Kandara stepped down next. Alik gestured to Callum, then took a quick look back with doubts filling his mind—too late, of course. They were committed now.

The medical display splashing onto his tarsus lens showed his heart rate climbing. He dismissed it and followed Callum across the rocky floor, unable to shake the sensation of vulnerability. The bulk of the *Avenging Heretic* blocked them from the other damaged ships lined up in the hangar, and he could see through the various feeds from outlying creeperdrones and sensor clumps that there were no quint anywhere near. Still, his anxiety didn't start to diminish until several minutes later when they reached the fissure in the wall that led to the cavern.

Somehow he'd misjudged the size of the fissure off the main passageway; the thick pipe trunks were taking up more space than he'd thought. Squeezing past them was something of a contortion act. *Which means getting out fast just ain't going to happen.*

Thankfully, the cavern past the egg tanks of fluid did match expectations—a dark, irregular space that was another couple of degrees colder than the passage. Alik lifted off his helmet and straight away saw his breath misting in the arid air. For the first time he breathed in the arkship's raw atmosphere, wrinkling his nose up at the sensation. It was surprisingly dry for something produced by biological systems, although he could smell mild, exotic scents that confirmed its alien origin. It was also several degrees cooler than the air in the *Avenging Heretic*.

Without really knowing why, he was ridiculously relieved by the pile of their equipment waiting on the uneven rock floor. Ten of the fake spider creeperdrones were standing beside it, along with a couple of the larger service creatures they'd used to deliver all their gear.

They took off their suits and pulled on thick tunics against the chill. Alik made a mental note to produce a pair of gloves in one of the three small initiators they'd brought to the cave.

"Are we ready?" Yuri asked. "Okay then, let's go."

Alik settled himself as comfortably as possible on one of the rock ledges and let his interface envelop his senses with the simulation. Once more, he was back on the fanciful bridge and watching Jessika activate the *Avenging Heretic*'s drive systems. The central display showed them the hangar with the array of damaged transport ships parked around them. A couple of larger Olyix maintenance creatures were clinging upside down from a thick pipe trunk on the ceiling, mandibles munching away at dead fronds. In the back of his mind, the *Salvation* onemind was a burble of impulses, like a distant waterfall—there, but without being directly present.

The *Avenging Heretic* lifted off the floor and swung around slowly, its nose a compass needle searching out the hangar entrance. There was nothing in the onemind's flow of thoughts; the hangar's perception simply didn't register the movement.

"Do you think we might just actually get away with this?" Callum asked.

Alik had to bark a laugh at the almost childlike optimism. "Not a fucking chance, my friend."

"The perception impediment in the hangar's neuralstrata is holding up fine," Jessika said. "The onemind doesn't know we're moving. The other ships do, but it's not their concern. Ships are semi-independent. I doubt they even have the mental syntax for rogue behavior."

"Maybe we should have stayed on board," Alik muttered.

The *Avenging Heretic* began to move forward—at walking pace at first, then slowly increasing speed. Alik was mesmerized by the hangar entrance as the sublime light of the galactic core shone in through the tunnel, basting the rock with a rich solstice glow.

"Ready to launch the Signal transmitters," Kandara announced.

"As soon as we're outside," Jessika replied. "I'm hoping there'll be a moment when we're clear of the rim and before *Salvation* notices we're in flight."

The *Avenging Heretic*'s nose pushed at the invisible pressure membrane over the entrance, and Alik could have sworn he felt the artificially combined air molecules slithering over the skin of his own torso like the stroke of an oily feather as the ship passed through. Then they were in space, with the massive rock wall of the arkship behind them.

"Now!" Jessika ordered.

The Signal transmitter vehicles were the best stealth technology Kruse Station could devise, combining human and Neána technology. The development team had utilized the concept employed by the Neána insertion ship to produce spheres four meters in diameter with a matte black body that was totally light absorbent. Internal heat sinks meant they maintained an ambient thermal profile, and their systems were shielded to prevent any electromagnetic emission. Instead of a gravitonic drive, they had an external layer of active molecular blocks, which meant the entire fuselage was a rocket motor with an exhaust of cold neutral atoms, which left only the faintest of traces. In theory, it should be no different from a gust of solar wind particles.

Alik caught a brief glimpse of the five covert transmitters as they left their silos—and that was only because the ship's sensors tracked their black outlines against the rock as they dropped away. His display came alive with the feed from the transmitter he was remote piloting. He triggered its surface blocks, propelling it farther away from the arkship, quickly building distance and velocity. Then he cut the drive, allowing it to coast along inertly. The transmitter's own sensors showed him the *Salvation of Life* receding quickly, its surface gleaming in the vivid silver light that ruled the star system.

"Explanation of your flight required."

Alik's limbs twitched with instinctive guilt as the *Salvation of Life*'s onemind queried the *Avenging Heretic*. Its thought came directly through the nodule of entangled cells. For now it was just a secondary level of consciousness; the arkship's main routines weren't even aware of the departure.

"On course for designated repair station," Jessika replied, along with an identification code of a station in the ring that she'd picked up as the assessment of each damaged ship was being conducted.

"You did not receive that designation."

Jessika increased the thrust of the *Avenging Heretic*'s gravitonic drive, allowing it to accelerate away at eight gees. The ship settled on a vector that aligned on the gateway. "Error," she answered. "Designation received and confirmed. En route."

"Incorrect. That course is not authorized. You are deviating. Return."

Alik could feel the timbre of the *Salvation*'s thoughts change as higher levels of its consciousness began to focus on the errant cargo ship.

"It's waking up to us," Yuri said.

Alik thought he sounded amused, or maybe excited.

"Following original designated instruction," Jessika insisted.

There was a pause for several seconds, then: "What are you?"

It was the *Salvation of Life*'s primary consciousness asking the question. Alik could feel the change, the enormous presence stacked up behind the query. Strange whispers began to slither out of its awareness, probing into the nodule . . . but Jessika blocked them easily.

"Neána," the *Salvation of Life* declared.

"Close, but you don't get to ride the unicorn," she retorted.

Watching through the Signal transmitter's sensors, Alik saw a dozen Deliverance ships abruptly break away from their escort formation around the arkship and accelerate hard in pursuit of the *Avenging Heretic*.

"You are one of the human constructs sent to Sol by an abode cluster," the *Salvation of Life* pronounced. "Why are you here?"

"For fuck's sake," Yuri told it. "How dumb are you? In what universe do you think *anyone* is going to answer that?"

"A human. I feel your thoughts, the uncertainty behind your bravado. Your instinct is right; the Neána have lied to you. We are your friends; all we want is to bring you to the greatest gift life can achieve. You will know the God at the End of Time. We will carry you to that glory."

"We've died in our millions fighting against our own Gods throughout history, and they don't even exist. What the fuck do you think we'll do to your God if we ever come face-to-face with it?"

"I weep at your bewitchment by such dishonesty."

"They're closing," Alik warned. The Deliverance ships were accelerating at fifteen gees, eating up the distance between them and the *Avenging Heretic*.

"My turn," Kandara said gleefully.

The *Avenging Heretic* released a cluster of Calmines from their silos. They used the same principle as Calmissiles: a fuselage that was ninety percent portal, but without having a spatial entanglement to a portal inside a star's corona, they didn't have a plasma drive, denying them hypervelocity maneuvering ability. Instead, they were equipped with a small active molecule section protruding from the portal fuselage. That provided sufficient thrust to fly them into the course of the Deliverance ships.

Kandara didn't have quite enough time to spread the Calmines wide enough. Only seven of the pursuing Deliverance ships struck them. Not that there was anything to strike. The holes in space sliced clean through the Deliverance ships in milliseconds. Seven violent explosions flared behind the *Avenging Heretic*.

Kandara's fist punched the air.

"Oops," Yuri mocked. "I thought you'd cleared all the debris out of this star system."

"You achieve nothing by this," the *Salvation of Life* said.

More Deliverance ships abandoned their escort duty around the *Salvation of Life* to chase after the *Avenging Heretic*.

Alik switched on the molecular block drive of his Signal transmitter, as did the other four. Undetected, the dark spheres began to fly farther away from the arkship, aligning themselves on the vast radio telescopes orbiting far outside the ring.

More Calmines dropped out of their silos. This time they only intersected one Deliverance ship.

"Shit. Sorry," Kandara grunted. "Missed."

"Come to us," the *Salvation of Life* urged. "We understand your panic and confusion. Let us welcome you into our home."

"Amp it up, Yuri," Callum said in an uncharacteristic snarl.

"We will never surrender," Yuri said. "Know this: We will have our vengeance. If not today, then your reckoning will come before the heat death of the universe. Life on every planet will combine to thwart the evil that you bring. Your God will die amid pain and suffering as it sees you fall in flames."

"Not bad," Kandara admitted. "A bit Old Testament, but . . ."

Yuri flashed her a grin and shrugged.

Nine Deliverance ships were still in pursuit of the *Aveng-*

ing Heretic. One fired an energy beam. The power was reduced from the colossal output it was capable of—intended to damage, to weaken.

The *Avenging Heretic* exploded in fury as Jessika released the magnetic confinement holding half a kilogram of antimatter. The radiation flash overwhelmed the fuselage of three Deliverance ships, which ruptured in a near synchronous cascade of ultraviolence. Two more tumbled away, ruined. Dead.

The brutal plasmasphere expanded, momentarily rivaling the galactic core's luminosity. Then it began to fade.

Alik watched it dissipate in silence, awed and disturbed by its force. Yet it was nothing compared to the power of the Olyix ships.

"Sweet enough, as funeral pyres go," Kandara said. "I couldn't wish for a better one."

"Jessika?" Yuri asked.

"I've switched the cell nodule's entanglement to purely passive. We'll still be able to perceive the onemind's thoughts, but that's all. There'll be no more loading our own quiet queries into the neuralstrata."

When Alik reached for the onemind's persistent background stream of thoughts, he found them muted. It didn't entirely displease him; having the massive alien's deliberations and memories weaving through his own brain had always left him on edge. Now all he could feel was the *Salvation of Life* directing a scan of the cooling ion cloud that was the remnants of the *Avenging Heretic*, its own puzzlement at how they had eluded it for so long, self-examination of its thought routines. A flicker of annoyance as it purged Jessika's neurovirus contamination from itself, restoring full perception to the hangar.

"Are we clear?" Callum asked nervously.

"I think so," Jessika said. "I can't sense much suspicion in its thoughts. Of course, it'll have analyzed the neurovirus and formatted countermeasures, so we'll never be able to use it again."

"Doesn't matter," Yuri said. "Once we trigger the Signal transmitters, our mission is over."

"You mean: successful," Kandara said.

"Yeah. Then we just have to keep our heads down and wait."

Alik let the bridge simulation dissolve and sat up. The cavern was a bleak contrast to the clean elegance of the bridge; even the *Avenging Heretic*'s too-small cabin was preferable. He hadn't been anywhere near a non-urban environment for decades, not since his last mandatory Bureau survival training course in Alaska's Denali Park—an area seemingly immune from the anthrochange warmth that gripped the rest of Earth. A week shivering in a sleeping bag at night, cooking on a thermal block that either burnt the food or left it raw, making snares that caught nothing, no showers, waterproofs that weren't, colleagues trying to be jolly, which made him want to punch them, and thick snow covering everything. Snow, he'd discovered, was not the white Christmas ideal everyone loved; it didn't make the excursion a fun-laden ski break. Snow halfway up a steep mountain was *cold*. It oozed through clothing, it made walking difficult, it hid treacherous ground that could twist ankles and break legs. It interred any dead branches that might have been used for a fire. Snow was shit. Now here he was, camping in a cave for what could be years; with a closed-loop waste recycling/food printing system that he *really* didn't want to think about. But at least there was no snow.

He walked over to the stack of equipment and switched on the food printer. "Who wants breakfast?"

They took it in turns to monitor the signal transmitters as they flew toward their allocated radio telescopes. Each of the targets had been chosen because they had a dish that was aligned on the section of space where Sol was located. Positioned correctly, the vessels could use a dish to focus their broadcast back toward Sol—though by the time it had traveled fifty thousand light-years, it was doubtful it would have the strength to be detected. Interstellar gas and the inverse square law would be severe debilitating factors.

Whether anyone would ever detect it became their main talking point. Alik shouldered the monotony of such a circular argument of unknowns as inevitable. He treated it like a stakeout. You didn't know the outcome, nor even when it would come, so you just waited patiently and tolerated your partner's bullshit. That was provided by Callum, who'd decided their mission was now pointless.

"Fifty thousand light-years," he complained. "We expected it to be two, maybe three thousand at the most. We're past the bloody galactic core here. We can't even *see* Sol."

"The longer it takes, the more powerful humans will become," Kandara said. "Think how much progress we made in the last five hundred years. And we'll have numbers on our side. The exodus habitats will expand exponentially."

"If they've got any sense, they'll head out in the opposite direction. I would."

"Great idea." Yuri laughed. "And how do they know what the opposite direction is?"

Callum gave him a glum look.

"We're committed," Jessika said. "All we can do now is wait it out."

"We planned on waiting for a year maximum," Callum said.

"Before we knew where the enclave star system actually was," Alik reminded him. "Now we just have to make the best of it."

"Bloody hell, man, we can't even go out of this cave."

"What do you suggest?" Kandara asked sharply. "Go and surrender to the Olyix?"

"We still have a mission," Yuri said. "Not just a mission—a purpose. When the human armada gets here, we have to show them where the five of us and all the cocoons are. That's what we focus on; that's all we focus on. Anything else is crap."

"A-men to that," Alik agreed—even though he knew it was all hopeless. *A hundred thousand years! Jez-us.*

After ten days, the Signal transmitter spheres were closing on the giant radio telescopes. They were just in time. The *Salvation of Life* was about fifteen hours out from the gateway. More than half of the sensor clumps they'd placed on the arkship's exterior had been lost. After the *Avenging Heretic* had exploded, the onemind had dispatched thirty quint in armor suits to scour the hangar for any further signs of human subterfuge. They went into every ship, no matter what condition it was in—a sight that put Alik in mind of SWAT teams busting into nark labs back in the day. Everything was suspect.

The *Salvation of Life* proved him right about that soon enough. After the search parties departed, Alik perceived the onemind's orders without any need to concentrate on the disparate threads murmuring away in the back of his head. This requirement was clear and singular. Every ship in the hangar was ordered off the arkship. They were given a trajectory, and in each case it was one that sent them down into the huge star's corona.

All the activity in the hangar had managed to sever half of the gossamer data threads that had been so carefully laid over many months. Thankfully, several had been laid over the roof, which gave them enough sensor clumps remaining to watch the enclave's gateway approach.

It was a phantom sphere a hundred kilometers across, surrounded by a swarm of Resolution ships looping around it like electrons circling their nucleus. If it hadn't been for them, he would never have known it existed. The silver light from the galactic core that shone so flamboyantly off their fuselages shimmered and twisted within the strange forces that defined the gateway's boundary. It was a bubble of emptiness with a monochrome aurora that he couldn't even be certain was there. But on the other side was the enclave: an area, or state, or realm—some otherplace—that the Neána said was a zone where time passed slowly. *Jez-us, I hope to hell they weren't lying about that.*

Its existence generated a satisfaction within the *Salvation*'s onemind that grew in proportion to its approach.

"Smug asshole," Alik said as he sat down on the stone ledge he'd claimed as his own.

The bridge enveloped him again. There were fewer data displays now, and the consoles were mostly blank shiny surfaces. *Still got the Goddamn blue trim, though.*

He reviewed the sparse data quickly. The transmitter sphere's telemetry was showing him it had used up more than eighty percent of the active molecular blocks that comprised its thick fuselage, losing more than half of its original size.

The image coming from the transmitter's sensors showed him the vast dodecahedrons washed in splendid silver corelight. The dishes were made up of hundred-kilometer hexagonal segments. He guessed they'd been mirror bright the day they were manufactured, same as human astroengineering structures. But centuries of exposure to space, and the star's intense light, had abraded the surface down to a dull white, with a few polished streaks remaining on areas where shadows lingered. *I wonder how long they've been here, listening for radio signals.*

"That's got to be the worst bad luck in the universe," he said.

"What is?" Callum asked.

"Being a species evolving on a star anywhere near here, the heart of the Olyix crusade. I mean, if you're living on a planet out where Sol is, at least you've got a slight chance. The Neána warning you, time to build a few escape ships, come up with mad plans like ours. But here, it's an instant response. One minute you're lifting your head up above the parapet to glimpse the wonder of the universe, then—*bam*—the next thing you know you're in a cocoon on board an arkship. You don't stand a chance."

"Maybe this is where the Neána came from," Yuri said. "They were at the same stage as the Olyix technologically, just a couple of light-years away, and saw what they were doing. They're not warlike, so they ran, and swore to warn any species they could find."

Jessika shrugged as they all looked at her. "Seriously, all of you. I. Do. Not. Know."

"Sorry," an abashed Callum muttered.

As the transmitter sphere drew closer to the radio telescope, Alik could make out flaws in the giant swathes of polished metal. The huge hexagonal segments were warped from thermal distortions so they no longer fitted together smoothly. Some had lifted; others had gently crinkled. Micrometeorites had punched small holes clean through, which had gone on to vacuum ablate, leaving the punctures with ragged edges, as if the surface was rotting like damp wood.

Alik waited while the onboard G8Turing steered the transmitter into position, thirteen hundred kilometers out from the center and off to one side. Theoretically, from there, any electromagnetic emission would be reflected toward the section of space containing Sol, boosting the signal strength in that direction.

"I don't know about anyone else's," he said, "but this radio telescope needs some serious maintenance."

"You're lucky," Callum said. "Mine needs scrapping and replacing altogether. One dish has a hole the size of Loch Ness."

"This is good," Yuri said.

"How?" Alik asked.

"It means there's not much Olyix activity out here. All their ships are concentrated over in the ring and around the wormholes. It'll take them time to fly anything out here when we trigger the transmitters."

"Mine's almost in place," Kandara told them.

"Jessika?"

"Five minutes. The transmitter's sensors haven't found any ships out here."

"These telescopes are big bastards," Callum said. "We don't know what's in the middle of them. Something has to be watching the receivers."

"The lack of ships and the state of the dishes is promising," Yuri said. "We might get away with a full broadcast."

"Ninety minutes, if we're lucky," Callum said. "But it'll take a miracle for anyone to catch it."

"They'll be watching," Kandara said. "They will."

Ten minutes later, everyone was in position.

"*Salvation* is going to go apeshit," Alik said happily.

"I hope so," Yuri said. "Stand by."

Alik checked the transmitter's position for the last time as the timer counted down. On zero, he triggered the Signal.

The center of each transmitter was a dense sphere of active molecules that formed a dynamic lattice to sequester individual anti-protons. The lattice was designed to deactivate in a long sequence, allowing a full-blown matter/antimatter annihilation, with the liberated energy burst powering a phenomenally powerful electromagnetic pulse. In theory, the deluge would last for ninety minutes.

Alik's entanglement link to the transmitter immediately ended as its delicate onboard electronics died instantly from the energy bombardment. "Well, something happened," he said. "Mine's out."

The others all acknowledged they'd lost direct contact with their transmitters.

"We're seven AUs from the nearest Signal," Jessika said. "It'll take an hour for us to see what's happened."

"If it worked, the *Salvation of Life* is going to know about it a bloody sight quicker than that," Callum said. "Every ship and station in this star system has entangled communications. They'll all know at once."

Alik closed his eyes so he could concentrate on the thoughts that whispered away at the back of his head. Sure enough, within a minute, one thing rose out of the onemind's babble to eclipse everything else—surprise and concern. It originated from the oneminds that governed the radio telescopes as they shared their perception.

He concentrated on the thoughts issuing out of the radio telescope his transmitter had reached. A tiny potent star hung above it, burning away at the upper end of the violet spectrum. Below it, the dish helped reflect and concentrate the Signal into a beam that was heading in the general direction of Sol.

"Goddamn, it worked," Alik said in a tone that betrayed his surprise. *We got something right.*

"Happy for you," Kandara growled.

As Alik examined the onemind's thoughts, he saw four of the Signal transmitters were now intense violet sparks, while the fifth— Something had gone wrong with the annihilation procedure. All the anti-protons had escaped their lattice confinement at once, producing a massive explosion, most of which was in the form of gamma and X-ray emissions—an outpouring of energy that for a brief instant rivaled that of the Olyix star. Already the dodecahedron of dishes was starting to crumple from the rampant flare, the curving continent-sized surfaces melting and fracturing. He saw long cracks tearing open, splintering the dishes even as the surface facing the antimatter explosion started to boil away. Then the closest viewpoint of the disaster vanished from the one-mind's thoughts.

"What happened?" Callum asked.

"My transmitter core got overenthusiastic," Kandara grumbled.

"Come on, stay positive," Jessika said. "Four of them are working. If the active molecules maintain cohesion, they'll last for almost another ninety minutes."

"But without mine, we've lost twenty percent of the broadcast power."

"There's certainly enough left to piss off the Olyix," Callum said contentedly.

Alik had to smile at the furious thoughts churning within the arkship's onemind. They'd been right about the radio telescopes not having any ships nearby. Eighteen Deliverance ships and eleven Resolution ships were being ordered to divert and intercept the signal generators. But the closest were more than an AU away. Even at maximum acceleration, it would take them a couple of hours to reach the radio telescopes, by which time the Signal transmitters would have exhausted their supply of anti-protons.

They carried on reading the onemind's thoughts until the last Signal transmitter flickered out. In total, the Signal had been broadcast for ninety-one minutes and seventeen seconds.

"It was a good strength," Jessika said. "Any exodus habitat with a decent sensor array should be able to receive it."

"A ninety-minute window in fifty thousand years' time?" Callum said bitterly. "Sure thing. Let's crack the champagne open and party."

"Oh, lighten the fuck up," Alik told him. "You can sense how disturbed the Olyix are. Even if humans don't pick up the Signal, other species will. Half the galaxy will know *something* is here. And anyone who's fleeing an Olyix invasion the way the Neána tell them to will have a pretty good idea who and what that something is. It's the beginning of the end, man."

Callum ducked his head. "Maybe."

Eight hours later, the *Salvation of Life* arrived at the gateway. The escort ships no longer spiraled exuberantly around it; there was no celebration. The onemind's thoughts had descended into a dour formality.

The remaining sensor clumps on the arkship's exterior showed them the barrier approaching—an insubstantial hemisphere refraction haloed by the galactic core, growing until it dominated space outside. Then they were passing through, their passage kicking up a delicate splash plume of silver scintillations.

GOX-QUINT

SALVATION OF LIFE GATEWAY ARRIVAL

I fucking *knew it*! Those sneaky little human shits put together some kind of dark operation. We should never trust them. Never.

They must have used a Neána neurovirus against the transport ship somehow and subverted its onemind. Just like Soćko did thirty years ago. They flew it into the hangar while we were retreating from Earth. There was a lot of confusion that day. We never did understand why they didn't attack all our positions simultaneously. They could've launched those deadly portal missiles at the *Salvation of Life* first. Not to destroy it—that would kill too many of their own, and they are laudably sentimental. But they could have taken out the wormhole generator. We would've been stranded, all alone. Well, now we know what they were actually doing. Everything about that assault was deliberately chaotic, thousands of our ships fleeing their attackers; even the onemind didn't analyze the maneuvers in any detail.

I paused from my endless task, supervising the containers with their myriad humans, and extended my reach farther into the wonderful union with the onemind. It was urgently reviewing its hangar memory. That ship took off from Salt Lake City, and there was an intense human attack there. Memories were incomplete, inadequate, with too many gaps. We were stupid. No: *It* was. Forgiving.

Now we pay for our compassion, for treating the humans with love and respect. Meanwhile, their antimatter-powered radio devices broadcast our position to the whole galaxy. There is nothing we can do about that now. The closest ships are over two hours away.

I don't understand the reason for the broadcast. The Sol system is fifty thousand light-years away. They cannot be calling for help. This is a setback for us, not a defeat. Our gallant Resolution ships will return to the humans' pitiful homeworld and settled planets within thirty years. All remaining humans will be liberated from their wasted lives so we may carry them to embrace the glory of the God at the End of Time. There will be no "rescue" for those we already hold.

So . . . why? Why this? Why expend this effort, surely every resource they possess, just to bring those radio transmitters here? Humans will never receive their broadcast. Ah. *They* won't . . .

I opened myself fully to the onemind. "It is the Neána," I declared. "They are behind this."

"Your reason for deciding this?" the onemind asks benignly.

"That broadcast is extremely unlikely to be detected by any human group that eludes our kindness. However, we know the Neána are spread wide across this galaxy in their treacherous nests. They listen as we do for transmissions from newly emerging species. They will know what that signal means, where it is originating."

"Not just the Neána," the onemind contemplates in an unguarded moment.

Deep memories from the arkship neuralstrata. We see the Katos—red blemishes traversing the elegant starscape, the destruction they inflicted upon us when they divined our true honorable mission. Worse, we felt the demise of valiant oneminds as our welcome ships were shattered and burned by the Angelis war fleet. The sadness of loss that lingers in every Olyix mind to this day.

"We should be able to find out the true intent behind this broadcast," I said. "The humans must still be on board. They can be questioned."

"The subverted transport ship was destroyed. No neurovirus distortion could forge that; verification was external. I have now purged the contamination from myself and confirmed total integrity. The remaining ships from that hangar are gone, flying into the star. Their trajectories are being monitored. There is no illusion anymore. The humans perished with their ship."

"Suicide in humans that dedicated to their mission is unlikely. I know. I understand humans very well."

"Your knowledge of human psychology is acknowledged. You shared it with me, and now I utilize your own routines in my analysis. There is nowhere further they can hide within my structure. Quint and sub-sect server organisms have searched the hangar for any continuing signs of human activity. There are none. They are dead."

The onemind is shitting on me from a truly great height. It doesn't fucking *listen*. "They are not."

"Your reluctance to accept my authority is troubling."

"I am simply offering likely possibilities. If humans were on board that ship, they will have attempted to survive."

"And, alternatively, if the ship was governed by a G8Turing? If there was a metahuman Neána on board? No. The regrettable incident is now closed. Rejoice; we are about to enter the enclave."

"I rejoice. Will the gateway's onemind watch for approaching hostile alien ships?"

"Of course. It is already determined that the gateway star system's watcher sensors will be refurbished. New short-range sensors will be built in to enhance our observation of near-space. Now recommence your duty. Our situation has returned to normal."

But it hasn't. That arrogant motherfucker will get us all killed. Those alien vermin are still on board, skulking about somewhere. And I am going to find them. I am going to prove the onemind wrong. I'll enjoy rubbing its smug face in that. Who knows, the Olyix fullmind might even reward me with elevation to a onemind—not in a Resolution ship, but a full arkship like I deserve. Wouldn't that be something?

MORGAN

FINALSTRIKE MISSION, YEAR TWELVE

Dellian and Yirella, along with the rest of the fleet crews, had spent twelve years in the toroid-shaped domain. Twelve years while the history faction remodeled the thirty fleet ships. They also increased the neutron star's defenses, adding concentric layers of sensors and portals out to three light-years, ready for any ships coming from the Olyix sensor station, sixty-seven light-years away. Within the domain, those events played out across a total of six days. Immanueel had reversed the speed that time flowed from the accelerated rate that had matured the biosphere into ancient delightful parkland to the same slowtime that was used by the Olyix enclave.

Dellian had to admit, that was a whole lot better than getting dunked in a suspension tank again. "So do you think they can timeshift the fleet when we're *inside* the wormhole?" he asked.

On the last day before they left for the enclave star, he and Yirella were walking through one of the domain's forests. It was something they'd done every day of the hiatus, enjoying an epoch that was probably the closest they'd ever get to old Earth's environment. Bizarrely, it seemed more natural than Juloss ever had. He'd decided that was down to age, which possessed a reassurance all of its own. Some trees in the forest were giants, hundreds of years old. So they'd explore the not quite overgrown paths and climb some of the stately trees and finish up with a swim in one of the big rock pools.

An altogether pleasant experience, until today. With the time flow normalized so they could access the outside universe directly again, Ainsley's android had come to visit them.

"The corpus guys know their shit," the white android said. "If everything goes to plan, we're actually going to be at the enclave in a few weeks—our time. Can you believe that?"

"No," Dellian said flatly.

"Easily," Yirella said, and gave him the look.

"Oh, come on, Dellian," Ainsley said. "Don't tell me you aren't interested to see the weapons upgrades they've been working on. Damn, if they've built you a combat suit like Yanki from Prefect Space III, I'll stuff this android in one and join you storming the *Salvation of Life* myself. They were awesome."

"Okay. I have no idea what you're talking about."

"Prefect Space III was a game matrix when I was . . . Well, when I just had an ordinary human body. It came out back in about 2100, I think. My memories didn't magically improve when I finally expanded into the Factory ship; all I remembered then is all I'm ever going to remember. Mind you, I do have perfect access to all those memories now."

"So were you dying?" Yirella asked.

"Hell, no. I'd had plenty of full cellular rebuilds by then. My body was in good shape. Our rejuvenation techniques on the exodus habitats were pretty good. The early ones back in Sol not so much. My neurons got screwed over at the start. Nothing big time, but enough to change me. I had a couple of flaky centuries back then, let me tell you."

Dellian gave the white figure a surprised glance. "You mean your original body—the actual you—is still alive somewhere?"

The android's face managed a thoughtful frown. "I don't remember. There's a memory of me on a bed in some fancy clinic; Emilja was there, some of my family—Gwendoline, for sure. Then I reactivated in the ship. But, two of me? Fuck no, that would just be weird. I'm pretty sure I wouldn't have done it. There's only me, and this is it—the genuine Ainsley Zangari, accept no substitute. My core identity is running in an exact copy of my original neural structure, but most of my thinking takes place in quantum arrays; that's what gives me speed and ability in a fight."

Dellian grinned. "And that's the non-weird part?"

"Hey, grab what the universe has to offer, kid."

"So your body's dead? I'm sorry."

"Don't be. It lived for thousands of years, and not in some Goddamn domain-time cheat. I lived them all for real. And I can do it again."

"Wait. What?"

"See, this way my personality is frozen, locked into what it was the instant my body passed. The ship's neural core doesn't have the kind of randomness that biological brains are subject to. I'm unchanging. So, when all this is over—and assuming I survive—I have a choice. I can carry on as the ship, or I can clone myself a new body and transfer my mind back into it. I'll be me again, exactly the same as before."

Dellian risked a glance at Yirella, knowing what he'd see: a face devoid of expression—except maybe a slight crinkling around her flat nose. It didn't matter; he knew exactly what she was thinking. *What about your soul?*

"Continuity seems to be a theme here," she said, "on quite a few levels. Did you know about this group of ultra-Utopials Emilja put together?"

"Kind of. I knew she and some level one Utopials had formed a political group, a loyalist movement. Again, the memories aren't too firm. I know Emilja and I were concerned by the lack of success in the exodus habitats. When we fled from Sol, we believed we'd be laying siege to the enclave within a thousand years. Well, that never happened. By the time we put the Factory together we knew we had to change the whole aspect of the exodus. Our technology had plateaued, but it was good enough to allow humans to adopt the Neána approach to surviving the Olyix. I never knew who she'd recruited, but we agreed on a program of soft influence with long-range objectives. We'd keep our civilization going, but slowly change the goal, turning the generation ships away from planetary life. Gotta admit, though, I wasn't expecting it to be quite so soft and slow. People like your Kenelm . . . sie could've been a bit more proactive."

"That's not the impression of you that I got at Vayan," Yirella said. "You were focused on attacking the enclave, not fighting a protective campaign to keep the Olyix away from this part of the galaxy."

The android's plain face managed to approximate a pensive expression. "Yeah, well. I might not be able to change my mind, but I'm not a Turing with preset operational targets. All I ever wanted, from the day the *Salvation of Life* turned up at Sol, was to nuke those Olyix bastards into oblivion. This was my greatest chance."

"Did the Factory know that when they installed you in a ship?"

"Emilja did. It doesn't matter. There are plenty of other Factory ships in these parts that can dump a shitload of grief on the Olyix if they start sniffing around."

"How many ships?" Dellian asked.

"Dunno. That's strategic information. But we know now that there are more than just me; that Signal from the Lolo Maude is proof of that. Lucky coincidence, huh?"

"What? That the other Factory ship beat the Olyix?"

"No." The android faced Yirella, his face unnervingly blank. "That you'd decelerated mid-flight. Those fleet ships weren't built on a government contract, you know."

Dellian started to open his mouth—

"Every component built by the lowest bidder," Ainsley told him. "That's how they used to build space rockets, back in the day. Made riding them kinda interesting. You just sat on top of a pillar of fire and fury wondering which part would fail first."

"I wanted to give the neutron star civilization as much time as possible to develop before we arrived," Yirella said. "Decelerating from relativistic speed, then accelerating back up again, added years to our flight here. A non-critical unit failure was a harmless way to achieve that."

Dellian clenched his jaw. *Saints! I should have worked that one out.* He didn't dare look at Yirella.

"Got to love the irony," Ainsley said. "As soon as they

cracked exotic matter manipulation, the corpus humans literally had as many centuries as they wanted to take."

Yirella shrugged. "Hindsight."

"But we're here now," Dellian said.

"And so are the Olyix," Ainsley said cheerfully.

"Immanueel has detected them?"

"Yep. Eleven Resolution ships, two hundred and eighty AUs out and closing; they're down to point two light speed. And they're all carrying a wormhole terminus. There will be more Resolution ships backed up inside the wormholes, too."

"They got here fast," Yirella said.

"We're sixty-seven light-years from the sensor station," Ainsley said. "They knew we'd come here as soon as we kicked their asses at Vayan. It's the culmination of the whole Strike plan, and the Olyix know that better than everyone by now."

"I have to question how many human societies would actually do that when they pick up a Signal, or pulled the enclave location from a onemind," Yirella mused. "I mean, if your closest neutron star is a hundred and fifty light-years away . . . why bother? Leave it to someone else. You probably wouldn't get there in time anyway."

"Irrelevant," Ainsley said. "The corpus humans are going to strike in another twenty-three minutes."

"They're already out there?" Dellian asked in surprise.

"Oh, yeah." Ainsley produced a disconcerting grin. "They used portals to send ships through behind the Olyix. Now they're accelerating at about a hundred gees to catch them while the Resolution ships are decelerating."

"And they're stealthed?"

"Let's just say they're quite hard to detect. We don't know the absolute capabilities of the Resolution ships, but Immanueel is quietly hopeful."

"You destroyed all the Resolution ships at Vayan," Dellian said. "I'm sure the corpus humans can do the same here."

"No question about it, kid. It's just how fast they can kill them. Think of this as a big trial of the corpus armada's capabilities before we get serious and go visit the enclave."

"But the sensor station is going to know they've suffered

a momentous defeat," Yirella said. "Once the wormhole generators are destroyed, the wormholes will collapse. All eleven wormholes collapsing together will tell the Olyix that humans have developed something formidable out here—especially after Vayan and whatever Lolo Maude did to the Olyix at the other Signal star."

"Bring it on," Ainsley said.

"I want to actually watch what happens," Dellian said. *In a way I can understand*—but he didn't say that out loud.

"Popcorn's ready and waiting at the congress hall," Ainsley said.

Dellian used his databud to request a portal. Within seconds, one dropped down onto the path and expanded.

They walked through it into the hall. Immanueel's strikingly lofty body was already there, along with a good number of fleet humans who'd accessed the news. The wooden chairs had gone, leaving everyone to stand as they watched a big tactical display that was projected into the air before the central column. Today the prismatic light inside the crystal was noticeably subdued as the corpus humans concentrated on the approaching Resolution ships.

Dellian and Yirella made their way over to Immanueel.

"How's it going?" Yirella asked.

"No deviation in the Resolution ships' trajectory," they replied. "We believe they haven't detected our forces, yet."

Dellian studied the big display. The graphics were easy enough: a clump of eleven scarlet icons with violet course vectors crawling toward the glittering emerald dataclump that was the neutron star. Behind them, arrow-shaped formations of violet attack cruisers were racing after the Resolution ships. It took a moment for him to grasp the scale; the eleven Resolution ships were occupying a bubble of space more than an AU in diameter. The cruisers were already traveling at point four light speed, and accelerating hard.

"What are you going to attack them with?" he asked.

"First barrage will be simple kinetics," Immanueel said. "The cruisers can fire them at relativistic velocity. There will be no plasma exhaust or gravity wave emission for the Resolution ships to distinguish. Once they become aware of our assault, we'll switch to active weapons. That should come between ten to a hundred milliseconds after detection."

Dellian's instinct was to make an incredulous grunt.

"We need to be fast," Immanueel said. "Given enough time, the Resolution ships can simply close the wormholes around themselves and fly back down them to the sensor station, or wherever the other end is. That, if you remember your history, is what Alpha Defense forced the *Salvation of Life* to do above Earth, once the *Avenging Heretic* was safely on board."

"Yeah. But . . . how long do you think they'll need?"

"We are working on one to one-point-five seconds. As they approach the neutron star, they will be very alert for our response. That would include an immediate escape trigger. It's what we would do."

He couldn't even imagine how many factors the corpus humans were incorporating into their attack scenario. "You don't really need us at all, do you," he said quietly.

"This is just basic orbital mechanics," Immanueel said. "Simple math. The enclave will be a lot more complicated."

"Huh."

"If you do not wish to join us on FinalStrike, we will understand."

"Oh, we're coming with you, all right," Yirella said as the display's projection light sent faint strokes of colors playing across her face. It heightened how intent she was—a determination that always captivated and unnerved Dellian.

He exchanged a knowing glance with the white android, which raised a whole new level of questions. *Is Ainsley actually looking through those blank eyes?*

When it happened, the attack was completely anticlimactic. The scarlet icons simply vanished. That triggered some cheering and clapping across the hall, but otherwise people just accepted the outcome tamely. Dellian was almost resentful they had no immediate sensor coverage; it took several seconds to get a visual image of the Resolution ships exploding. Even then it was just white-sphere-on-a-black-background—nothing to really indicate the true violence of the spectacle, the success they should feel.

"Did the wormholes collapse?" Yirella asked urgently.

Immanueel nodded. "Yes. The Olyix will not be able to return here for sixty-seven years. So the sensor station will believe—until we arrive there."

Dellian watched the tenuous white plasma blooms diminishing. The tactics in play here were too much like a horribly advanced chess game that he could never quite fathom, making him thankful that his own part was just going to be storming an arkship and killing quint—nothing complicated. Destroying the Resolution ships' wormholes had been a misdirection by the corpus armada, intended to keep the Olyix concentrating on the enigma of whatever dwelled at the neutron star. They'd be desperate to return—in force—to confront the challenge. In reality, thirty-four years ago the corpus humans had launched a starship, carrying a wormhole, toward the sensor station. It would arrive decades before any Olyix force returned here, catching them unawares and unprepared.

"What happens if the Olyix have a second wave of ships behind the ones you've just taken out?" he asked. "Or a third—or more?"

"We will remain alert for any further ships approaching," Immanueel said. "There will be an unknown number of Olyix ships materializing in real space between here and the sensor station as the wormhole collapses around them. Some might decide to travel here rather than return. We do not anticipate them being a problem."

Yirella stared keenly at the fading explosions. "Good. We can start the real fight back now."

Two hours later, Dellian walked through a portal back into the rebuilt *Morgan*. The ship was completely different from the one that had left Juloss. Where before it had been a stack of spherical grids, this iteration was a streamlined five-kilometer cone of the same protective copper mirror shell that encased all the other neutron star ring particles. Its base was a simple shallow hemisphere, fluoresced by the aquamarine light of an advanced gravitonic drive, with a rim that had sprouted long scarlet and black needles like a crown of bloodied thorns.

A layout unfolded across Dellian's optik. The forward section was mostly hangar space holding a range of weapons and ancillary craft, while behind that were all fifty-two decks of the life support section, with the engineering deck aft. That was it. The *Morgan* no longer had any of the complex asteroid mining and refining equipment, nor the von Neumann replicator systems to begin a new civilization. This was a purebred warship now. There was no compromise, no allowance for failure. He had to concede the logic was impeccable. If they lost at the Olyix enclave, there would be no running away and hiding to regroup somewhere safe amid the lonely stars. They'd be dead or worse. But if—*when!*— they won, there was an open future with the human race reunited in victory and rich in possibility.

That outcome was so close Dellian was practically living it as he walked along the circular main corridor of deck thirty-three to the cabin he and Yirella had been assigned. The floor was flat, which he wasn't used to, but this version of the *Morgan* didn't spin to provide gravity.

"Artificial gravity is only one function of manipulating exotic matter," Yirella said approvingly. "It'll provide timeflow control in here, too. They've really mastered this technology."

"Yeah," he said. "You know, I'm really not convinced they need us."

"They don't. But I need to go."

"Sure. I'm with you on that, Yi." The decision hadn't been that difficult, at least not for him. And thankfully the rest of the squad had chosen to face FinalStrike together—though a good portion of the warship crews who'd arrived at the neutron star had chosen to go their own way and build habitats adrift in the vast gulfs of interstellar space. Surprisingly, Kenelm had chosen to stay with the *Morgan*.

Dellian didn't resent those who'd left, nor even the ex-captain for staying. When they did finally arrive at the *Salvation of Life*, he only wanted the truly dedicated to be storming it with him.

He sank down on their bed—bigger and softer than before. The walls were blank, awaiting Yirella to format their texture.

"How long do you think you'll need to adapt to all the armor upgrades?" she asked.

"A couple of months, at least. I've been reviewing the capabilities. They've gone micro and macro. Some of those weapons could take out a whole squadron of huntspheres, while the subtle ones can wipe whole sections of the neural-strata."

"Saints, you be careful using anything that interfaces with a onemind again."

He spread his arms wide. "I learned my lesson, trust me. There's some kind of failsafe in these new systems."

"Riiiight."

"There is! A nuanimate routine analyzes any impulse coming out of the neuralstrata. It's like an independent corpus sub-aspect—smart but not self-aware."

"Well, listen to you: the coding master."

"I just read the instructions. But the tough part is going to be training the cohort to deal with all the new hardware we've got. That's a whole fresh set of response reflexes we've got to build in. It'll take time."

"Well, that's the advantage of controlling time. You can have as much or as little as you want."

Dellian propped himself up on his elbows to look at her. "I can think of a few other things we could use all that extra time for."

"I'm sure you can," she said with a roguish grin.

"No! Well—yes. But no, I meant we could do what all those neutron star people did, the . . . what did Immanuel call them, naturalists? They lived for thousands of years. They had a life where they were never burdened by the threat of the Olyix. We can have that life."

"Everyone can have that life, Del. Once we liberate them from the enclave."

"Yeah. I suppose so. Put it like that . . ."

"But I do understand." She sat next to him and started rubbing his back between the shoulder blades.

"Doesn't it bother you how . . . *different* the corpus humans are?" he asked.

"Bother me? No. I'm a bit in awe of them, to be honest."

"Saints, really? So would you elaborate yourself? Become corpus? Like they've done?"

"Not today." She flashed a flat smile, which did nothing to reassure him.

"But you've thought about it?"

"Haven't you?"

"Not really. But . . . Saints! In this place, with all their domain timeshift technology, you could walk out of here and come back an hour later my time, having spent fifty years a full corpus. I'd never know."

"Yeah. This timeshifting is hard to get your head around, isn't it?"

"Sure. Me. With my thick head."

"Don't be like that. You have a beautiful head. I know. I've been inside it."

"Oh, crap. We really are going to do this, aren't we?"

"Well, the corpus weapons will do most of it for us, but yes." She inclined her head solemnly. "We're going to do this. We're going to face the enclave."

"We were too cocky before. Even if we'd won at Vayan, can you imagine us going up against the enclave with ships like the *Morgan* used to be? We would have been cocooned in the first minute."

"Maybe we still can be. Who knows what the Olyix are capable of? In that respect, going to face them now is no different than before. It was never going to be the *Morgan* alone. The Strike plan was always for humans to gather at a neutron star and combine forces to attack the enclave. And that's what we've done."

"What you've done."

"I armed us with hope, that's all."

"Saints! How about we go living those four thousand years, Yi? We could do that, you and me, have that life. Then after we've lived everything there is, we go kick down the enclave door."

"No, Del. However wrong Alexandre's generation was to create us: Here we are. And we have a purpose, even if we had no choice. And we're hardly the first humans to be in this position."

"Well, here's hoping we're the last."

——

The squad gathered around a couple of big tables in deck thirty-three's canteen, which someone had textured to resemble a Parisian Left Bank café circa 1920, all high arched ceilings and flickering gaslights inside frosted glass shades, with a long polished wood counter along one side—an effect spoiled only by having food extruders instead of stewards wearing stiff white tunics. The tall windows, which ostensibly opened out onto the city's famed Boulevard Saint-Germain, had clouded over with tactical displays of the neutron star system.

Dellian sipped his hot chocolate as he watched the history faction prepare to depart the neutron star. Like everything in the disk around the star, the wormhole generator was a big nondescript particle with an undulant copper surface protecting whatever machinery was within. As he watched, the covering peeled back with a sinuous flourish to reveal a maw glowing with the distinct violet radiance of Cherenkov radiation. He was moderately disappointed that the shimmer didn't curve back into an infinite vortex.

"How far does it extend?" Xante asked.

"The history faction launched their carrier ship toward the Olyix sensor station twenty-two years before we arrived," Tilliana said. "And we've been here twelve years, so the ship is already thirty-four light-years away, give or take. It's only got another thirty-two to go."

"I'm finding it hard to believe there were only ever two factions here," Ellici said. "History and egress. Out of a hundred thousand people? Come on, that's not realistic."

"Their factions are a broad church," Tilliana said. "And don't forget there was a whole bunch of naturalists, the ones who didn't elaborate up to corpus level."

"Oh, hey, the ring particles are moving, look," Uret said.

Dellian glanced over at the displays. The particles closest to the wormhole were accelerating toward it, with more following. The whole movement reminded him of a shoal of playful fish smoothly following the leaders.

After an hour they could see the entire ring was on the move, every particle heading for the wormhole.

"So the whole ring is coming with us to invade the enclave?" Janc said.

"Every particle, yes," Yirella confirmed. "They're either warships or specialist weapons. It's an armada, and our little fleet is a part of it. Finally!"

Alexandre's icon appeared in Dellian's optik. "Stand by," sie said. "We're launching toward the wormhole terminus."

Data in the optik showed him the *Morgan* was under acceleration. He frowned when he saw they'd passed ten gees. The gravity felt absolutely stable, as if they were on a planet.

"Maybe we should have had a test flight or twenty first," Uret said. "I mean, what would've happened if the compensators didn't work?"

"All the fleet ships were extensively tested while we were taking our break in the domain," Yirella told him. "They ironed all the bugs out."

"Er . . . what bugs?"

Her lips lifted into a faint smile. Dellian watched her closely. She was sitting with Ellici and Tilliana at the other end of the table from him, a distant expression on her face, eyes closed.

It was a pose he was seeing a lot more lately. She was otherwhere half the time, her body a spirit that moved through this world without any real grounding. While her mind . . . He knew she was using the neural interface to link directly into the *Morgan*'s network. It gave her a much greater perception of the digital universe than any databud could. His own interface had remained unused since his treatment. Several times he'd gone down to the *Morgan*'s clinic, ready to have it extracted. Each time he'd paused at the door and walked away. *I want to be her equal . . . or at least not be regarded as inferior.*

The visual displays filling the café windows were showing all one hundred fifty of the very large particles, the ones with the powerful gravity wave emissions. They were starting to move in closer to the neutron star itself. More than half of them were changing orbital inclination, rising out of the ecliptic plane so that they were evenly dispersed above the dark surface.

"They're forming the cage," Yirella said.

Dellian didn't have a clue what she was talking about. He picked up his almond croissant and took a bite. "What cage?"

"The major particles are high-power gravitonic systems that are going to contain the neutron star during transit. They'll also act as negative energy conduits, same as every ship that flies inside a wormhole."

"Transit?" Uret asked.

Yirella opened her eyes and smiled at her friends. "So I'm guessing none of you bothered to access the full mission plan?"

Tilliana grinned. "Of course they didn't."

"Takes a lot of power to hold a wormhole open across sixty-odd light-years, let alone all the way to the enclave," Yirella said. "Really, a lot."

"Oh, Great Saints," Dellian blurted as mission data finally zipped across his optik. "It's coming with us. They're bringing the neutron star to the enclave."

"To be more accurate," Yirella said, "they're going to attack the enclave with the neutron star. It's the ultimate magic bullet."

"Against what?" Falar demanded. "I know everyone keeps saying we don't know what's inside, but there's got to be thousands of different Olyix structures. All the arkships storing cocoons, for a start."

"There's only one target," Ellici said, "and it doesn't get any bigger. The enclave has to have a star to power it. If you kill the star, you cut the power. Best way to kill a star—"

"Hit it with a neutron star," Yirella finished for her, smiling gleefully. "Boom! Nova. Probably followed by collapse into a black hole if the enclave star is big enough."

"You're kidding, right?" Uret demanded.

Yirella's index finger sketched a circle around her head as she smirked. "Is this my kidding face?"

"Saints!"

"This is a war, people. Win or lose, it's the last one humans will ever fight. And it's not one we're going to win with half measures."

It took a day and a half for all the corpus particles to fly into the wormhole. Once the majority had entered, the *Morgan*'s fleet—all seventeen remaining ships—slipped in after them.

Dellian was in the café again, watching the displays showing a feed from external sensors. When they were a thousand kilometers from the wormhole terminus, the *Morgan*'s negative energy conduits—small, blade-like spurs—slipped out of their recesses across the fuselage. Acceleration dipped down to point-one gee, guiding them along their course. The other ships of the fleet took up position behind them. Then Ainsley came gliding in behind the formation, its white fuselage reflecting the wan violet light of the wormhole's Cherenkov radiation.

The *Morgan* slipped past the wormhole's throat, and every visual image died simultaneously.

"What the Saints . . . ?"

"We're not in natural space-time anymore," Tilliana told him as she tucked into a breakfast of pancakes, maple syrup, and berries. "Whatever's outside the hull doesn't propagate photons."

"So how do we know where the other ships are?"

"Their mass shows up as distortions in the *Morgan*'s exotic mass detectors."

Dellian changed his optik's input feed, so he was looking along a simple white tube leading away to the vanishing point, with gray smears ahead and behind, like dense clots of mist. Then the tube surface deformed, with ripples running along it. His imagination filled in a judder as they passed the *Morgan*. Behind them, a black sphere was filling the narrow tunnel, forcing it to warp around its bulk. All he could think of was a snake swallowing a big rat, the bulge slowly working its way along.

"The neutron star," Yirella announced in satisfaction.

Something about having the neutron star racing along right behind them was deeply discomforting. But then he hadn't quite been prepared for the whole wormhole experience. Looking around the table, his friends hunched in their seats, nursing various cups of tea, coffee, and juice, that concern was something they all seemed to be sharing.

"We need to start training," Dellian announced. Anything

to take his mind off what was outside. Not that there was anything outside, not even a vacuum. *Which is the whole problem.*

Tilliana smirked. "Good. We've been working up new scenarios for you boys. The welcome ship at Vayan gave us the basis for some realistic environments to simulate for you when you're in the egg. This'll be fun."

"Fun?" Xante asked cautiously.

"For me and Ellici."

The corpus armada emerged from the wormhole half a light-year away from the Olyix sensor station. All the squads were on alert as the *Morgan* dropped back into space-time. They'd joked and grumbled as they suited up three hours before passing through the terminus, blustering through the knowledge that if the Olyix were waiting, it would be over so fast they'd probably never know. But if there was a delay, a skirmish between evenly matched ships, there was a remote chance they'd be needed to play a part.

So Dellian led them onto a troop carrier, where they waited, and waited . . . Tilliana and Ellici were in their tactical situation room on deck twenty-four, with a dedicated munc-interfaced genten feeding them prodigious amounts of real-time sensor data.

Once again, Yirella had nothing to do. She waited in her cabin, lying on the bed, with the walls detextured. Her neural interface connected her directly into the *Morgan*'s network. The corpus humans who'd refashioned the warship had built in a full-capacity union for her. Riding the network channels was a seriously liberating experience, especially as she used a quantum array as a buffer to the vast quantity of available information. It was similar, she supposed, to the way the muncs' neural instinct filtered data for Tilliana and Ellici. Except the processing power in the array also boosted her consciousness.

In this state it was hard to justify remaining as a single flesh body, the advantages of elaborating up to corpus status were so obvious.

There's still time. All the time I want.

She began to compartmentalize her newly expanded mind, each segment monitoring a separate block of information—the wormhole, the corpus armada ships, the neutron star's cage, the squad's troop carrier, Dellian in his new utterly lethal armor suit, his cohort at ease in their new attack body casings. Her primary attention flicked effortlessly between them. *I really am a guardian angel this time*.

Immanueel's presence impinged on her cognizance, a phantom hello, acknowledging her presence in the network.

"Can I observe in concert with you?" she asked.

"I would welcome your company," they replied.

She shifted her focus, moving into several (but not all) of the particles that housed aspects of Immanueel's corpus. Some were little more than carrier craft for warships whose weapons could devastate whole moons. Others had more complex mechanisms.

"I didn't realize you were this . . . I was going to say big, but it's more like: expansive."

"I am what I want to be," they replied courteously. "Perhaps after FinalStrike I will reconjugate into something less aggressive."

Together they watched as the armada began to emerge from the wormhole terminus. As they passed the throat, their copper surfaces pared back, exposing the ships within and allowing a greater range of sensors to examine their new environment. They were six light-months from the Olyix signal station—a modest L-class star with an airless, rocky planet orbiting two AUs out, and a Neptune-sized ice giant huddled away in the cold thirty-two AUs distant.

When the wormhole carrier ship had decelerated into this location two years ago, the history faction had dispatched a squadron of stealthed ships on toward the Olyix outpost, each one holding an expansion portal. They'd flown into the star system undetected. Now Yirella watched through dedicated links as they slowly glided into position, closing on their targets.

"That is impressive," she murmured grudgingly. Sensors on the stealthed ships were showing her detailed images of the Olyix structures. They locked onto the station itself as it orbited two thirds of an AU from the L-class star. It was a nest of seven concentric bands, spinning slowly. Their surfaces shone an intense purple in the sun's lemon-tinted light, as if they'd been milled from a solid block of metal.

"So that's an Olyix habitat?" she said. The outermost ring was two hundred kilometers in diameter.

"It would seem so. Given their technology level, we're surprised they need something this large to operate an outpost like this. Perhaps it is related to how many biological server constructs they appear to use."

"So it's a home for a onemind, and . . . what? A stable of constructs?"

"Possibly. But there is no question there is plenty of activity here."

Yirella followed the station's orbital track. Eleven huge radio telescopes were visible, pentagonal dodecahedrons that put her in mind of a clump of symmetric sunflowers, but two thousand kilometers wide. They were spaced equidistantly around the star, allowing them to scan interstellar space for any innocent radio broadcasts from emerging civilizations.

Those she ignored. Her concern was spiked by the number of Resolution ships holding position fifty thousand kilometers from the big multi-ring station. The squadron had adopted a protective formation around a welcome ship, a rocky cylinder thirty five kilometers long.

Her perception enclosed it, magnifying the sight until it hung in the center of her conscience like a detailed ghost. Its profile was unpleasantly familiar from their encounter with a near-identical ship at Vayan.

"I wonder how many humans are cocooned on board?" she mused.

"Unknown," Immanueel said. "We conclude it was assigned to the new war fleet en route to us. They thought they could capture us."

"Most likely," she agreed. After examining the Resolution ships, confirming they were the upgraded version, her main interest was the star's equator, where a loop of matter was spinning around the seething corona, partially occluded by an unnatural storm of prominences that its presence whipped up. "That's got to be the generator to power their wormholes. Saints! The energy they're producing!"

"Indeed."

She switched focus to the wormholes that circled lazily around the station. Thirty-seven active ones, presenting as pools of Cherenkov radiation gleaming sharply against the blackness of interstellar space. Trailing farther along the orbital path, and drifting out of alignment, were eleven dead hemispheres of cold machinery, their delicate exposed elements fraying with vacuum ablation over the decades. Behind them were another two inert hemispheres slowly circling around each other in a ghostly dance.

"Those eleven in the first clump have to be the termini for the wormholes you destroyed," Yirella said.

"Yes. And presumably the remaining pair were the termini for Vayan, and the lure world where they encountered the Lolo Maude."

"And the active wormholes? We're assuming the largest is the one that leads back to the enclave."

"The others presumably lead to the ships currently flying to the neutron star and the Signal star. They'll want to eliminate all sources of resistance."

"Yeah."

She watched as three stealthed corpus ships drifted in toward the largest of the Olyix wormholes. After their two-year flight, they were now within ten thousand miles. Dark puffs of inert molecules effervesced gently out of them, performing final course corrections.

"No indication the Olyix have detected us," Immanueel said. "Everything is going to plan."

Yirella had to wonder how much anxiety she was subconsciously leaking through the neural interface. Or perhaps Immanueel just knew her too well. She pulled her attention back.

All around the *Morgan*, specialist systems and armada warships were converging on the expansion portals that were entangled with their twins in the stealth ships. They began to form up in their designated assault sequence, and she concentrated on the five negative-energy generators that would target the wormhole that led back to the enclave. If they didn't get through, or if they failed to take control of the wormhole, the armada would have to take the long way around. They were utterly critical.

She finally understood why humans on old Earth had assigned deities to the constellations. It was pleasing to believe there was a higher power you could beg to circumvent fate. Useless . . . but pleasing.

Saints, but I wish I wasn't so smart.

"Here we go," Immanueel said.

The lead stealth ship approaching the enclave wormhole was less than a meter across. It had shed its external layer of molecular blocks in an unsymmetrical sequence, taking on an irregular shape so that any detailed scan would show a natural-appearing lump of asteroidal debris. The course it was on would take it twelve hundred meters south of the generator mechanism, approaching at three thousand seven hundred nineteen kilometers an hour. Close, but not dangerous. The corpus expected the Olyix structures to have impact protection—a gravity distortion field if nothing else, deflecting space fragments away harmlessly.

Data zipped through Yirella's mind, delivered by the quantum array that operated at a seemingly instinctual level. The generator was indeed sitting at the center of an inverted gravity swirl. But there were no other active measures—yet.

The stealth ships flashed in to the closest approach, their courses bending slightly as they skipped off the boundary of the gravitational deflection field like spinning stones bouncing along a lake. They curved around the hemispherical wormhole generator, one on either side of the glowing entrance, while the third followed the camber of the machinery. At two kilometers out, the portals expanded.

Five negative-energy generators flew through the portals, *fast*. Defense cruisers corkscrewed around them, ready to ward off any form of attack, be it energy-based or physical. Immanueel wasn't concerned by that. The only goal was to establish their own grip on the wormhole structure inside a second.

For Yirella, aloof on her digital Olympus, that instant stretched out interminably thanks to the quantum computer's hyperfast presentation, giving her old brain cells a jolt as she struggled to cope with the massive data input. The event hit her like an ice-cream headache, each aspect painfully clear.

As soon as they emerged through the portals, the five generators interfaced with the throat of the wormhole, their negative-energy output locking the opening in place and providing enough power to maintain it. Less than a second later, they were buffeted by a severe gravitational distortion, coupled with a ferocious bombardment of energy beams. Simultaneous with that, the Olyix generator cut its own negative-energy emission. Without that, the wormhole should have collapsed. It didn't.

Once the defense cruisers confirmed the wormhole had retained its integrity and was under corpus control, they retaliated. The Olyix generator fractured abruptly as the entire bulk was subjected to a massive graviton pulse, twisting the internal structure into an impossible physical alignment. Then the deformation reversed. The entire generator structure shattered, jagged splinters streaking outward. Thousands bounced off the copper shells of the corpus ships, ricocheting back wildly. The remainder formed an expanding debris cloud scintillating in the tawny sunlight.

"We got it!" she exclaimed.

"We certainly did," Immanueel agreed.

At the heart of the twinkling knot of rubble and gas, the violet glow of the wormhole's Cherenkov radiation remained steadfast.

The remaining ten stealth craft infiltrating the star system expanded their portals. Two light-years away, the history faction's copper-skinned armada swarmed through—a deluge that lasted five hours. With Ainsley leading one of the formations, they accelerated in sharply toward the Resolution ships.

SAINTS

OLYIX ENCLAVE

They stayed in the bridge simulation as the *Salvation of Life* passed through the gateway. Yuri took a puzzled moment to examine the images being fed to him from the sensor clusters on the arkship's hull. At first he thought it was just a multicolored smear—an instrument malfunction, or maybe some kind of spatial deformation like the interior of a wormhole? Then his brain finally grasped the *scale,* and he recognized what he was seeing.

The smear resolved into monumental veils of gas twining around each other in a slow, almost sensual, sashay, fluorescing in spectacular hues as they crawled around their prison. A nebula, then. Caged by the enclave, a spherical zone that gave a good impression of infinity but which the G8 Turing measured at about ninety AUs in diameter.

"Fuck me," he grunted. Five AUs away, the star at the center of this artificial micro-universe, just visible through the thick currents of dust and gas, was a twin of the one outside, over one and a half times the size of Sol, and burning an intense white below a highly agitated corona. Yuri had never seen so many sunspots and prominences contaminating a star. Vast braids of plasma were leaping out of the chromosphere, some soaring up vertically over a million kilometers before twirling down in epic cascades of incandescent rain.

This time the star had five rings wrapped around it. The innermost was spinning around the equator in the same direction as the star's rotation, while the second one was just outside that, inclined at twenty degrees, and spinning in the opposite direction.

The three outermost rings were also inclined at progressively steeper angles, with the outermost encircling the poles. Unlike the solid inner pair, they were composed entirely of opalescent light that shone brighter than the corona underneath.

"Exotic matter?" Callum speculated.

"That's not the usual Cherenkov radiation wavelength," Jessika said. "But given the energy level involved in maintaining temporal flow manipulation across something as vast as the enclave, it's got to be a variant. The impression I'm getting from the onemind is that they're the generators, and the inner pair of rings are powering them."

"Man, I'm not sure I can get my head around this," Alik said quietly. "Every stage of this trip we're seeing something more impossible than the last. Maybe humans shouldn't have gone down the technology route. Shoulda just stuck to the caves on the savanna. Kept it simple, you know."

Yuri couldn't recall seeing such an amazed expression on the FBI agent's face before. And somehow he couldn't even snark; he was finding the enclave just as imposing himself.

"We're not quite in a vacuum anymore," Jessika said. "That nebula has a measurable density. Take a look aft of the *Salvation*."

Yuri called up the correct sensor view. She was right. Behind them the gateway hung motionless like a black version of the spectral bubble outside. As the arkship accelerated away from it, they were stretching out a long tail, like an oceangoing ship of old scoring a bio-phosphorescent wake through nighttime water.

"Why?" Kandara asked. "Is this *stuff* connected to the temporal flow?"

"No," Callum said. "The enclave is very finite. There's nowhere for the solar wind to escape, so it just churns around in here absorbing all the star's surplus energy. In a billion years it'll be a proper atmosphere—one of hydrogen, but pretty bloody thick."

"And hot," Jessika said. "And radioactive. The whole enclave will wind up resembling the interior of a red giant star. But hey, hopefully we won't be here that long."

"A billion years in this time, or outside time?" Alik asked.

"No way do we care," Kandara said, with a sly grin. "Even I never planned on living a billion years."

"Inside time—but that was just a guess," Callum said. "Actually, all they have to do is switch the enclave off for a day and let the nebula blast away into interstellar space, then switch it back on again."

"Oh, well, if you put it like that . . . Simple."

"It doesn't matter how things work in here," Alik said. "No one gives a shit. All we have now is the mission. We stay alive and free for as long as we can. And maybe at the end we get to tell a rescue ship where we are. That's it. Period."

"There must be some way of knowing what speed time is flowing at in here," Yuri said.

"Only if we can compare it with the outside rate to get a baseline," Jessika told him. "Which we can't."

"Crap."

"It doesn't matter," Alik persisted. "Concentrate on the mission. We're here to guide a human armada to the *Salvation*, right? Which actually we lucked out on, because fuck knows you can't see jack in here. Any invading ships will need to know where we are. We have a genuine purpose, people."

The bridge's main display swept the nebula aside and revealed the inside of the cave. All of them were sitting around on the rock ledges they'd claimed, unmoving.

The perspective was odd, Yuri thought, affecting him like a mild dose of vertigo. He was in the simulation looking out at himself, whereas in reality the image he was seeing only existed inside his head. The schizophrenic version of standing between two mirrors and seeing an infinity of yous.

Jessika had centered the camera on the transmitter the *Avenging Heretic*'s initiators had built, a simple black disk a meter wide, strong enough to blast a message across a solar system, with power reserves to last for an hour.

We'll never get that long.

But a few minutes should be enough. Any armada that slammed its way into the enclave would have sensors capable of picking up a human broadcast.

"Okay," Yuri said. "So we work out the best way to get it to the hangar entrance."

"That's a fluid situation," Kandara said. "We don't know what will be in or around the hangar when the armada arrives."

"So start with worst case," Alik said. "It's got armored quint standing guard in there."

"Standing guard?" Yuri snorted. "What is this, a medieval castle?"

"Quint in one of those flying spheres is way more worst case, anyway," Kandara said.

"There won't be anybody paying any attention to the hangar," Callum said. "The *Salvation of Life* is going into some kind of storage. No invasion force is going to get here for thousands of years. The Olyix already think we're dead, so the onemind won't be looking for us. Actually, if we get really lucky, the onemind will have let the hangar's biological systems die off by then. It doesn't need them; it doesn't need the hangar. All the *Salvation* has to do now is keep the cocoons alive."

"Congratulations," Alik told him. "That is the biggest crock of shit I have heard since we left Earth. In fact, since I don't know when."

Yuri bit back on a laugh as he saw Callum's pale face darken from petulance; even his freckles had vanished in the flush. "All right." He held up a hand to Alik. "That's the option we'd like to happen. But, Callum, we plan for worst case, okay? It'll give us something to do, if nothing else."

"Sure, whatever."

"I should be able to track down the physical location of this area's nexus," Jessika said.

Yuri frowned. "The what?"

"Nexus. It's like a network junction in the neuralstrata.

Take that out, and the onemind can't perceive or control the whole zone."

"Won't it just use entanglement with its quint and service creatures to see in?" Callum asked.

"Yes, but those are restrictive viewpoints. Taking out the nexus will give us a big tactical advantage."

"Okay," Yuri said. "See if you can find the nexus. If we can reach it, then we'll have it as an option. Otherwise we need to consider the easiest way to position the transmitter."

Kandara pointed at the black disk. "Put it in some kind of drone, one that can fly, and fly fast. We can get it outside before the *Salvation*'s onemind can react."

"More than one drone," Callum said. "We need some redundancy here."

"We need to know the armada's here first," Jessika said. "That means keeping track of the onemind's thoughts."

Yuri grimaced at that prospect. "Yeah."

"Let's see where we're heading before we start making any plans," Kandara said. "If it's inside some kind of big storage warehouse, we are truly screwed."

"A warehouse?" Callum said. "For arkships?"

"You know what I mean."

"I'm not getting that intimation from the onemind," Jessika said. "Just a sense, kind of like a contentment, that it'll be joining others."

"We're definitely heading somewhere," Alik said. "And the *Salvation* is still accelerating."

It took a day for their destination to become apparent. Orbiting seven AUs out from the sun was a gas-giant planet. Not that the sensors could obtain a visual image of it to start with; all they could see was a bright patch lurking deeper in the nebula where they were heading. But it had a tail that curved elegantly along ten percent of its orbit—a strange blemish in this mini-cosmos that was suffused with light. It was as if someone had taken a knife to slice through the nebula, cutting open a vein of inner darkness.

"How?" Alik asked simply.

"Impact," Callum replied, studying the small amount of data the G8Turing was extracting from the images. "The gas giant is plowing its way through the nebula, and its magnetic field is acting like a buffer, bending the clouds around it. Then when ions and electrons hit the field, it accelerates them, which heats them, so the plasma expands away— which is why it's a darker zone relative to the surrounding nebula. It's basically a version of the Io plasma torus around Jupiter, but the magnitude here is something else again."

"Is it dangerous?"

"Hell yes, if you don't have radiation shielding. And thermal baffles. You need to watch for electrical discharges, too. The worst part is that sparkle at the tail's extremity. See it? That's basically lightning forks about the same size as a moon. Get zapped by one of those brutes, and it's terminal game over."

Alik brightened. "So it's a potential weapon?"

"Nah, the arkship is big and solid enough to weather it even if you could somehow lure it inside the tail. The static would make your eyes water, mind."

"We don't want to disable the arkship," Yuri reminded the FBI agent gently. "There're a billion humans living on board."

"Call that living?" Alik retorted.

"Wait till we get close enough to see the buffer effect," Callum said happily.

They were eleven million kilometers out before they could see through the enhanced glow of the nebula surrounding the gas giant.

"A super-Jovian," Jessika announced as the figures started to resolve. "Two hundred thousand kilometers in diameter. But only forty times the mass."

"Failed star," Callum said. "Not quite big and dense enough to ignite. But hot."

"So is the nebula going to slow it down enough to not crash into the star?" Kandara asked.

"Given time," Jessika said. "But the nebula is only technically not a vacuum. For all the resistance it puts up, the gas giant has the same inertia as god. That really would take a hundred billion years to brake it out of orbit."

"Maybe," Callum muttered quietly.

Yuri could see he was studying the astronomical data intently. As they drew closer, the image improved. The gas giant had acquired wings. Vast elliptical arcs of bright rose-gold plasma currents curled around its phenomenal bulk—the result of a potent planetary magnetic field interacting with the mist of elementary particles that it was slamming through.

"It's like a science text illustration," Callum said. "You can actually see the magnetic flux."

"The planet's ring is wrong," Jessika announced.

Yuri checked the display. The gas giant had a single ring, two and a quarter million kilometers above its highly agitated cloudscape, which put it just outside the fringes of the magnetosphere's illuminated bow wave. Normally gas-giant rings orbited above the equator; this one was polar, and shepherded by a rosette of five small moons. The gaps between them were filled by thousands of individual light-gray motes. They were big—relatively—for a ring. There were none of the gravel-sized particles and dust grains that made up the rings of Saturn.

"Is that what I think it is?" Yuri asked.

Jessika just nodded.

"Jez-us," Alik said. "They can't all be arkships, can they?"

"Looks like it," Callum said.

"How many?"

"The G8 is estimating fifteen thousand, assuming placement is constant. We'll be able to get a more accurate count as we approach."

"Fifteen thousand!"

"Yeah."

"That has to be a mistake."

"Why?" Jessika said. "Because you think it's too high?"

"Well . . . I don't fucking know. Fifteen thousand!"

"The Olyix have been doing this for a long time," Jessika said. "Consider, the sensor outpost we came through is approximately fifty thousand light-years from here. That means it took the Olyix at least that long to fly a wormhole-carrying ship to it. And that's assuming they didn't expand their outposts in stages. Then there's the unknown of how long it's been there. Do you really think it's likely to have picked up Earth's radio signals the first year they arrived?"

"Holy shit. Fifteen thousand species taken captive?"

"It won't be that many," Yuri said.

"How the hell do you know that?"

"The human race wouldn't fit into one arkship; there's too many of us. And even a species as arrogant as the Olyix will need redundancy. So say they spread a captive race over two or three arkships—"

"Why so low?" Alik demanded. "Why not ten, or why not jam five species into one? Why—"

"Hey, calm the hell down, okay? This is just a *what if*. Let me have five, okay? It's a starting point is all I'm saying. So five ships per species, that gives us maybe three thousand different types of aliens."

"Three thousand evolutions cut short," Jessika said flatly. "Three thousand species denied their future. Three thousand destinies destroyed. It doesn't matter what ethics you have; that ring is the greatest crime it's possible to commit in this universe."

"Do you think your people will be in there?" Kandara asked.

"You're my people," Jessika snapped with uncharacteristic anger. "But my creators, the Neána? Yes, one of those ships will be the prison for those of them that didn't escape in time."

Yuri almost smiled at Kandara's little flush of awkwardness. "Jessika nailed it. The Olyix have been doing this a long time. Maybe a hundred thousand years, and maybe a lot longer than that. It would take them time to expand across the galaxy. They didn't go from this one star all the way out to the rim in a single surge."

"So we should be grateful it's not more than three thousand?" Kandara asked.

"I don't think gratitude comes into this. I think this whole situation is too big for emotion. All we can do is deal in facts."

"Observe and move on, huh?" Callum asked. "Don't let it get to you."

Maybe the others didn't catch the edge, but Yuri did. *He still hasn't let go of Savi and Zagreus. A hundred years, for*

THE SAINTS OF SALVATION 313

fuck's sake. "Like Alik said, we have a job to do. A worthwhile one. We need to concentrate on that."

"Sure. Yeah, right."

The *Salvation of Life* altered course over the next couple of hours, rising up out of the plane of the ecliptic so it could decelerate into polar orbit around the gas giant. As they drew closer, there was no mistaking the composition of the ring. Every one of its particles was another arkship, though the sizes did vary. Most of them had acquired their own protracted fluorescent halo from the magnetic bow wave effect, a more intense violet than the gas giant's gilded shimmer below their orbit.

As they maneuvered to rendezvous, sliding into a large gap in the ring, the *Salvation of Life* began to amass its own nimbus. Simultaneously, they lost the long tail of unquiet vapor they'd generated flying through the nebula.

Yuri was aware of the onemind's contentment returning to enliven its thought routines, the same self-assurance it had possessed right up until the point they'd triggered the Signal. It was among its own now, exchanging welcome thoughts with the other successful arkships in their eternal storage orbit. A validation of a pilgrimage completed under extremely difficult circumstances. Arkships in the ring appreciated and understood what it had been through, more so than any of the oneminds outside. Those who had not yet proved themselves.

Bitchy, Yuri thought.

And behind the cozy thoughts percolating through the ring was the greatest union of all: the fullmind. A summation of all that was Olyix. A loving guide, directing their destiny until they arrived at the end of time.

"The priest-king," he said out loud.

"Hey," Kandara announced. "It's come back."

"What has?" Yuri asked.

"The odd quint."

He pulled up the feed from the sensor clusters inside the hangar. Now that all the transport ships had gone, it seemed a lot bigger than it had on their voyage to the enclave. It was almost like viewing a still hologram, the thick weave of root-like tubes clinging to the rock walls and ceiling, with meager twigs sprouting slim leaves. Serpentine lines of bioluminescent cells embedded along the surface of the bark illuminated the big space in a uniform orange-tinted light that banished shadows.

The hangar hadn't changed since the plethora of service creatures and armored quint had searched it on the day the *Avenging Heretic* flew away on its doomed escape maneuver. Apart from once, when a quint visited and slowly walked around the whole area.

Now it was back.

"What's it doing?" Callum asked.

The quint was standing in the middle of the hangar floor, its fat, disk-shaped body swaying in a ponderous circular rhythm as if it alone was hearing a slow dance beat. Yuri wondered if its golden annular eye was scanning around like an attentive radar sweep in time with the motion. Its skirt of flaccid manipulator flesh flopped about idly, though small peaks rose and fell along the rim without ever really forming any real appendage. He watched the thickest of the five legs, ostensibly the leading one, flex with an almost nervous twitch, the kind a terrestrial animal would have as a precursor to a charge.

"It's . . . anxious?" he ventured.

"That's a bunch of bullshit," Alik said. "I'd say it is stressed; angry about something."

"You can't equate its body posture to ours," Jessika insisted.

"Yeah? Tell me it's not worked up about something. I know agitation when I see it."

"Fight or flight reflex," Kandara said. "I'm with Alik on this one."

Yuri just managed to avoid giving Callum an amused glance at her loyal support. "It's there for a reason. Everything they do has a reason. They don't have our . . ."

"Whimsy?" Callum suggested. "Imagination? Poetry? Individuality? A soul?"

"Sure. All of that crap. Jessika, anything you can determine about it from the onemind?"

"I doubt it. The deliberations of a single quint are essentially lost in the onemind thought flow. Too small to matter. Only the sub-sub-sub thought routines handle them."

Before he could ask her to try, she'd closed her eyes, concentrating. Yuri returned his attention to the odd quint. Distinguishing between quint bodies was difficult; there were very few individual characteristics. Given they were all produced in a convener, with every cell in their body stitched together to a standard template, they should be identical. But they did have occasional blemishes, a scar, or differences in the faint color striations inside the translucent manipulator flesh.

Everything their sensors viewed was recorded in a dedicated memory store. Yuri told his altme, Boris, to run a comparison.

"It is not the same quint body that was here last time," his altme replied. "The manipulator flesh imperfections are different."

"But it's behaving strangely, like the last one."

"Then it's most likely to be the same quint, but this is a different one of its five physical bodies."

"Right."

"I have nothing," Jessika said, her tone thoughtful.

"Okay," Yuri said. "Well, thanks for trying."

"No, you don't understand. I can't find the hangar—our hangar—in the onemind's thoughtflow."

"Huh?"

"Let me show you."

Yuri closed his eyes and accepted the simulation. It wasn't the bridge anymore; she'd brought him into her own interface expression. He was immersed inside the onemind's vast thoughtflow, literally inside a stream. A column of water that rushed past him, impulses from his skin telling him he was damp and cold. The rippling silver surface that was all around him was awash with poorly glimpsed images slipping past. He wanted to concentrate on them, but they were too fast and he couldn't focus.

"This is how you perceive the onemind's thoughts?" he asked.

"Yes. Don't you?"

"No. This . . . I'm more haphazard." It made him wonder just how different her mind actually was. *Maybe Kandara is right to be suspicious?*

"It's just not here," Jessika said.

They broke through the surface like a spawning fish leaping upstream. Emerging into chambers within the arkship. Multiple jumps, none of them lasting a second. The new surroundings barely registering before they were gone again. The tunnels. Chambers filled with biomechanical systems. Skyscraper stacks of cocoons, tended by ugly service creatures. Gloomy caverns unused since leaving Earth. Hangars without ships. Hangars with ships—all of them similar. None of them *their* hangar.

Yuri jolted upright on his rock ledge, staring around intensely as his mind sought to reorient itself, place him where he should be in the universe. He sucked down air, as if he'd truly been underwater for too long.

Kandara was giving him a strange look. "You okay?"

He nodded, not quite trusting himself to speak.

"There is nothing from our hangar," Jessika said calmly. "The impulses from every sensory cell in the hangar have somehow vanished before they reach any of the onemind's most basic routines, and they certainly aren't incorporated in its memory. We only know this because our sensor clusters can see the quint in there. Nothing else can."

"Did someone kill the nexus?"

"This has nothing to do with the nexus," Jessika said. "If that was burned, then the neuralstrata would be denied over a much greater area. This blind spot is specific to our hangar and the passageways leading to it."

"Why, though?" Callum asked.

"I don't know," she said, frowning. "Something has to be blocking the onemind's perception."

"Another neurovirus?" Alik asked in surprise. "There's another dark-ops team on board?"

"No way," Kandara said. "It took the combined resources of Alpha Defense and every settled world to get us on board. There is no second mission."

"Whatever is doing this is more subtle than a neurovirus," Jessika said. "The onemind doesn't know that it doesn't know. I don't get it. You can't get that deep into the autonomic routines. Or at least, I can't."

Alik's taut face crumpled up in confusion. "You mean odd quint is hiding from the onemind?"

Jessika shrugged. "When you've eliminated the impossible, whatever remains, however improbable, must be the truth."

"So what the fuck is it doing?"

MORGAN

OLYIX SENSOR STATION

The battle had lasted three days. It wasn't one giant fight between the two opposing sides; essentially it was over within the first two seconds when the armada's generators captured the wormhole that led back to the Olyix enclave. After that, it was basically a mopping-up operation. There were dozens of Resolution ships guarding the seven concentric rings of the Olyix habitat. They were no match for the superior numbers and weapons of the history faction, but surrender was clearly not part of the Olyix genetic code. Every one of them fought to the end.

Some Resolution ships tried to escape, presumably to try to reach and warn other Olyix outposts. They started accelerating outsystem hard within minutes of the armada emerging through their expansion portals. They had to be chased down, which took days. Ainsley took the lead on catching two of them.

The station's defensive formation of Resolution ships was eventually wiped out, leaving the seven rings exposed. Troop carriers from the *Morgan* flew in, escorted by armada battleships. The human squads even got into the rings, fighting their way through the honeycomb of chambers inside. They were backing up teams of corpus mobility weapons, which the squads had nicknamed "marines." Working together, they'd managed to corner and subdue individual quint bodies. None of the raids lasted long. The Olyix had fought back in a frenzy, their huntspheres demolishing whole sections of the rings' interior in their desperation to resist.

· It ended badly for the Olyix, with the corpus armada attack cruisers using antimatter blasts and graviton pulses to smash up the station rings and vaporize the larger surviving chunks. The rapidly expanding debris cloud absorbed the vapor plumes that used to be Resolution ships. With the station eliminated, attack cruisers swooped on the giant radio telescopes. Once they had disintegrated, the armada's attention turned onto the giant hoop spinning around the star's equator. A flotilla of fifty battle cruisers powered into a three-million-kilometer orbit above the extraordinary artifact. The corpus humans were interested in analyzing its composition and structure; their probes determined the outer structure had a unified quantum signature.

"You mean the shell is one atom?" Yirella asked.

"That interpretation is too crude," Immanueel said. "It is an expansion of classic duality, which in effect makes it a singular wave while simultaneously unifying multiple particles. Both states co-exist within the modified quantum field. A clever solution to the stress that the loop is subject to—not only the extreme radiation and thermal loading from its proximity to the sun, but also for something that large retaining its physical integrity while it spins. Ordinary matter would simply break apart."

She watched dispassionately as Ainsley arrived in orbit two million kilometers above the star. His white fuselage had turned silver, making it look like a fragment of the star itself had broken free to hang above the rowdy corona. The corpus exploratory flotilla backed off fast, high-gee acceleration propelling them into the safety of the expansion portals. They emerged within the umbra of the star's single rocky world, where the majority of the armada was flocking around the safety of its Lagrange 2 point.

Ainsley fired a lone missile armed with a quantum-variant warhead. It detonated barely a thousand kilometers above the loop's upper surface. The superhot gases of the chromosphere warped abruptly, forming a twister-vortex around the missile as they underwent dissolution. Then the effect struck the loop.

The entire edifice shattered at the speed of light, the annihilation effect racing in two waves around the circumference in opposing directions. A trillion fragments flew outward, blazing like nuclear comets as they went spinning off across interplanetary space and then beyond. Ainsley dodged them by simply rising up out of his ecliptic orbit.

"Great Saints," Yirella whispered. "We are become death, destroyer of stars."

"Not yet," Immanueel said. "But soon."

"The devastation," she said, surveying the expanding debris cluster that was once the seven-ring habitat; the smaller glowing haze patches that had been Resolution ships. Nimbi of whirling rubble evidenced where the sedate radio telescopes had once orbited, while the radiation bursts from collapsed wormholes were already shrieking their demise out across interstellar space. "The scale is frightening."

"Come now, corpus and Olyix are Kardashev Type Two civilizations at war over the future liberty of a galaxy. Our battlefields will awe and perplex alien astronomers for millennia to come, no matter what the ultimate outcome. If there is any validity in our struggle, it is that magnificence."

"I guess so. Nobody will ever forget us now."

"*Ever* is too long. But we will leave our mark one way or another."

"Do you think the God at the End of Time can see what we've done?"

"If it can, then we will have failed to kill it before it is born."

"Paradox."

"Always."

"I like to think of it as a condemned man on death row, watching the dawn arise on his execution day. It knows it will cease to exist, but there is nothing it can do to stop the sunrise."

"It will try. You know that, don't you?"

"I do. But it's not here yet."

"No. Your sun is still rising."

The noise and swirls of movement made for a hard impact on Dellian as he walked out of the troop ship. For all the high-stress charging around inside the Olyix habitat ring, the quick and lethal contacts with the enemy, adrenaline and terror, their combat had been inaudible. His helmet insulated him from the probably deadly sounds of high-energy discharges—beam, kinetic, plasma-blast. A quiet war, then, if not particularly civilized.

Then on the ship traveling back to the *Morgan*, there wasn't much room, so movement was at a minimum. But now here in the hangar, raw mechanical noise blared like a rock concert. The lighting was harsh, the air smelled metallic, and the remotes and the awesome corpus marines he'd fought alongside raced around on unknowable duties. He almost wanted to head on back into the sanctity of the troop carrier and wait for the commotion to die down. Almost. Because there *she* was, standing at the bottom of the ramp, a bright smile lifting her face as soon as she caught sight of him. Her specter of worry and concern was withdrawing into her lustrous eyes, so fast he thought he'd imagined it. So maybe he was only projecting what he wanted to see; after all, she more than anyone knew that he and the squad had come through unscathed.

He scurried down the ramp, where she bobbed about excitedly and flung her arms around him, kissing him exuberantly. Smiles and happy jeers encircled them, and Yirella extended her welcome-home grin to take in the rest of the squad.

"You're all safe," she said. "Thank the Saints."

Dellian saw the uncertainty flicker behind her happiness and knew what she was thinking. This is just a sensor station, a tiny outpost that was taken by surprise and superior numbers. Next time it's going to be real. Next time nobody can know who'll be coming down the ramp after—if there's even going to be a ship with a ramp. Like her, he hid the worry deep.

They hurried back to their cabin like the overeager kids they'd once been—too long ago now. Fucked hard and fast on the bed. Had a meal and a bath and fucked again. Slept. Spooned, less frantic teens now, more loving and sensual.

"Did you watch us?" Dellian asked as they headed for the shower together.

"Yeah," she said as the warm drops rained over her scalp, running together in soapy streams down her back. "Tilliana and Ellici are good. Plus, your training helped. You're tight now, not like back at Vayan."

"Not so naïve?" he teased.

"That too."

"Yeah. I was pleased with everyone. Though I still think we're surplus to the armada."

"They're not patronizing us. They are so elevated now I doubt they take hurt feelings into account."

"Right." He said it, but didn't believe he'd sounded convincing. Then hands slippery from soap gel came sliding over his chest, and he could banish his doubts again.

Dellian watched the feed in his optik as fragments of the Olyix power ring reached the rocky world. Silent blooms of their impacts peppered the dayside, sending gouts of debris shooting upward for tens of kilometers, obscuring the ancient landscape that had remained unchanged for a hundred million years. As the dust began to settle, nothing remained of the ancient canyons and dry mares and worn mountains; they'd been replaced by overlapping craters whose centers still glowed as their new lava lakes slowly cooled and solidified.

The devastation made him clench his stomach muscles in reflex as he and Yirella walked around deck thirty-three's main corridor to a portal hub. Outside the *Morgan*, in the shelter of the Lagrange 2 point, the armada ships increased power to their gravitational deflection effect and waited for the lethal swarm to pass. He knew they were safe— technically. Nonetheless, that level of destruction chilled him; it was so much greater than anything the squad did.

A portal took them into a xenobiology research facility housing one of Immanueel's aspects. They walked straight into a huge central chamber constructed out of translucent pearl-white walls that broke it up into a wide spiral of hemispherical cells. To Dellian, it looked a little too much like the biological technology the Olyix used. When he got close to any of the curving walls, he could just make out a burgundy filigree of veins below the surface. The similarity made him uncomfortable.

"Engineering always provides one definitive solution to a problem, right?" he asked as they walked in. "We work through methods and prototypes until we find how to do the job properly. I mean, there aren't two ways to build a generator or a processor junction."

Yirella gave him a glance that conveyed mild puzzlement. "As a general rule, yes."

"So . . . eventually corpus humans are going to wind up with the same technology as the Olyix? It's the plateau theory, isn't it, that some things just can't be improved any further, so it becomes universal, never changes?"

"As a general rule, yes. What's your point?"

"Well, if everything we do drives us in the same direction, doesn't that mean we might wind up like them? The Olyix?"

"No! Whatever made you think that? Why would we want to go around the galaxy enslaving other species?"

"It kind of adds a purpose to life, doesn't it? I'm not saying it's a good purpose," he added quickly. "But it's infected them; it gives them something to build their immortal lives around. I mean, look at Kenelm and all the others like him. This cause they had, to maintain Utopial philosophy down the generations, it kept him focused, gave him something to live for. Causes are dangerous, Yi."

"I know that. But, really, Del, we don't think like the Olyix. They're alien, remember. Not just in their biology and culture, but the way they think, too."

"Are they, or did they just shape themselves to fit the crusade that the God at the End of Time gave them? That's what you can do if your biotechnology is so advanced it allows you to morph your own body for convenience. And that's what we've got now, isn't it? We've got the potential to live forever if we want to. But I'm not sure we're built for that, not as we are. Our minds can't cope with us lasting that long, so we'd have to change them. Just like the corpus humans have done. Our outlook will have to evolve to cope with extreme lifespans. And what about all the people we're going to liberate?"

"What about them?" she asked sharply.

"Well, y'know." He shrugged expressively, hoping not too much shame was showing.

"No, Del, I don't."

"Oh, come on. They're not as . . . well, as *enlightened* as we are. The times they grew up in were different."

"And?"

Dellian was really starting to wish he hadn't begun this conversation. "Okay, the kind of people Saint Alik was dealing with—the New York gangs, for one. They're not the kind of people we can give full access to an initiator, are they? Really, I mean. Hell alone knows what they'd build!"

"Human civilization is always regulated, Del. It's how it maintains itself, the eternal balance between freedom and authority. We all live in the middle, obeying the rules for the common good."

"Maybe," he grumbled. "But the people from Earth might not be as accepting of limits when they see what we've accomplished, what our technology can provide."

"You're being very judgy all of a sudden."

"Hey, you're the one who normally has contingencies for everything. I'm just asking the question, that's all."

"A lot of things will have to be agreed if FinalStrike is successful. We can start with some kind of citizens' convention, I suppose, to agree a new constitution. When that happens, we can talk about introducing initiator restrictions, like the Neána did for their society."

"Okay. But I'm not convinced that attitudes will change."

"Are you saying we *shouldn't* liberate the humans who were captured?"

"No! But, it's just . . . nothing is easy anymore. When we left Juloss, I thought there'd be a couple of battles—tough ones—but after that it would all be over and we could all settle somewhere together and have a normal life."

"It wouldn't be the first time someone won the war then lost the peace. But really, Del, we have to win it first. Then we can start thinking what comes next."

"Yeah, but we will have to change ourselves. That's what worries me, Yi: what we'll become."

"If we change ourselves, and control how we change, we can keep hold of our souls. I'm not sure the Olyix did that."

"I hope you're right. But we've been pretty monomaniacal about spreading terrestrial DNA across the galaxy. That's a form of conquest, too."

"Not going to happen, Del."

He wanted to believe her. But not even Yirella could see clearly through so many variables. So he had to go on faith instead. That was easy. "Okay, so back to this tech equivalence. I was wondering if the Neána are hiding in slowtime enclaves, if that's what their abode clusters actually are? What if they're heading for the heat death of the universe in parallel to the Olyix, and one day both of them will finally confront each other?"

"Great Saints, Del, where's all this coming from?"

"I dunno. Just trying to think outside of training and what we're doing. I want the big picture, Yi. Like you have. But I don't think I can do that being me."

"Del . . . are you thinking of elevating up to corpus? Is that what all this is about?"

He shrugged limply. "I wouldn't want to do it alone. If I did, that is."

Her hand came down on his shoulder, making him halt. He found himself looking up at her face, and the sorrowful expression she wore. "You're not dumb, Del. You don't need this right now. We have a vital role in FinalStrike."

Again the doubt, but the words did comfort—especially coming from her.

"Afterward," she said, "if you still really feel like this, then we'll elevate to corpus together."

"Saints, you'd do that? Seriously?"

"Yes. And you know why?"

"I never understand you."

"Because it's reversible. If it's wrong for us, we just come back to being us."

He had to grin. "I thought you were going to say something about destiny, or love, stuff like that."

"Right." She licked her lips. "You only want to try it because all your bodies would be having sex together."

"Hey! I never thought of that. Wow!"

She sighed in martyred exasperation. "Come on. Before your brain melts. I want to see what Immanueel's got for us."

Twenty of the research facility's cells contained quint bodies. They'd been immobilized on top of a weird stool-like pillar, with their stumpy legs encased in black sheaths that were fused to the floor and a steel bracelet that encased their mid-torso skirt of manipulator flesh. Their neck and lower head were also collared by metal, leaving the apposition eye peering out above. Actinic white light shone down on them, which somehow added to the discomforting impression they were being crucified.

Less surprisingly, the Ainsley android was in a cell with one of them. It and Immanueel's big humanoid body were crowding in on the suspended quint: a timeless image of impassive scientists studying a specimen.

"Making good progress," Ainsley said as they came in. His featureless white hands were applying small scarlet hemispheres to the alien's translucent flesh. Dellian could see fibers had sprouted from the base of each of the little gadgets to weave around the dark organs inside; they were all heading for the core of the torso where the brain sat. Somehow, he could tell the quint's golden eye was unfocused.

"Progress to what?" he asked.

"Memory extraction," Immanueel replied. "Unfortunately, none of our marines managed to isolate a ship's central neural array before the onemind eradicated itself."

"Same problem I had back during the Vayan ambush," Ainsley said. "As soon as the onemind realizes its integrity has been compromised by intrusion systems, it does the honorable thing and suicides. With something as massive as an arkship, which has a neuralstrata the size of a skyscraper, that takes time, and I could extract some memories. But the Resolution ships here were quick, and the habitat onemind had plenty of warning. It erased its critical memories before you guys even busted your way inside it."

Dellian stared at the quint, keeping his face neutral. "But the quint didn't suicide?"

"They did not," Immanueel said. "At least not all of them. The squads and marines used a lot of entanglement suppression when you took the Olyix station, which breaks up the union between quint bodies. Once one is isolated from the other four in the unit, it becomes more averse to suiciding. I'm assuming that's a residual instinct from when they were natural animals with a single body each, not this rigid elevated version. That hesitation was what allowed you and the marines to stun them."

"And those filaments you're using? They suck the memories out?"

"Essentially, yes. But we do have to allow them a level of consciousness to animate their minds. They try to resist."

"Does it . . . feel pain?"

"No. They eradicated the whole concept from their bodies when they became quint. The nervous system is more like a data network. The body knows if it suffers damage, but it doesn't interpret it the same way we do."

"Okay." He wasn't sure if he was glad about that or not. Torturing an enemy combatant went against his principles, but this was an Olyix. It deserved punishment—not that he had the slightest idea what was appropriate for the cosmic-size crime they were committing. "So what have you got? Actually, what are you looking for?"

Immanueel's tail flicked languidly. "Information on the enclave star system is our primary objective. Firstly, confirmation it is where we believe it to be."

"Well, fuck you very much," Ainsley grunted.

"Which it seems is correct—thank you."

"Forty thousand light-years away," Yirella said wistfully.

Dellian exchanged a glance with her. He could see how daunted she was by the distance, but it didn't bother him. It was just a number. They had the route there, and a method of reaching it through the captured Olyix wormhole. They could take as much or as little time as they wanted traveling. Numbers were irrelevant.

"Yeah," Ainsley said. "Ten thousand years, and we finally

have a target. Statistically, we shouldn't be the first humans to take them on. But hey . . . those are the breaks."

Yirella's gaze hadn't moved from the immobilized quint. "The Neána must have done something like this. Soćko and Saint Jessika had so much information on the Olyix."

"Out of date information," Ainsley said.

"That was inevitable," Immanueel countered, "given the scale of events. But the basic facts are sound. Sadly, there is a hierarchy among the Olyix, with a quint created outside the enclave just about at the bottom. They don't know much."

"I thought they had an egalitarian monoculture society," Dellian said.

"You thought wrong, kid," Ainsley said. "Looks like evolution kicks up the same old shit no matter where in the galaxy you start off at. The quint are the lowest of the low in the Olyix civilization—worker drones, basically. But they do have a degree of autonomy."

"Free will?" Yirella asked sharply.

"Nah, this is more like the ability to come to low-level decisions away from a onemind's guidance. Just like every religion or ideology, you're free to do what you want as long as it conforms to the governing commandments. But it does allow them to progress up the ladder—another leftover of natural selection. Darwin would be proud of these little shits."

"So they can start to question what they're doing?"

"I suppose. In theory. But for a quint to change its attitude and beliefs, they'd have to be exposed to different ways of thinking, something to make them challenge their indoctrination. That never happens. Like you said, they live in a monoculture."

"What the hell is the next rung for a quint, anyway?" Dellian asked in fascination. "Six bodies?"

"A onemind," Immanueel said. "They transplant you into something pretty basic like a transport ship where you toil away loyally, and if you do a good job you get another promotion. Deliverance ship maybe, then up to Resolution ship or an outpost habitation station, arkship, welcome ship, a manufacturing base. But even those have different levels. If you begin your existence outside the enclave, you only get inside the enclave once you have fulfilled an invasion crusade and brought back the treasure of another species."

"Which is a problem for us," Immanueel said. "We have quint memories of the enclave star system, but none of these quint ever went through the gateway into the enclave itself. They have no firsthand knowledge."

"But you've found memories of the enclave star system?" Yirella asked excitedly.

"Yes. Recent ones, only a few years old."

Dellian used his databud to call up the data Immanueel and Ainsley had extracted. The primary of the enclave system was a large white star devoid of any planets. Instead there was a single impossibly dense ring orbiting five AUs out, backdropped by the splendor of the galactic core.

"The ring is rubble," Immanueel said. "Unnaturally large segments, too. They broke their planets apart to allow easy access to the available mass."

"Kardashev Type Two and a half, if you ask me," Ainsley said. "Re-engineering a star system, for Christ's sake! And that's just to prepare yourself for the crusade."

"We knew it would not be easy," Immanueel replied.

Dellian's optik provided a picture of the gateway itself. In his mind he'd envisaged a great technological orb, maybe protected by fearsome energy cannons that could blast a minor planet apart. True, the number of Resolution ships circling around it was formidable, but the gateway itself was hard to distinguish, as if it were nothing more than a ball of dark water reflecting the blaze of corelight.

The sight of it chilled him. So much history. *Humans have waited ten thousand years just to get this glimpse. Longer than the recorded history of humans on Earth, for Saints' sake. The sheer effort and suffering it's taken us to get to this point is humbling. I don't think I'm worthy.* "The gate to hell," he said softly. "Do you think we knew all along? That this was so big, so momentous, that it somehow wormed its way into our collective racial memory?"

"Could be," Yirella said.

He knew she was just humoring him, which put a bite of anger in his voice. "Immanueel, do any of these quint memories confirm the Saints were killed? I . . . I want to know."

To know it wasn't just propaganda, a lie to break me as part of the neurovirus. He saw Ainsley and Immanueel look at each other. A strange physical characteristic, considering they must be connected at some unimaginably high data rate.

"There is a level of deep knowledge in every quint brain," Immanueel said. "A racial memory, similar to us learning critical points of our history. It is a way of best understanding ourselves."

"They're dead," Ainsley said. "They got to the enclave star system on the *Salvation of Life* and made a break for it in the *Avenging Heretic* when they realized they would be discovered. But they managed to take out some Deliverance ships before they got hit. Imagine that! They set out using the most primitive technology—the best we had at the time, but nothing compared to what we have now. It was a fucking miracle they even got on board the arkship to start with! Yet they made it all the way to the Olyix enclave system, the first humans to see it. It was sheer ballpower that got them that far. And they sent the Signal, too. They did everything we tasked them to do, against the most ridiculous odds in the universe. It takes something to impress me, but those guys were genuinely the best of the best. They really were Saints. I'm proud I knew them."

Dellian's databud played the one file that was available. He watched a fuzzy vision of a Signal transmitter blazing away in front of a massive radio telescope. It was a weird visual inversion of natural astronomy, as if a star were orbiting a planet.

"So the original Signal is on its way to us," Yirella said reverentially.

"Yes," Immanueel said. "It will reach this part of the galaxy in about thirty thousand years' time."

"I wonder if it will be strong enough to detect?" she pondered.

"It should be."

"We should keep watch. We owe them that much."

"If humans are still free, I expect we will build quite a creed of expectation around the arrival of the Saint's Signal. It is a truly magnificent symbol of our fortitude and spirit."

Dellian played the file once again. *Thank you*, he told the Saints silently. *You've showed me we can prevail even in the bleakest of times.*

After a moment of respect, he drew a breath and started to concentrate on the layout of the enclave star system with its multitude of ships and industrial hubs. "So now what?"

"Now every corpus aspect will convene to formulate our assault strategy," Immanueel said. "We invite you to join us in a determinative congress."

Sure, like we can contribute, Dellian thought sullenly.

"Thank you," Yirella said. "Our priority has to be reaching the *Salvation of Life* and all the other ships holding human cocoons."

"The scale of the enclave star system, and its resources, is at the upper end of our projections. We understand the primacy of liberating the cocooned. However, if that proves unobtainable, our fallback position must be the successful elimination of the Olyix' ability to continue their crusade. Humans can resume a more normal existence if this nemesis is destroyed."

"No," Yirella said. "I can't countenance this. We exist to liberate our cocooned cousins."

"And every effort will be made to achieve this. But, genesis human, please consider the nature of the weapons that are going to be deployed—by both sides. Somewhere in the gateway system are mechanisms for breaking apart entire planets."

"In the past," Dellian said.

"Yes. But we cannot ignore the possibility that they still exist. The sheer number of Deliverance and Resolution ships available to deploy against our armada means that the destructive energies to be unleashed is phenomenal. And that is just on the Olyix side. We are bringing a neutron star to this battlefield to fire into their star. There *will* be a nova—probably a supernova. Our losses will be significant. You must prepare yourself for casualties."

"Casualties, yes. Failure, no."

"We will develop the best possible strategy. There are still too many unknowns to guarantee victory. I'm sorry, but this is not a war that will result in absolutes. Like the Saints, we will endeavor all we have to accomplish the mission. That is all our ancestors can ask of us: that we tried our best. And this *is* the best, our omega."

"We know," Dellian said before Yirella could start arguing. He *knew* her. "And we stand with you. All the squads do."

"Appreciate that, Dellian," Ainsley said. "So let's get that new congress of determination started, shall we?"

SAINTS

OLYIX ENCLAVE

Callum took the bowl of salmon and asparagus risotto out of the food printer's base slot and put it in the microwave that he set for ninety seconds. While that was heating up, he waited for the printer to finish conjuring up his garlic bread. The microwave *ping*ed, and he opened the door to inhale the meal's aroma. Faint traces of vapor were rising off the glistening rice. It smelled wonderful—

Bloody hell!

"Hey, those sensing cells on the pipe trunk leaves outside, are they olfactory along with everything else?" he asked ur gently.

Jessika and Yuri were slouched on their rock shelves, receiving the dream that was the onemind's thoughtstream. Kandara and Alik were sitting together, him with a beer, she sipping a white wine. They all looked at Callum.

"Well?" he asked, one hand gesturing to the steaming bowl. "Does the onemind have a sense of smell inside the *Salvation*?"

Jessika glanced at the risotto and frowned. "There are some leaves budding off the trunks that are sensitive to atmospheric composition. I wouldn't call it smell, exactly. The ability is used to detect if there's an imbalance in the gas mix—too much carbon dioxide building up, that kind of thing."

Callum stared down at his risotto suspiciously. "Yeah, but the molecules this is giving off have a terrestrial signature, right? The onemind must have a record of them."

Now everyone was looking at Jessika. "Possibly," she admitted. "I'm not sure about the sensitivity levels, mind."

"If we're cooking food in here for a couple of years, there's damn well going to be a buildup of smells, that's for sure," Callum said. "They'll drift into the corridor outside. Food smells always do. I remember walking through Edinburgh late on Saturday nights."

"What are you saying, man?" Alik asked. He held up his beer. "I have to give this up?"

Callum shrugged. "Water is neutral."

"Fuck that!"

"Cold food is less effervescent," Kandara said thoughtfully.

"Effervescent?" Alik sounded astonished.

"Evaporation. Hot food gives off more odor."

"You're saying we eat Goddamn cold sandwiches for ten years?"

"Callum may have a point," Jessika said.

"Jez-us H. Christ almighty. No fucking way."

The food printer flashed a ready light, and the garlic bread slid out of the slot. Callum gave it a guilty look.

"Garlic is quite strong," Yuri said. "Worse if you heat it."

Callum badly wanted to glare at Yuri, who was clearly channeling the devil at peak temptation. But that would've given Yuri a win.

"Seriously, cold food?" Alik asked. "What about—aww, crap—coffee? No! Come on, man."

Kandara nodded sagely. "I think Callum may be right. We shouldn't take the risk."

"I am *not* spending what's left of my life drinking . . ." Alik shouted—then took a breath and spoke quietly. "Water."

"Vodka has little effervescence," Yuri said with low amusement. "And is best served iced in the correct Russian way. Even fewer stray molecules given off that way."

Alik gave a cry of disgust, throwing his hands up.

Callum awarded the garlic bread a last resentful gaze and

dropped it in the toilet pan. The flush swirled it away into the atomizer unit at the bottom of the nutrient formulator. At least there was nothing he could do about the risotto now but eat it.

"The G8Turing should be able to suggest a decent low-emissive menu for us," Kandara said.

"Wait." Jessika held a hand up. "There's another ship arrived: the *Liberation from Ignorance.*"

Startled, Callum's limbs locked in an idiot pose, fully laden fork just centimeters in front of his open mouth. "At the gas giant?"

"No. Into the enclave. It just came through the gateway. I can feel its thoughts being unified within the fullmind. Oh, shit!"

"What?" Yuri asked sharply.

"They sent a . . . they called it a Reconciliation Fleet, to Earth. The *Liberation from Ignorance* is the first to come back. It's full."

"Full?" Callum said. He knew what she meant, but still . . .

"Of cocoons."

"Oh, Christ, no. How can that be? We've only been here— Oh. Right. Slowtime. It must have been years outside."

"Couple of decades, at least," Kandara said. "More when you take the wormhole flight time to Sol and back. Say thirty."

"We've not been in the enclave two full days yet," Alik protested.

She directed a mocking smile his way. "Really slow time."

"What happened?" Yuri asked.

"Earth fell," Jessika said. "They sent in thousands of Resolution ships. They broke the city shields. They cocooned everyone left on the planet. Billions of us. Billions!"

"What about the settled worlds?" Alik asked.

"The *Liberation from Ignorance* feels sad, sort of incomplete," Jessika said. "Our terraformed worlds were practically deserted when the Olyix arrived. The exodus habitats had all portaled out, and the Olyix couldn't find out where."

"Thank God for that," Callum said. "They did it. They got out across the galaxy. There's still hope." Somehow he was wiping moisture from his eyes, not knowing how it got there. *The kids are safe. Damn, they'll be old by now; the grand-kids will probably have children of their own. At this rate it won't be much longer—not even a week—and they'll have lived more years than me. And they'll never know I'm still alive, that we made it.*

"That went better than I expected," Yuri said. "They got out—Emilja and the Zangaris, even Soćko, presumably. They know what they have to do. We got the easy assignment, now."

"Easy?" Alik challenged.

"Sit and wait," Callum said. "And work out how to call the human armada. When it comes."

Callum had a fitful sleep that night. In his short, vivid dream he walked through nighttime Edinburgh, back in the good old days, him and his pals, making their way to someone's flat after the pubs had closed. The paved clear routes were slick with a cold rain washing down from the Scottish Highlands, reflecting jagged streaks of streetlighting and holo-gram ads. Then the lights went out one by one, leaving him alone, staggering through a canyon of stone buildings, their walls shifting out of alignment. There was some light re-maining in the dwindling city—the windows of kebab shops and chippies and burger joints and pizzerias and noodle bars. People were crammed inside; elements of grills and ovens glared lava-orange, casting occult glows over drawn faces—faces that were losing their features, melting away to ovals of flesh. And the fat smoke rose from charring food, billowing up into the extractor fans. Jets of rank smog flooded out across the street, their stench unavoidable. And in the gutters, rodent noses twitched behind the bars of the drains, pushing up toward the source—

"Cal?"

He cried out as the dream juddered away. Jessika's face was poised above him, concern on her gentle features. "You were crying out in your sleep," she explained. "Bad dream?"

"Something like that. What time is it?" He unzipped the side of his sleeping bag. Cool air slithered over him. *I need a thicker sleeping bag.*

"Five in the morning, on the ship's time we're keeping."

"Uh, right. Thanks. And sorry." The light in the cavern was a minimal glimmer, allowing the shadows to loom large, compressing his world still further. Just like in the nightmare.

"The G8Turing has reconstituted the formula for milk," she said. "It's less of an aerosol with its molecules now. I can warm some for you, if you like."

Warm milk. What am I, five? Bloody hell. Maybe Alik is right; some sacrifices are too great. Best to go out in a vapor plume of decent Scotch. "Thanks. I appreciate it." He rubbed his hands together before cupping them and blowing hard on his dry palms. "I'm cold."

"Get used to it," she said as she fussed around the food printer.

"Damn. This isn't how I thought it would end. I was hoping for the bang, not the whimper."

She put a mug in the microwave. "There's another ship arrived."

"Christ, now what?"

"It's called the *Refuge of Hope*, and it's scooped up humans from the exodus. I think they came from two new planets."

"Shit. The exodus? Man, that's bad. They're hunting us, then?"

"Yes. I'm sorry, but it was inevitable. They are fanatics."

"Damn, I wonder who it was."

"I can try and filter a little deeper."

Callum took the mug she was offering him. "Thanks." The liquid tasted of nothing: warm white water.

"There is one thing that the fullmind is examining in a primary consciousness routine," she said. "They're concerned. They know about the exodus and what its goals are."

"The exodus goals? You mean, that humans are supposed to be building up our military strength to fight back?"

"Yes." She hesitated. "And more."

"More?"

"They must have interrogated people, extracted memories directly from their brains. The Olyix know who we are. The five of us are featuring pretty heavily in the fullmind's thoughtstream."

GOX-QUINT

SALVATION OF LIFE

Nullifying the neuralstrata's perception in the hangar is an easy accomplishment, a few simple misdirections in the autonomous routines of the local nexus. I don't enjoy concealing my activities from the onemind, but I don't have a choice; the onemind is mistaken about its priorities. Those bastard humans are still alive in here somewhere, so I've got to do what I've got to do.

Everything that's happening is just more proof I'm right. I'm amassing the information brought to us by the redoubtable *Refuge of Hope*, who carries so many of this vile human race. Didn't expect that, did you, you little shits? Didn't expect us to come chasing you across light-years and centuries. We've seen it all before, you know, all the treachery and villainy overrated simians like you represent. We know how to deal with you.

You will be brought to account for yourselves at the end of time. There is no escaping that noble destiny we are charged to deliver.

I mean, did you really think your pitiful little brains could outsmart us, even with those fucking Neána scum pushing you, lying to you, giving you false hope and better technology they probably stole from us or the Katos? No, my deluded friends. That's not how this universe works. Not at all.

And how dumb was that plan anyway? Run away and

breed like deviant rats until there are enough of you to swarm our enclave? Have you no intelligence at all; can you not even try to imagine what we have amassed to defend ourselves? We have been shepherding and saving other forlorn, misguided races since before your squalid zero-sentient ancestors even learned how to use fire.

So you sneaked your way on board? So fucking what, assholes? Nobody's ever going to hear your Signal. Not over that distance. You lost.

And now all I need to do is finish my one final cleanup assignment. Because I'm going to find you, no matter how long it takes. I am going to kick your loathsome—

—

Oh. Interesting. That's it? That's them? The best of the best? You call them saints now? Really? Them? You've got to be fucking kidding me. I've had bodies that are already dead and rotting who would be a better choice.

Still, that means you're mine now; I fucking own you. And I'll enjoy every second of it. I might even hook into the local environment biostructure plexus to smell your fear when I find you. And, yeah, I know I should hand you over for a cozy little suspension in the limbo ships until we reach the end of time. But, hey, accidents happen, and your bodies are feeble; they damage easily in a fight. I know that. Do I ever! I'm *good* at it, too.

See, the trick to hunting terrestrial animals is putting yourself in their position, adopting their mind-set, understanding their motivations. Once you are centered in that place, their options become clear to you and their moves easy to anticipate.

When I draw out the memory of the stolen transport ship from the neuralstrata, I know the exact position it rested on the floor. I stand where the nose was, pointing toward the wall. I feel it, build the memory into a solid vision. I am the transport ship. They move inside me. They skulk. Shuffle from day to day. Their primitive brains spark dully as they formulate their pitiful plans.

Everything the humans did on the day they launched their S-Day attack against us was designed to put that one ship on board the *Salvation of Life*. Big deal. It took everything you had, cost every last fusodollar—your entire output from every industrial station, all your dirty political deals, just to place five people here in this very hangar.

And here they remain—somewhere close. Don't you? I know it, even if the *Salvation of Life* won't acknowledge that. That onemind is too far up its high and mighty ass to listen to me.

Well, I know you now. Saints.

Yuri Alster, a has-been secret policeman and alcoholic miserabilist incapable of relating to another human.

FBI senior special detective Alik Monday. Professional ass-licker to politicians, the most corrupt high-level fixer you can get.

Callum Hepburn, disgraced engineer, weakling and moral coward, Emilja Jurich's court eunuch.

Jessika Mye. Neána construct. Not even alive by any definition.

And Kandara Martinez. Oh, Kandara, you think you're tough, don't you? Ms Virtue, a black-ops illegal murderer of gangstas. So badly damaged by your parents' death, your ruined mind has to be controlled and calmed by drugs, lest your own fury burn you up.

I will find you, Kandara. I promise I will find you and finish what you and I started on Verby. I'm going to remind you what your kind used to call me back then when I moved among you. It was a good name, too, because every human knows, Cancer always gets you in the end, *bitch*.

MORGAN

OLYIX SENSOR STATION

The day before the armada's departure, Yirella visited Immanueel in their centrex. She walked in cautiously, anxious as always not to skid on the glossy floor. The shapes that made up the hemispherical wall seemed different somehow, more rounded this time, a little less mechanical. As before, she tried to work out which was Immanueel's big biophysical body. For some reason, her pattern recognition was poor today.

"Are you well?" Immanueel's voice asked.

Yirella turned full circle, trying to get a lock on where they might be. The little lights that slid along the cracks were of no help. "Doing okay, like always. Nervous that we're about to go kick Olyix butt."

A chortle echoed lightly around the chamber. "Methinks you have been spending too much time with Ainsley."

"You're probably right. I like his confidence. I find it soothing."

"Some say confidence. Others, ego."

"Yeah, but think what he's accomplished in his life. He was born in the twenty-first century, for Saints' sake. He created the Connexion Corp, helped Emilja push through the exodus. And here he still is, a warship that makes even you guys edgy."

"Born rich, and leveraged his way into exploiting portal

technology. Then he bought politicians. Connexion was the pioneer when it came to establishing rock-squatter asteroids as tax havens, which helped maintain Universal culture across Sol."

"Humans are not born equal; we all have different abilities. His we really need right now, like the Juloss civilization needed me and the boys."

"I acknowledge the necessity of difference among us, and encourage it. If it were a currency, every human would have been rich since the dawn of our history."

She caught a movement. One of the wall shapes was moving slightly faster than the others, its profile changing, the light beads sliding away from it. "I came to ask if you had pulled anything else out of the quint brains. Specifically, the history of the enclave star system?"

"Ah. Our quest to find the origin of the tachyon message? Well, I have good news: It proceeds apace. The enclave system is indeed the home star of the Olyix. Alas, I could not determine how long ago they heard the message from whatever entity they named the God at the End of Time. However, the Olyix do appear to have been on their crusade for over two million years."

"Saints! They must be close to invincible by now. The Angelis fleet was running to another galaxy. Even the Katos were avoiding direct confrontation. Does that make us the dumb ones?"

The shape stopped moving for a moment.

"An interesting assessment," Immanueel's voice said. "In the time the Olyix crusade has been active, they have invaded and captured over three thousand alien races. The exact number is unknown to us, as details like that are not important to quint. They do so lack our unquenchable curiosity about the universe. Perhaps if you are born, or created, into a society that has been unassailable for so long, you no longer feel the need to ask questions, for all have been answered already."

"Yeah. That would certainly account for their arrogance, the belief that they're right. I just can't stop thinking about how much damage they've caused in cosmic ecological terms. It's devastating."

"Unlike our own expansion, which has been scattering terrestrial DNA across a sizable portion of the galaxy."

"Touché." She watched Immanueel's outline resolve as their biophysical body reached the base of the wall. "So you don't think it was a God then, sitting up there in the future?"

"I consider it extremely unlikely. Which I admit sounds like an agnostic answer rather than a definitive atheist assertion. More likely it is some remnant of the Olyix trying to reinforce a temporal loop to bolster its own position."

"More paradox."

"Not entirely. The fate—or destiny—of the Olyix are undoubtedly linked to this entity. Consider this: Who else would know where to aim the tachyon beam? This entity would have to know both where the star is in that time, and that there is someone there to receive it. Not to mention using a language that the pre–crusade era Olyix will understand."

"Gods are omniscient," she mused.

"Indeed, so why do they need captives from the past to be brought to their altar?"

"You mean, why does a next-generation Olyix need them? That's likely what this is. We will need to ask it."

Immanueel's biophysical body straightened up as they detached themself from the wall. Their tail was the last part to be free, and flicked around in celebration. "Ah, I always enjoy taking my first breath. It is an experience I associate with my old singlebody waking from slumber."

She gave their tall body a bemused grin. *Talking about gods . . . "*You've scheduled departure for seventeen hours."

"We have, yes. Is there a problem?"

"No. I just wanted to check you think you have everything you need. We can wait here as long as you like while your manufacture systems build more weapons."

Immanueel's urbane face produced a beatific smile. "If FinalStrike cannot be accomplished with what we have now, it cannot be accomplished at all."

"Okay, then. I just wanted to ask. I'm officially here to tell you the advisory council thinks four days is enough flight time for us."

"A day for each year, then. Very well, we will manipulate

the time flow inside your ships accordingly. May I ask what you intend to do during that time?"

"The squads will have one final day of training. Then it's just going to be gym work and contingency planning. It should bring the squads to peak efficiency when we reach the gateway star."

"Commendably efficacious. However, I was referring to you, dearest genesis human. What will you do during Final-Strike?"

"I'll watch. There's nothing else I can do by then. We either win or we don't. I've done everything I can now."

"Indeed you have." Immanueel reached down and took her hands. "There is no need for you to come with the armada to the enclave."

"No! Don't even go there. I am not abandoning my friends and my Dellian. I never will."

"The genesis human would consider every rational proposal."

"Good luck finding her."

"You haven't even heard what I'm suggesting."

Hating herself, she said: "Go on."

"A subgroup of my aspects could break away and become independent."

"Wait, what? I thought that was . . . not exactly illegal, but frowned upon? Corpus humans don't divide up, do they?"

"Not normally, no. But one way or another, we face the end of an era. We have done everything we can to ensure the survival of our species, and the egress faction has guaranteed that some humans will remain forever free. If this armada of ours fails to defeat the Olyix, then we will not survive the weapons that are being deployed in the last battle."

Yirella took a shaky breath. "Okay, I wasn't expecting you to be quite that blunt. But that's not how we should venture into this. Pessimism never won any battle."

"Ah, yes, a Dwight D. Eisenhower quote, I believe."

"You believe right."

"I do not go into this with pessimism, Yirella. Objectivity is my creed. And given the odds, a fallback would be prudent. You could create a secondary version of yourself as well."

"Fuck! No way. Absolutely not."

"If FinalStrike is successful, we would simply remerge with our originals. If not, you live."

Yirella squeezed their hands warmly. "Without anything to live for. No, Immanueel, I see you are kind and sweet, but no. Whatever fate has waiting for us at the enclave, I will embrace it with the people I have shared my life with. And I'm glad you're now one of them." She stood on tiptoes and kissed them gently on the cheek. "Thank you."

Ainsley's android was waiting outside the deck thirty-three canteen like a forlorn statue. Yirella slowed as she saw him and produced a mournful smile. She knew why he was there.

"Join us," she said. "The whole squad's inside. Your friends."

"Your friends, you mean."

"Fire forged friends, and all that. They'd be glad to see you. We're watching the armada form up. It's becoming something of a tradition."

"Another reason I can't stay."

"Yeah, I accessed the formation plan. You're taking point."

"Gotta have someone at the front who'll shoot first and ask questions later."

"A later that's never."

"That'd be me. You got an argument against it?"

"No." She shook her head, studying his blank white face for any intimation of expression. "Immanueel told me there are some of your weapons they can't replicate."

"Yeah, the part of my armamentarium that came from the Katos. I don't remember much of them from the Factory era; I guess that was edited out of my memory for security. But they've taken the understanding of phase matter up to the celestial level. Trust me, these are the swords Gods use to smite the unrighteous."

"Interesting. So why didn't they ever go head-to-head with the Olyix?"

"Same problem we have, I guess. If we lose, the Olyix gain the technology. Makes it a fuck of a lot harder for the next guys who come along."

"That makes no sense. Why give it to you, then?"

"I'm supposed to be running a guerrilla campaign, remember. Factory ships like me were supposed to hassle the Olyix in this portion of the galaxy so the exodus descendants can finally catch a break. Out here in the big dark, they'd never be able to catch me like they never caught the Katos mothership. I've got evasion techniques like you've never seen. See what I did there?"

"Oh, dear." She grinned fondly even as she winced. "So we're not likely to ever find Sanctuary?"

"No."

"Well, thank the Saints for that. If we can't, neither can the Olyix."

"Yeah." His white lips crinkled up, head nodding slightly, an imitation of awkward.

Yirella let the pause drag on until she shared the moment. "So . . . I'll see you on the other side."

"That's a date."

"You take care, point man."

"I will. Yirella, you know he's crazy about you, right? The boyfriend."

"Yes."

"Just checking. Sometimes you start to take things like that for granted without even realizing what you're doing. And I was married fifteen times, so I really do know what I'm talking about here."

"Saints, Ainsley Zangari—a romantic. That's not in any history files I've ever accessed."

"Seeing high school sweethearts always makes me happy. And there ain't much happy in this galaxy right now. I'd hate to see another little bit die."

"I think I get the high school reference, but it's okay; you don't need to worry about me and Del."

"Good. I'm going to go now. I'll see you in a week or so. When this is all over."

She fought the hardening muscles of her throat that were making talking so difficult. "I'll see you in a week."

———

"You all right?" Dellian asked when she walked into the café with its arched windows letting in the warm Parisian sunlight of late spring.

"Sure." She gave him a reassuring smile, as real as the canteen's textured environment, and sat at the table with the rest of the squad. "So what's happening?"

SAINTS

OLYIX ENCLAVE

Kandara hadn't made a list. Not exactly. But . . . if she had, then the way Callum made a gurgling, sucking sound every time he concentrated would be right up there at the top. Or the food. After twenty days of cold, bland food, her stomachache was nearly constant. Then there was Alik's slow-boiling anger. Yuri's sullenness. Only Jessika seemed relatively unchanged.

So perhaps she is just a sophisticated AI after all.

It wasn't just the crap food and the confined space and the boredom that was preying on everyone. The news from outside the enclave had been getting progressively worse—not helped by the slowtime inside the enclave, which meant that news from outside arrived in bursts, with centuries of activity compressed into dense updates.

They'd all been horrified when they learned how the Olyix had started to capture the ships and worlds humans had thought they were building in secret as they fled across the galaxy. Privately Kandara started to suspect that it was over; that they'd lost. And after a few days it was obvious she wasn't alone with that thought; everyone's mood was darkening further, flames burning up the last of the air. The only thing keeping them going now was routine; building the drone transmitters had come to resemble a workfare scheme in her mind. It was pointless but kept them occupied. *Three fucking weeks, and we've completely lost our shit. Mother Mary!*

"Guess who's turned up again?" Jessika exclaimed.

Kandara didn't bother to look up. She and Callum were running tests on the latest transmitter drone before they knitted up the casing. The initiators had produced all the components, but without an assembly bay they had to be put together by hand. Precision work—which was difficult even with the small manipulator rigs the initiators had provided first. On the plus side, she reflected, it kept Callum busy, so that was less moaning they all had to listen to.

After a couple of false starts, they'd refined the design of the transmitters to the shape of a streamlined manta ray a meter long, with a sharp intake grid on the front instead of a mouth, and twin ion drives at the rear. With its flexible-camber wings it was designed to maneuver fast once it reached the passage outside, then flip into some elusive acrobatics in the hangar in case anything hostile was waiting there, before streaking out to freedom through the main hangar entrance. Once outside, the drones would call the invading human armada, revealing the location of the *Salvation of Life* in its storage orbit.

Except time outside had stretched and stretched until it had become an abstract. As far as they could make out, close to ten thousand years had passed. That figure didn't connect with her at all. She'd begun to wonder if her glands were malfunctioning and she was living in some kind of dream state.

When Zapata, her altme, did shift the test data to one side, Kandara accessed the hangar's remaining sensor feeds. Jessika was right; Odd Quint had returned. It began its lumbering walk around the hangar, a black stonelike orb held upright in a protuberance of its manipulator flesh, like a priest with an offering. *Or maybe an Olyix with a hard-on.*

"What the fuck is it doing this time?" Alik asked.

"Same as it always does—nothing," Callum replied.

"No," Kandara corrected him. "This is the second time it's brought that orb. That has to be significant." Over the last couple of weeks, a quint (or the many bodies of a quint) had returned eight times to perform its strange examination of the hangar, its behavior singling it out and earning it the nickname. Every time, Odd Quint had neutralized the neuralstrata's receptors so it remained unseen by the arkship's onemind. If they'd been on Earth, she would have said it was engaged in some type of criminal activity. *Smuggling human artifacts, maybe? Or could it be an alien nark dealer?* But despite knowing ridiculously little about Olyix culture, she didn't believe that. There was a purpose behind its constant appearances. And a covert one at that, which made her very uneasy.

"The orb has to be some kind of sensor, or recording gadget," Yuri said.

"But Odd Quint doesn't apply it to anything to analyze," Callum complained. "It can't be a Geiger counter, can it?"

Kandara studied the way the quint was holding the orb up, the manipulator flesh shifting it from side to side, a motion that was partly obscured by its tilting walk. "It's waving it," she said. "Mary, you might have been right about the food smell, Cal. I bet that gadget takes air samples."

"Shit." Alik gave the cavern's jagged entranceway a guilty glance. "How sensitive can it be? I mean, like, bloodhound good? If it is, we are royally screwed."

"Anything we can do, so can they—and then some," Yuri said.

"If that sensor was as good as a bloodhound, Odd Quint would be here already, along with the rest of its bodies," Kandara said. "So maybe we've got some time."

"Oh, here it goes," Jessika said.

Kandara watched as Odd Quint started to walk along one of the smaller tunnels leading away from the hangar. They didn't have any sensor clusters hidden in the tunnel's trunk pipes, so all they could see was the quint slowly enveloped by the thickening shadows, the orb still upheld.

"Definitely smelling for us," Kandara said.

"I can buy that," Alik said. "But why doesn't it want the onemind to know?"

She gave him a troubled glance. "I don't know."

"There are eleven tunnels and corridors out of that hangar," Yuri said. "So it's only a matter of time till it passes the entrance to our cavern. If that orb has any decent level of sensitivity, it'll smell us."

"We should kill it," Kandara said.

"That's a real dumbass idea," Alik said. "You step out here and shoot that mother, the rest of us'll have ten minutes max."

"I'm not so sure," Kandara said. "There's still no neural-strata coverage of the hangar, right?"

"No," Jessika agreed reluctantly.

"So?"

"So? It's a fucking quint. One of five," Alik snapped. "You shoot it, the other four are sure as shit going to know about it."

"Yeah, but are they going to tell?" She gave him a grin that was pure taunt—very superior. It was a mean tease—especially if you knew all Alik's buttons, which she did. But being cooped up in this rock jail was driving her loco.

Alik's mouth opened, then shut; he looked at Yuri for help. "We're not doing this, right? Tell me we're not."

"We don't know if whatever Odd Quint is doing is illegal," Yuri said slowly, "or heretical, or whatever brings down the local gestapo. But it's obviously not totally aboveboard."

"You cannot gamble our lives on that. Jez-us! We still got us the mission." Alik gestured at the four completed transmitter drones, their sleek stealth-gray shapes soaking up the cavern's low light. "Getting these outside is our priority, right?"

"I wasn't planning on going *mano a mano*, asshole," Kandara said. "We rig up a creeperdrone and use a stinger. The biotoxin Alpha Defense worked up from Soćko's formula will kill a quint, right, Jessika?"

"It should do, yes. I can't give absolutes."

"And if we use a creeperdrone"—she gestured at the row of inert spider creatures—"we can get an entanglement suppressor up close. Then the other four bodies won't even know for certain it's dead."

"So then what? You know they'll just come down and investigate."

"Bad news for them."

"You cannot be fucking serious?"

"Have you seen where we are?" she shouted, both arms flung out to deride the cavern. "Do you have any idea how deep this shit is? Drowning depth, okay? The Olyix are scooping up every generation ship we fly now. We're losing. Has that even registered with you? We are *losing*! This does not have a good ending, not for us. We are not walking off into the sunset, Alik. There is no sunset, because there is no Earth anymore to have a sunset on. They killed it—they murdered our world! All we have left now is our righteous vengeance. And in Mary's name, I swear I will make them fucking pay. Before I am done, they will curse their *God* for ever sending them its message."

Alik looked at her in shock, a diminutive twitch bending the corner of his mouth. She'd never seen that before. On anyone else, it would have been a full jaw drop.

"Hey." Jessika put her arm around Kandara's shoulder. "Take a breath. It's okay."

"Oh-fucking-kay? *This*? This is okay?"

"Absolutely. Get this: A ship's just arrived from one of the Olyix monitor outposts along the expansion wavefront. The fullmind is startled. It's never been startled before, not like this."

"What about?" Yuri asked.

Jessika closed her eyes. "Something's happened out there. They thought humans had set up another lure planet, Vayan, so they sent a welcome ship with a batch of Resolution ships. The wormhole collapsed as soon as they got to Vayan. Someone hit them hard."

"Finally," Kandara breathed. For a second the tension in her thoughts actually slacked off.

"Wait," Jessika said, and her hand rose in an involuntary reflex. "A neutron star. That's weird."

It was all Kandara could do not to scream at her. "What's weird?"

"The rotation speed changed."

"You can't change a neutron star's rotation speed," Callum protested.

"It's changed," Jessika insisted. "The Olyix sensor outpost made careful observations. Something is out there at that neutron star. Something powerful. The fullmind knows the plan is for humans to assemble at the nearest neutron star once the Signal has been received. It's dispatching a harmony fleet." Her eyes opened, showing puzzlement. "But we're too far away. Our Signal couldn't possibly have gone that far yet."

"We need to be ready," Yuri snapped. "Callum, get that last transmitter drone finished. Kandara, we might have to deal with Odd Quint."

"I am so ready for that!"

"Come on, man," Alik said, "they're forty thousand light-years away. Even if these neutron star people crush the harmony fleet, it'll be forever until they get here."

"Twenty-five years—their ship time—if they travel at point-nine C," Callum said. "For us, that's probably six months to a year. But it gives the Olyix outside the enclave forty thousand years to build up their defenses."

"And the same time to track their progress," Yuri said. "And intercept them."

"They changed a neutron star's rotation," Jessika said with a lot of emphasis. "That's Kardashev Type Two right there—probably the high end of it, too."

"And the Olyix aren't?" Alik asked. "Do you even remember what's powering this enclave? Generator rings around a fucking star."

"I'm just saying it won't be that easy to intercept them."

"You ask me," Callum said, "this is the first piece of good news we've had since Feriton called us together for the assessment mission to Nkya. I'm with Yuri; we need to be ready."

Kandara grinned softly at that miracle. She and Callum finished running diagnostics on the transmitter drone components and instigated the casing knit. They usually ran more tests, but decided there was no point. If the tests showed a problem, there would be no time to correct it. So just finish up and hope it worked.

"This is what you call a real all-up test," Callum muttered as the upper casing segments closed up and fused together along the drone's dorsal spine.

Kandara was about to reply when she felt a frisson of

surprise within the *Salvation of Life*'s onemind. When she tried to read it raw from the thoughtstream, instead of clarity, she felt a backwash of alarm.

Jessika looked around with an incredulous smile on her face. "They're here."

FINALSTRIKE

Dellian knew there was no way he could tell he was in a slowtime flow, yet some annoying little instinct kept telling him there was something subtly wrong with his universe. The armada's journey down the wormhole would take four years, real-time—depending on how you define real. But for the *Morgan*, it would only be four days. His brain kept searching for signs that something was wrong.

"More like portents than signs," Yirella said with cheerful mockery on the first night. "Portents are imaginary, after all. Time is always constant to the observer, Del. Forget about it."

He couldn't, of course. Every paranoiac little sense he had, the hair-trigger responses he'd developed in combat training, were constantly alert. Being vigilant for so long was draining. He also stubbornly refused to use any of his glands to clear the nonsense away chemically, earning another eye roll from Yirella.

And now here they were, only a couple of hours out. His anxiety had made him rise early, needing to be ready. Because if their artificial time had been misjudged somehow . . .

Yi's right, I am an idiot.

With its long storage racks stretching away under gloomy lighting, the cohort hiatus facility on deck seven put Dellian in mind of a warehouse. As he walked down one of the aisles he could feel the resonance in the floor from all the support machinery.

After the last training simulation, his cohort had been resting up for two days. He almost wished he'd been doing the same as they traveled to the enclave star system, but then he knew almost everybody on board was in an equally hyped-up state. All those final update briefings provided by corpus humans, data stripped directly from captured quint brains—and between those meetings, lots of frantic, needy sex.

"You know this isn't goodbye blues sex, don't you?" Yirella had said last night as they clung to each other in bed. "I mean, we're both nervous about FinalStrike; that's natural. But it's not the ultimate battle."

"Huh?" was all he could manage in a twilight created by the textured cabin in the Immerle estate woodland—the exact same one he'd been assigned in their senior year.

"There is so much we have to do after we liberate the *Salvation of Life* and all the other humans in the enclave," she told him earnestly.

"Yeah. We've got to get them home for a start."

"Maybe. But the corpus humans don't need us for that. If we're going to end this threat, we have to take down the God at the End of Time itself."

He rolled around on the bed to stare at her in surprise. *Does she ever inspire anything else?* "Saints! What?"

"It's still out there, Del, lurking up in the future. There's nothing to stop it sending messages to all the surviving Olyix, restarting the crusade all over again. Apart from us, of course. We can stop it."

"Us?"

"Somebody has to. I don't see the Neána stepping up, do you?"

"But . . . how?"

Which was when she told him about the tachyon detector that the corpus humans had built for her. When she'd finished, he didn't know if he was going to laugh or cry. "But if we kill the God's home star now," he said slowly, his brain as always light-years behind her, "that means it won't be around to send the message back to the Olyix. So Earth won't be invaded, the exodus will never happen. We won't be born."

"Paradox. I know. It's fascinating how many theories there are about this, isn't it? But don't worry. If it is a temporal loop spun off by a time machine creating an alternative universe, us breaking that cycle will stabilize our timeline. We just carry on, but in this reality the God at the End of Time doesn't send a message back to the Olyix, so there's no further split, no new alternative Earth that suffers the same fate yet again. At least, that's what Immanueel and the other corpus humans postulate."

He was horrified by how eager she sounded. Horrified that they would begin their own monomaniacal crusade. He'd committed his entire life to FinalStrike knowing that afterward—if he survived—he and Yi could go and live an ordinary life on a new world, or maybe even Earth itself. Now this.

FinalStrike isn't going to be the end for Yirella. Saints, she's never going to stop, not until she's seen the last Olyix in the galaxy dead and their God exterminated.

He'd sat up in bed and rested his head in his hands, feeling the same numbness and despair he'd known when he'd heard of Rello's death.

Yirella's arm went around his shoulders, and she hugged him. "What's wrong?"

"Wrong?" he barked. "Fuck the Saints, Yi, don't you ever just stop? Don't you ever think about what anyone else might want?"

"But killing the God-entity before it's born will make us safe, Del."

"You sure about that? Because I don't know, Yi. I'm too dumb to figure out quantum timelines and which reality is real. And don't try explaining, not tonight, okay?"

"I just wanted you to know tomorrow that I'm always going to be there, trying to think up answers," she said meekly.

He nodded, not trusting himself to look directly at her. "Sure. Hey, I knew that anyway. You're the one stable thing in my world."

"That's my line, Del, I'm the one who relies on you."

After that, of course, he hadn't slept well. In the morning he did his best to make it up to her, eating a nice eggs Benedict breakfast together before leaving with plenty of hugs and kisses and a good show of reluctant yet glad to be *finishing* this. Except he wasn't. Being scared shitless about the fight was one thing; despair at what came after was something else again.

Saints, but I am one screwed-up mess.

He came to a halt at the section of the racks that held his cohort. They were in new casings now, designed by the corpus humans. Still being stubborn about not using his neural interface—this morning of all mornings—he used his databud to activate the cohort. They were like flattened black eggs the same length as his own body, but made out of porcelain and inlaid with slim silver hieroglyphs. Smaller than before, then, yet managing to look even more efficiently deadly.

With drive systems powered up, they rose out of their cradles and eased forward. Dellian reached out and gently ran an appreciative finger over the curving nose of the closest. They were all abruptly circling around him, nuzzling affectionately like metallic puppies. He was reliving the easier times when they were just muncs, sleeping with him in the estate dormitory, comforting and warm and adoring. Understanding him as he understood them, when knowledge was pure instinct.

Even now they could read his unhappiness; he could tell from the subtle angles they hovered at, the gentle pressure applied as they rubbed playfully against him, their little shakes of contentment as he stroked their cool casings while his hands felt only their short gray-and-chestnut pelt. His mind could hear the familiar soft hooting sounds they used to make.

"Thanks, guys," he said. "We'll get through this, okay?" He stood up straighter and gave them one last pat each. "Okay then, let's"—he grinned—"lock and load."

Farther down the rack, the cohort's exoarmor came alive. Another innovation courtesy of Immanueel and their friends. The corpus all swore they didn't model the exoarmor suits on hellhounds, but Dellian was pretty sure they were just covering their embarrassment at going full-on-nerd battle-gaming. After all, it wasn't like the Olyix were going to be intimidated by cybernetic beasts from human mythology. But, Saints, surely any living creature would find them menacing?

Twice the size of a human, massing a good quarter of a ton, with four standard terrestrial limbs and two prehensile tails—which in just about any combination could claw their way along a narrow arkship tunnel if they didn't have a clear flight path. They even had a wedge-shaped head on a stocky neck, containing sensors and weapons, while the shell was woven through with energy deflector fibers and atomic bond enhancers, leaving them capable of surviving a tactical nuke at close quarters.

The cohort settled their ovoid casings into the exoarmor's shaped recesses, and the petal lids snapped shut over them. Limbs flexed, running through test procedures; a multitude of weapon nozzles telescoped out, then back again. The cybernetic hellhounds landed and formed up in an eager pack, their adaptive feet making clacking sounds on the smooth floor.

"Nice." Dellian smiled down at them. His own hulking armor suit was farther along the rack. He walked toward it, just as Janc and Xante appeared at the end of the aisle.

"Saints, I thought we were early," Janc exclaimed.

"And that's why some of us are mere squad members, while I'm squad leader," Dellian told them.

They jeered him loudly before the three of them hugged. It meant so much more today. He'd always thought leading the squad on their Vayan ambush mission was as intense as life got. But this . . . *the Olyix enclave*!

Uret was next, followed by Falar and Mallot. More squads were turning up in the hiatus facility, activating their cohorts. The noise level built steadily. Dellian was glad of the activity; he could concentrate on routine, making sure everyone had run their equipment tests. His own armor suit needed a replacement rear left visual sensor—the ultraviolet receptors were below optimal—while Xante's needed a new magpulse rifle projectile feed tube. All their equipment was designed with multiple redundancy modes, ready for whatever damage they were punished with in combat, but he wasn't going to allow anyone to move out at anything less than full operational capacity.

Just before they got into their suits he made them gather in a circle, arms around one another's shoulders. *We need to be this close. It might be the last time we ever see one another in the flesh.*

"We left pep talks behind on Juloss," he said. "And face it, I'm crap at speeches anyway. But we've trained for this our whole lives. Saints, this is what we were born for! So I know we're going to watch one another's backs and do the best we can—especially for the poor bastards we're here to liberate. All I want to say is that I'm glad it's you guys that I'm facing this with."

The group hug tightened—almost as much as Dellian's throat. He wiped away some tears from his eyes, not trying to disguise it. He wanted them to see how much they meant to him. Looking around, he wasn't the only one overtaken by the moment. That felt good, too.

His suit was standing in front of its storage and maintenance alcove in the rack, chest segments open. Intellectually, he still wasn't comfortable with the arms and legs. This brute was so big that his own limbs wouldn't be long enough, so the corpus humans who designed it had provided its legs and arms with three joints apiece, giving him extra knees and elbows. The extremities were governed by his own physical kinesis—walking, running, reaching, lifting—as extrapolated by an integral genten to provide perfectly coordinated movements.

A maintenance remote brought a small set of mounting stairs out for him, and he climbed up, twisting awkwardly to get inside. He slipped his legs down the tunnels of spongy padding that felt like oiled leather until he was sitting on the haunches' cushioning. Then there came the bad bit, *fitting* the waste extraction tubes—as usual accompanied by some serious grimacing. Finally he was able to push his arms into the suit's sleeves. The suit went to active level one, and the loose padding in the arms and legs contracted around his skin, gripping firmly. There was no separate helmet. Instead his neck and head were completely enclosed by the top of the torso, reducing vulnerability. Its upper section hinged down and locked, triggering a long moment where he felt as if he'd been imprisoned in a medieval iron maiden.

Graphics and camera feeds swarmed across his optiks, and his databud confirmed full integration. Systems data swirled green. A quick double-check on the ultraviolet receptors, and he initiated full-motion possession, which allowed his physicality to puppet the suit's movements. So . . . a shadow-box review for the arms, run on the spot, twist and sway and crouch in a seriously naff dance routine. From the claustrophobia of a second ago, he was now liberated, weighing nothing as he floated gracefully along the aisle.

Every display remained green.

He kept an eye on the rest of the squad, confirming their telemetry as they finished their screwy assessment calisthenics, half smiling at the way everyone's cohort kept their distance, as if they couldn't quite believe what they were seeing.

He opened the mission comms icon. "Ellici, Tilliana, comms check, please. Switching to multiple redundant linkage."

"We got you, Del," Ellici answered. "Hardened em encryption, omni and directional, plus multiple entanglement rotation. Stand by. One hour to wormhole exodus."

If everything goes okay, he added silently. "Thank you, tactical." He raised his arms as if he were performing a blessing. "Okay, squad, let's get down to the armory and load up. Embarking in twenty minutes." He started walking toward the portal at the far end of the aisle, secretly rather pleased at looking like a full-on badass demon, his hellhound pack following eagerly.

Yirella found the *Morgan* distinctly unsettling that morning. The ship's quarters were big—deliberately so— giving people space. You normally couldn't tell if there were a hundred people in the chambers around you, or none. But now, walking along the curving corridor, she knew she was alone. If you were part of the *Morgan*'s crew you had one of two jobs: You were either a squad member, or you were in one of the tactical command cabins. No exceptions—apart from her. Even Alexandre was with Ellici and Tilliana as they approached the end of the wormhole.

Parting with Del wasn't helping her mood, either. She thought she'd done the right thing telling him all about the tachyon detector, the prospect of eliminating the God at the End of Time in this era, of the intriguing complexity of quantum temporal theory. But it hadn't gone down the way it had played in her mind: his fascination, enthusiasm. And certainly no admiration for her enterprise and determination, which she'd privately looked forward to. *You selfish idiot,* she cursed herself.

He was going out to face a physical fight far worse than last time—and that's if they even got through the gateway and into the enclave. The last thing he needed was uncertainty and complexity.

But that was my goodbye gift. Fool!

He'd smiled and been affectionate this morning during a breakfast he'd barely picked over. At least she'd recognized the anxiety shadowing his thoughts. It had taken all of her self-control, but she hadn't pressed him about it—*what do you think, what are you feeling?* He didn't need that, didn't deserve more of her wild ambitions. So maybe she had helped.

"For fuck's sake," she shouted down the deserted corridor. "This is not about you!"

I should be in tactical. I should be capable of being in tactical. I should have made a lot of different choices.

But my choices brought us here.

The strength drained out of her as she went into the deck thirty-three canteen. It was pleasantly warm, the air scented with coffee and cinnamon. On the other side of the windows, the Boulevard Saint-Germain was waking up to a spring morning. Vibrant flowers in baskets decorated the façades of the other bars and cafés, the road was slick with water from a cleansing night rain, and cyclists were pedaling along with cheery smiles on their faces.

Yirella caught sight of herself reflected in the glass. Hunched shoulders, which with her height looked just pathetic; face that was beyond miserable and sliding into broken. She glared at her reflection. "Pull yourself together. He needs you."

The food printers produced some croissants, and she made coffee. Columbian: black, strong, bitter. She held the cup in her hands and slumped back in the chair, eyes half closed, and began to sing.

I saw Earth reclaimed
Got me a ride back
An old ship, can't reach near light
Earth where once we came
Earth where we all belong
Earth where life is strong
Oh to be—

"Mind if I join you?"

Yirella squealed as every limb twitched in shock. Her lurch sent coffee splattering over the table and onto her trousers. "Saints! I didn't know anyone else was on this deck." *And it had to be hir!*

"Sorry, didn't mean to startle you." Kenelm hurried over with a handful of napkins and started dabbing at her trousers. That only made it worse.

"Give me that." She scowled and began wiping properly.

Abashed, sie began mopping up the puddle on the table. "I haven't heard that song before."

Yirella blushed. "It's from back when we were just kids." Which was good enough; no need to tell hir she'd gone through a big music phase when she was in therapy. Writing lyrics kept her mind busy and diverted from the problems that jailed her.

"It's good." Kenelm was standing over the table, looking lost. Sie wore a simple blue-and-green tunic that could so easily have been mistaken for a uniform.

Someone was having trouble adjusting to their lack of status.

Yirella gave up. "You'd better sit down. It's going to be a long day."

"Thank you." A remote collected the clump of soaking napkins, and sie sat down, leaving an empty seat between them. "I've spent two thousand years waiting for this, but I know they'd be apprehensive with me on the bridge."

"You say bridge, I say comfortable main council room. Sometimes I think our fabulous resources have tempted us down the wrong route. Maybe we should have stuck to the kind of structures our ancestors had. You *knew* you were going to war in the old ocean navy battleships."

"You knew your chances of surviving weren't too good, either," sie countered. "Those days are badly over-romanticized."

"You're probably right."

"Different era, different requirements. The gentens will handle most of the battle."

"But it's reassuring having people in the loop to make the final decisions," she insisted. "There's a psychology about facing the enemy. You need to have belief in your own ability, but not one that verges on hubris."

"I think the Vayan ambush cured us of hubris," Kenelm said.

"Yes. But I'm worried about Del."

"That's natural. It's good."

"Really? I might have said the wrong things before he left. I should be more . . . empathic."

"Oh, please. I've never seen any couple more synchronized than you two. It's like you're each other's munc. You know half the time the pair of you don't actually speak in full sentences when you're talking? You don't need to."

She frowned. "We don't?"

"No. It's funny and endearing. The rest of us are always left playing catch-up."

"Oh."

"One mind, two bodies. Or a quint missing three."

"Don't say that."

"Sorry. Bad joke."

"What was she like?" Yirella asked suddenly. "Emilja, I mean? I can't believe you knew her. She's history for me, not something we can ever connect to."

"I have trouble remembering that far back, to be honest. Sometimes I think my life before Juloss is just a dream. But . . . she was tired, that's what sticks the most now. I don't mean lack of sleep tired, but weary. Exodus just wasn't working as a concept, and it had taken everything she had to make it happen in the first place. So she'd spent eight thousand years watching it fail. Can you imagine that? Eight thousand years seeing hope slowly fade away, being beaten down century after century. All those Strike ships and generation ships we sent out into the galaxy, and all they gave back was silence. But she weathered it, even though she was trapped by her own vision."

"That's why she founded your group?"

"Yes. She knew we had to change, yet our own rigid cultural stability made that difficult."

"So you're actually a rebel?"

"Yeah." Kenelm smiled wryly. "I guess you could say that. In my own way. I was never against you, Yirella. It was just that you wanted to change so much so quickly. It was reckless."

"Yet here we are. With the corpus humans' armada and about to FinalStrike. The first humans to ever get this far."

"Yes. A fantastic achievement. But did you ever stop to think what would happen if it went wrong? You gambled with a whole human civilization. You once asked what gave me the right to guide the *Morgan*'s future away from Strike. That was a modest realignment compared to this."

"But it worked."

"It gives us a chance, granted. But worked . . . ? I hope it does, because I don't think there will be another human attack against the enclave. Ten thousand years, and this is the only one."

"I don't know," Yirella said, toying with the coffee cup. "If your group's strategy worked, there are a lot of humans safe in the dark out there. But they won't hide away forever. It's not in our nature. As you have discovered."

"Touché."

"If we fail, there will be others. The Factory ships will give what's left of the exodus expansion a breathing space to regroup."

"Maybe," Kenelm said. "But for what it's worth, I think this is the best shot we'll ever have." Sie grinned disbelievingly. "A fucking neutron star!"

"Yeah." She ordered the printers to produce a new round of coffee and croissants. "Ten minutes." There was a nervous tremor in her voice that no amount of willpower could banish.

"Let's take a look."

Yirella used her interface to summon tactical displays into the café windows. The cozy mirage of Boulevard Saint-Germain faded away, replaced by bright schematics. More data slipped directly into her mind, adding comprehension.

The wormhole representation was a tunnel made up of white walls, with subtle imperfections as if they were falling through the eye of a hurricane, allowing her to track their progress. Ainsley was the lead ship, slowly rotating as he flew forward. Behind him were seven specialist ships containing negative-energy generators to assume immediate control of the wormhole when they arrived in the gateway system. Chasing them hard were more than a thousand warships and weapons platforms, assigned to defending the wormhole terminus. The armada would need to leave through the wormhole after FinalStrike was over, which meant it would be subjected to a ferocious assault by the Olyix.

The rest of the armada followed, with the *Morgan* class ships in the middle. As before, the neutron star was at the rear—an ominous presence that always seemed to be edging closer to the armada.

Yirella opened Ainsley's icon.

"Welcome aboard," he responded immediately. And she was flush with the sensation of speed leaking down the link into her neural interface—an exhilarating power plunge, spinning around for the sheer joy of it, a kingfisher on its dive. There was also a deeper sensation: the pent-up power of his phenomenal weapons bestowing an urbane confidence.

The end of the wormhole was visible now—a black speck some indeterminable length down the swirling white tunnel, but expanding. Ainsley leveled out his roll, and the speed seemed to increase. "Thirty seconds," he said in perfect contentment.

"Whatever happens," Yirella said, "I'm pleased we met."

"It's been too short, kid, but oh boy did we hit this universe hard."

Ainsley flew out of the wormhole. There should have been a noise, Yirella thought, like a sonic boom but for when you punctured the fabric of reality to get back in—a detonation of light and sound that hadn't been known since the big bang. Instead: nothing. The utter absence of sound as if her ears were in a vacuum. But there was light . . .

"Oh, you beautiful Saints," she whispered.

Ahead was a huge white-spectrum star, looped by a splendorous ring that shimmered as if it were the child born of two diamond worlds colliding. But behind that was the true majesty of the Olyix homestar: the galactic core stretching halfway across space.

Ainsley's external sensors found the spectral gateway itself, two and a half AUs away.

"At least it isn't on the other side of the star," Yirella said.

"Still got to get there," Ainsley retorted. "That's going to be fun."

A second after Ainsley, the generator particles reached the terminus, producing their own negative energy to interface with the existing pattern that held the wormhole open. Just as they'd done back at the sensor station, they established control over the exotic matter structure even as the Olyix cut power to their own generators. The terminus remained open.

Ainsley's acceleration was so brutal he shone like the sun as the solar wind struck its discontinuity boundary. More than five billion perception fronds burst out from his hull, saturating space to provide unparalleled resolution. Seven Resolution ships were already closing on Ainsley at eighty gees. He selected a degenerator pulse, and a speck of ultra-dense matter collapsed into pure energy, which was channeled into seven beams. Seven Resolution ships detonated in glorious violence.

A fraction of the overspill degenerator pulse energy transmuted into an omnidirectional radio blast. "Hello, motherfuckers," Ainsley announced to the entire Olyix system. "The humans have arrived. Sorry we're late. But now we're here, let's party."

As soon as the fronds went active, Yirella's tactical display started to expand. "Oh, hell," she grunted. "Are you seeing this?"

"We expected nothing less," Immanuel replied calmly.

The fronds were now perceiving a spherical volume of space half a million kilometers in diameter, with the wormhole terminus at its center—a zone populated with eight hundred seventy-three Resolution ships. All of them were now in motion. Hundreds closest to the terminus were closing on it, while eighty converged into a battle formation to pursue Ainsley.

Armada ships were swarming out of the wormhole, attack cruisers establishing a defensive perimeter around the generators, obliterating the Olyix systems and nearby ships. Missiles and graviton beams speared out from the incoming Resolution ships, countered by nucleonic barriers and antimatter missiles from the attack cruisers. Ultra-high radiation flooded out from hundreds of matter-annihilating explosions, creating a lethal energy storm around the wormhole terminus that reduced all unprotected mass to its subatomic particles, adding to the radiative deluge. Even the fronds' perception failed amid the colossal overload. Continuous waves of missiles streaked through the chaos. Defense cruisers died, but still more of the armada poured out of the wormhole, reinforcing any gaps in the protective cordon they were establishing, while squadrons of heavy-duty battle cruisers plowed through the hypercharged arena to strike at the incoming Resolution ships. Controlled by corpus sub aspects, they were extremely maneuverable and extensively armored. After the first twenty encounters all resulted in the Resolution ships being destroyed, the remainder of the Olyix ships began to take evasive action. Waves of teardrop-shaped Calmissiles accelerated out from the tightly packed formation of battle cruisers, raking short-lived black contrails in their wake as they devoured the plasma they flew through. Within seconds of being fired, their acceleration wound up to an incredible thousand gees. The closest Resolution ships didn't have time to react before the first salvo sliced clean through their fuselages. More distant Resolution ships increased their evasion tactics to watch the Calmissiles flash past, their colossal velocity swiftly taking them beyond the outermost shell of Olyix ships assigned to guarding the wormhole terminus. Some Resolution ships used suppression projectors, killing the Calmissiles' entanglement, exposing the raw structure of the small vessels that were instantly vulnerable to both abrasion from ultra-velocity interplanetary dust and ordinary X-ray laser fire.

"That's good," Immanueel said as they lost the eighteenth Calmissile. "We have the ranging on their suppression technology. Phase two deployment strategy is now being modified accordingly."

Yirella watched more than five hundred Calmissiles dwindle away out into the star system, difficult even for the sensor fronds to follow. Only their internal communication links allowed the armada tactical network to track them.

After a minute of flight, during which he eliminated nineteen Resolution ships, Ainsley increased his acceleration up to two hundred eighty gees and vectored around in a massive parabola until he was heading straight back toward the wormhole terminus, powering headlong for the formation of a hundred seventy Resolution ships that had been chasing him. Even though she knew what was about to happen, Yirella found herself gripping the arms of the café seat.

With twenty-five seconds before he reached the Resolution ships, Ainsley triggered another degenerator pulse. This time, his entire energy output was routed directly into a monster electromagnetic discharge, temporarily blinding the multitude of sensors tracking him, denying his opponents critical data for a couple of seconds.

"Oh, Saints," Yirella moaned. She could see Ainsley's course vector as he streaked back toward them; he was going to fly past the wormhole terminus with barely two thousand kilometers' separation distance at a terrifying speed. *If this doesn't work . . .*

Ainsley brought the ultradense matter shield up from energized suspension to deployment status. At that point, he was seventeen thousand kilometers from the formation of Resolution ships and closing *fast*. When he reached fifteen, he triggered the shield.

The shield massed roughly the same as a medium-size

moon. In its phasefolded state, it was a disk thirty meters in diameter and one centimeter deep. It unfolded at point-nine-five light speed, expanding out to eighty thousand kilometers in diameter and one hundred microns thick. Boosted quantum equilibrium ensured every compositional atom shared the same state, unifying them.

The Resolution ships didn't have any time to vector away; they crashed into what was in effect a two-dimensional moon with a closing velocity in excess of nine hundred kilometers a second. Their impacts were simultaneously distributed and absorbed by the entire mass. Star-hot debris plumes were bulldozed out of the way by the shield's unstoppable inertia, forming relativistic rivers across its surface before cascading over the edges.

Five seconds after the last impact, Ainsley refolded it.

Yirella let out an involuntary scream as she watched the incredible shield rushing at deadly speed toward the wormhole terminus. It eclipsed the entire galactic core, smothering the blazing star, even most of the glittering ring was obscured. Some animal level of her brain told her such a thing couldn't possibly be real.

Then it shrank away as fast as it had emerged, and Ainsley swept past the wormhole terminus. Three seconds later, the shield sprang out again. Dozens of Resolution ships inbound toward the wormhole smashed apart as it plowed through them, graviton beams and antimatter impacts useless against its artificial structure.

"Told you it'd work." Ainsley chuckled. "The Katos really know how to manipulate matter." He folded the shield away again and performed another three-hundred-gee maneuver back to the wormhole terminus. "You guys ready?" he asked the corpus humans.

"Confirmed," Immanueel said. "Beginning phase three."

The generators holding the wormhole open began to accelerate at two hundred fifty gees, heading for the gateway. The armada cruisers englobing it matched their speed. Ainsley took up his point position again. Another salvo of Calmissiles was launched, racing on ahead to form up in a protective umbrella to intercept the incoming Olyix ships.

"Ten hours to reach the gateway," Yirella said. "There's a lot that can go wrong in that time."

"Not just for us," Kenelm replied. "Our attack profile will force the Olyix to divert resources away from us."

"I was never sure about this part," she admitted. "If it was me defending the enclave, I'd throw everything I had into preventing us from reaching the gateway. If we kill the enclave, it's all over. They can take the other losses."

"I disagree. If we destroy their wormholes, the galaxy will have millennia before they can venture out again in their obscene crusades. That will give newly evolving species a chance to become starfaring, and for the Neána to make contact first."

"Yeah," she mused. "About that . . . I'm not so sure being subtly manipulated by the Neána is necessarily the best option for anyone."

"It's *an* option—which is more than most species get at the moment. Besides which, we're talking about immediate tactics. The Olyix oneminds will have to decide how badly they want to keep the wormhole network. My guess is: pretty bad."

"Saints, I hope so. The more I'm reviewing our sensor data, the bigger their resources seem to be." She looked away from the tactical displays to see Kenelm's tense expression.

"They've been actively running this crusade for a couple of million years," sie said. "Even if they've plateaued or stagnated—whatever you want to call it—they've had all that time to prepare for an assault. Because they knew damn well that someone would eventually come here to challenge them."

"It doesn't matter now. If we win, the galaxy will be free of them. If we lose, well . . . we won't be around to care."

"You are such an odd fatalist."

"Yeah, I know."

Yirella glanced back at the displays playing within the windows. The huge flotilla of Calmissiles that were racing out into the gateway system was now over a quarter of a million kilometers away and spreading wide. Forty percent of them were heading straight in for the gateway, while the remainder were targeting the ring, fanning out so they would cover every industrial station. Sensors were showing her thousands of Olyix ships accelerating toward the invaders from across the system. The majority were on course to intercept the wormhole terminus, while the rest were outbound to confront the Calmissiles.

"Multiplying," Immanueel announced.

Again, there were few visual clues, even from Ainsley's sensor fronds, leaving Yirella to rely on the armada's tactical network. The portals covering the Calmissile fuselages expanded out to half a kilometer in diameter. Hundreds of additional Calmissiles flew out of each one. It was like a firework starburst, but inverted, with lightsinks rather than dazzling flares. The newcomers also started accelerating away at a thousand gees. Five minutes later, they too expanded and released another batch of Calmissiles.

"Half a million active portals effected," Immanueel said ten minutes later. "That should occupy their ships, if nothing else. We'll have complete access to the entire system in twenty-four hours."

Despite having tens of thousands of ships and thousands of industrial stations in the ring, the Olyix seemed uncertain where to direct their forces. As Yirella predicted, every ship within an AU of the gateway headed there to defend it, while the remainder were dispersed to deal with the proliferation of Calmissiles.

Approach speeds were a big factor. Resolution ships simply didn't have the kind of acceleration that could catch the Calmissiles. They had to go for head-on interceptions, using entanglement suppression with supreme accuracy. The armada tactics were simple enough. If a Resolution ship was flying to intercept, the Calmissile would maneuver to strike it. While they were still ten thousand kilometers apart, the Calmissile fuselage portal would expand so that a battle cruiser next to the portal's twin would open fire with graviton beams or ultra-powered X-ray lasers. If they missed, it didn't matter; the Resolution ship would be traveling away from the gateway system at a velocity that would take too long to cancel before it could return to the ring or anywhere else it could be of use. The same went for a Calmissile that succumbed to suppression and broke apart from solar wind collision shock. It had diverted the Resolution ship from defending strategic assets, so it had achieved its goal.

Despite the scale of the armada forces, and the importance of reaching the gateway, Yirella kept focused on the seven thousand Calmissiles that were heading in for the star. It wasn't an obvious maneuver; their course vectors should be interpreted as taking them to the ring on the far side of the star from the wormhole terminus. But they were critical to the assault plan. In total, it would take them three hours to reach the corona, by which time the Olyix might realize their true goal. But if it did take them that long, she knew, it would be too late.

Three major squadrons of mixed Resolution and Deliverance ships attacked the wormhole terminus as it sped across the system. Tactically, they faced the same problem as the ships trying to tackle the Calmissiles. Closing velocity gave them a single chance, and the armada could see them coming, plotting their trajectories with remarkable precision. Multiplying Calmissiles backed up by battle cruisers took care of two squadrons, while Ainsley's phasefolded shield devastated the third.

Eighty-seven Resolution ships were orbiting the huge star, thirty million kilometers above its equator and the titanic black power ring that was spinning fast above the fringes of the corona, stirring up a necklace of gigantic prominences. As the seven thousand strong formation of Calmissiles streaked in, their target now obvious, the Olyix finally responded to the incursion. Every ship they had within fifty million kilometers accelerated toward the threat at their full ninety-gee acceleration. Even if the Calmissiles punched a thousand holes through the power band, it wouldn't have had much effect on such a vast structure, but the Olyix clearly weren't taking any chances.

"Too little, too late," Yirella murmured in satisfaction.

The Resolution ships were good, and by now the Olyix were refining their techniques, clumping three Resolution ships together and triangulating the entanglement suppression effect. They started picking off the Calmissiles on the fringe of the formation, but the armada only needed one.

When it was fifteen million kilometers above the star, the Calmissile stopped accelerating. Its fuselage portal expanded, and Ainsley slipped out. He fired eight missiles with quantum-variant warheads at the power band.

"Eight?" Yirella queried.

"We have to be very certain," Ainsley replied, then slipped back through the portal to resume his escort duty at the wormhole terminus.

The first two q-v missiles detonated squarely on the power band. It disintegrated so fast, the remaining six missiles never even had a target.

She'd seen it before, but Yirella still watched in appalled awe as the power ring shattered and died, flinging out its uncountable multitudes of fragments, tumbling radiant daggers the size of Earth's moon.

All across the gateway system, the Olyix wormholes died, cutting them off from their galaxy-wide empire of sensor stations.

"We did it!" she exclaimed in delight. "It will take them centuries to build another power ring, and they're locked into this system until they do!"

Kenelm nodded cautiously. "Safer," sie said. "There are still thousands of Olyix stations out there, and look what we built with just the resources available on the *Morgan*."

"No," she said, shaking her head. "We've broken their grip. They'll diverge now, just like we did. The monoculture is broken." *And I'm going to make sure their God can't restart it with another message.*

"The gateway is still intact."

She pulled the latest sensor data out of the tactical network. The gateway sphere was unaffected by the loss of the power ring. "We were pretty sure killing the power ring wouldn't affect the gateway; it has to be powered from inside. So the corpus conjecture was right. There has to be another star in there."

"Which means this was a binary star?"

"Yes. That . . . may be a problem."

"The nova?"

"If we hit the enclave star with our neutron star, then the enclave boundary itself will fail. You'll revert to a binary star system with one star going nova. That will probably trigger the second, too."

"So we'll wind up with a supernova."

"High possibility, yeah. And if it does, the radiation will kill everything for fifty light-years. So we really have got to safeguard the wormhole terminus. It's the only way any of us are getting out of this alive now."

"So let's hope we can get into the enclave."

Now that the Olyix had learned how Calmissiles could be trojans, allowing the armada ships access through them, their tactics changed. Deliverance and Resolution ships that had been racing to intercept Calmissiles heading for the ring abruptly diverted to head for the Calmissiles flying to the gateway, while thousands of the ships assigned to guard the gateway left their passive englobement formation to join the attack against the incoming forces.

Calmissiles began to vanish from the tactical display at an increasing rate.

Yirella frowned at the data. "How are they doing that?" she asked.

"Collision," Immanueel replied. "The ship oneminds are sacrificing themselves. The Resolution ships are aligning directly on the Calmissiles. That way, the suppression effect will definitely reach the Calmissile even though there will be no time for the Resolution ship to move out of the way."

"But we have a hundred and twenty thousand Calmissiles heading for the gateway. And us! They have . . ."

"Twenty-eight thousand ships within reach," Immanueel said.

"Saints! And they're all going to suicide? They really are fanatics, aren't they?"

"Our Calmissiles will have to decelerate. Reduced closing velocity will give the Olyix forces a tactical advantage."

"But we still have a numerical advantage, right?"

"For the gateway assault, yes. We can deploy another two multiple salvos, but ultimately they have more ships. We need to get inside the enclave before they arrive."

The armada used the remaining salvos when the Calmissiles closed to within twenty million kilometers of the gateway. That distance had become the Resolution ships' killing field. At reduced velocity, the Calmissiles were far more susceptible to the suppression effect. Hundreds, then thousands, started to vanish from the tactical feeds. The remainder expanded their portals, and thousands more Calmissiles came flashing through. There were far too many for the Olyix to stop.

Just before stage four was due to begin, Yirella opened Dellian's icon. "How's it going down there?"

"It's boring, and the armor itches."

"Oh, poor you. But at least everything's going according to plan."

"If it's going according to plan, why did I have to be in armor for a day before we reach the gateway?"

"Wow, peak miserable. If things hadn't gone according to plan, the wormhole would've collapsed, the *Morgan* would've been dumped back into space-time somewhere close to the gateway star, and ten thousand Resolution ships would be hunting us down. So suck it up, you in your luxury comfort blanket, mister."

"You have a very weird concept of luxury."

She grinned. "Not at all. The croissants this morning were the wrong shade of golden; so there you are: I share your suffering."

"Oh, great Saints!"

"The battle cruisers are portaling to the gateway in two minutes."

"Yeah, I'm watching the tacticals. It's looking good."

"Loss numbers are top end of the projection, which I don't like, but yes. So far we're holding it together."

"You're going to monitor the squad, aren't you? When we go in, I mean."

"Monitor, yes. But that's it."

"I know. Tilliana and Ellici are the best. It's just, you're my guardian angel, that's all. You know that."

"I'll be watching."

Thousands of Calmissiles were decelerating to rendezvous around the ephemeral gateway. Seven Olyix fortress stations were orbiting above it, along with a final defensive shell of nine thousand Resolution ships. Every Calmissile expanded their portal, and armada battle cruisers started to fly through.

The fight lasted for two hours. Debris and energy eruptions saturated the space around the gateway, which at times glimmered as bright as the star as it refracted the actinic explosions in short-lived unsymmetrical waves. But by the time the wormhole terminus and Ainsley matched orbit, there were no Olyix left within ten million kilometers of the gateway. Tens of thousands of Resolution ships were en route from across the entire system.

"They're abandoning everything," Yirella said. "Most of their stations in the ring have only got a few dozen defenders left."

"It's going to be tough protecting the gateway once we're through," Kenelm conceded. "If we can get through."

"The defenders only have to cover us for a while—just enough for us to put phase four in motion."

"Our sensor probes report the boundary to be open," Immanueel said. "The interface is a simple pattern of negative energy that does not appear to be harmful."

Yirella regarded the shimmering orb with immense distrust. "That strikes me as unlikely. There's got to be something on the other side to attack us when we pass through."

"Yes, but not yet. Time is slower inside the enclave. They might only just be registering our appearance. It will take days, if not longer, in their timeframe, to assemble a defense fleet."

"Once we're inside, it won't take so long. We'll all be in the same time flow."

"Yes, but until we're through we have an advantage."

Yirella reviewed the hordes of approaching Resolution ships. The numbers were bad news. "We have to safeguard the wormhole terminus. It's our only route out of this system afterward."

"Acknowledged," Immanueel said. "Once the neutron star has exited, we will withdraw the terminus from this system at high acceleration. At the very least, the Olyix will have to split their forces. We conclude that most will enter the enclave in pursuit."

"Okay. So when are we going in?"

"Right now," Ainsley said.

Yirella felt her heart rate bump up. Fighting their way across the gateway system had been tense, but she had confidence in their warships and tactics. This, though—this was truly a step into the unknown.

She used her neural interface to pull in as much real-time tactical data as she could. Battle cruisers were taking up position outside the gateway, with large particles flowing out of the wormhole terminus. As soon as they emerged, their copper coating swirled away to reveal weapons platforms, adding to the protective layers building up.

"See you on the other side," Ainsley said.

She wanted to say, *wait, no, be careful*—just something that might help, might let him know she cared. But the big white ship accelerated smoothly and slipped easily through the shimmering surface. Seconds later, a stream of armada battle cruisers followed. The wormhole terminus was maneuvered until it was holding position a mere two kilometers above the gateway's ethereal surface. Thousands more battle cruisers accelerated out of the wormhole and vanished immediately into the enclave.

"Any response?" Yirella asked desperately.

"None," Immanueel replied. "I have no contact with any aspects of my corpus self that have gone through. In fact, this aspect group is now in a minority; our intellect is shrinking. It is an unusual circumstance, and one I find disconcerting. Being separated into two conscious entities is unnatural."

She exchanged a look with Kenelm. Having Immanueel confess that was somehow demoralizing.

Most of the armada was now inside the enclave. Or through the gateway, anyway, she told herself. Oh, Saints, what if it's the most elaborate trap in the universe? What if any species that manages to break free of the initial invasion is lured here? What if

The *Morgan* accelerated forward, quickly clearing the wormhole. Within seconds its nose was entering the tenuous photonic bubble of the gateway. She couldn't intervene. She couldn't stop this now even if she used every network subversion she possessed.

"Ohhh, shit!"

Eyes jammed shut to deflect the agonizing death blow as fire and fury ripped the *Morgan* apart.

Nothing.

She looked around. Tactical displays were building swiftly as the *Morgan* regained contact with the armada and . . . Ainsley. *Yes!*

But there was surely something wrong with the visual image; the café windows were showing a swirl of colorful clouds. It was as if they'd emerged into a gas giant's atmosphere. Which she knew was wrong. She just couldn't judge the perspective—to start with.

"Great Saints, it's a nebula," she gasped.

"You made it, then?" Ainsley said.

Yirella let out a long breath of relief. "That we did. So what local intelligence have you got for us?"

"Even my sensor fronds are having trouble seeing through this murk. They're spreading out now, so we should get a more comprehensive picture, but it's not easy. The good news is: There aren't many ships in here, and none of them are close to us. The star has got two power bands wrapped around it, and some other bands above them, which I'm guessing are the exotic matter generators creating this place. There's only one planet in here, a gas giant; that's the patch of the nebula that looks like it's on fire. It's got a massive energized ion tail, and thousands of small moons in a polar orbit, which I'm assuming are arkships. Should be able to get some decent resolution on that soon."

"And the Olyix have no large force of ships here?" Yirella asked. That just didn't seem possible.

"This is one big thick nebula, kid. There could be anything hiding in here, especially if it's not under acceleration. I am detecting some odd . . . twinkles appearing."

"Twinkles?"

"Points of light that appear, then vanish. Random distribution."

"Radiation impacts on nebula particles?"

"I don't know."

"Are they a potential threat?"

"Still unknown. Any more dumb questions?"

She pressed her lips together, not quite in amusement.

"We will dispatch a trio of battle cruisers to the nearest *twinkle* coordinate to investigate," Immanueel said. "But the rest of the armada needs to move now. The Olyix will soon be arriving in force behind us. We will set a course for the gas giant. That will suffice until our knowledge base of the enclave expands."

The transmitter drone lifted on three small thrusters, each one producing a tiny spire of icy blue static below its fuselage. It slowly rose to head height, then steered itself carefully around the cavern.

"That'll do," Yuri said. "It works." In his mind, reluctance was warring against eagerness. *To get this done. To finish it.* But as he had learned so painfully during his career, rushing into a hostile situation never produced a good result.

"Man," Alik grumbled. "The Wright brothers had a bigger first flight than that."

"To be fair, they had a bigger beach," Callum said. "And we've had centuries of flight experience since then."

"I'm sure the brothers would be very proud of all of you," Jessika said. "But there are a hell of a lot more human ships in the enclave now. They're starting to move away from the emergence point. We need to do this."

Yuri eyed the three other transmitter drones lying on the rumpled rock floor. "How many should we send?"

Callum gave him a puzzled look. "Well . . . all of them, of course. We're not going to get a second chance."

"One," Kandara said. "We send one. And the instant it gets outside we send the others."

"We send them all," Yuri said, ignoring Callum's mildly surprised expression. "Today is not the day for pussying around."

"Eggs," Kandara said. "Basket. One."

"I'm with Yuri on this," Alik said. "We need to get out there and *shout*. It's why we're here, for Christ's sake."

"Fucking testosterone," Kandara grumbled.

"Jessika, how far away are the ships?" Yuri asked. In his mind he could see what the fullmind perceived: a vast swarm of intruders in a neat formation, flowing smoothly through the nebula. There were several different types, which the Olyix were slowly categorizing.

"They're in a big cone formation with that white ship, the one the fullmind is nervous of, at the front. It looks like they're accelerating on a course toward the gas giant. They're coming to us."

"Time to arrival?"

"The fullmind estimates a couple of hours."

"Hours?" Callum asked. "It took us days to get here after we arrived in the enclave."

"They're warships," Jessika said. "I wasn't kidding when I said they were fast."

"And they'll be pointing a lot of sensors our way," Alik said.

"Okay, then," Yuri said. "Let's do this."

"Nexus first," Kandara said. "The fallback. You must always have a fallback."

I know! "Yes," Yuri said. "Alik, could you pilot them, please?"

"Sure." Alik settled onto his rock ledge and closed his eyes. Five of the creeperdrone spiders stood up and flexed their legs.

"No server creature activity in the tunnel outside," Jessika said. "And Odd Quint is still blocking neuralstrata perception around the hangar. Clear to go."

The creeperdrones lined up and scuttled out of the chamber.

"How long?" Yuri asked. The neuralstrata nexus Jessika had identified was along one of the other corridors leading from the hangar, so the creeperdrones would have to go back there first. In total, the chamber with the nexus was nearly two kilometers away.

"As long as it takes," Alik said through gritted teeth, his eyes still shut.

Callum held a hand up toward Yuri. "Let's just stay calm, shall we?"

Almost, he almost said: *I am calm.* But he made an effort to stay quiet. His one comfort was that the others would be equally stressed. *Just a few hours now, and this is going to be over—one way or another.*

"The fullmind is doing something," Jessika announced.

"What?" Yuri and Kandara asked simultaneously.

"Some kind of weapon." A frown creased Jessika's forehead. "But not a weapon. No. The enclave is a weapon. I don't understand. It thinks it can stop the fleet."

"We need to warn them," Callum said. The remaining three transmitter drones rose up.

"Wait!" Yuri said. "Nothing we can say will make any difference. If they get attacked, they'll fucking know about it, okay? We need to concentrate on telling them where we are. And to stand any chance of that, we need to be able to take out the nexus. Alik, how long?"

"Ask me that again, motherfucker, and I swear I will bring them back here and burn your ass to ash!"

Yuri shrugged at Callum, then he closed his eyes and got Boris to pull up a tactical map. The gossamer strands unwinding from the back of the creeperdrone spiders provided high-quality images from their eyes. They were already approaching the hangar.

A burst of shock emanating from the fullmind broke his concentration. He tried to focus on the thoughtstream, only to be overwhelmed by what looked like a . . . blob? It was moving through the enclave's nebula. Instead of brushing aside the vast curlicues of multicolored gas, it seemed to be sucking the strands in. "What the hell?"

"Fuck me!" Jessika exclaimed.

Yuri didn't know which surprised him most—the fullmind's alarm or hearing Jessika swear. "What is that thing?"

"A star."

"Huh?"

"It's a neutron star! The invaders have brought a neutron star with them. It's going to hit the enclave star."

"No way," Callum said. "That'll . . . Bloody hell!"

"That'll what?" Yuri asked in a tightly controlled voice.

"Nova," Jessika said. "If we're lucky."

"Lucky?"

"Technically, it's a smart move," Callum said. "It'll destroy the power rings on its way into the star, which will kill the enclave. So we'll be dumped back into space-time."

"Oh, Mother Mary," Kandara said. "We'll be right next to the gateway star."

"Next to is a relative term," Callum said. "But yeah, it's a binary system. And if a star this size is going nova . . ."

"It'll trigger the other one," Yuri realized.

"We may wind up in the middle of a supernova."

"But these invaders must know that, right?" Alik said. "They'll have an escape route planned out."

"Of course they have," Jessika said. "The invasion ships are heading here, where all the arkships are. So they've got to have a strategy."

"All right," Yuri said. "So let's help them. Alik?"

Alik glared at him, then immediately shut his eyes again, his hardened skin crunching up into a frown of concentration. When Yuri checked, he found the creeperdrone spiders were leaving the hangar now, heading up the corridor that would take them to the chamber where the nexus was. Two of them were scurrying along the floor while the rest were racing along the web of trunks that covered the walls and ceiling, traveling almost as fast. Yuri had to admit, Alik had quality piloting the things.

When he checked the sensor clusters in the hangar, they peered up the corridor where Odd Quint had gone—nothing moving there.

"Do we go?" Callum asked. His body was quivering, as if he were about to start a race.

"This invasion is going to take hours to play out," Yuri said. "And Alik will have the creeperdrones in place in just a few minutes. So let's not screw this up because we can't wait, okay?" He ignored Callum's groan of disappointment.

"The fullmind is rallying," Jessika warned.

When he tried to make sense of the thoughtstream, all Yuri could grasp was pressure. Somehow the fullmind was squeezing the enclave—a process that was absorbing a phenomenal amount of energy and placing a dangerous strain on the star's power rings. He didn't understand any of it. So . . .

Concentrate on what can be achieved.

The creeperdrones had finally arrived in a huge cavern that was filled with machinery, living pipes, and large city-block-sized tanks. A grim throwback to the time of Earth's oil refineries, complete with dank puddles, dripping junctions, and thin layers of grubby mist. All five of the creeper-drones swiftly scaled a weird, twisting glass and carbon pillar, clambering around bulges where fresh green fronds merged with the tightly packed fibers inside.

"Okay, I got this," Alik said. "I can blind the neuralstrata in this whole section as soon as you give the word."

"Callum, Kandara," Yuri said. "You're on."

The drones headed out of the cavern in an easy sashay, their tiny blue ion plumes soaring up the spectrum toward a near-invisible violet. A soft gust of air marked their flight, but they were almost silent. They swept into the tunnel beyond and arrowed toward the hangar. In that huge empty space, they seemed utterly inconsequential. It took them seconds to cross the floor and pass into the open entrance.

Then they stopped, simply hanging in the air, ion jets throttled up to maximum, not moving.

"What the fuck?" Yuri exclaimed.

"Oh, bloody hell," Callum said. "They hit the membrane. It's turned solid."

"But we flew in easily," Alik said in protest. "All the transport ships did; and back out again."

"That was when there were ships using the hangar," Callum said. "The onemind must've kept the membrane looser then. It's hardened now to prevent any atmosphere leaking out. That means the drones can't get through it. Nothing can."

"What do we do? We have to get those transmitter drones outside."

Yuri glanced over at Kandara. Judging from her expression, she already knew what he was going to say.

"We go into the hangar and physically take out the membrane generator."

None of the Olyix ships in the enclave were flying on a course to intercept the armada. Some had, right at the start; then the neutron star punched through the gateway, and they'd swiftly altered course.

"Are they waiting for reinforcements, do you think?" Yirella asked.

"We are uncertain of their tactics," Immanueel said. "None seem to have followed us through the gateway. That is strange, given the number of ships they have in the system outside. There may be a large presence of Resolution ships in the enclave that we have not yet detected."

"But they have to know Ainsley will take out the power rings, just like he did in the gateway system. They have to deploy against us fast if they want to try and stop that. Unless . . ." *No, surely not.* "Have they accepted they've lost?"

"From what we understand of the Olyix character, that is extremely unlikely."

"Yeah." She reviewed the neutron star again and tried not to let it chill her. The cage generators had performed their last course correction maneuvers and had disengaged, leaving the neutron star to fly along its final trajectory. At its current speed, it would take two days to reach the enclave's star. "I always thought bringing the neutron star was overkill, but now that I've seen what the Olyix have built here, I think you made the right call."

"It is our guarantee should Ainsley fail; it will destroy the star and the enclave. Whatever the outcome for us, this will ensure the Olyix cannot rise again."

"Well, let's just hope we can accomplish more than that."

"Thirty minutes to deceleration point," Alexandre announced. "Stand by for troop ship deployment."

Yirella opened the squad's icon. "Good luck, you guys. May the Saints be with you."

They replied with cheery comments. As soon as she accessed the sensors inside the troop ship, she realized how meaningless the visual feed was. Dark, lumpy machinery gripped by industrial-grade clamps, hanging in a gallery jammed with a profusion of cables so tangled they could have been shat out by a giant diarrhetic spider. Nothing human visible; no emotional connection to be made. No last images of faces.

But I remember them. And that's what counts.

She switched to the *Morgan*'s external cameras, watching the troop ships launch out of their tubes—fat ebony wedge-shapes with twin spears extending out of the prow that cut a sharp profile against the meandering gyres of the iridescent nebulascape. They accelerated away to take up a bracelet formation a thousand kilometers out.

That was when she saw the twinkles fading in and out of existence, as if the *Morgan* were flying through a sparse galaxy of microstars.

"Hey, did we find out what those things are?" she asked. "They look like some kind of blemish in the enclave continuum, something that twists the light."

There was a long pause, then she heard Immanueel say: "Finding what those things are."

"What?"

"Confirming aspect integration."

"Immanueel?" She turned to frown at Kenelm, who seemed equally puzzled. The *Morgan*'s network began to run analysis on the armada's secure communication links.

"Ainsley, are you in contact with Immanueel?"

"Partial contact. There's some kind of glitch. The Olyix are jamming our links. Running analysis."

Yirella checked the tactical status display. "Ah, okay. I'm having trouble accessing your fronds, too."

The café lights flickered, then stabilized. Yirella gave them a puzzled glance. Part of her tactical display froze, then the figures and graphics accelerated, becoming nonsense blurs. "What the hell? Are they virusing our network?"

"Ainsley?"

"Saints!"

"The *Morgan*'s genten isn't responding," an alarmed Kenelm said. "The local management array is running this section of the ship. It looks like the network nodes have dropped out. There was some kind of massive data transfer generated internally, so the safety routines activated and isolated each physical sector of the network."

"Saints! How are they doing that? How did they get a virus into our systems? The corpus completely rebuilt the *Morgan*."

The look sie gave her said all she needed to know. They

were both thinking the same thing—that somehow Olyix agents had infiltrated the expansion. *And I know one person who's been with us a long time, so long no reliable records exist. Just a picture in a book . . .* She used her interface to check where the nearest personal weapons were—the deck below. *So if I have to improvise?* The café had plenty of cutlery.

Stay calm. I don't have any proof. Yet.

"I don't know," Kenelm said. "But the genten will counter and purge any virus."

"Right." She nodded, hoping sie couldn't read her doubts. "Ainsley, we think the *Morgan*'s been virused."

Ainsley's icon remained on, but there was still no reply. She used the deck's sub-network to acquire feeds directly from any hull sensors it could reach. The view was restricted, but several troop ships around the *Morgan* were visible keeping position a thousand kilometers out. They looked okay. In the distance was the white dot that was Ainsley. She could see the swirls of disturbed gas it had created as it ripped through the nebula. Directly behind it, their motion had arrested in mid-churn. But around the big white ship, the outer fronds of the turmoil looked as if they were still fluctuating. It was hard to be certain. The curious warped lightpoints had thickened and multiplied around Ainsley; there were so many they were disrupting the view.

"Oh, Saints!" She brought the focus back. The twinkles within the armada formation were appearing in greater numbers, their vivacity brightening. "This isn't a network virus. They're doing something to us."

"What?"

"I don't know. It's like . . . Oh, shit! Tilliana?"

There was no answer.

Yirella hurriedly activated the general communication icon. The ship's internal secure links were hardened against any form of electronic warfare. "Anyone? This is Yirella. Is anyone on the *Morgan* receiving this?"

The displays told her the links were open, but no one was responding.

"What's happening?" Kenelm asked.

"That twinkling we can see, it's a lensing effect from

blemishes in the enclave's continuum," Yirella said. "The Olyix are changing something in here. I think they're slowing time around the armada." *But why is that affecting our internal network?*

"Hellfire."

When she used the sensor feed to check on the neutron star, it was enveloped by a shimmer of distorted light. Here, though, the glimmers seemed warped and fuzzy, fluttering like living things in torment. The nebula around them was fluorescing brighter than she'd seen it before.

"I need to talk with Tilliana and Ellici. We have to get to their tactical command cabin."

Kenelm nodded reluctantly. "Yes."

"It's on deck twenty-five. Let's go."

They left the canteen together. As they walked, Yirella tried to examine the ship's network diagram. "I don't get this," she complained. "The safety routines are blocking inputs from some decks where the data rate is extreme, while some are dead."

They arrived at a portal hub. Yirella stared around in dismay. The edge of every portal was glowing red, while the centers had become black and solid-looking. She'd never seen them in that state before.

"That sucks," Kenelm said.

"Right." Her interface pulled up a schematic of the *Morgan*'s decks. She knew the general layout of the life support section, but the exact details were vague. *That's what happens when you use portals all the time.*

The life support section had three main service support shafts running its full height up through all the decks, providing routes for pipes, ducts, and cabling, along with a spiral stair winding around the wall, and a central column that remotes could ride up and down. They started off toward the nearest one. Yirella used her interface to check if there were any available connections to a transmitter on the hull. It was possible; she had to route power from an emergency cell to a backup communication module and use alternative data cables to give her a solid connection.

She stood still and concentrated on setting up the procedure.

When she did reach the transmitter management routine, it didn't have any navigation feed, so she couldn't use a direct beam, because she didn't have a clue where Dellian's troop ship actually was in relation to the *Morgan*. So general broadcast it was. *I will help you. I will be the guardian angel you need me to be.*

"Calling squad leader Dellian. This is Yirella in the *Morgan*. Are you receiving?"

There was no reply. She loaded in discrimination filters and ordered the unit to expand the reception spectrum. Her reward was a flurry of static. She overrode the safety limiters to increase the power to the transmitter as high as she dared.

"This is Yirella on the *Morgan*. We're suffering communication difficulties. I think the Olyix might be changing the time flow. Is anyone receiving me?"

Still nothing. She called a few more times, with no result. The nebula, one giant field of ionization, must have been blocking the signal. So she left her message on repeat and loaded a monitor routine to review the receiver output.

"I can't get anything," she said dejectedly.

Kenelm wasn't there.

She frowned and looked around. "Kenelm?"

Sie was nowhere to be seen. Yirella told her databud to send out a ping. Kenelm's databud didn't respond. *That's not possible*. A ping was databud to databud, with a kilometer range. *But sie was here a moment ago.*

All the mistrust she'd had for Kenelm surfed back in on an adrenaline wave. Her skin grew hot, heart rate soaring upward. Fight-or-flight reflex dropped her into a kind of crouch, half-forgotten personal combat maneuvers bubbling up in confusion. She whirled around, hunting urgently.

The brightly lit corridor curved away behind and ahead, completely empty. Innocuous, yet suddenly incredibly sinister.

There was nothing she could use as a weapon. For a second she considered running back to the canteen and arming herself with the cutlery. *Yeah, a cake fork; that'll help. Saints!*

Three meters ahead there was a junction. According to

the ship schematic, it led to one of the support shafts. She fixated on the junction and whatever lurked beyond as she crept along nervously, feverish thoughts alive with all sorts of nightmare scenarios. A glistening hive of monsters bulging out of the door to the shaft. Huntspheres blasting along the corridor at supersonic speed, chasing her down. Del's cocoon dangling from the ceiling like some moldering chunk of spider food.

Stop it.

She peeked around the junction, pulling her head back fast in case something took a shot at her. *Because targeting systems are really that slow. Come on, pull yourself together.* The brief image she glimpsed made her squeak in shock. Slowly she shuffled forward to place herself in the middle of the junction, facing toward the support shaft door thirty meters away.

Five meters along the corridor, Kenelm was sprawled facedown on the floor. She knew it was Kenelm; the body was wearing hir green-and-blue tunic. But sie'd been dead for a long time. Yirella could see hir head, the shrunken desiccated skin, tufts protruding from a skull that had decayed so far there was very little left. A disgusting stain had spread out from it, organic fluids long since dried.

But . . .

Hir feet were swollen and discolored, the flesh a vile mid-putrefaction green.

All Yirella could do was stand there staring, muscles rendered useless by shock and incomprehension.

The Olyix haven't slowed time, she realized. They've speeded it up. But how did that kill hir?

It made no sense. If Kenelm had walked into a zone with a faster time flow, then sie would simply live at that rate. Just like the *Morgan* had lived at a slower rate while they were flying along the wormhole.

She examined the body again. The swollen feet were wrinkling up, the flesh darkening, while the head's paper-like skin was diminishing away to nothing as wisps of hair fell to the floor.

"Different rate," she whispered. "It's a gradient."

The zone of faster time flow didn't have an abrupt border.

It built over a few meters from the ordinary rate where she was standing to one where a human corpse decayed in barely a couple of minutes. A databud file told her that kind of decay would take years.

Great Saints! She took an involuntary step backward. The gradient, short though it was, would be utterly lethal to any living thing. All the parts of your body would be living at different rates as you moved through it. Circulation would be impossible, nerve impulses from the faster sections would flood into the slower ones, overloading axons to burnout while the misfiring synapses of the brain would scramble every thought.

She gagged as bile surged up into her throat. Initial inertia would sustain your motion across the gradient. But . . . parts of you would have been dead for a year, while the rest was still alive as you started to fall.

Yirella dropped to her knees and threw up violently. Even now she couldn't take her eyes off the corpse.

That's what was happening to the *Morgan*. They'd jumbled the time flow so it had been segmented. Some areas were fast, and some were slow; it was why the network dataflow increased from some sections while others slowed so much they didn't even register. It would be the same with all the corpus aspects. It was not a straight communications failure; they were all separated in time. Alone.

Being briefly separated into just two consciousnesses as all their aspects flew into the enclave had left Immanueel badly perturbed. Now each of their aspects would be solitary. All the corpus human aspects would be divorced. A disconnected armada.

She took a juddering breath, spitting out the last of the bitter juices from her mouth. Slowly she backed away from the junction, terrified by the fate that awaited any unsuspecting soul crossing the boundary. Then she stopped. She had no idea where the other aberrative time flows began.

Think. There must be a way of spotting them.

First was a review of the network failures. Sure enough, the corridor to the service shaft had no operational connection to the section around her. Using that as a baseline, she began to plot other blank areas of the life support section. A pattern began to build. It was reassuringly simple. The *Morgan* had been divided up into layers—some slow, some normal, some fast. Comparison of data rates as the network collapsed told her just how different the flows were, but that was only an approximation. She knew the general area where the time flows changed, but there was no way of telling the exact position of the boundaries.

So what would give them away?

Yirella switched her optik to infrared, at the highest sensitivity. The air around her had currents. Purified air at an exact temperature of twenty-one degrees Celsius gusted out of the vents along the floor, while vents along the top of the wall sucked it back in to run through filters. They were slow currents, barely visible. But there were enough minute temperature variants to distinguish the general circulation movements.

She looked down the corridor toward the stairwell. Beyond Kenelm's corpse, the air was moving like a gas giant's supersonic cloud stream. She gave it a respectful nod and backed away a little farther.

The normal time area she was in seemed to be four decks deep, and over half the diameter of the life support section. A file showed her the zone that now incarcerated her was all living quarters—individual crew cabins, some lounges, canteens, a gym, a medical bay, and various compartments of support machinery. There was no power coming in from the ship's main generators; everything was running off local backup quantum cells. A quick calculation for one inhabitant showed the decks she was trapped in could provide life support and reprocess nutrients to print food for the next three hundred seventy-two years—assuming optimum equipment operation. There were no initiators to provide spare parts should anything major fail. Then she realized she had no way of moving between decks. The portals had shut down, and she couldn't get to the service shafts where the stairs were.

"Oh, Great Saints."

Yirella went back to the canteen. Without the network, Boulevard Saint-Germain was stuck on a loop, condemning the happy, stylish Parisians to walk through their fresh new morning every seven minutes. The irony of sitting in a temporal bubble watching their closed time cycle was strong enough to burn. She switched the windows off.

Now what?

She wasn't sure the corpus aspects were smart enough individually to solve this. They had mastered time flow technology back at the neutron star, creating the domains, but the enclave was on such a colossal scale they would need to combine again to counter it. The obvious—in fact, the only—solution was to destroy the power rings around the star. Without them, the enclave would fall. But the contrasting time flows were a plague that stopped any of them from acting, let alone flying to the star to attack the rings.

So . . .

She needed to reunify the *Morgan* somehow, to banish all the different time flows. Once it was operational again, she could start to fight back.

The life support section had its own time flow unit; they'd spent the journey through the wormhole inside it. *If I can switch that on, it could shield us from the Olyix's temporal distortions.* But of course she couldn't switch it on, because the *Morgan*'s network was down—and even if she did, that would just protect the life support section from the attack. *I need the whole ship, everything inside the hull unified.*

Visualizing the ship like that, surrounded by a protective envelope that repelled the distortions, triggered an idea. At a fundamental level, the internal continuum of the enclave was no different from that of the wormhole. They were both a manipulation of space-time by a complex pattern of exotic matter. The *Morgan*'s negative-energy conduits also channeled that pseudofabric, allowing the ship to fly along a wormhole. And there were hundreds of conduits all over the fuselage. If she could activate them, and realign their function to deflect the temporal distortions, the *Morgan* would contain a single time zone again.

But it was a chicken-and-egg problem. You had to provide the ship with a single time flow in order to activate the conduits—which would give the ship a single time flow.

"I hate paradox," she announced to the canteen.

The fuselage conduits had to be activated simultaneously.

That might just be possible if each section's sub-network knew when to switch them on. But to do that would mean having to get a message into each section and load the instructions into the local sub-net. Trying to move between time flows was a death sentence. "For humans," she shouted triumphantly.

She immediately sent a ping to her cyborg. "Oh, fuck the Saints." It was no use; the cyborg was in storage in a compartment down on deck forty-six, three time zones away. Completely out of reach. So she pulled an inventory of every remote device on deck thirty-three. More than a dozen small janitor remotes were available, and even three small maintenance units, plus . . . "YES!"

She almost ran, but forced herself to keep a sensible pace while using the optik interface to watch for any sign of a boundary she hadn't plotted. The unused cabin was five doors down from the quarters she and Dellian shared. *Makes sense.*

The door opened, and she peered in. Lights came on. There, sitting inertly on the untextured raised rectangle of the bed, was the Ainsley android. Her interface immediately connected her to it. The chest cavity contained a huge neural array, which was in standby mode. She carefully selected the routines she'd used before, when she'd elaborated her consciousness out into the *Morgan's* network. This time it would be different; this time she wouldn't stay connected to the android.

The process to elaborate up to corpus level, to become more than one, was complicated. Part of the time she was impatient for it to run, while the rest of the process was spent fearing her personality pattern and memories weren't just being duplicated, they were being methodically stripped out of her biological brain to be absorbed by the android's array. Stupid to think that, of course, but still very much her own foible.

In the end, there she was—two Yirella minds, held together in perfect harmony by a single high-capacity link. She cut the link.

She opened her eyes to stare at . . . the android. *Thank the*

Saints, I'm the original me, the real one. She saw the android turn down the corners of its lips.

"Sorry," she said.

"I'll be you again," it said. "When this is all over."

"That's down to you now. Maybe you won't want to be."

"You know the answer to that, and you know you're just voicing a concern to have it denied, thus gaining reassurance."

"Yes."

"So I won't. Corpus is clearly not for us."

"Not now. But you and I are asunder. Every instant from now on, the divergence will widen. And in the fast flow sections, you're going to exist for years—decades, possibly. The difference will become . . . extensive," she said.

"As soon as our aspects rejoin, there will be no difference."

"I am not an aspect. I am Yirella."

"We are."

"No. You're an artificial personality operating in an array that was never designed for you."

"Yet here I am." The android stood up, then glanced down at itself and grinned. "And it's not just the array that's different."

"Oh, Saints." But there was nothing she could do to stop her own grin; her lips quirked in exactly the same fashion. *Maybe thoughts have an entanglement all their own, more spiritual than quantum?*

"We'd better get on with this," the android said.

"Yeah. I thought you should go through riding on something. I'm not sure even you are capable of coordinating yourself while transiting through a gradient."

"I know. A chair might work."

"Yes." There was no point in her saying anything else. She'd spent the time her memories were being copied thinking about the practical aspects of getting to the stairwell. Therefore: It had.

The android picked up a chair from the canteen, one with casters, and carried it effortlessly. When they were back at the junction, it sat down, facing Kenelm's corpse. The decay had progressed. Hir skeleton had obviously fallen apart as the joints detached from each other, subsiding into a jumble with the tunic deflating around it. Hir skull had rolled to one side, empty sockets staring up at the ceiling.

Yirella gripped the back of the chair and pulled it back, testing how easy it was to roll.

"Make sure you don't hit the skeleton," the android said.

That didn't even deserve a response. "Ready?" she asked.

"Rhetorical question."

Yirella braced herself and ran at the junction, pushing *hard*. She let go—and stopped abruptly, arms waving for balance. *Do NOT fall forward*. The chair rattled along, sliding easily into the boundary, where the frantic air currents whipped around it. Passed the skeleton—

And the android vanished. So fast it didn't even leave a blur.

Yirella let out a long breath of relief. The chair remained in the same position for a few seconds, then—she thought she saw something behind it, a shadow moving with the speed of a lightning bolt. A small wheeled platform with a single column standing vertically in the middle appeared, racing out of the boundary. The Ainsley android was standing on it, along with a quartet of similar androids—genderless this time, and with a skin color remarkably similar to her own.

"What happened?" she asked.

The four black-skinned androids dismounted and hurried off along the corridor.

"Hey," she spluttered in outrage.

"I'm really sorry," the Ainsley android said, as it left the platform.

"What? Why?" That it was acting defensively was giving her a bad feeling.

Her personal icon appeared in her optik. She hesitated to open it, guessing the memories were going to be bad. "Just tell me this. Can we deflect the time flows?"

"I believe so, yes. Our others have gone to begin the process."

Yirella opened the icon—

———

—the sensation was like waking, consciousness rising from foggy darkness, bringing with it the memories of who she was and what she'd done to restore her identity. She self-identified—there were no doubts, no biochemical anxiety for the Ainsley android. Nonetheless, its passage through the gradient was excruciating. Its internal network suffered an avalanche of glitches, while the array in its chest underwent random failures. She thought she was losing her mind . . . which in a way she was. She countered by putting the precious memories into deep store while she traveled through the gradient, the chair's little caster wheels taking agonizing days to complete a single rotation. Full awareness rushed back in as the crazy time fluxes smoothed out, and time was whole again. She stood up and hurried into the stairwell, climbing up to deck twenty-five. It had aged. Some of the lights were dark. Every air grill had engendered dust streaks rising like black flames on the walls. Colors had faded on doors, walls, trapping her in a world of bleak pastels. The floor outside the tactical cabin had lost its tread, the thin laminate worn down to the metal below.

How long? she wondered.

There was no one in the cabin. But there had been. A huge dune of rubbish filled more than half of the room—mainly old meal trays with smears of food that had long since dried and hardened but still gave off a putrid stench. *Wait. Huh? The android has a sense of smell? Why?* She hurriedly shut the door again. They must have been using the tactical cabin as a rubbish dump. Then the size of the pile registered. *Saints, how many trays were in there? Hundreds? No, more like thousands.*

How long?

"Tilliana. Ellici. Alexandre?" she called. No reply. The android's management routines were complex; she had to concentrate to use the communication architecture. There was a functional sub-net in this section, though some of the nodes had dropped out. A maintenance log icon expanded, supplying her with failure details. The nodes had started to crash eleven years ago.

Eleven years? She expanded the log's details. Her mouth opened to cry out in dismay, hand coming up to cover it. The disassociation was complete. The hand was white—her hand—and for a moment she couldn't understand why. Then she remembered she was in the android body. Strange how she'd adapted within minutes. But the shock of realization had been great enough to break that cozy accommodation. According to the log, the nodes had originally disengaged from the *Morgan*'s full network ninety-seven years ago.

"Oh, Saints, no. No, no, no!" *That cannot be right.*

She began to run, opening every door. The tenth compartment was a canteen. There were a lot of meal trays piled up here, too, fresher than the conference room. Not all the food was dry, and the smell was intense. The wall panels around the food printers had been removed. Somebody had repaired the machines; two had been opened up and partially dismantled, their intricate components plumbed in to the remaining printer with crude hoses and cables. She accessed the printer's menu; it was very limited, mainly soups and soft bread rolls. Some fruit flavors were still available, and the dairy option could produce milk and cheese. Solids were error-tagged; they only came out as a paste now. All the nutrient tanks were redlined, with barely five percent left.

Yirella staggered back out of the canteen. There was a clinic on the deck below; if Tilliana, Ellici, and Alexandre had survived, they'd need that. She made her way down the stairwell, forcing herself to hurry. The clinic door was open, its mechanism not working. Inside, the five medical bays had all undergone repairs, their casings removed to expose the delicate systems inside and the rudimentary alterations that had been performed on them. The android body didn't have the routines for involuntary muscle shudders, but she certainly felt as if she'd shivered.

She went back out into the corridor and looked down at the floor, seeing worn tracks. There were several cabins that had been used. The first she went in was dark, its texture walls inert; the same with the second. As she approached the third, she could hear orchestral music. When the door opened, it was so loud she hesitated on the threshold before she went in. The cabin's texture had reproduced Turin's splendid Teatro Regio opera house in its original eighteenth-century form. The auditorium was full of men and women in formal attire, while a full orchestra played in the pit and ostentatious players in authentic costumes bestrode the stage. A subroutine identified the performance as *La Bohème*.

Sitting in the front of the stalls was an old woman wearing an extravagant lace-embellished gown Yirella associated with the kind of cantankerous dowager always to be found in a Jane Austen novel. If it hadn't been for that fanciful gown, Yirella could've easily imagined the woman had walked onto the *Morgan* straight out of the Neolithic age. A visual subroutine gave a forty-three percent probability it was Tilliana. When Yirella really concentrated, she could pick out the characteristics she'd known all her life, aged and worn by nine decades.

She sank to her knees beside Tilliana. "Till? Till, is that you?"

An aghast Tilliana looked at her and began a pitiful wailing. "Who are you? You're not part of the cast. I didn't texture you. Are you Olyix? Have you come for us?"

"No, I'm not Olyix. I'm very human, I promise."

The orchestra stopped playing, and up on the stage the actors became still. Yirella tried to ignore the way the whole audience was now staring at her.

"It's been so long," Tilliana said. "I know this is your punishment, making us suffer for coming to the enclave."

Yirella reached for Tilliana's clawlike hands, only to have them jerked away. "No, Till. I'm not Olyix. I'm Yirella, but I'm riding the Ainsley android. Do you remember me? Do you remember the android? We thought it was so funny when we arrived at the neutron star, so childish of Ainsley, not wearing clothes."

"Ainsley? Ainsley was so fine. A ship that could've been built in heaven itself."

"Yes. Yes, he is a fine ship, the best. And me, Tilliana, do you remember me? Yirella?"

"I remember Yirella. We lost her when we came to the enclave. We lost everyone. They all froze outside; unmoving forever. The Olyix are making them wait until the end of time while they punish us. But they're making us live through all of those billions of years. It's because we were in tactical, you know. That's what we decided. We were in charge, so they blamed us. We're the only ones left." Tears began rolling down her cheeks.

"I'm not lost, Till. I'm still here. The Olyix have screwed with time inside the *Morgan*. You've lived so much longer than us. But I am Yirella. We grew up together on the Immerle estate. Alexandre was our mentor, remember? Is Alexandre here? Is sie okay?"

"Oh, no, dear. Alexandre has been dead since that very first day."

"No!" She couldn't help the cry of dismay. For an array that struggled to perform emotional routines, that was a blow so raw she knew she must be trying to cry. It was useless; those particular impulses went nowhere. Ainsley hadn't included tear ducts in the android. "How? How did sie die?"

"Sie tried to walk into another section. We didn't understand. Sie just fell over dead, but sie never decayed. Hir body's still there. I think so, anyway. I haven't visited for years, now."

"And Ellici? Is she still alive?"

Tilliana gave a mournful nod. "She's still alive. But it was all too much for her. She hasn't been herself for a while now. It's been hard, you know. Life can be such a burden when there is nothing you can use it for. Sometimes I think I should just let it end, but she needs me to look after her. So I have my shows and my music stored in what's left of the network. Perhaps that was a mistake."

"No. It wasn't. I'm here now. We're going to get out of this."

"I don't think so, dear, I don't know who you really are, but there's no way out of the enclave. It is eternal."

"Can I see Ellici, please? I'd be very grateful."

"I suppose there's no harm." The Teatro Regio and its phantom audience of opera enthusiasts slowly faded away into neutral textured cabin walls. "Help me up, dear; my arthritis is quite troublesome now. The clinic's pharma dispenser stopped working a while back. I couldn't repair it anymore. There aren't any initiators in this portion of the ship."

"I know." She helped Tilliana get to her feet. It was easy enough; the old woman was so thin. Yirella was surprised and a little disturbed by how little she weighed. Once she was upright, Tilliana continued to grip the android's arm for support. By the time they reached Ellici's cabin, the exertion was causing her to tremble continuously.

"You go in," Tilliana said. "I'm a bit tired. She can be exhausting."

The doors opened, revealing a dimly lit room. It wasn't textured in a way Yirella recognized. No cultural classic home, no historic city vista just outside. The walls were a thick silver-gray cushion, as was the floor, and even the ceiling, apart from a few inset strips that radiated the diffuse light. There was a toilet basin—also padded, inside and out—and a small sink alcove that appeared to have been scooped out of the wall.

The only other thing in the room was the bed, a raised rectangular slab. Thickly padded. Ellici lay on it, dressed in a dreadfully filthy, thin one-piece suit that Yirella recognized: a space suit's skin layer, a garment designed to keep body temperature stable and extract human waste. Her knees were drawn up against her stomach and her hands were drawing invisible pictures on the padding. Not that she seemed to be looking at them; her eyes were unfocused.

"Oh, no," Yirella moaned. The sight of her vibrant friend reduced to this was too much. She'd always accepted that they'd stay together for ages yet, staying the same thanks to the ability to rebuild and rejuvenate their bodies. Maybe in time, perhaps back on Earth reclaimed, they'd eventually go their separate ways. But there would be decades of warning. This, though—this was the cruelest weapon the Olyix had ever attacked the humans with. There had been no warning, no time to prepare. "We'll make it better," she whispered. "I'll fix the *Morgan*. The clinics will work again. They'll heal you."

Physically, perhaps—but she knew more than any of them how deep the mental scars reached. The Ellici and Tilliana she'd known were gone forever now.

She backed out of the room, saying nothing as the door slid shut again.

"I'm sorry," Tilliana said. "It was too much for her. The waiting, the emptiness. They broke her."

"I understand." Yirella faced her old friend. "What about the other tactical stations, the other squads? Are you in contact with any of them?"

"No. Every way in and out of this part of the ship has time boundaries."

"Okay. I want you to sit tight. I'll do what I came here for."

"Oh. Why are you here?"

"To fix this. It might take me a while, but I'll be back, I promise."

She helped Tilliana back to her cabin, then pulled up a status display from the worn-out sub-network. Good news and bad news; there was plenty of processing capacity and a decent reserve in the power cells. The negative-energy conduits on the fuselage remained functional; they just needed operating instructions.

What she still didn't have was a working initiator. There were three on deck twenty-two, but the sub-network didn't extend there. It was on a different time flow. She ran an inventory check for remotes and found three cargo trolleys available. Two worked.

A minute later she was in a different stairwell shaft, sitting on the trolley as it clamped itself to the central column. Looking down past her dangling feet, sight switched to infrared, she saw the billowing air currents scudding about at what appeared to be a slower rate. She ordered the trolley to lower at maximum speed so she'd get through the gradient as quickly as possible.

This time the discontinuity didn't seem so bad. She wondered if deck twenty-two had a slow or fast time flow.

The lights were in standby mode, giving off a dim green glow. And there was something wrong with the air; it carried a musty scent. Her infrared vision showed her the grills were barely pumping out any fresh air at all. Another standby mode.

She connected to the sub-net and reviewed the logs. The nodes had been isolated from the network for sixty-three years. So, slower than the section incarcerating Tilliana and Ellici, but still fast compared to the one she'd started in. The gradient would be enough to kill a biological body trying to cross over.

When she reviewed the log data, she saw the sub-net had waited for a year, during which there had been no power demand from any equipment. The atmosphere had remained unchanged with no carbon dioxide to scrub; no doors had opened; no movement was detected. The management routine had put everything into full stasis mode and waited for further instructions.

Yirella provided them.

The engineering compartment was already brightly lit, with fresh air blowing hard out of the grills when she arrived. The three cylindrical initiators were running internal pre-commencement checks. Yirella connected to their management arrays and loaded in the android design, then began to modify it. Some raw material simply wasn't available, so she verified substitutions. After that there was Ainsley's unnecessary anatomical fixation to . . . smooth over. Also, if this was her first shaky step elevating to corpus, the new androids shouldn't have Ainsley's profile.

Once the design was finalized, she activated the initiators. Fabrication took eight hours. One of the initiators glitched halfway through the procedure—when she opened the cylinder's lid it looked like a burned corpse was inside—but the remaining pair kept working.

Five days later they'd produced thirty androids of herself. It was a strange sensation when each of the new aspects came online and started sharing her thought routines. She could feel her awareness expand as her mind acquired additional processing capacity—which wasn't quite the equivalent of a greater intellect, but certainly helped problem solving—in particular, quantifying the negative-energy patterns that the *Morgan*'s conduits would have to direct. With that determined—in theory—she set about formatting the routines to load. The new androids also came equipped with a quantum logic clock, accurate enough for her to synchronize the channel activation across differing time flows.

She dispatched twenty of them across the ship, with two primary missions. The first was to make contact with any other surviving tactical teams, while the second was to track down working initiators that could build more of herselves. The *Morgan*'s sleek conical profile was five kilometers long, which she estimated would now be subject to at least two hundred fifty different time flows. At least the androids didn't need space suits to move through the sections in a vacuum, so they should be able to position themselves evenly throughout the ship.

Two of them remained with the initiators to keep on producing more aspects. Seven accompanied the Ainsley android aspect back to the deck where Tilliana and Ellici lived, where three stayed, providing companionship and practical help to her two friends. The remaining four went back with the Ainsley android to where the original Yirella was waiting—

—she swayed about as if caught in a blast of wind, the experience of living so much in the space of seconds almost taking her to her knees. "Fuck the Saints," she moaned. But at the end, all she could see was Ellici and Tilliana—her smart, funny friends reduced to age-ruined shadows of the amazing people they used to be.

When she blinked the sticky moisture out of her eyes, she saw her own mournful expression on the Ainsley android's face. The rest of the knowledge it had brought back was sloshing about inside her head like storm waves hitting a rocky shore. "The conduits?"

"We'll activate them in another three minutes," the Ainsley android said.

Of course. The memory was there; she just had to concentrate. If those first twenty androids she'd sent into the ship had found more initiators, then there should be more than a thousand of her aspects positioned across the *Morgan* by now, all ready with their operating instructions loaded into conduit managers, and emergency power rerouted. If not, the two of herselves she'd left behind on deck twenty-two would have produced more than two hundred more androids by now, which should just be enough to activate all the conduits. It was all down to timing, governed by the quantum logic clocks.

As she absorbed the situation she became very aware of how her attention was struggling to cope with the six aspects now on deck thirty-three that were linked up into one personality. It wasn't that the images from six different pairs of eyes, and other more extensive senses, were confusing. It was rather that she couldn't quite process all her aspects' thoughts in unity. Her brain simply wasn't wired for it, despite the corpus routines doing their best to smooth the perception and thoughts into one.

"I think Immanueel and the others modified the neural structure in those biophysical bodies of theirs," she said out loud. "This is going to give me a headache despite all the filtering I'm applying."

"Hang on in there," her Ainsley android aspect replied. The other four aspects signaled their support and sympathy, reducing their own input to the common personality to help.

She was starting to worry just how she'd cope if the *Morgan* did liberate itself from the time flows and hundreds of aspects joined her personality.

There are worse things.

And she wasn't quite sure where that thought originated— her organic brain or the multi-aspect personality that she had elaborated up to.

I'll take it, though. Because it is mine.

A countdown in her optik told her there were ninety seconds left. She accessed the hull cameras just in time to see the negative-energy conduits rising up out of their recesses in the *Morgan*'s shiny copper fuselage. As she looked at the lean curve and menacing point of the spurs, all she could think of were the ears of the morox that had attacked Del after the flier crash back on Juloss. The shape triggered way too many nerves.

There were twenty seconds left on the count, with the aspects loading the pattern format into local management routines, when awareness burgeoned into her mind, deriving from the plural personality—a gentle mental nudge to a weak biological brain. It wasn't just the spurs on their section of the fuselage that were rising. The cameras were showing them standing proud across all of the *Morgan*.

"Saints," she gasped. "It worked. *I* worked." The countdown reached zero. A tremor ran through the deck, and her optik was deluged by icons detailing node status and recovery routines going active. Her personality aspects expanded at a phenomenal rate as the network reintegrated, elaborating her to seventeen hundred aspects. *Corpus level!* She was scattered throughout the ship: in cabins, engineering bays, hangars, the dark spaces between tanks, wedged into machinery modules, airless interzones pressed against the fuselage, clinging to structural beams. All of her aspects interfaced with arrays and power systems, supervising the conduit patterns, scanning the nebula, arming weapons. Alarmingly, she could see the power drain from the conduits was absorbing almost all of the *Morgan*'s generating capacity to repel the time flows. They'd have to operate at redline limits just to accelerate, and as for beam weapons . . . She had to order them to power down. They couldn't fight—not if they wanted to stay clear of the time flows.

Thirty-seven hers were tending to ancient tactical personnel who had endured decades of miserable imprisonment in their isolated decks, while another fifteen were trying to calm squad tacticians who'd been in normal time flows or slow ones and who hadn't even noticed anything was wrong yet.

Operationally, the *Morgan* was running at about seventy percent capacity, with machinery that hadn't been powered up for decades taking time to get back online, while some equipment was so worn it would need replacing entirely. But it was a warship, designed to keep functioning and fighting when it was damaged.

"Armada status!" Yirella demanded. The main tactical display refreshed as the network reacquired the full sensor suite. For some reason she could analyze it calmly, no longer the Yirella who used to quail at the thought of taking an active part in advising the FinalStrike itself. *Probably because only one aspect suffers hormonal stress, while the other seventeen hundred are pure analytics. That's what I call a decent balance.*

The armada was besieged by photonic disfigurements, every ship the center of a shimmering cyclone of flickering microstars. "The squads," she gasped in relief as she saw the troop carriers were in plain sight, still holding position a thousand kilometers out from the *Morgan*. None of them were being accosted by twinkles. *Too insignificant*. The thought angered her. *Just you wait*.

Her comms were receiving calls from every squad leader—including Dellian. All of them were desperate to know what was happening. She talked to all of them simultaneously, ordering them back to the *Morgan*, where they'd be safer inside its hull, protected from errant time flows.

At the same time she was also monitoring a squadron of eighty Resolution ships picking off the armada ships quickly and easily. More Resolution ships were flooding through the gateway behind them, accelerating toward the armada to add to the carnage. Nothing could fight back; the corpus warships were paralyzed by the different time flows twisting through their structure. They were being struck by graviton pulses and nuclear missiles and energy beams, detonating into vivid swirls of incandescent vapor that expanded out like a distorted cluster of weird tumors as their destruction times varied.

While her android aspects handled tactical, her original body opened Dellian's icon. "Hey, you. How are you doing?"

"Yirella! Saints! What's happening? Are you all right?"

"I'm fine. The Olyix hit us with a weird time weapon. That's why you've been ordered back to the *Morgan*. You'll be safer inside."

"Right. Yeah. Listen, Ellici and Tilliana aren't responding. Do you know if they're okay?"

She steeled herself for the lie. *A white lie, though. The squads cannot have distractions when they get into the arkship*. "Yes, they're okay. Tactical's really busy right now, so I took this job."

"Thanks, Yi. So is FinalStrike over? Are we retreating? We can see the armada ships being destroyed."

"No, Del, we're not retreating. The corpus humans are going to start fighting back. We know how to beat the Olyix weapon. Our ships will be liberated."

"Thank the Saints for that. After all this, we can't back out now. We can't."

"I know. I'll call you back."

"Sure. Thanks for stepping up. I get how stressful this must be for you."

"No problem." She closed Del's icon. The relief from hearing his voice was profound. She granted her original body a moment while her corpus personality finalized strategy. They really did need to liberate the armada fast. Otherwise this freedom wasn't going to last long—

The *Morgan*'s generators were nearly all back on line, providing close to a full power output—enough to power a whole continent back on old Earth. Her lips twisted into a smile. "Fire on those Saints-damned twinkles," she ordered the *Morgan*'s network. "Every graviton beam we've got." She needed to see what impact the weapons would have. The twinkles were just loci within the enclave's slow-time continuum. There was nothing physical there to be blown up, but she was fairly confident they could be distorted, their temporal effect broken.

Graviton pulses swiped through shoals of twinkles, scattering them like a tornado hitting a pile of leaves. The troop carriers swept in through the scintillating lightstorm, returning to their hangars. As soon as the last one was back on board, Yirella accelerated the *Morgan* at eighty gees, streaking toward the closest battle cruiser. They came alongside fast, graviton pulses bombarding the dense throng of scintillating blemishes that surrounded the long copper-sheathed shape. "It's working," she said gleefully, as fractured auroral curlicues scythed away from the battle cruiser's hull.

Immanueel's communication icon appeared, routed through the armada's secure links. "What just happened?" they asked. The battle cruiser was only a single aspect, but the contact was profoundly reassuring. She sent the file she'd composed. A second later the battle cruiser's negative-energy conduit fins were sliding up through the copper hull.

"I'll get Ainsley," she said. "You clear the rest of the armada."

"At once," Immanueel replied.

The battle cruiser speed-blurred in her sensor images as it shot away. The *Morgan* accelerated again, driving through the armada at three hundred gees, heading straight for Ainsley.

The Olyix had made a mistake, she thought, by not targeting Ainsley first. But as the Resolution ships coming through the gateway had caught up with the tail end of the armada, they'd started attacking the helpless ships there. *Bad strategy*.

By the time the *Morgan* reached Ainsley, Immanueel had lifted four more warships out of the disjointed time flows. They had each gone on to unshackle more; freedom was now growing geometrically. Judging by the rising intensity of the twinkles, the Olyix recognized the inevitable outcome.

At two kilometers long, Ainsley was shorter than the *Morgan*. That made Yirella extremely confident they could rip it clear of the distortions. But the Olyix had obviously realized the same thing. When they rendezvoused, the white hull was almost invisible behind a cloud of the diabolical sprites. The *Morgan* was firing gravitonic pulses almost continuously; Yirella's corpus personality had assumed direct command of the ship's systems from the genten arrays and diverted every watt from the generators into the negative-energy conduits.

It wasn't a battle many sensors could see, let alone interpret. But the counters the *Morgan* was deploying methodically peeled the clashing continuum disfigurements away from Ainsley, creating a dark zone around the pair of them.

Finally, Ainsley's white icon appeared.

"Motherfucker! Those sneaky little shits. Parts of me lived for a thousand years. Nothing worked. It was like being smothered for eternity. That . . . *Goddamn*. I'm having to delete entire memory clusters. It's too painful. Fuck them! They crippled half of my mind, and the other half didn't even know. I'm going rip them a new one bigger than their star. I am going to neurovirus every quint and make them eat the onemind neuralstratas—"

"Ainsley."

"—when I am finished with them they won't even be a boogeyman legend in this galaxy. I'm going to—"

"Ainsley."

"Jesus fuck. *What*?"

"Ainsley, we need you. Please." She watched negative-energy fins telescope smoothly out of the white fuselage. The ship's winglike structures were briefly sketched by a complex web of glaring scarlet and turquoise lines that swiftly softened to a subliminal tessellation.

"Right. Yeah. Fine. I'm realigning my mentality. I've got most systems under control. Fuck! Even some of my units have time ablated. Hell, if that'd gone on much longer, they could've compromised the phasefolded systems. Performance is returning."

"Ainsley, the Olyix are going heavy on targeting the neutron star with this temporal distortion crap. I think they're trying to slow it down. So I need you to take out the power rings. We have to kill the enclave. Now."

"Got it. Yirella?"

"Yes."

"What happened to you?"

"I went corpus. It was the only way to overcome multiple time flows."

"Okay. Well . . . uh, thanks, kid."

"You're welcome. Ainsley—"

"Yeah?"

"Tilliana and Ellici got trapped in a fast time flow. It finished them. They're alive, but they lived in it for ninety years."

"Oh, Jeez, no. What about the boyfriend?"

"He's good. He's alive and back on board the *Morgan*."

"Okay. I'm going to take down the power rings. See you at the arkships."

"Yes." She watched Ainsley depart, scoring a long, dark line through the nebula. When she checked, the total elapsed time since she'd rendezvoused with him was two point eight seconds. *So there are some benefits to elevation, then.*

The tactical display showed her the rate armada ships were being recovered was increasing dramatically. Ten minutes later the liberation was complete, even though she felt sick at how much glowing wreckage was clotting this whole section of the nebula—a swirling radioactive monument to their hubris. *So many ships destroyed, so many aspects lost.* But now attack cruisers were beginning to engage the Resolution ships that were still pouring in through the gateway, creating a new maelstrom of wreckage among the energy-saturated plasma of the nebula.

"We have to leave now," she told Immanueel. "We can accelerate harder than the Resolution ships. We'll leave fifteen percent of the armada to engage them while the rest of us get to the arkships."

"Agreed."

The course was already plotted. The *Morgan* began to accelerate at five hundred gees.

SAINTS

SALVATION OF LIFE

Kandara slipped the light armor jacket over her environment suit and twisted the seal button, feeling it lock down the side of her rib cage. An initiator had fabricated it for her the first week they moved into the cavern, providing customized active firing apertures for the peripherals in her forearms. She glanced down at it and shook her head in dismay at the way it barely covered her hips. *About as much use as that chain mail bikini Sumiko used to wear in her* Stella Knife *series.* The jacket would protect her vital organs from a kinetic impact or energy beam strike, but that was all. *Ah, who needs limbs anyway?* She clipped the heavy-duty magpulse pistol to the jacket's belt, raising an eyebrow in challenge at Yuri's look of exasperation.

"Well, what were you going to kill the membrane generators with?" she asked him.

He held up a powerblade machete. "I'm simply going to cut the power. The last thing we need is to get into a firefight with an Olyix huntsphere. It won't end well. You of all people should appreciate that."

She really didn't want to think of *that* encounter on the McDivitt habitat. "Not a huntsphere, no. But Odd Quint is probably skulking somewhere along that corridor. It hasn't come back yet."

"She's right about that," Jessika said. "The hangar's perception is still being neutralized, which means Odd Quint is still in the vicinity."

"You don't have to come," Kandara told them. "I can handle this."

"I don't know about you lot," Callum said, "but I think we should stick together now. We've come this far. I don't want to . . . well, be left behind when the human warships arrive."

To die alone, Kandara filled in for him. Which was fine; it was exactly what she was thinking.

"I'm with you on that," Alik said and lifted his helmet on.

Yuri nodded crisply and handed him another of the machetes. "It's for the best."

"Thanks, man."

"Oh, bloody hell," Callum grumbled and held out a hand. A smiling Yuri gave him a machete.

"Don't I get one?" Jessika asked wickedly.

"I'd prefer you to monitor the onemind," Yuri said. "Any warning you can give us . . ."

Kandara grinned and put her arm around Jessika's shoulders. "After they vaporize Yuri, you can always use his."

"Screw you," Yuri grunted.

Kandara swore she could see his shoulders sag in a gesture of reluctance as he opened a small case and took out a magpistol along with three spare projectile clips.

She chuckled. "Fucking typical. You should be a politician: Don't do as I do, do as I say."

"Last resort," Yuri said defensively.

"Absolutely," Alik said and held up a maser carbine.

"Jesus wept," Callum exclaimed.

"Now I'm happy," Kandara said.

"We go to the hangar together," Yuri said. "We do this together, we come straight back. Okay? Move out."

Kandara said nothing as she slipped her helmet on, but . . . *I'm clearly not the only one who's accessed too many interactive combat dramas.*

She made her way cautiously around the egg tanks in the outer portion of the rock chamber. The feed she was looking at through her tarsus lens came from two creeperdrones waiting in the tunnel outside. One carried an entanglement suppressor and a dart gun loaded with the biotoxin, while the other had an extra row of sensors that were showing her enhanced images of the tunnel. She inched her way forward and took a quick look around the fissure's jagged rim.

"Clear."

"Something's happening," Jessika said. "The fullmind's attack on the human ships: It's not going according to plan."

"Good!"

"They're breaking free of whatever it hit them with."

"Let's just concentrate on the hangar, please," Yuri repri-manded.

"The onemind's perception is still neutralized."

Kandara squeezed through the fissure and stepped out into the gloomy tunnel. The pair of creeperdrone spider creatures were five meters away. There was nothing else in sight. She glanced up at the pipe trunks suspiciously. The winding tubes of crinkled bark seemed so innocuous, almost a woodland scene, taking her right back to the long walks she used to have with her parents in the mountains above Tavernola when they visited the head office.

Focus!

She took a couple of steps toward the hangar. Nothing else in the corridor was moving. She scanned around with her helmet opticals turned up to full sensitivity. The infrared patterns were benign—not even the glowing pinpricks of in-sects you'd get in a terrestrial landscape. She carried on, hearing the others emerge behind her. She held back on be-rating them for making such a racket.

"Hey, Allk?"

"Yeah?"

"Do you think we should just send the creeperdrone we armed into the tunnel after Odd Quint and switch on the entanglement suppressor?"

"Why would we do that? We want to get in and out fast, not chase some phantom threat. We'll deal with Odd Quint if it gets in our way. Don't complicate things."

"I'm not complicating anything. But Odd Quint is a threat. It needs eradicating."

"We've been through this," Yuri said. "We don't under-stand Odd Quint. So leave it alone."

"That's a dumb attitude. I do understand it. Odd Quint is tracking us. It's . . . it's like an Olyix version of a dark agent."

"Unlikely," Jessika said. "All Olyix quint act on orders from their oneminds."

"Then why is it blocking the onemind perception in the hangar?" Callum asked.

"Because it's a dark agent," Kandara repeated stubbornly. "It's independent, somehow."

"Maybe," Jessika said, but she sounded uncertain. "I'll give you that it doesn't behave like an ordinary Olyix."

"I wonder how it learned to act like this," Kandara mused. "What led it astray?"

"The Olyix do possess a level of natural ambition," Jessika said. "Most sentient species have a variant. It's a universal part of nature's toolbox, acting as an evolutionary catalyst. And proving themselves is how a quint gets selected for onemind status. So maybe . . . it thinks hunting us down is its route to promotion?"

Kandara considered that. "Have any new quint come on board since we arrived here?"

"No. The *Salvation of Life* is self-sufficient. Its systems simply grow new quint bodies whenever one ages out."

"So every quint on board was part of the Olyix's Earth crusade. Mother Mary, I'll bet Odd Quint was part of their saboteur teams, and now it's got sort of their version of PTSD. It picked up some bad habits back on Earth, like secrecy and human-style greed, maybe a dash of our paranoia."

"Are you saying Odd Quint is Feriton?" Yuri asked sharply.

"Oh, bloody hell, yes," Callum said. "His mission for Connexion had him sneaking around the *Salvation of Life* just like this. He could be reliving it."

"That's a bit of a stretch," Kandara said. "There were hundreds—thousands—of Olyix infiltrating us for decades. It could be any of them."

"It doesn't matter," Alik said. "We're aware of the problem, that's all that counts. If Odd Quint gets in the way, we kill it. If it doesn't get in the way, we take out the membrane, and it'll get blown out into vacuum. Either way, we don't go looking for it. We keep our objective as simple as possible."

Kandara knew he was right, but it didn't make her feel any easier about having a quint lurking around somewhere.

The creeperdrones moved into the hangar and spread out. She paused again, ten meters back from the hangar. Images from the creeperdrones and the sensor clumps on the ceiling showed her the familiar scene of a deserted hangar.

Pistol drawn, peripherals armed, she walked up to the entrance. Everything she saw confirmed what the feed was showing her. "Area clear," she told the others.

Training took over, and she slipped around the rim, pistol in a double-handed grip, tracking between potential threat points—and ending up aimed at the tunnel mouth where Odd Quint had last been seen. Target graphics splashed into her tarsus lens, locking onto hypothetical hostile locations. She could feel the peripherals in her arms poking at the jacket fabric, ready to fire in an instant.

The four transmitter drones were hovering over by the wide hangar entrance. She could see the slight static haze in the air of the membrane where the pipe trunks thinned out around the start of a two-hundred-meter passage of naked rock that angled down to the enclave. The shifting glow of the nebula beyond was just visible, casting wavering pastel streaks on the rock walls.

Ignoring the drones, she hurried across the floor to the tunnel where Odd Quint had gone. The others followed her out.

"Alik," she said, "I could do with some cover here."

"I got you."

While Callum, Yuri, and Jessika ran toward the membrane-covered entrance, Alik sprinted after her. She stopped two meters short of the tunnel and flattened herself against the wall. Alik pressed himself against the weave of pipe trunks behind her.

"The creeperdrone still can't see any activity in there," she said.

"Good. Listen, we need to secure ourselves to something solid, ready for when they kill the power to the membrane. Gonna be worse than a Kansas twister in here when decompression hits."

"Yeah." She studied the tunnel entrance, which didn't

seem to have any machinery even close to it, just more pipe trunks leading back into the gloom. "They've got to have some kind of emergency air lock door, right?"

"I guess. We would."

"Yeah? So I can't see anything that looks like a door."

"Maybe something fancy inside the trunks? It'll just pop out."

"Mary, I don't know. Hey, Jessika?"

"Yes?"

"Have they got emergency pressure doors in here?"

"I have no idea."

"Shit."

"They must have," Callum said. "Why would they not?"

"Riiight. Have you found the generator power leads yet?"

"No! Give us a bloody chance. Christ!"

Kandara zoomed her helmet opticals in on the other three, who were scuttling about near the membrane, waving sensors over the sinuous pipe trunks wrapped around the big entrance. She cursed silently. It put them in line of sight of the tunnel she was guarding. If Odd Quint was in there, it would have a clean shot at them.

She took a slim harness cable from her belt and passed it around a thick pipe trunk. She pulled hard; it held. It'd probably take her weight, she decided.

"Got one," Yuri said. "Organic conductor cable. Looks like a thick green vine, see? It leads to this unit here."

"I'll check the other side," Callum said.

"They'll have a backup cable," Jessika said. "Probably more than one."

"And a backup membrane generator, too," Callum said. "Stands to reason. I would."

Kandara wanted to shout at them to hurry. *Get a grip. They know what they're doing.*

All across the hangar ceiling, the slim lighting strands began to get brighter. A lot brighter. Her suit helmet had to apply filters to block the glare.

"Oh, Mother Mary!" She brought the pistol up to cover the tunnel opening, squeezing so tight it was a miracle the grip didn't shatter. Apertures along her jacket sleeves opened. The light was just as intense in the infrared spectrum, producing a uniform brilliance that jammed her sensors. *Not a coincidence.* "They're coming!"

She concentrated hard on the feed from the creeperdrone sensors. The tunnel illumination was as bright as the hangar, but there was no movement in there.

"Alik."

"What?"

"Kill the nexus."

"What?"

"The neuralstrata nexus. Kill it. Now! We have to stop the onemind seeing what's going on in here."

Her tactical monitor routines detected movement in the hangar behind Alik. She spun around, crouching—

GOX-QUINT

SALVATION OF LIFE

I observed through the neuralstrata as the four little flying machines swooped across the hangar and struck the entrance membrane, stopping them in midair. With my gentle misdirection diverting the local nexus, the extraordinary sight didn't reach the onemind. Even if it had, I don't think the onemind would have paid any attention. The human armada was breaking out of the temporal distortions we'd ensnared them in. Now Resolution ships were being destroyed, as moments ago they had been the destroyers. That alone was profoundly worrying to the fullmind, absorbing every facet of its intellect. To me the arrival of the humans in such appalling force was indicative of its betrayal. How could our leadership have been so ignorant, so complacent, so *fucking stupid*?

Our sacrosanct wormhole routes into the galaxy were lost. Our pious fleets decimated by terrible human weapons. Our hallowed enclave—the sacred core of our purpose, the reason we exist—invaded. Violated by animals who barely qualify as sentient. They brought a *neutron star* to kill our sun, for fuck's sake.

All because the fullmind would not deign to think the unthinkable: that we were not secure against the Neána and Katos and others whose ships had escaped being welcomed into our glorious pilgrimage.

The truly pitiful fullmind orthodoxy: How could we have been chosen by the God at the End of Time if it did not believe us to be supreme? And how would our God not know, up there in the future, about any dangerous challenges that we would face? If we, its chosen ones, were placed under a genuine threat, it would warn us with another message, allowing us to eradicate that threat before it developed.

Our fullmind believes it understood the divine. What bullshit arrogance! An arrogance that has condemned us. We have to prove ourselves to our God, not the other way around. Any fuckwit knows this.

So now the exquisite history of the Olyix will be extinguished along with our existence. By humans. *Humans!* The dumbest species in the galaxy—subverted, manipulated, and nurtured for millennia by the bastard Neána.

That might be the fate that awaits my fellow quint, but I'm not going quietly into the darkness and barbarism of a galaxy denied our benevolence. I will not fail our God. I see another path for myself now.

The Saints' little flying drones can't be an anti-arkship weapon; they're too small. Besides, they would never dare damage the *Salvation of Life*, not with all the humans on board. So they must be some kind of communicator. There are thousands of arkships and welcome ships here in limbo; the humans will not know which one is the *Salvation of Life*. The sneaky little shits hiding in here must be trying to call to their own kind for help, just as they did outside the gateway. Doing the same thing over and over again, because their inferior brains have no imagination.

But they didn't understand about the membrane and how it is strengthened to seal the atmosphere in now that the *Salvation of Life* rests in limbo. It stopped their drones. So they'll have to come into the hangar themselves to cut the membrane power, or—given their basic mind—shoot the generator.

The remaining four of my bodies abandoned their assigned tasks and headed for the hangar.

If the fullmind cannot stop the neutron star—and it doesn't believe it can—it will impact the enclave sun. The power rings and exotic matter rings will be destroyed, and ultimately the sun will nova, along with the sun outside. Everyone will have to leave—or die. In such a situation, the human fleet will no doubt devote themselves to saving our limbo ships. Their emotion-driven devotion to those who have not yet converted to our God's grace is a profound strategic weakness—yet another of their failings.

They don't deserve the life this universe bestowed.

And I am clearly the one our God at the End of Time has chosen to deliver divine retribution upon those who have enabled this catastrophe. If I am to maintain my purpose here and now, it will be to fight the profane invaders until the end. Every one of them killed now will be one less who lives to contaminate the time of our God.

The Saints must have some kind of surveillance devices in the hangar.

I couldn't be sure they hadn't seen me, even though I'd done nothing to betray my objective. So I planned for that. They'd watch the tunnel I was in to see if I came back. The schema of routes through the *Salvation of Life* is easy enough to follow. The hangar had twelve different entrances. I excluded the one the flying machines came out of and picked four others.

The quartet of my bodies arrived and made their way along them, watching keenly for any sign of the despicable intruders. It didn't take long. My perception inside the neuralstrata revealed the five Saints—awkward, badly evolved beasts scuttling out of a crack in a tunnel wall, wearing primitive pressure suits. They had a couple of fake server creatures with them, not Olyix in manufacture. I recognized the technology: creeperdrones. The criminal filth I utilized on Earth deployed similar machines in raids and petty fights.

My quartet of bodies moved gingerly down the tunnels I selected, edging close to the hangar. Only three of the humans were carrying real weapons: two pistols and a maser carbine. There were also some long powerblades, which would be useless in a fight against me. The weapons my bodies were carrying were considerably more powerful, but I knew from our last encounter that Kandara was extremely dangerous. I'll have to be cautious around that one.

My quartet approached the hangar. Ahead of me, two of

the Saints guarded the tunnel I was searching when the armada arrived; the other three were examining the area around the membrane generators. I activated my weapons and prepared to shoot. The Saints weren't aware my quartet was almost on them, which gave me an advantage. But first I wanted to give myself an even better advantage. I extended my influence within the local nexus, no longer just passively misdirecting its perception filters but adapting the autonomic routines.

I ordered the hangar's light level to rise to its maximum. My quartet raced forward into the glare while the humans were still confused. Body two emerged first, firing a multi-blade kinetic at Alik Monday, who was crouched beside the tunnel entrance. One of the FBI agent's legs was severed above the knee; the other was badly flayed by the cloud of spinning blades. He toppled over, spraying blood.

Human bodies: such a flawed evolution pathway. No other species we've welcomed has such a high nutrient fluid circulation pressure.

I lost body two. Kandara had been crouched beside Alik Monday and reacted with a speed we weren't expecting, returning fire with a pistol she was carrying. *Bitch!*

Body two was struck and its internal organs were abruptly shredded. I felt shock and the impossible intimation of supreme pain—dulled by knowing it wasn't real. But I'm still *infected* by human autonomic routines from my time —*too, too long*—running missions on Earth, when I incorporated their gross bodies into my quint and even grosser thoughts into my mind to help me blend into their culture.

Kandara shot body two with a wyst bullet. Its legs lost rigidity, and it fell to the hangar floor. The weight on impact ripped the damaged midsection skin apart, and it burst open, sending out a sticky wave of pulped tissue.

My remaining four bodies all froze in shock. That's a fucking human reflex—again. No true Olyix should do that. I have got to purge myself properly once this is over.

Then I lost contact with the local nexus. The hangar light dropped to normal levels. I didn't understand what had happened. *Did the nexus fail? Or . . . had the onemind discov-*

ered my misdirection? But its thoughtstream remained fixated on the approaching armada.

Bodies three, four, and five laid out a continuous fire pattern, strafing the areas where the Saints had been. They'd scattered; Kandara and Yuri were returning fire from the cover of tunnel entrances. Body three was hit, a leg wound. I spun it around fast, galloping as best I could for the tunnel it'd just emerged from. So nearly made it—

Bullets penetrated the brain. I lost body three from unity.

Motherfuckers!

I was using body five to hammer the area around the hangar entrance with proton pellets. Callum and Jessika Mye, the Neána metahuman, had taken cover there. Long sections of the hangar's biostructure erupted in static-blasted splinters and liquid. Lightning bolts snapped down from the ceiling as the pellets' energy sought to equalize, gouging out smoking punctures in the rock floor. I shifted body five's aim and shot one of the little dark drones. The machine's power cell detonated instantly, its blast wave sending everyone— bodies four and five, and all the Saints—tumbling across the floor.

Unity ended.

I was alone in body five. *Not possible.* I knew body one was safe, away from the hangar; I could not be reduced to just one unless body four had been eliminated. Yet I only had this single body. I saw body four scramble upright fifty meters away from me. We looked at each other. In a crazy gesture, I extended my manipulator flesh toward it. And it was doing the same. Yet our thoughts could not connect.

Some of my manipulator flesh was still gripping the proton pellet gun. I struggled upright, hunting for a target. One of the little creeperdrone fakes was on the ground beside body four, its legs already bending to right itself. I brought the pistol around, target locks bracketing the device. But before I could fire and blast the thing apart, a small green flame flickered out of an anatomically incorrect orifice on its upper body.

Body four swayed around, juddering as if it were being physically assaulted by invisible foes. Its manipulator flesh formed a long tendril ending in an elongated sucker. I watched, helpless, as it began to clout the sucker against a small dripping wound on its upper body, as if trying to slap out a fire. No injury that small should conjure up such a frantic reaction. Body four's legs began to jolt about, kicking wildly. Its manipulator flesh expanded in random surges, the tendril losing cohesion.

I knew it was experiencing the impossible: agony. But Olyix quint do not feel pain. Our bodies are too advanced. We do not suffer like basic animals, like . . . *humans*.

I shot the creeperdrone. The proton pellet demolished it in a blaze of scorched tatters. It must have been carrying an entanglement suppressor. The thoughts of body one and body four reunified with mine. *Thank fuck for that*. We became full Gox-quint again. No . . . part of us was dying; we could feel our brain dissolve as the toxin bit deep into our cells, spreading like wildfire. Precious memories that only that body contained were lost, ripped away into darkness.

It was not pain but terror body four felt. Terror at the outrage, as every memory it had left fled into the brains of bodies one and five. That terrible jumble of chaotic routines and recollections that was Gox, all of us past—Gox-Li, Gox-Mandy, Gox-Esfir, Gox-Suzanne, Gox-Namono, Gox-Yua, Gox-Azucene, Gox-Renpa, Gox-Keerthi, Gox-Niomi, Gox-Myriana, Gox-Galina, Gox-Annukka, Gox-Ornella, Gox-Chailail—the behavior routines, the very essence of the human females we had subsumed to act their role, transforming into the perfect quint human body: Cancer. We were all one, yet utterly discordant amid the turmoil of distress and fear. I felt no physical pain, but from our alien origin I knew true dread.

I tried to scream at the torturous death body four was suffering. Body four's manipulator flesh sent up hands, human hands, shaking them in fury at the universe.

"What is happening?" the *Salvation of Life* onemind demanded, for I had let my mental guard down. "Why are you in that hangar? What are humans doing there? How did they get inside me?"

"FUCK YOU!" I retaliated amid my anguish. "You did this to us. You! I told you the humans were still here. I fucking told you."

"Gox-quint, restrain yourself."

I made a supreme effort to regain equilibrium, squeezing the alien demons back into their correct place, deep, deep in my beautiful, perfect Olyix mind. They are nothing to me—instructions on subterfuge, an open book I once let fall, glimpsing pages fluttering in the dying light, a few meaningless phrases. Nothing more. Not real. Not me.

I banished entanglement with the *Salvation of Life*. I *renounced* it as the useless failure it was.

I watched body four topple to the ground. Dead.

Movement amid the smoke and ruins of the hangar. Yuri was advancing cautiously, slinking between the irregular protrusions of biostructure. I blasted away in his direction with both weapons. Answering shots streaked through the smoke and static blasts. Rock chips and shards of biostructure whirled around body five. Several struck, causing insignificant damage.

I ducked body five back into the tunnel and ran fast, keeping low. But it is not body five anymore. It is body two. I am no longer quint, quad, or trio; I am duo now. And that will never change, not now the last day of the Olyix has arrived.

Do not laugh, humans. I hear you. I taste your bitter joy. Deep inside my mind where your contemptible remnants cower. I know you. But this is your end, too. For this is the time of my glory.

I killed one of those bastard Saints, injured others. She will never let that lie, not Kandara. Soon she will follow me into the lonely vastness of the arkship—my home for centuries. Fool that I was, I loved it for all that time, and so its schema is embedded in my mind. Now it will become my killing field.

SAINTS

SALVATION OF LIFE

Kandara skidded across the hangar floor, boots plowing debris and sticky nutrient fluid away. She came to a stop, crouching over Alik. She stared aghast at his stump, the ruined leg beside it. Blood was pumping out of both in great gouts.

Oh, sweet Mother Mary, nobody has this much blood in them.

Deadened fingers clawed at the medipac on her thigh. It was so ridiculously small, and Alik's godawful injuries would challenge an entire ER crash team.

"Need help!" she yelled. "Bring your medipacs. Now! Alik? Oh, Mary! Alik, can you hear me?"

Somewhere behind her, Yuri was still firing his pistol into the corridor where the last quint had vanished.

Alik's body juddered weakly as he coughed. The seals on his collar clicked open and the helmet dropped off to one side, clattering onto the rock.

Kandara had seen death claim people before, seen the desperation and loss in their eyes. And here it was again.

Zapata used its field medic routines to analyze the damage and splashed up a triage sequence on her tarsus lens.

That's not going to be enough.

"Hey, you free tonight?" Alik whispered. Blood dribbled out between his lips.

"Don't talk!" She shoved the first emergency tourniquet clamp directly onto the tattered end of his femoral artery. It annealed to the artery and contracted, slowing the blood loss but not stanching it altogether. The second clamp was hard to pull out of the medipac. She shook it free angrily and slammed it into the gore of the horrific gash on his remaining leg, trying to maneuver it onto the source of the blood. Her suit gauntlets were never intended for a task this delicate; she was sure she was just causing more damage.

Medical diagnostics from Shango, his altme, splashed across her tarsus lens, turning her world disaster red. The tourniquets didn't seem to have made any difference. Jessika arrived, her medipac already open. As Kandara attached another tourniquet to the leaking femoral artery, Jessika applied a bladder of bloodsub to Alik's neck, a vampire jellyfish going for his jugular. "We need to keep his organs oxygenated," she said as the bladder started to contract. "This is going to take all the bloodsub we've got."

Kandara read the combination of drugs Zapata wanted fed to Alik and plugged a pharma module directly into the plasma bladder. It was difficult; hot tears were distorting her tarsus lens, warping its displays. Alik's icon splashed across the deepening red view.

"Stick with the mission," his calm voice spoke directly into her head. "Get the message out where we are."

"I'm going to get you into the cave," Kandara told him. "It'll be okay. The initiators can help. You'll be fine, Alik."

The medical display flashed critical alerts as Alik's organs started to fail. His eyes rolled upward.

"Jez-us, Kandara," he sent over the interface, "grant a dying guy his wish. Blow the membrane, get the drones outside, then go kill that sonofabitch Odd Quint for me. Kill it good, all its motherfucking bodies. You got that?"

"I'm on it, just as soon as we get you stable."

"No!" His body shook feebly. "I fucking want this." A big glob of blood oozed out of his mouth, and the hard muscles his face had been remade with finally turned slack.

The medical splash from Shango went dark.

"Fuck!" Kandara screamed. She didn't know if she did it

straight away or if she'd been staring mindlessly at Alik's corpse for an age. Her whole body was numb from raw fury.

"Uh," Callum said, "I could do with some help."

Kandara scanned around, ready to yell her filthiest insults at him. Alik was dead. Didn't he understand that? Dead. Traveled fifty thousand light-years to die in pain and blood and ignominy.

She saw Callum slumped against the wall amid a tangle of mangled pipe trunks, with their glutinous juices pulsing out in anomalous rhythms. His left arm was bent at a bad angle, the environment suit sleeve torn from shoulder to elbow. He was pushing a klingskin bandage onto the wound inside, a feeble rubbing motion that seemed to be having no effect. She thought she could see a sharp dagger of broken bone sticking out of the flesh, but everything was so red it was hard to tell.

"Hell!" Jessika yelped. She snatched up her medipac and ran for him.

Kandara glanced back at Alik. People were supposed to look peaceful when they passed. Alik didn't.

Good.

She picked up Alik's carbine and hung the strap over her shoulder. Then she stood up and started walking toward one of the three dead quint bodies—the one that had blown up a great swathe of pipe trunks and rock wall with its gun. "Yuri, did you get that last quint?"

"I don't think so. I can see about a hundred meters along the corridor. There's no body."

Kandara told Zapata to run a check on the remaining three transmitter drones. "Keep watching. I'm going to try and flush it out."

"Kandara—"

"Keep watching," she insisted. "And everyone, tie yourself down. This is going to be fierce."

She picked up the Olyix gun. It was about the size of her forearm and must have weighed ten kilos. Instead of a handgrip, one end forked apart into prongs that ended in two large scalloped bulbs, which she'd seen the quint's manipulator flesh envelop. No trigger, but there was a circle of five rubbery buttons. She hefted it up, using a knee to support the barrel.

"No," Yuri warned. "Don't."

Kandara ordered the drones to hover right in front of the membrane. They slid obediently through the thin strands of grimy smoke that now layered the hangar's air.

"Oh, shit," Jessika grunted. She quickly finished sealing a pressure patch over Callum's torn sleeve, then grabbed at his harness cable, attaching it to her belt.

Yuri was running across the floor to the end of his cable. "Wait—"

Kandara aimed the big gun's muzzle at the wall around the membrane and pressed one of the buttons. Nothing. Second one. *Third time lucky.*

It fired. A small white flare at the end of the muzzle, then a lightning ball was exploding out of the pipe trunks, sending electron tendrils crackling across the disintegrating bark. The membrane glared violet.

"Wait, for fuck's sake," Yuri shouted; he was doubled over, fumbling with his belt or something.

Kandara pressed button three again. Again. Again!

Inside the helmet, her yell was louder than the roar of detonations. She marched the strikes around the side of the big entrance, destroying every chunk of Olyix biotechnology on the wall, and a good portion of the rock underneath. The hit on the membrane generator's last power cable came without warning. One second the membrane was there, glimmering like a window framing a clear sunset sky, then it vanished.

Atmosphere howled out into the vacuum, creating an instant blizzard from the debris clutter across the floor. The dead quint bodies started to roll and slither, picking up speed before finally sailing out of the hangar entrance amid the rushing gas streamers. Kandara hadn't quite expected the force of the wind to be so powerful. She flung herself down on all fours—not that traction counted for much, certainly not given the puddles of brown goop rippling across the floor. She had to use the harness cable, pulling herself along hand over hand to reach the rock, where she could get a decent grip in the gnarled pipe trunks. She prayed to sweet Mary that the cable would hold.

Quick check around, and there was Yuri, doing the same thing as she was, still at the end of the tunnel where the last quint had gone. He'd managed to hang on to his pistol, which was more than she'd done with the Olyix gun. That'd gone twirling away to oblivion along with its previous user. By the side of the entrance, Jessika and Callum were clinging to the knotty strands of bioware, her arm around his waist as his feet kept lifting off the ground.

"Yuri?" Kandara called. "Anything?"

"Not yet," he replied. "Did the transmitter drones make it?"

Zapata reported it had a signal from the three drones, though it was weak. The image from their sensors splashed across her vision, and she was looking at a jumble of vivid nebula billows and worn-gray rock as they careered around one another. Ion rockets were firing at full thrust to try to stabilize the drones. Tiny ice crystals and chunks of bark spun around them, spewing from the dark slit in the curving cliff of rock, swinging chaotically in and out of view. A lot of the image was taken up by sweeps of the gas giant's heat-enraged cloudscape, and the golden glow of the bow wave wings that embraced it. The drones' inertial guidance systems calculated the section of the nebula where the human fleet ought to be and focused their antennae on it.

Kandara ordered them to start sending, and added her own channel to the prerecorded message. "Calling the invasion fleet. This is Kandara from the *Avenging Heretic* if any of you even still remember us. We made it. We're on board the *Salvation of Life*, along with all the cocoons—everyone they took from Earth before S-Day. They're alive. Mary, am I glad to see you. But you coming here has kicked off the mother of all shitstorms. We're cornered and could really do with your help. Now, please. We're in the hangar that—"

A dark, curving shape slid into the feed's image, silhouetted against the planet's beautiful bow wave, and every drone icon vanished from her tarsus lens, along with their image feeds and telemetry.

"Ahh, Mary," she complained. "Well, the drones worked. Let's just hope humans still use quaint old radio."

The hangar's atmospheric pressure had dropped severely. All twelve of the corridors and tunnels that led off into the arkship were now acting like rocket exhausts, with powerful fountains of white gas firing out across the wide hangar, only to be sucked away through the big entrance. At least it meant the force that was tugging at her had reduced to a mere gale. She could almost stand upright, but the slippery floor was treacherous, and now the slick pools of fluid were bubbling off into the violent thinning atmosphere.

"Mary, their starships have flown across the entire galaxy and they haven't got health and safety protocols? Where the hell are the emergency doors?"

"Kandara!" Yuri barked. "It's coming."

She fought her way across the hangar floor, keeping as low as she could. There were still dark flakes *zing*ing through the thinning air, twigs and leaves and small fibrous tubules torn from the arkship biotechnology, each one with a punch like a cage fighter when it struck her.

Yuri started firing his pistol along the corridor when she was still thirty meters away.

The edge of the entrance next to him blew apart in a cascade of rock shards as it was hit by energetic gunfire from somewhere within. Yuri went sprawling, then rolled smoothly back into a crouch, pistol held steady on the corridor.

Like he's done it before, Kandara thought admiringly. She lurched for cover amid a tangle of broken pipe tubes that were swaying alarmingly, bringing the carbine around ready. The jet of mist roaring out of the corridor started to fluctuate, its subtle fluorescence dimming. A quint was bumping along the corridor wall, legs skittering frantically on the rock floor while its manipulator flesh surged out in thick pseudopods, trying to grapple onto the wall's undulating pipe trunks and fluttering creeper fronds, but the malleable translucent flesh wasn't strong enough to hold the quint's weight against the tremendous force of the atmospheric tsunami howling into the hungry vacuum beyond. One protuberance still held a weapon, which it was trying to aim at the still smoldering corridor entrance close to Yuri.

"Mine," she bellowed. The carbine's slender orange target graphics splashed into her tarsus lens, and she brought the weapon around carefully, tracking . . . She fired straight into the quint's manipulator flesh, searing it deep. In response the flesh cratered as it tried to avoid the burn. She moved the carbine a fraction, scorching again, each time ruining more of the manipulator flesh.

"What the hell are you doing?" Yuri demanded. "Go headshot. Kill the bastard!"

"I am killing it," she growled. "But not the nice way."

Another salvo of accurate maser shots, and the crippled, smoldering manipulator flesh lost its grip. The quint body was ripped off the wall by the torrent of air, tumbling crazily, legs still kicking.

Kandara stood up, bracing herself against the wind, and gave it an almighty forearm jerk. *Yeah, you saw that. You know. I did this. I finished you, fucker. Me!*

The quint body slammed through the hangar entrance, smacking into the rock several times as it went. Kandara never even flinched at the brutal impacts.

"Happy now?" Jessika asked.

"Oh, Mother Mary, yes. I truly am." She saw Jessika and Callum still clinging together and started crawling over to them. Three of the unruly atmosphere jets were between them.

"Don't move," Jessika said. "We're okay."

"Right." She started to look for a safer route. But they all involved climbing up the wall and crabbing her way over the tunnel entrances mere centimeters from the jets. *Crap.*

"They're fading," Yuri said.

"What?"

"Look. The pressure's dropping."

Sure enough, the jets started to shrink, losing their vigor. Within a minute they had finished. The hangar was in a vacuum.

"Finally," Jessika said. "Some health and safety protocols."

Kandara started toward them. She only got a few paces before realization hit and she stopped, scanning around.

"Aww, Mary! No." Alik's body was nowhere to be seen. He'd been blasted out into space.

She thought she might cry again, but there was nothing. No emotion. Either her gland reigned supreme, or the sheer intensity of everything that had happened had scoured her clean of feelings forever.

When she finally got over to Jessika and Callum, Yuri was already there. Everyone was examining Callum's arm.

"It's okay," he insisted. "I'm fine."

"Yeah, you will be," Yuri said. "It's not serious."

"What?"

Kandara chuckled dryly at the indignation in the old man's voice. She suspected he wanted to argue with Yuri, make the universe right again.

"But—" Yuri said. "I am concerned about maintaining the suit integrity. That patch is medical. It's not supposed to repair a rip like that in a vacuum. So keep as still as possible. I'm going to wrap another patch on top, then we need to get back to the cavern. The initiators can extrude something better for you until the human invasion fleet arrives."

"Not arguing," Callum said. He didn't even object to Jessika helping him slowly to his feet as he held his arm out stiffly.

Kandara slung the maser back over her shoulder and loaded one of the spare clips of wyst bullets into her magpistol. *Only one clip left now.* Callum's powerblade machete was hanging off his belt. She unclipped it and fastened it to her own.

"What are you doing?" Yuri asked.

"Haven't you been counting?"

"What are you talking about?"

"Odd Quint. *Quint.* There's five of it. We only took out four bodies." She pointed at the tunnel the first quint had gone into. "That one never came back."

"We're in a vacuum," Jessika said. "They're tough, but they still need to breathe."

"And yet here we are," she snapped. "I'd be worried if maybe we were in a spaceship, you know—the kind of vehicle that would carry some piece of equipment that allows quint to survive in a vacuum. Sort of a: Space? Suit?"

"You know what's on the other side of whatever emergency door is up there, don't you?" Yuri said. "Every quint on the *Salvation of Life*—and all of them are going to be very keen to find out if we survived."

"Yeah?" Kandara patted the carbine. "Well, they're about to discover the hard way."

"Please," Jessika said. "Don't do this. We've won. I can see it in the onemind's thoughtstream; the human ships are so close now. And you know Alik wouldn't want you to do this."

"Cheap shot."

"But true," Callum said.

Kandara stood completely still. The vacuum around her had taken away all the subtle noises that she normally never noticed, making the sound of her heart implausibly loud inside her helmet. It was a fast beat. She desperately wanted to eliminate the last of Odd Quint's bodies. *So I do still have feelings, even if they are only vengeance and anger.* "I'll just check the tunnel. Okay? That's all. I won't go past whatever emergency door is sealing the far end."

"Kandara . . ." Jessika said wearily.

"On Mother Mary's life, I swear I'll stay in the vacuum. But I have to know if the last Odd Quint body is there. And if the onemind is sending a battalion of quint down here after us, you won't believe how fast I can run away."

"Be careful," Yuri said. "Please."

She grinned at the concern in his voice. "Middle name."

MORGAN

Virella couldn't bring herself to go back into the *Morgan*'s main council room. The memory of everyone sitting there—talking, arguing, making impassioned suggestions for FinalStrike—was too vivid. So she was sitting in the deck thirty-three café yet again, with the Ainsley android on the other side of the table. None of her other android aspects was present. She wondered why that was. *Some kind of sub-conscious insecurity? My own androids are too much of me to reassure me? I need outside validation?*

Oh, stop it.

The tactical situation wasn't all bad. The *Morgan* was still plagued by twinkles, but they were only minutes out from the gas giant now. Even decelerating, its tremendous velocity was ripping through the nebula plasma, leaving a long contrail of emptiness roiling in its wake. The rest of the armada formation was expanding, ships heading for rendezvous with individual arkships. And Ainsley was approaching the power rings at a speed that was chilling her skin. He wasn't decelerating at all. The residual plumes of nine Resolution ships were still dissolving behind him, while the white ship was all but invisible at the center of an impenetrable cluster of fluctuating twinkles brighter than the corona it was approaching.

"What are you doing?" she asked. "That vector you're taking is dangerous."

"Making sure."

"Ainsley . . ."

"The Olyix know what I'm going to do. They're trying to suffocate me with time flows, kid—really trying. I'm at maximum power output deflecting them. And, face it, my maximum can punch a hole through Jupiter. If I fire a q-v missile, the flow variances in this twinkle clusterfuck would cripple it as soon as it gets outside my hull."

Even now, her corpus personality—the most rational mind she'd thought possible—just didn't want to process what she knew was inevitable. "So how are you going to kill the power rings?"

"Up close and personal. Only way. Deliver the q-v myself."

"You can't. We need you. There are thousands of arkships here. We have to save them."

"You got this. The technology the corpus retro-engineered out of my mentalic subsections works well on oneminds. Remember what I did to the welcome ship at Vayan? You can fly those big mothers out of here without me easily enough. That's what this is about, it's why we're here: to save those poor bastards who've been cocooned."

"I need you."

"And I need you to survive. To do that, I have to kill the enclave; you're not going to get home otherwise. Resisting this time flow shit is too big a strain; it's going to kick our asses eventually. Without it, you've got a decent chance."

"Oh, Saints, Ainsley. What about the shield? Can't you use that? If it hits the inner ring at your current velocity, the inertia will destabilize its precession. It'll start to drop into the chromosphere, and that'll be catastrophic."

"The shield is backup, kid—because I cannot afford to fuck this up. When I hit the ring, the shield will be on board; it still has the same mass, remember. So either the q-v warhead will get it, or the shield mass will. Either way, we win."

"You won't." But she knew it was no good; she could see Ainsley wasn't altering course. There was no emotional appeal that would make him reconsider. He had reached a healthy fraction of light speed now and was starting to red-shift.

"Call it job satisfaction. That's always been my motivation. You should have seen how we partied back in the day every time we pulled off a deal. Man, we could've shown the Romans a thing or two about decadence."

"Ainsley?"

"Get the *Salvation of Life* home, Yirella. But before you do, find out where the Olyix God is hiding. Say hello to the bastard from me, okay?"

"Oh, Saints."

The tactical display showed her Ainsley approaching the innermost power ring. She watched in dread. Given his phenomenal velocity, the margin for error was minute. If Ainsley hadn't got the course completely right there was no time now to correct. *Saints, that means I want the ship to hit.*

It did.

Ainsley got the timing perfectly, triggering the q-v warhead nanoseconds before any impact obliterated them, but close enough to affect the ring fabric: an impact like a bullet hitting an ice sculpture. The ring shattered, flinging out a massive halo of destruction that swarmed out across the ecliptic. As it disintegrated, the three outermost rings of exotic matter flickered, then vanished. At the same time, the iridescent sparks blockading the armada ships were abruptly extinguished.

Where Ainsley hit, the shield expanded—an unnatural black circle against the coronal glare. It began a slow tumble, flipping over and over as it flew onward through the deranged pirouetting prominences before splashing into the chromosphere. Gargantuan spumes of dense plasma flared up around the disk, folding over to engulf the intruder, dragging it down into the unknown depths.

Then the radial blast of fragments hit the second ring at the two points their orbits crossed. One of the collision areas retained its integrity, while the other broke apart, leaving an unstable mega-loop spinning half a million kilometers above the corona. The first fluctuation took what seemed like an age to build, but then the ring did have a circumference of over eight million kilometers. In reality, the deformation was astonishingly fast, and kept building. In less than five minutes the first fissures began to appear, swiftly followed by a chunk a quarter of a million kilometers long breaking off.

"Trajectory?" Yirella asked hurriedly as a second massive fragment joined the first, hurtling outward. Vectors appeared in the tactical display, showing their trajectories. With the second ring orbiting in a twenty-two-degree inclination, any debris from its disintegration wasn't going to pass anywhere close to the gas giant. More fissures split open in the tormented second ring, sending another group of fragments peeling off into space.

"The enclave's exotic continuum has dissolved," Immanueel said. "We're back in real space-time. I am entangled with my aspects that are accompanying the wormhole."

Yirella looked across the table at the Ainsley android. It was so difficult having his face right there in front of her. The aspect simply smiled meekly and mouthed: "Sorry. No."

Some stupidly juvenile part of her mind had expected him to have backed up, and *voilà*, his mind would decompress into the white android's neural array. She had to accept it; Ainsley was gone.

But not forgotten.

Outside the *Morgan*, the nebula clouds glimmered unchanged. Yirella magnified the visual sensors to their maximum resolution. "I can't see any stars."

"The enclave was ninety AUs across," Immanueel said. "Light from the outside will take hours to reach us."

"So we have no idea where the gateway star is?"

"Well, thankfully it didn't materialize in the middle of us. We should be grateful for that."

"Yes. I suppose so." She realigned the sensors on the arkships in their polar orbit. "The neutron star's going to reach this star in another eight hours. We need to find the *Salvation of Life* and get those arkships out of here and into the wormhole."

"My aspects at the wormhole can now observe the enclave nebula."

"What?"

"It is visible to them; the outer edge is intersecting the debris ring in the gateway star system."

"Saints, that's closer than we expected."

"Yes. Which has advantages and disadvantages. There are still tens of thousands of Resolution ships in the gateway system. They can reach us easily now."

"But the wormhole's close as well. We can—"

Then the *Morgan*'s sensors detected a radio signal emanating from the gas giant's polar orbit. And *everything* changed.

GOX-QUINT

SALVATION OF LIFE

I just made it to the secondary atmosphere containment sheet as it began to unfurl across the tunnel. The pressure that the air jet was exerting against body one was extreme. My manipulator flesh extrusions could barely maintain a grip on the tangle of biostructure that webbed the tunnel's ceiling and walls. By digging my feet into the crannies between individual tubes for extra stability, I managed to haul myself along in fitful increments as the *Salvation of Life*'s air hemorrhaged out past me. If I slipped, I would tumble down the tunnel like a kinetic projectile in a rifle barrel, just as body five was doing in its corridor. The vigor of the air stream—clotted with dangerous slivers of broken biostructure—was already overcoming body five's grip. I just couldn't get a decent hold on the biostructure, and my Goddamn feet were slipping on the floor. The proton pellet gun was making my predicament worse. I had to keep hold of it, which was impairing my balance and the amount of manipulator flesh I could apply to the wall.

Body five was getting close to the end of the tunnel when kinetic projectiles struck the wall beside it. I returned fire, blasting the end of the tunnel with proton pellets.

I experienced the first burst of damage to body five. Its nervous system registered the attack as a section of cells in my manipulator flesh dying from a massive thermal input, as was correct. But my mind . . . My mind somehow interpreted it as pain. Pain from a fierce, stabbing burn. It was all I could do to maintain my manipulator flesh in its composed shape. What I wanted to do was *flinch*.

"Shit!"

"Gox-quint," the *Salvation of Life* onemind demanded. "What is transpiring?"

"Fuck off!"

The pain had made me lose concentration, allowing the entanglement to resume. I slammed my mind closed to that useless turd.

More burns punctured body five. I started to tremble in shock as I forced myself to hang on. The beam weapon, which had to be a fucking maser, continued its assault. More and more manipulator flesh was ruined until I could hold on no longer.

Body five took flight, buffeted by the unrelenting blast of escaping air to tumble helplessly down the tunnel and out into the hangar. I was expecting a kill shot to body five's brain. Two Saints were in full view as I plummeted past, both holding weapons. I braced myself, compelling my mind that there was no pain. Quint do not feel pain, only humans.

There was no kill shot.

As I spun haphazardly, I saw one of the humans leaning into the storm. It gave me a forearm jerk.

You motherfucking bitch-whore! I'll kill you. I'll kill the whole fucking lot of you. I'm going to blow the *Salvation of Life* to shit with nukes and take every single one of your devil-spawned species on board with me. You're dead! Fucking dead!

Body five struck the wall of the hangar entrance. Hard. I was so dazed, body one almost lost its grip. It took everything I had, but I held on. I had to. I was going to finish Kandara if it was the last thing I did. There were more impacts as the venting atmosphere slammed me against the rock, again and again.

When body five was eventually swept out into the vacuum of the enclave, it was wrecked, the brain barely functional. But the pain had gone. I swiveled around and around, seeing the elegant colors of the nebula clouds, then the vast curving shell of the *Salvation of Life*. Air streamed out of body five's gills, forming a strange gray spiral as if someone were slowly wrapping a misty ribbon around me. Then the sight began to dim.

I lost body five.

There is only me left.

A containment sheet had already begun to close off the tunnel, emerging from its dehiscent pod in a mass of muscular crenulations dewed with viscous yellow fluid. Once free, its movements started to speed up. I made a frantic effort to reach it and clambered around its edge while there was still room. It was the first of three sheets in the tunnel, each a short distance apart, all squeezing shut. The air surge reduced to nothing around me.

I opened a tiny entanglement with the onemind, passively reading its thoughtstream Alarm was dominating its consciousness—alarm at the incoming human fleet, alarm at the destruction of the power rings, alarm at the course of the neutron star, and alarm at events within its hangar. A company of reverent quint was on its way to embrace the surviving humans and inquire what they had been doing. It actually considered that they might hold information relevant to the situation outside; it even offered this option to the fullmind, who responded encouragingly.

These dumb assholes.

I prised my way through the second containment sheet and opened the reserve repository of space suits. The one I removed flowformed around me quickly. Its neurofibers imprinted on my nerves, making it one with my movements. I picked up the proton pistol and made my way back through the containment sheets and into the vacuum. I wouldn't have long. The company would be here quickly, and they would be heavily armed, ready to subdue the remaining Saints.

Several of the overhead biostructure's luminescent strands had been damaged or simply ripped away by the frenzied depressurization, but there was enough light to see by. Nutrient fluids dripped from rips in the tubules, creating tacky puddles on the floor that were bubbling away in the vacuum. The corridor curved away ahead of me. I enhanced the space suit's visual sensors into the far infrared and ultraviolet spectrum, then bundled in magnetic readers—the radiation monitor and radio detector. Without the perception points of my other bodies to accommodate, interpreting that many senses was profoundly easy. It was as if I had brought daylight into the tunnel, with a multitude of embellished colors painting every facet in distinctive tones.

That's why I noticed the infrared traces from fifty meters away. They were patches on the floor, their heat radiating back to ambient, but definitely human footprints. One person had come this way and then returned.

I slowed. Up ahead, leading into the curve, the light from the strands was almost nonexistent, as if they'd been ravaged by the depressurization gale. And yet it was the only section to suffer like that.

She was good, I'll grant her that. I pushed myself against the wall and advanced carefully. There was a bright infrared glow coming from the gaps between a portion of the biostructure pipes. In there with it was a small, tight knot of magnetic flux lines—the kind a human weapon's power source would emit.

An ambush. Crude, but a decent attempt, given the circumstances.

I moved fast, driving forward and bringing the proton pellet gun up, firing three shots directly at the heat source. The energy flare of their detonation overloaded the space suit sensors momentarily. It didn't matter; the whole section of wall and biostructure was pulverized, with glowing embers jouncing along the floor to sizzle away in the puddles. There was so much infrared emission I had to reduce the sensitivity.

I halted beside the new crater, with its lopsided rim surrounded by broken stems of biostructure gasping out puffs of vapor. On the floor was a tattered human armor jacket, missing an arm. A mangled maser carbine was attached to it

THE SAINTS OF SALVATION   445

by a strap. But there was no actual human, no shredded flesh
nor burned bone, no boiling blood.

Shit!

I turned—tried to—but shock had numbed my legs.

I am an Olyix quint, for fuck's sake. I DO NOT suffer
shock— Oh.

SAINTS

SALVATION OF LIFE

It wasn't the smartest thing Kandara had ever done, and she knew it, but by now she was past caring. Call it obsession, call it finishing the mission—no, call it what it was: straight-up vengeance. Humans were finally hitting back, just as the Strike plan had always envisaged.

Time for me to contribute to the active stage of the mission.

So she'd turned off the gland and let her mind run free.

And Mary, does it feel gooood.

Unrestricted for the first time in decades. All she worried about now was being too confident. Or maybe that was the paranoia rising to the same levels as every other unchained psychosis. Whatever.

As soon as she started up the corridor, she began to run through options. She didn't have anything like the usual level of weapon systems that were her basic minimum for any sharp-edge op back in the day. Four peripherals: an upper-arm smart grenade launcher—good, but size constraints meant only three mid-energy grenades in the magazine; forearm kinetic barrel, with explosive bullets; forearm nerve-block emitter; and a wrist spool of monomolecule fiber. Even when the gland kept her calm and rational, she'd always had a deep distrust of the monomolecule—an invisible thread that could cut through a human body with the

slightest pressure. Every dark-operative's nightmare—
especially if you didn't have the correct sensors to warn you
it was up ahead. Her tarsus lenses were ultra-grade; they
should be able to see the Mary-cursed stuff if a strand got
loose. But she was wearing her damned helmet, so that was
no use. The kinetic was okay, but her magpistol with its wyst
bullets packed a much bigger punch. The nerve-block was
an unknown. (Jessika always said it should work on an
Olyix, but it was as yet untested.) The grenades were a defi-
nite plus—or minus; they gave off a strong power signal if
you had the right sensors.

She ordered the launcher to eject all three grenades,
wincing at the hiss of escaping air as the suit slit parted to let
them out—a quick sting on the exposed skin. Once they
were out, she placed them amid the pipe trunks. As a last
resort, she could trigger them by remote and bring the whole
place down on Odd Quint. Because it would come for her.
She *knew* that. They might be different species, but it was
easy enough to see your own kind in a mirror, however great
the distortion. Her grin at the knowledge was feral. Somewhere up at the other end of the corridor, Odd Quint would
be readying itself for their final encounter.

So here she was in an alien arkship in a time-skewed enclave, where she'd arrived by traveling down a wormhole for
fifty thousand light-years, ten thousand years after fleeing
her home, battling a religious extremist alien with a grudge.
Cool.

Around her, the pipe trunks with their sporadic fern
leaves and matting of lianas were sagging from the walls and
ceiling, splintered and broken. They leaked sludge onto the
floor where the vacuum boiled it away, making walking
treacherous. The corridor curved away ahead, but she and
Odd Quint would see each other from fifty meters away. So
it would come down to being the fastest draw, like a pair of
old Wild West gunslingers. What she needed was the ultimate in sophisticated hardware that human and Neána technology could produce. She studied the mass of alien
biotechnology smothering the rock, a displacement primor-
dial jungle at dusk. *Or I could just go full human primitive—*

There were doubts—so many doubts—seething away in

her brain. For the first thirty seconds, crammed upside down into a gap between pipe trunks in the ceiling, she'd felt elated. This was her true self—cunning and ready to unleash violence, heedless of risk. The state she was born to be in. But then flaws in the plan began to manifest, gnawing away at her confidence. Suppose Odd Quint didn't have any infrared sensors? Because you really shouldn't short out a maser carbine's power cell just to produce a thermal signature, as its safeties struggled to contain the feedback. That was never going to end well. Wrapping it in the armored jacket to contain the heat emission was also dumb. Suppose she needed the jacket for protection?

So many things that could go wrong.

Such a bad idea.

But if it worked . . .

Mary, this is why I needed the gland: clarity.

Her position meant she couldn't look along the corridor; all she could see was a small section of sticky floor directly underneath. Any sliver of her helmet exposed outside the irregular surface of tattered bark would have given her location away to the most simplistic sensor. So she waited in growing physical discomfort as her thoughts churned and her body grew hotter and hotter. Her environment suit's thermal regulator was turned off so the heat her body generated couldn't escape and betray her.

Even though she was expecting something like it, the explosions caught her by surprise. Kandara *yipped* in shock—a sound that was alarmingly loud inside the helmet. Every muscle turned rigid as the nest of pipe trunks surrounding her rocked. Her whole body juddered downward a few centimeters as the stems comprising her tangled nest slackened off.

She held her breath, knowing *this* was the crux. Below her was a quint in a gray space suit that looked as if it were made from fish scales, walking cautiously toward the pulverized wall—exactly where she'd wedged the jacket. She fired the nerve-block. Her hands let go of the pipe trunks she was holding, and she bent forward, straining to push her head out of the nest. Brittle, smoldering strands snapped around her shoulders, and she wound up with her whole torso hanging down while her legs strained to anchor her. The sight that greeted her was upside down, revealing the quint quaking as it stood over the shredded armor jacket.

She brought both arms up, target graphics splashing into her tarsus lenses. Peripheral kinetics shot the weapon Odd Quint was holding, smashing it apart. Simultaneously, her magpistol fired three times, sending a wyst bullet into three of its legs. They blew apart in gouts of flesh and space suit scales, sending Odd Quint toppling to the ground.

Kandara gripped the sturdiest pipe trunk with both hands and eased her legs out, allowing her to drop to the ground in a smooth dismount. In front of her, Odd Quint's two remaining legs were skittering wildly, but all the motion did was spin it around. Her altme switched on her suit radio, even though she suspected Odd Quint's suit didn't even have radio. And to hell with any part of the arkship that could pick up the signal.

"Bleeding out through your leg stumps, huh? That's a bad way to go. I know. Let me help." She brought up the power machete and swung the blade. Her aim was true, severing one of Odd Quint's remaining legs.

The crescent of manipulator flesh that was still intact rippled in torment, trying and failing to form appendages. Kandara swung the machete again, taking off its final leg. "I've spent my life taking down fanatics. Humans, Olyix, we've both got sick fucks like you ruining everything for the rest of us. And you all make the same mistake. You think our decency makes us weak, makes us easy targets. Do you still think that?"

She brought the machete around, ready to slice off some of the manipulator flesh. On the wall, the few surviving tatters of leaf fronds fluttered in the wind.

Wind?

A gust of atmosphere blew along the corridor. It was weak, lasting barely a couple of seconds, but it had to come from somewhere—like an emergency pressure door opening and closing.

Oh, sweet Mary.

Jessika's icon splashed across her tarsus lens. "It's coming, Kandara. The onemind is sending something into the hangar for us. Get out of there. Now!"

Kandara fired her magpistol into Odd Quint, five wyst bullets mashing every internal organ and finally its brain.

Her tarsus lens splashed the helmet sensor image of the corridor behind her as she jogged away from the dead quint. Right where it curved into a vanishing point, jagged shadows were flowing along the bulging walls. She sprinted past the grenades, then triggered them.

Debris slammed into her back, sending her sprawling painfully across the dark slick of simmering fluids. Several caution icons splashed amber, but her suit integrity held. She forced herself up onto her knees, wincing at the pain. When she twisted around, the corridor was blocked by a pile of rubble.

"Are you okay?" Jessika asked.

"Just about. I stopped them. And, Jessika, I got it. I killed the bastard that shot Alik."

"All right. We've put a pressure balloon on Cal's arm. It should hold. You need to get back here."

"Yeah. On my way."

It took an effort, but she managed to get up onto her feet. She swayed around—although maybe it was the corridor wobbling around her. She couldn't be sure.

Chunks of rock rolled down the pile blocking the corridor. "Huh?" She blinked, trying to understand what she was seeing. More rock was rolling down, pushed out of the scree by dark worms.

"Oh, Mother Mary."

The worm shapes fell out of the holes they'd made and started slithering along the ground; more started to wriggle through behind them. There must have been hundreds of the things. She'd seen them enough times on feeds from Earth's cities right after their shields collapsed. *Capturesnakes*.

Kandara turned and ran.

DELLIAN'S SQUAD

ENCLAVE

Dellian was doing his best not to let his worry show. Body posture easy; he was in his armor, clamped into the troop carrier's rack, an immobile nonhuman metallic statue. Nobody could read anything from that. Voice, though . . . that might be a giveaway. So he only talked to the squad in short, emotionless sentences. *Because no one will be able to tell anything from that. Right?*

It had all been going according to plan. Arrival in the enclave star system. Flying through the gateway. Deploying the troop carrier. That was when the weird crap began. They lost comms with the *Morgan* and the rest of the armada, except for other troop carriers, and even that contact was intermittent.

Then Yirella contacted the troop carrier and ordered them back into the *Morgan,* where they'd be safe. Delight at hearing her voice, knowing she was okay, was immediately blunted by the rest of the tactical situation. The Olyix had done *something* to the enclave, creating temporal havoc within the armada. Resolution ships had come pouring through the gateway to devastate the helpless corpus warships. And worst of all, Tilliana and Ellici were in the clinic. They were okay, Yirella assured the squad, but needed treatment. She was taking over tactical.

Another reason Dellian was glad he was inside his suit:

He knew he'd be swapping perturbed glances with the rest of the squad. Yirella was brilliant, and frighteningly determined, but maybe not the best to be directing them under pressure. And pressure didn't come any greater than this.

The whole squad cheered when Ainsley destroyed the power rings, killing the enclave, but Dellian's command channel showed him the terrible price that victory came with. He didn't share it with the squad; he couldn't allow them to be distracted when they arrived at an arkship.

Yirella ordered the troop ships to launch again. Then came the truly crazy news, which he immediately dismissed as an Olyix trap—and a nasty one, too.

"The Saints are dead," he told her over the secure channel.

"Our analysis of the message gives it a seventy percent probability of being genuine. It was Saint Kandara."

"The Olyix have had ten thousand years to put a perfect fake together."

"But why bother?" she argued. "We're here. We're going to put our squads into the arkship. If it's a fake message, we'll know right away."

"Yeah, when the arkship explodes and takes all of us out with it."

"Again, what's the point, Del? They must know we're going to win this part of the campaign. We will take the arkships. And they'd know we'd be skeptical of any message, especially one that cuts off. All that's going to do is make you even more alert and cautious when you get on board the *Salvation of Life.*"

"When *I* get on board?"

"I can assign that hangar to someone else."

He gritted his teeth in dismay. He'd lived with that image of the *Avenging Heretic* dying in a flaring nuclear hell for too long. It was his reality. This news was opening up old wounds, and the worry that he was setting himself up for an emotional fall. *But if there's a chance, however tiny . . .*

"Thanks," he said. "I appreciate that."

"You're welcome. Stand by."

The *Morgan* altered its trajectory slightly, curving around to match orbits with the source of the brief message. The arkship in polar orbit that was supposed to be the *Salvation of Life* did match the parameters of every record from old Earth. Not that it was much different from any of the other arkships and welcome ships encircling the gas giant.

The armada battle cruisers flew on ahead to attack the Deliverance ships that were clustered protectively along the polar orbit. Dellian watched the clashes. They seemed so irrelevant—small flashes of bright white light, as if the last twinkles were flaring their way to death. It seemed remote, somehow. The troop carrier's sensors were providing him with an excellent image of the planet's gargantuan magnetic bow wave wings. In contrast to the carnage the armada was inflicting, he found them utterly beautiful, shining like multiple halo wings as the world circled endlessly through this strange realm.

"The defense ships have been cleared," Yirella told him. "You're go for entry."

The troop carrier accelerated in toward the massive cylinder of rock, bringing back too many memories. Small explosions were blooming all across the rock as the attack cruisers destroyed the *Salvation of Life*'s defense systems. Now that they were close, there were patterns in the rock—strata lines and small craters that corresponded to the old records. The jagged rim where the rear quarter had been separated to reveal the wormhole terminus was an exact match.

"They couldn't fake that, could they?" he asked.

"Theoretically yes," Yirella said. "But they had no reason."

"Other than that they've been expecting us."

"Do you want to abort?"

"No."

The troop carrier swooped around the arkship and eased its way into one of the craters circling the midsection. The crater floor had a rectangular entrance cut into it, with a tunnel that curved up into the interior. It was barely wide enough for the troop carrier to fit in.

Twenty seconds later they emerged into a hangar.

"What the Saints happened here?" Falar asked.

"Explosive decompression," Xante said. "That's probably why the message got cut off."

454 PETER F. HAMILTON

"The emergency seals activated," Mallot said. "It's a hard vacuum now."

"Egress, pattern three," Dellian ordered. "Assume hostiles."

"Don't you mean hostages?" Falar said.

"Pattern three."

"Yes, sir."

Eighteen different hatches opened in the troop ship's fuselage. The cohort leaped out, speeding into the big empty hangar. Several of them nuzzled up at the sites of the most violent damage, where there'd clearly been a lot of gunfire.

"Proton pellets," Dellian read off his optik display. Which was almost a relief. Their armor's mirrorfabrik carapace could withstand those quite easily. You'd get shaken up inside, but the cohort would take care of the attacker swiftly enough.

"Let's get a picture of what's up those corridors," Dellian said. "Falar, Janc, Uret, take the left-hand side of the hangar. The rest of us: right."

The cohorts began to scamper into position, splitting into duos at the start of each gap that led out of the hangar. There was nothing in the immediately visible parts. Small airborne drones floated along the hangar roof and hovered by each tunnel entrance. They drifted in.

"I got a burst of air here," Xante said. "The emergency seal up there may be failing."

"Okay," Dellian said. "Whatever happened in here was recent, so let's be—"

An explosion registered up the tunnel.

"Delta cover," Dellian declared. It was all he could do not to smile. His cohort might be able to read his every intention, but his friends were equally empathic. They were already deploying as he gave the order.

Xante and Uret jumped and clung on to the ceiling. Clawing up into the battered pipe trunks, they were joined by a dozen of the cohort. Dellian himself leaped back under the troop ship, where one of the landing struts acted as a barrier. The rest of the cohorts fanned out, some sinking onto their haunches ready to lunge at whatever came out of the tunnel.

"Visual," Xante yelled. "It's a . . . Saints! Human."

"Confirm," Dellian told him.

"Human shape. Mass and thermal authentic. Crude suit design, not armor. Small weapons."

Dellian studied the image in his optik, feeling his heart rate climb. Either this was an astonishingly detailed lure that even Yirella could only dream of, or— "Okay, back away. Let them come." Two shoulder-mounted cannons slid up and aligned on the tunnel entrance.

"You getting this?" he asked Yirella.

"Yes."

The space-suited figure charged into the hangar and immediately saw the exoarmor hellhounds that were the cohort, hunched down poised to jump. Its reaction verged on comical—limbs flailing, desperately trying to slow. Boots slipped on the floor slicked by juices, and it fell on its ass, skidding along.

Dellian's suit detected a radio signal.

"Shit shit shit," a woman yelled. "Jessika, I got made. They're everywhere."

"Hold fire," Dellian commanded. His suit genten was flashing up a voice pattern match. For a moment his throat wouldn't actually work. "Saint Kandara?" he gasped. "Is that you?"

"What?" The suit shifted around fast, pistol swinging in a wide arc, switching between the two closest cohort exoskeletons. "Who's that?"

That's military training, was all Dellian could think. "I'm squad leader Dellian," he said. "I'm under the troop carrier. I'm going to stand up. Just . . . let's take this easy."

The pistol swung in his direction. He held his arms above his head and stood.

"Are you things actually human?" Kandara asked.

"Well, yeah!"

"Mary, limbs got strange since we left. And you're big, too."

"No, this is just my suit."

The rest of the squad was emerging from cover.

Kandara rolled around abruptly, pointing her pistol along the corridor she'd come from. "I hope it's a combat suit!"

"Are you really Saint Kandara?" Xante asked breathlessly.

"Fuck," she yelled. "Here they come."

Sensor alarms from the aerial drones went off. A dark tide slithered out of the tunnel. Dellian stared in shock at capturesnakes right out of the history files. The squad and their cohorts opened fire.

SAINTS

SALVATION OF LIFE

Callum was trying to keep his cool. Not easy. He'd been tense for so long now that he was frightened any attempt to relax and go with the flow would make him cry. Not that it mattered, because no one would see it. Nothing human. Or nothing he recognized as human, anyway.

Kandara had led a squad of invasion soldiers to the cave—two types in frankly terrifying exoskeleton armor. The first were human-ish, with limbs that had too many joints, while the second were a pack of demonic robot warriors arisen from nightmares. Both were too big to get in through the gap in the tunnel wall unless they ripped the rock apart. By the look of their suit limbs, they probably didn't even need weapons to do that.

His arm was throbbing badly by then—the kind of drug-dulled pain that was frightening because the sedative couldn't eliminate it. And the ridiculous balloon Jessika had fabricated in the initiator made it look like he'd got his arm stuck inside a beach ball.

The squad escorted them to the hangar, where a ship from the human armada was waiting. Their leader was called Dellian, whose voice over the radio came across as a strange mix of teenage excitement and religious reverence. *And why the bloody hell does he keep calling us Saints?*

That question died on Callum's lips when he saw the hangar. The firefight had left it strewn with the wreckage of busted capturesnakes and huntspheres that'd been cracked open like metallic eggs—eggs whose insides were a churn of molten metal and plastic . . . and charred quint flesh.

It was a vivid contrast going into the troop carrier, which was like being inside a machine where every surface had been coated in black chrome. But when the airlock sealed and the atmosphere came up to pressure, Dellian sank to his first set of knees, and the top of his armor hinged up.

Callum studied the young man intently; there was something not quite right about the features that he couldn't define. Head too . . . wide? Or maybe the thick neck was too short? He gave up trying to work it out and unlocked his own helmet.

"It's really you," Dellian said. "Saint Callum."

Yuri and the others took their helmets off, and Dellian stared around with a dazed expression, then started crying.

"Come on," an embarrassed Callum said. "We're not that bad looking."

"You don't understand," Dellian said, grimacing as if he were in pain. "I saw the *Avenging Heretic* explode. We thought you were all dead."

"You saw it?" a frowning Jessika asked.

"Yeah. I kind of got neurovirused by a onemind. That image was part of breaking me."

"Well, fuck," Yuri grunted. "So you've been fighting the Olyix for a while, then?"

"All my life. All of us have. And you were our inspiration, the five of you—our Saints. What you did, sacrificing everything to challenge the Olyix, it has been our guidance since our ancestors fled Earth. I'm so sorry we didn't get here in time to save Saint Alik."

"Saint Alik," Kandara said with a wry smirk. "How about that?"

"You know what he'd say about it, don't you?" Yuri said.

"What?" Dellian asked.

"He'd be very honored," Callum said quickly, before Yuri could reveal Alik's true opinion.

"Uh, we need to get you to the *Morgan* now," Dellian said. "It'll be safer for you, and Saint Callum can get his arm treated in one of our clinics. I have to go and lead my squad into the *Salvation of Life*. We're part of the clean-out phase."

"Clean-out?"

Dellian's guileless face hardened. "Yirella is dealing with the onemind, but we're going to exterminate the quint on board."

Callum shrugged, which made him wince. "Okay then."

A portal expanded at the far end of the cluttered chamber. "I'd like to talk to you," Dellian said. "Afterward. If you don't mind."

"Sure."

So they went through the portal. It was like walking back into a corporate headquarters, though perhaps the walls were whiter than any Connexion office block, the air filtering not so sterile. And the people . . . who weren't people, in the biological sense. They were greeted by epicene androids with black skin, a good half meter taller than even Yuri. The androids were all called Yirella, which didn't help clarify anything. But they showed Callum and the others to a clinic. That at least was reassuringly normal, though the medical equipment was a lot smaller and sleeker than anything he'd seen before.

Several other bays were occupied. Callum was sitting on a bed opposite a pair of amazingly old women. Even back on Earth in his time, only the poorest people had ever looked that old.

"What happened to them?" he asked the two androids helping to remove his space suit.

"Victims of war," one of the androids replied. "Fighting the Olyix meant a lot of sacrifices. I wasn't expecting it to be so . . . brutal. It has been very personal for me."

"Yeah. I'm starting to realize just how much I've left behind. We really are time travelers, aren't we?"

The Yirella android who had just removed the protective balloon from his arm nodded thoughtfully. "Yes, I suppose so. Though it is a one-way trip, I'm afraid," she said.

Callum couldn't actually look at his arm; the damage and protruding bone made him feel sick. Another android appeared, white, and smaller than the black ones, with an anatomy that was definitely male. It even wore a pair of green shorts. It was holding a long blue sleeve that looked as if it had been knitted out of fat silk.

"What's that?" he asked, then looked at the android's face. *"Ainsley?"*

"Not anymore," the white android said. "Sorry, I'm also Yirella. I just thought it would be more reassuring for you to have a familiar-looking aspect in a medical environment. This must all be very disorienting."

"Yeah, well, you're not wrong there. This—none of this—is how I expected our mission to end."

"What were you expecting?"

"Not to get this far, frankly. I'm still suspicious that this is a dream, and my brain is really in an Olyix cocoon."

"Trust me, you're not."

He lay back as the android with Ainsley's face gently slipped the blue sleeve over his arm, plugging its tubes and cables into a silver pillar at the top of the bed. His phantom pain finally vanished as the sleeve inflated; he sighed in relief. The tubes began to sway as fluids flowed along them. One was a horrible brown color. He looked away again.

"So what happens now?" he asked.

"My other aspects are dealing with the *Salvation of Life* onemind."

"Dealing with?"

"Killing it. I need to take control of the *Salvation*'s main systems so we can maintain the cocoons."

"There are other arkships carrying human cocoons. Five, I think."

"I know. The armada is already engaging them, as it is all the Olyix ships here. There are thousands of different species imprisoned in cocoons or their equivalent. We have to save them all. It is our duty and honor to do so. We're going to take them all with us, back across the galaxy to the expansion wavefront."

That took Callum a moment to process. "Do you have that kind of . . . capacity?"

"Just. We have taken more losses than expected. But the corpus armada prevails. An aspect will replace each onemind."

"Er, *aspect*?"

"Corpus humans are people who have divided their minds into many aspects, each of which resides in a different vessel—biological bodies, quantum arrays, machines, warships . . ."

"Androids." He was having trouble accepting what she was saying. *Too much strangeness.*

"Some, yes. Now their aspects are starting to occupy the arkships as their oneminds are eliminated. And very soon we will have to leave."

"I know; you brought a neutron star with you. It's going to hit this star, isn't it?"

"Yes. And it will soon turn nova, which in turn will trigger its twin. There is an eighty-two percent chance the two combined will produce a supernova. It is our moral obligation to ensure none of the Olyix's victims are left behind."

"I'm bloody glad to hear that. You're frighteningly advanced, so it's comforting to know you put so much emphasis on ethics. They are so easy to abandon in times of war."

"I am pleased I can reassure you. We owe you so much."

"Not really. The Signal we sent won't reach Earth for another forty thousand years. So many people sacrificed so much to get us here. The gamble we took . . . And in the end, you found your way here without us." Callum found his throat was all hot and tight; tears were building in his eyes. Stupid, but . . . This life he was now living was not something he'd ever expected. In so many ways it was an afterlife now, forever separated from those people he'd loved and lived with. He began to laugh, which turned into sobs.

The white android's hand touched his shoulder. "Are you all right?"

"Yeah. I think reality is catching up with me. I've just realized the only contemporaries I've got left in this brave new world are Yuri, Kandara, and Jessika. Bloody hell: the relic squad."

"The living are not relics. And you will soon be joined by billions from your own time. You are going home, Saint Callum. And when you do, you and the other Saints will be revered on the Earth rebuilt, along with every human world we settle."

462   PETER F. HAMILTON

"For what?" It came out with more bitterness than he expected—or wanted.

"You guided us here, Callum, you and your fellow Saints. You are the star we followed into the night. You are the heroes from our deepest legends. We—me, the squad you met, all the other squads who have traveled across half the galaxy to be here—we were all born for this one moment. How do you think we felt when we heard Saint Kandara's voice and followed her broadcast here to the *Salvation of Life* itself, the greatest evil humans have known? The legend of you gave my generation the most precious gift ever, as it gave all the exodus generations before us. You gave us hope, Saint Callum. And we were right to believe in you, for none of you gave up, did you? You did your duty right to the end. Can you imagine how profound that is to those of us living through what has become the end of days?"

"I didn't ask for any of this, you know," he said meekly.

"I know. None of us did. And possibly for the first time in my life, I am glad I exist. Because of you, Saint Callum. You are the reason I live. You are my life's validation. Thank you."

"You're very welcome. But I've got to warn you, we do not deserve your admiration."

"We'll see. Even with a wormhole that'll take us to within ten thousand light-years of Sol and the old settled worlds, it's going to be a long voyage."

"Back to Earth," he said in wonder. "Do you think we'll make it?"

"Yes. Effectively, this part of the war is over. We've won. Humans now possess the only wormhole leading away from this star system. It's the one that brought us here, and it's currently accelerating away faster than any of the Olyix ships pursuing it. They can't catch it now."

"But we can?"

"Oh, yes. A lot of very smart people put this campaign together."

"I look forward to meeting them." He hesitated as his arm began to itch under the blue medical sleeve. "We're really going to go home?"

"Yes."

YIRELLA

MORGAN

Yirella didn't quite trust herself to meet the Saints in the actual flesh. She was pretty sure her original body wouldn't be able to stop gushing with admiration and she'd make a total fool of herself. Even her android-housed aspects were thrilled to be in their presence.

She helped them out of their space suits in the clinic and ran basic scans to make sure they were all right, marveling at how accurate all the stories were about them. Callum so world-weary, yet still with a core of optimism— a good man at heart, numb from their incredible mission. Yuri, all gruff and professional, working hard to keep his relief from showing—but no reticence about being suspicious. Jessika, so cool and enigmatic, human with a classy hint of Neána. Perfectly composed at where she found herself. But no, she said sadly, she didn't know if the end of the enclave would mean the Neána abodes finally emerging from hiding. And Kandara, one tough dark-ops mercenary, a genuine professional killer, her lethal qualities only held at bay with neurological chemicals. Having aspects standing next to her, talking normally about the *Morgan* and what was happening with the armada, was a situation Yirella found darkly exciting. *She's killed people. Bad guys, terrorists, but still other humans.*

All of them were fascinating, and she wanted nothing

more than to talk to them for a decade solid. People who had lived and walked on old Earth. But now she had aspects inside the *Salvation of Life*. Thousands of corpus marines were helping the squads and their cohorts chase down and eliminate quint bodies and most of the service creatures. And three other machines advanced with them—mentalic aspects, little more than relay units for her corpus personality. They each made their way through the corridors and chambers of the arkship, hunting out a nexus. When they found one, they inserted a batch of needles that swiftly meshed with the neuralstrata nerve fibers.

"Hello," she said.

"Human, but not. I feel your mind, your thoughts are ordered like a machine."

"Some of me is, but that's really not relevant right now, is it?"

"Why do you do this? Why have you brought so much death and destruction to our haven? We love you."

"You know what, let's just cut the crap. You've lost. This is my offer. Relinquish control of the arkship freely, and I will allow some of your quint to establish a colony. They will have no memory of their history, no knowledge of the message from your God, but your species will survive."

"I feel you investigating my memories. What are you looking for?"

"I see you erasing your memories. What are you trying to hide?"

"We are open to you, now and always."

"I never did understand your level of fanaticism. You would rather die than be given a second chance. That's extraordinary."

"I am a single unit in the Olyix fullmind. Part of me will live on no matter how many of us are killed by your slaughter here today. This will not end our divine purpose. It is eternal."

"No, it's not. I've heard your God's message. It's bullshit."

"Yet still you hunt through my mind. Is that what you seek? The message from the God at the End of Time? This I offer freely. It is our gracious task to bring it to all life that lives in the light."

"Don't need it, because I already had a taste at Vayan. But I admit I am curious. Surely by now you've realized the universe isn't cyclic? The only thing that's waiting up there in the far future is heat death, not rebirth bringing a new light. You've had long enough for your astronomers to determine that—so many millennia. Us humans got there after just four centuries of studying the cosmos."

"Dear human, we have held the truth for so much longer than that."

Yirella smiled. The association had worked; she could see the arrival of the message at the Olyix homeworld, this very binary star, two and a half million years ago. "So you have. Thank you."

Finally, a bloom of uncertainty appeared in the onemind's serene thoughts. "You wanted to know the time when the God at the End of Time blessed us with its message."

"That is part of what I seek, yes."

"Why?"

"So I can use it to defeat you."

"You cannot defeat a God. The nova your neutron star will create will eliminate this star system, but we have thousands of outposts across the galaxy. Each of them will flourish and grow into a new enclave. Each will continue our crusade."

"Yes, I was concerned that might happen. And I see you really believe that. So know this. We will deal with any survivors, and every attempt they might make to resurrect your despicable crusade. We have the ability now, and friends. So many friends, thanks to you." She felt the onemind erasing vast sections of itself, a retreat that made her own incursion into its personality so much easier.

"The locations of our valiant outposts are gone now. Dear human, my descendants will meet yours out there one day. This battle is merely one amid a war that will last until our God arises."

"I know."

"Then end your sacrilege. Stop this profane attack. It is not too late for your redemption. Humans now have the ability to travel to the era of our God in your own vessels. Join our pilgrimage as loving equals."

"You have ruined the evolution of thousands of species—billions upon billions of lives lost. And it was you personally that oversaw the death of my homeworld; almost as many people died from collapsing city shields as you stole. You've killed my friends, and your senseless zealotry is forcing me to make decisions that will never bring me closure, let alone happiness. After all the evil you have unleashed, you ask me to be merciful? And you still haven't realized, have you? It wasn't a God that sent your message; it was the devil, you psychotic shit. Now die."

SAINTS

MORGAN

Of all the things Yuri wasn't expecting to find in a super-technology warship built by some very weird post-humans, he had to admit a roaring twenties Parisian café would be close to the top of his list.

Nonetheless, that was where he and Jessika and Kandara and Callum had wound up. They sat at one of the wooden tables where remotes served them the best food he'd tasted in . . . well, a long time.

As they ate, the big arched windows showed tactical displays. The corpus armada had killed the oneminds in every arkship above the gas-giant world; squads backed by machine marines had occupied every arkship and welcome ship containing human cocoons. More marines had continued to overrun the other vessels with imprisoned aliens, but they were running out of time to implement the next phase of the mission.

The neutron star was going to impact the big white-spectrum star in another ninety minutes. A vast fleet of Resolution ships was forming up on the fringe of the nebula. And the armada had expended most of its Calmissiles.

"I can't believe they still call them that," Kandara said, shaking her head in apparent dismay.

"Why wouldn't they?" Callum asked. "The Higgs boson, Einstein's theory of relativity, Robson's progression, Rindstorm's door, Newton's law of gravity. So many break-throughs are named after their inventor."

"But they're important historical figures," Yuri said with a straight face. "The giants of human science."

"Then I'm in good company."

Jessika and Kandara both laughed at him. Callum ignored them, drinking his beer in an attempt at silent dignity.

Yuri used his altme to call up a visual feed from the *Morgan*'s fuselage sensors. They were keeping station with the *Salvation of Life* along with twenty much larger attack cruisers from the armada. A swarm of small insectoid craft was hopping across the rock, attaching a multitude of dark hemispherical machines to the arkship's surface. In the background, points of light sparkled through the nebula's beautiful polychromatic clouds. For a moment he was concerned the twinkles had returned, but then he realized that—one by one—the stars were appearing as their light crawled across the empty expanse that used to be the enclave. Sure enough, as the arkship swept over the gas giant's equator, he saw the galactic core rising from behind the planet as if it were the universe's most intricate jewel moon.

There was an outbreak of whispering over by the café's counter, a heated discussion just below comprehension threshold. Yuri refused to look around, but Kandara did. She leaned in across the table. "The kids are home from school," she muttered in amusement.

When he did deign to glance in that direction, Yuri saw Dellian and a group of other young men clustered together, their argument stalled as soon as they saw him looking at them. Despite the obvious ethnic variances between them, they had a peculiar sameness—all of them squat and broad-shouldered, not so much Olympian-fit as carrying the kind of excess muscle Earth's bodybuilders used to get from embracing a full illegal tox development. They also shared the same vaguely guilty expression as they stared at Yuri's table.

"Join us," a grinning Kandara said before Yuri could object. But then, after so long spent with just the five of them, some fresh company wasn't such a bad idea.

Dellian's squad and several more of their friends hurried over.

"This is an honor—" Janc began eagerly.

"Don't," Yuri said, holding up a finger in warning. "Just don't. And we're not Saints, either."

"Yes, sir."

He let that one go.

"So what state is the *Salvation* in?" Callum asked.

"Secure," Dellian said. "Yirella eliminated the onemind, so we have continuity in maintaining the cocoons. And we've eliminated a lot of quint."

"Yeah," Uret said glumly. "But as we know from the Vayan ambush, it's going to take months to track down the last of them. Those arkships are the biggest three-dimensional maze in the galaxy; there are a million places inside where you can hide unnoticed."

"Look who you're telling," Jessika said.

Uret blushed.

Kandara raised her glass of wine, regarding it intently. "So, you organize hunting parties?"

"There are teams of marines on specialist tracking duty," Xante said. "And remotes will install a comprehensive sensor network throughout every chamber and corridor. But we're scheduled for duty rotations to that detail. It helps keep us fresh."

"It's going to take most of the flight to be sure we got them all," Janc said. "Last time, we transferred all the cocoons over to our habitat and got out of there fast, but we can't do that this time."

"Last time?" Yuri asked.

"Yeah. We got ambushed."

"Right. We knew the Olyix were raiding the expansion wavefront. There are five more ships here storing human cocoons."

"And thousands of other species," Jessika said. "I understand from the Yirella androids that they're all coming with us?"

"Away from here, yes," Dellian said. "They'll be flown to the other end of the wormhole, then we'll see what we do. Yirella was saying she thinks we should all settle stars close together, form some kind of grand interspecies alliance, in case the Olyix ever come back."

"Bold move," Yuri said. "But suppose some of those species are even crazier than the Olyix?"

"Please excuse Yuri," Callum said. "He always thinks the worst."

Half of their rapt audience nodded eagerly. "We know."

For once, Yuri was at a loss for a rebuke.

"It'll take a lot of work," Dellian said. "We need to find out all about them. But statistically, there will be some we'd want as neighbors."

Callum raised his glass and finished the beer in a couple of gulps. "Time will tell. In the meantime, what kind of beers from the future do you boys recommend for an old-timer?"

YIRELLA

MORGAN

Yirella's corpus personality observed the deck thirty-three café through sensors. She still hadn't used her original body to meet the Saints. It was sitting quietly in the captain's formal reception room along with a clone of herself. Immanueel had spent the last hour growing it for her inside a fast-time domain that was barely larger than the womb-vat. An initiator growing her a biologic body would have been a simpler solution, but she didn't want to be that cheap. This body had to be perfect in every respect; *he* deserved that much.

Both aspects were anxiously watching corpus ships and machines racing to install exotic energy conduits around the outside of all the huge Olyix ships they'd captured. Simultaneously, she kept a great deal of her attention focused on the progress of the neutron star. It was less than an hour out from the corona now. Vast rivers of nebula dust were flowing into it, flaring like solar prominences as they sank into the oblivion of its black horizon. As lightstorms went, it should have been spectacular. Yirella found it ominous.

"We're cutting this fine," she said.

"We are on schedule," Immanueel said calmly.

"Assuming nothing goes wrong. Don't fall into the hubris trap. We're not the Olyix. We need to leave now; you can finish fixing conduits to the arkships later."

"Very well. We concede your point, genesis human."

Yirella didn't quite know what to make of that. Immanueel only used that honorific when they were being formal. "Did I just annoy you?"

"No. The opinion of the genesis human is always treated with respect—even more so now you have chosen to elaborate."

"It's not a full elaboration. I'm not ready for that."

"We understand. We remember when we began the process. It takes considerable mental adjustment."

"Yeah."

"We are flying the portals into place now."

Yirella concentrated the majority of her aspects on the feeds from across the armada. Another advantage of being many: You could really appreciate the bigger picture.

Far away, the wormhole terminus was englobed by more than a thousand corpus attack cruisers. Unable to match its initial acceleration, the Resolution ships chasing it had fallen a long way behind. Most of them seemed to be decelerating. It was hard to tell; they only just registered on the billions of sensor fronds the wormhole had scattered in its wake. She read the distance in surprise. "How long were we in the enclave?"

"A relativity question that has no correct answer—especially given how the Olyix fullmind manipulated the enclave time flow."

"The wormhole terminus is three quarters of a light-year away," she said. "We must have been in there for months."

"Yes, but it means that the closest Resolution ships are nearly seven thousand AUs behind the wormhole. That is to our advantage."

"It certainly is."

"The evacuation is starting."

Expansion portals opened in front of every arkship, bathing them in a lush sapphire light. Yirella's personality was still operating within the *Salvation of Life* neuralstrata—albeit with a great many protective routines and cutoffs in case the onemind had left behind any darkvirals. She had given up trying to activate its gravitonic drive. Whole sections had been decommissioned, with components fed into the Olyix equivalent of disassembly reactors, ready for the mass to be recycled. Some of the older arkships didn't even have the chambers that housed the drive anymore; they'd all been repurposed to help support the cocoons.

All she could do now was ensure the power supply to the massive cocoon vaults was maintained, keeping over a billion human brains alive. As responsibilities went, she hated it.

An attack cruiser positioned itself a kilometer in front of the arkship and established a wide distortion boundary. The portal itself began to move backward, swallowing the *Salvation of Life*.

I'll never see the neutron star hit. We're going to outrun the nova light all the way back to Earth. Shame. It should be pretty spectacular.

The remaining attack cruisers and the *Morgan* followed the *Salvation of Life* through the portal. Yirella took a last look at the elegant nebula clouds framed by a thin blue rim. Once the ships were all through, Immanueel deactivated the portal.

Yirella rearranged the feed from the *Morgan*'s sensors. A coma of flaring interstellar dust was forming around the *Salvation of Life* as the lonely molecules collided with the attack cruiser's protective boundary and disintegrated into their elementary particles. A hundred thousand kilometers ahead, the wormhole was open and waiting.

"So now you have one decision left," Immanueel said. "Do you tell him?"

Yirella rose to her feet, her original body and her new clone standing facing each other. "I can't. He deserves the life we were promised. I refuse to deny him that. I love him."

Twenty-seven decks below, in one of the *Morgan*'s cargo chambers, she'd gathered all her android aspects together. She withdrew from them now, feeling them turn quiescent, their functions shutting down. Immanueel took over the *Morgan*'s network as she left that; then she handed over control of the *Salvation of Life* to them.

And then there were two.

Double vision—both images of herself, both aspects utterly identical, even wearing the same clothes. *Because I cannot afford to be honest with him.* Out of all the eeriness that came from being a host of corpus aspects, this was the most poignant.

A portal expanded at the end of the reception room. Immanueel's biophysical body came through, ducking down sharply, their tail quivering to maintain balance. "We're ready," they told her.

"Thank you." She gave their dark, mottled body a gentle hug.

"Are you sure you want to do this?"

"Yes. I have to. He will never understand. Nor forgive."

"He might. He loves you."

"No. I know my Del. His war is over now. After everything he's done, everything that's happened to him, I cannot ask him to do more."

"What about you? Is this what you deserve?"

"Deserve? That simplicity no longer applies. As I learned long ago, if you are in a position to make the choice, you have the right to make it."

"You are the true genesis human."

Yirella in her original body straightened her back and accompanied Immanueel into their centrex ship. Her mind twinned and separated. She looked back at her clone through the glowing rim of the portal and lifted a hand in parting. "Take care of him."

It was quite a party that had developed by the time Yirella got back to the café. Nobody could resist just dropping by to meet the Saints, who after an almost believable show of reluctance had bravely settled into accepting their idol status. Talk was loud, and the Latin music louder.

Yuri was still at the table, facing down Janc and Xante; a heap of sticky shot glasses had piled up between them, along with two empty bottles of vodka so cold they were still covered in frost. Yuri poured a fresh trio of shots from a new bottle as he explained some heroic mission he and Kohei had run once upon a time to save the world from terrorists or revolutionaries or mad ideologues. Yirella was seriously impressed how steady his hand was, while Xante could barely see his shot glass, let alone pick it up.

Callum was having a terribly earnest conversation with Ovan about the Don's last amazing season in the Scottish first division before he'd left Earth, while Kandara was teaching Uret and Falar how to samba—really samba—much to their audience's whooping approval.

Dellian was chatting enthusiastically to Jessika, the pair of them looking up at a window's tactical display. Yirella slid her arms around him, resting her head on his shoulder where it belonged. "Hello, you."

"Finally!" he exclaimed and kissed her happily. "I wondered where you'd got to."

"It's been a busy time."

"Yeah!" His smile faded. "Tilliana and Ellici?"

"Alive. We can rejuvenate their bodies, the same way we recovered everyone on the *Calibar.*"

"Great!"

"Their bodies, Del. Their bodies will recover. But there's not much of them left."

He nodded despondently. "Right."

Yirella smiled at Jessika, who was giving her a calculating look. *Almost as if she knows.* "Pleased to meet you."

"Likewise. And thank you."

"I have to ask: Did you know, when you arrived on Earth? Did you think we'd be the ones who beat the Olyix?"

"Nothing is certain. But I had confidence."

"Right. Well, and here we are."

"So what happens next?"

Yirella gestured at the window and brought up a visual image of the wormhole terminus. Arkships were sliding into its open throat one after the other. "In about three minutes we go in there, and four years later we come out at a small star that used to be an Olyix sensor station It's not anymore; the armada saw to that. Then it's a ten-thousand-light-year trip to Earth the long way around."

"So easy—if you say it quickly."

"You've been there—to Earth, I mean. We haven't."

"It was in quite a state by the time I left. It's going to take some rebuilding."

"We can do that," Yirella blurted. "We've had practice terraforming so many worlds. We can rebuild it. Ainsley used to laugh at me when I said things like that."

Jessika raised a tall cocktail glass. "Sounds like him."

"Yeah."

"There are a lot of Olyix still alive out there. You know that, don't you? Their ships and industrial stations here; all their outposts across the galaxy. This isn't over. I talked to the *Salvation of Life* onemind briefly once, back when we arrived at this star and it thought I was inside the *Avenging Heretic,* just before the Deliverance ships blew it up. I felt its fanaticism."

"I know. But destroying the enclave is the beginning of the end. For them."

"I hope so," Jessika said.

"Starting now. All those armada ships on protection duty around the wormhole terminus? They're about to go dark."

"Dark?"

"Once the last arkship is safe inside the wormhole, the corpus humans will close it, just like the *Salvation of Life* did when you forced it to flee from Earth. Then all these dark warships will quietly circle back around and start tracking the Resolution ships. The Olyix can't stay here now. Their stars will go nova, maybe even supernova—then who knows, a black hole? They have to leave in order to live. And they'll travel to their outposts. Our warships will follow them. And—when they're light-years from anywhere—strike."

"Bloody hell," Jessika muttered. "The corpus humans will do that?"

"Yes. Their aspects will separate and multiply; they're prepared for it. We have a duty to protect the innocents in this galaxy, to make sure they have a history."

"Is that what humans are going to do now?"

"You did. Passively, when you came to Earth. We're not passive."

"I'm human," Jessika said sorrowfully. "As I always say: just like you."

Yirella studied her through narrowed eyes. "Of course."

"It could be quite something, having a galaxy with thousands of different species in contact with one another. So different from the isolation and loneliness we've had to endure for the last two and a half million years."

"Yes! We can establish wormholes and portals to link all the stars again like Connexion did, but on a huge scale. A loop of stations right around the galaxy, so we can travel among all the species and cultures, and just . . . *live.*"

"You're a dreamer, Yirella."

She hugged Dellian tight and smiled down at him. "I've been accused of that before."

Dellian kissed her. "Come on. It's almost time."

The party paused. Everyone crowded around the windows, watching as the *Morgan* flew toward the wormhole. Drinks were clasped to chests in anticipation.

"Like Hogmanay," Callum said happily.

Yirella frowned and turned back to look at Jessika. *How did she know the Olyix crusade started two and a half million years ago?*

Someone started a countdown. Yirella put the question to one side and hurriedly grabbed a glass to join in. Ahead of them, the *Salvation of Life* slipped into the wormhole, swallowed by extrinsic darkness. Negative-energy conduits rose up out of the *Morgan*'s fuselage.

"Three. Two. One!"

The wormhole enveloped them, and the windows went blank. The cheering was ecstatic; the drinking epic. Yirella made sure she kissed everyone in the café, then started dancing, laughing at Dellian, whose enthusiasm outranked his grace. Finally they wound up just holding each other tight, swaying gently amid the riotous dancing queens and disco jivers.

At the end of it all, when the music was slow, and glutted bodies were sprawled everywhere, she bent down and kissed him properly. "I love you," she said. "I never want to live without you." Then she started crying.

Her beautiful Dellian smiled up at her, his face as adoring as it had been ever since they were five years old. "Silly thing," he said as a finger caressed her tears away. "Nothing can separate us. And what a life we're going to live in a galaxy you made happen."

Her thoughts slipped oh-so-briefly to her other aspect—the one she'd left behind to accompany Immanueel, the one who would finish her quest. *Because if you can't trust yourself, then who can you trust?* "We're together now," she told her love. "And we always will be."

RETURN FLIGHT

MORGAN

The *Morgan* didn't have actual viewports, not ones you could look through. Of course it didn't; it was a warship, designed to withstand nuclear blasts, hypervelocity impacts, and intense energy beam assaults. But during the voyage home, everyone realized they wanted to *see* the world that was legend, not just watch a projection of it, however excellent the resolution. So during the hiatus when the armada emerged from the wormhole at the L-class star that used to be the Olyix sensor station, a slight redesign was instigated. A curving transparent blister now rose out of the smooth hull, as if it were beset with a tumor.

Kandara waited until the first rush of sightseers had all had their fill of the system's eerie blue ice giant before she ventured a look. The observation lounge was spartan compared to the rest of the starship's quarters with their texture surfaces. She couldn't really even tell she was inside. The dome was optically perfect, invisible unless a star's glimmer caught it at an acute angle to create a minute diffraction halo. As far as her natural senses could make out, she was standing on the hull, naked to space.

The armada ships and their appropriated Olyix arkships were orbiting the star's solitary ice giant—thousands of lightpoints forming a slender ring a million kilometers above the frigid cloudscape. She watched the dull, slow-moving hurricanes of ammonia crystals swirling gently so far over her head, occasionally harassed by the flicker of lightning blasts. That was when she started working out the scale. Some of those storm swirls were the same size as South America, which meant the speed they were spinning wasn't so sluggish after all. And as for the power in each lightning bolt . . .

She heard footsteps approaching, someone deliberately making their presence known. So someone who knew not to creep up on her. "Hello, Yuri." She hadn't seen much of her fellow *Saints* during the trip back down the wormhole; not that they'd sought her out, either. A welcome break.

Thanks to the slowtime flow within the *Morgan,* it had only taken a week to get here. She'd spent most of it with Dellian's squad—nice kids who were starting to relax properly for the first time in their lives. Like her, they didn't know what the hell they were going to do now, which made them all kindred souls.

"Quite a view," Yuri said as he stood beside her.

"Not really, but it's the first time I've actually seen the outside in ten thousand years. We were in Kruse Station for so long before the flight, then everything since we left has been a sensor feed into my neural interface. This viewing dome is an anachronism; sensors provide a much better view, and in higher resolution. But, Mary, this, this is *real*. It helps to ground me."

"Yeah, that many ships does put everything into perspective, doesn't it?"

Kandara nodded as she shifted her gaze to the long loop of glowing dots that arched sedately around the ice giant. The closest was a large one: the *Salvation of Life* itself. She had very mixed feelings about that. "Yeah. Here we are, back in a parking orbit right beside that bastard. Some rescue, huh?"

"A necessary step in the journey. I've been talking to Immanueel and Yirella. There is some debate as to what we should do next."

"I thought that was settled. We're going back to Earth, aren't we?"

"We are. Before the armada left, the corpus people dispatched several wormhole-carrying ships back there. More are now on their way to the original settled stars."

"There's an unspoken *but* in there somewhere, Yuri."

"The corpus humans have catalogued the arkships and welcome ships we brought with us. There are six thousand four hundred and twenty-three alien species in various kinds of stasis."

"Various kinds?"

"Yes. There's one that is entirely unhatched eggs— millions of them. Their world was in an elliptical orbit that lasts forty-five terrestrial years; so every generation lived for about thirty years, then died off at the onset of winter after they laid their eggs. All the Olyix had to do was drop in after winter started and scoop them up."

"That sounds . . . bizarre. How did they ever discover radio in thirty years?"

"Nature, it turns out, is quite neat. Apparently the egg yolk is some kind of chemical memory extruded by a gland in the adult brain. The embryos absorb it as they grow. So once they hatch, they simply move into the buildings their ancestors left behind, and have all the knowledge to make everything work. They understand science, too, and carry on the research."

"Okay, I'll give you that one: It is neat."

"Another one is a cold-blooded race that the Olyix have literally frozen in liquid nitrogen under extreme pressure. Then there's one that—"

"Yuri, I don't need a rundown of all six thousand species, thanks. What's the debate?"

"We have to decide where to send them."

"Ah."

"It's going to take ten thousand years for the starships to reach Earth; so we certainly have time to decide."

"Now I get it. We need to evaluate each species, and decree which ones we want living near human worlds. Oh, and I'm guessing what level of technology we provide, too?"

"Right. Some may be hostile. We have to be careful. In which case, we don't bring them out of stasis before we re-establish human society."

"Because they'd have ten thousand years to advance their own technology . . ."

"Yes."

"Well, I appreciate the thinking behind that. After all, another century and Earth would probably have been able to take on the Olyix. So who is going to make all these evaluations?"

Yuri gave her a modest shrug. "Immanueel is concerned that it shouldn't just be corpus humans. It'll be a council, with people revived from various arkships and eras. Yirella, of course. And Jessika should be able to bring a decent new perspective."

"Council? I think you mean a bureaucracy, don't you?"

"I found it quite reassuring. Even corpus humans, faced with a problem, instinctively form a committee."

"Presumably you're going to be on it?"

"I was asked. I have spent a lifetime in security, after all. And so have you."

"What? Oh, no. No. That's not the mission I signed on for. I've done my part."

"And in doing so, built yourself a reputation: Saint Kandara. You know no battle plan survives contact with the enemy. Besides, what else are you going to do for the next ten thousand years?"

"A time I fully intend to spend in a corpus domain with an exceedingly slow time flow."

Yuri's lips flickered with a smile. "Saint Callum's already agreed."

"Mary, color me surprised. And Yirella? You said she's on this committee?"

"Yes." Yuri gave her a shrewd look. "Why? Don't you trust her?"

"Sure. I trust her."

"See, this is the kind of instinct we need on the committee."

"It's not instinct, it's . . ."

"Prejudice?"

"Fuck you. But have you noticed how everything Yirella suggests is inevitably what happens?"

"Because she's smart."

"So are corpus humans."

"They do have a reverence for her that I find a little disturbing. It'll be good to have someone like you to act as a balance to her."

"Oh, Mary."

"Excellent. First meeting is in two days' time. The species catalogue is available for you to access."

"You expect me to review six thousand four hundred species in forty-eight hours?"

"They're grouped into preliminary categories. But I expect we'll be spending the first dozen sessions arguing what we do with the ones we really don't want in a neighboring star system."

"Sure."

"Then we have to decide what kind of human culture we want to establish when we do return everyone to Earth. With the power that corpus-level technology gives us, there will have to be restrictions on individual usage."

Kandara just glared at him, not trusting herself to speak. As always, she wondered just how effective her gland was. "Right," she snapped.

"Face it, who else would you trust with this? We are Saints, after all."

LONDON

FAR FUTURE

When he became conscious, Horatio screamed and screamed. His body fought the capturesnakes that were violating him, every limb conjuring up wild sweeping motions that strangely resulted in swathes of white cloth sweeping around him like sails caught in a storm. But even his frantic, terrified mind eventually realized there was something wrong about that—and there was no pain. He stopped thrashing and actually looked where he was: wrapped in a fresh white cotton sheet, in the middle of a big circular bed that curved up gently around him, preventing him from falling out. Two people were standing at the side of the bed, wearing stylish green tunics that marked them down as some kind of medics; their faces registered sympathy.

"It's okay," one said, smiling in reassurance. "It's over. The capturesnakes are gone. You're in recovery. And you're doing fine. Just try and settle. Take as much time as you need. We're here to help."

Something about the tone infuriated Horatio; the medic was aiming for assurance but was hitting patronizing. *Needs some proper empathy training.* Which made him bark a laugh, because being offended at someone who'd saved him from the Olyix was about as dumb as you could get. So he did indeed *settle*, and steadied his breathing. "What happened?"

Again the smile that didn't quite reach genuine sympathy. "You've been extracted from cocooning and re-bodied."

"Uh—" What that should have been was: Gwendoline disobeyed the rules and sent security agents through to snatch you from the capturesnakes. It was touch-and-go for a while, but the emergency clinics here on Pasobla are the best. "Where's Gwendoline?"

The two medics exchanged a glance. "Disorientation like this is common. I'd suggest you take a moment to prepare yourself for us to explain your status. But everything is going to be okay; I can't stress that enough."

"I'm not disorientated," he said in a dangerous voice. His hands rose up—not to clench into fists. No. But then he saw those hands properly and focused on his skin. His *youthful* skin. A startled cry, and he was sitting up, pulling at the sheet, exposing more and more of his body. It was perfect—slim, nicely muscled, limb movements fast and assured, no joint pain. The body from nostalgic memory—the one he used to see in the mirror in the best days of late adolescence. "What? *What?*"

"Take it easy."

"Don't fucking patronize me!" he roared. "Where am I? What's happened?"

"Okay. Simply put, the Olyix turned you into a cocoon. Then a long time later, you were rescued. Now you're back in the Sol system, on a habitat orbiting Earth. Right now, there's a huge ongoing operation to resced the biosphere after the damage the Olyix siege of the cities caused. Our dear homeworld was in a new Ice Age when we returned, but our geotechnicians think they've initiated a self-sustaining reversal."

"Gwendoline," he whispered.

"I'm sorry, but we don't really have any information about your history. We don't even know your name."

"Horatio. I'm Horatio Seymore. I lived in London. Right up until the day the Olyix returned."

"You're doing well, Horatio. It sounds like your memories are integrated. Can you tell me who Gwendoline is?"

"My wife."

"All right. Well, here's the good news. We've established

a family tracking agency. If you can provide enough details, they should be able to tell you if she's been re-bodied or if she's still . . . awaiting the recovery process."

"She . . ." He sank back down onto the curving bed. "She was on the Pasobla the day the Olyix returned."

"Oh. I'm sorry, then she won't be in any of the Olyix ships the armada brought back. The Pasobla left Delta Pavonis successfully and became part of the exodus."

"She got away, then?"

"Yes."

"How long ago?" he asked softly.

"It's been a long time. The Olyix enclave—their home star—was a considerable distance from Earth."

"Just bloody tell me. How long?"

"Approximately twenty thousand years."

Horatio wanted to yell that they'd got that wrong, or he'd misheard, or . . . But he knew he hadn't. *Twenty thousand years*. The tears came then, and he couldn't stop them.

NEW YORK

FAR FUTURE

Ten years after their starship returned to Sol, the four of them finally portaled down to their homeworld to visit what had been New York's Central Park, and would be again. The ground was still boggy from the sea water that had covered it until seventeen months earlier, so they stuck to the temporary pathway that had been laid out along the exact line of the mall, walking in silence. On either side of them, an army of pasty white synthetic bioforms, like squirrel-size caterpillars, were plowing their way through the briny mud, amassing salt and other unwelcome oceanic minerals in bulging filter stomachs, leaving purified soil in their wake. Smaller, more mechanical, genten remotes skittered among them, examining the old tree stumps uncovered after Manhattan had been drained, sampling and analyzing the wood, ready to replant the correct genus when the landscaping was complete.

When they reached the slope littered with the red bricks that had once been Bethesda Terrace, they paused and looked northward. Skeletons of new buildings were spiking up into the chilly azure sky. The distant kilometer-high towers along the Harlem River were complete, home to the first batch of revived New York residents, while the rest of the city was still under construction, progressing south block by block.

Jessika took it all in, feeling a weird kind of nostalgia and pride. *I helped these people. I did my job. Now I can finally live with them.* Of course, it was always going to be a challenge rebuilding New York. As they came out of the re-life procedure—and a considerable amount of therapy—its old inhabitants set about doing what they did best: arguing loudly—about levels of authenticity, what to re-create, what to consign to history. A surprising number wanted something radically new, a statement of how they should face the future, while some, who took a long, difficult route to accepting their new existence, simply didn't care.

She rubbed her hands against the cold, wishing she'd worn a thicker jacket. It was mid-August, but the winds blowing down from the glaciers covering the Great Lakes made summers here decidedly Nordic these days. But the ice was in retreat now, leaving behind a very different geography from what had been before.

Callum and Yuri had both gone in for the full rejuvenation process, spun off from the cocoon re-life procedure—itself a legacy from Neána biologic technology that she'd brought to Earth all those years ago. Jessika could only grin ruefully at the vanity her gift had enabled. Kandara, she was surprised to see, hadn't tuned her appearance back to a perpetual twenties like the boys. She seemed content to settle in her biological forties, still imposingly physical, but with a whole tribal elder vibe going for her now. It helped that everyone on the planet knew who she was thanks to the legend of the Saints, and now her gatekeeper role in the alien assessment committee set up by the Alliance Parliament. People would stop and stare in nervous awe when they saw her, as if she might banish them to the other side of the galaxy as she had so many species.

I wonder if she'd do that to me? Jessika hadn't confided in her friends—and certainly not to Kandara—but since the destruction of the Olyix enclave, she'd thought she was becoming more knowledgeable. There was information in her mind she was sure hadn't been there before. Not some massive download triggered by the success of FinalStrike, but an awareness of more than she'd known before.

So perhaps Kandara was right all along, and there is

some deep Ncána control routine in my subconscious. Or maybe I'm just becoming as paranoid as ordinary humans.

"You're looking good," Jessika told Kandara. "Still got your peripherals?"

Kandara's expression was contemptuous. "A couple of upgrades, yeah. I'm sure the corpus guys are doing a great job out there, blowing all the surviving Olyix shit up, but who wants to take the risk?"

"They'll never get close to us again," Yuri said. "Forty-two human settled worlds established. And fifteen hundred designated Alliance star systems beyond that, with another three thousand elected for potential bioforming. Now that's what I call a solid boundary."

"You mean buffer zone." Kandara smirked.

"Those stars might be part of the Alliance," Callum said, "but they're going to belong to aliens once they're fully bio-formed. You don't think that cages us in at all?"

"Now that's the Callum paranoia we all know and love."

"We have wormholes and portals stretching almost half-way around the galaxy," Kandara said. "We are not and never will be 'caged in.' Stop thinking in pre-spaceflight terms."

"News from the frontier," Jessika said. "Another eight human habitat constellations have emerged to make contact in the last six months."

"I know," Yuri said.

"Of course you do," Callum said, and saluted mockingly. "Adjutant-general, sir."

"Hey, they're my headache," Yuri shot back. "We have to assess what kind of culture they've developed. Emilja was a little too successful with her breakaway neolibertarian movement. There are some very strange ideas on how people should live out there."

"Well, let's just thank Mary she's not around to hear you call it that," Kandara said.

"Could be worse," Callum said. "They could be like the Jukuar."

Even Jessika shuddered at the memory of last year's crisis—the first quasi-military action the Alliance had been forced to launch upon one of their own.

"Mary!" a thoroughly pissed Kandara snapped, staring at

Callum. "One mistake, out of over three thousand evaluations. Okay?"

"It wasn't a criticism," Callum mumbled.

"How was my team supposed to know the adults could produce subspecies? The original Jukuar batch we revived agreed to the diplomatic framework of the Alliance, with all the non-aggression articles. Binding articles! They didn't need to birth a soldier caste."

"Scorpions," Yuri said.

"What?"

"You all know the morality tale. Scorpions do what they do because that's what they are. Jukuar families have their soldiers because that's their nature."

"Yeah, well, we know that *now*," Callum said.

"You can't blame them."

"To analyze the Jukuar genetic code to an extent that showed us they have a selective subspecies breeding ability would be phenomenally difficult," Callum said. "We're having enough trouble bioforming worlds for aliens with even moderately different biochemistry to ours. We've got to synthesize organisms from scratch to provide them with the nutrients they need."

Kandara gave Jessika a thoughtful stare. "Be nice if we had some help. Any sign of the Neána showing themselves?"

"No," Jessika said. "Not yet, anyway. But they will. One day."

"Well, they certainly know what we've done," Kandara said. "Every planet humans have settled in this crazy old Alliance of ours is broadcasting their opinions loud and clear across the galaxy. It makes the old solnet allcomments look sane. We're well and truly in the post–Fermi Paradox era now."

Callum chuckled. "So much intrigue, so many politicians demanding a democratic voice. *He* would have loved this, you know."

"Yeah," Kandara agreed. "He would."

"Damn right," Yuri said. "He was a DC man to the core."

"True," Jessika said, and looked around. To the south, along the markers for West 59th Street, the first few foundations had been sunk into the frosty black silt, displacing the old concrete pilings. Carbon girders were already rising up, assembled at impressive speed by genten construction remotes. "Do you remember when we were up there?" she asked. "On the Connexion tower roof, looking down at all the people praying on this terrace?"

"The birth of the incredible Calmissile idea," Kandara said.

"Oh, bloody hell, will you *ever* let that go?"

Jessika laughed. "The missile that won the war."

"Is this why we're here?" Callum asked.

"No," Jessika said. "We're here to remember him. Because no one else will."

"He's one of us, a Saint," Kandara protested. "Nobody will forget any of us. Mary, do I ever know that!"

"But they didn't know him, not like they do us. The four of us are practically the only government anyone can name."

"Us and Yirella," Kandara added gruffly. "If we're Saints, she's a fucking angel to the rest of the galaxy."

Callum gave a sheepish nod. "What do you think we should do, build a memorial?"

"Fuck no," Yuri said. "He would have hated that. He was a spook; he lived in the shadows. He lived *for* the shadows."

"It's enough that we come here for him," Kandara said. "Not every year, that would be maudlin, and I'm not lighting candles or crap like that, either. But we will keep doing this when we can. He would enjoy the inconvenience it causes us, if nothing else."

Yuri smiled. "Then here's to the inconvenience of Saint Alik Monday, with thanks from the galaxy he liberated."

YIRELLA2

LONDON

Yirella loved the snow. Even after living on Earth for two years, she still relished going outside to experience it falling magically from the sky. That was why she insisted their house be on the northern edge of London, giving her a panoramic view of the subarctic landscape. In its new incarnation, the ancient capital city was an amalgamation of cozy villages, intended to provide residents a strongly knit community, which was essential for those recovering. For all they were now blessed with perfect new bodies and a postscarcity interstellar civilization, the shock and abrupt transition from the invasion was overwhelming.

The village they'd settled in was called Lavender Hill. Homes were either solitary lodges, like theirs, or long stone terraces patterned in authentic Georgian style. The quaint architecture made her laugh, but the character did have a certain elegance, and it belonged in her mental image of London.

Standing in front of the curving bay window, she watched daylight fading from the comatose gray sky. The curving street outside was wide, with discreet lighting hidden amid the tall spruce trees. Snow had been cleared from the central pathway, but everywhere else it was a good thirty centimeters deep and compacted, while the boughs and twigs of the trees and bushes were varnished in tough ice. Autumn and winter lasted for a good seven months, and spring was often delayed. Everyone walked around wrapped in thick coats and long scarves, and moaned a lot about the cold. Yirella, who'd grown up in the tropics, relished all the snow and ice, the frozen lakes and frosted trees. For her, the vista was a romantic winter wonderland. Her only disappointment was that they were too far south to see the glacier that covered most of northern England.

It wasn't an opinion Dellian shared. He never complained. But she *knew*.

A figure was moving cautiously along the central pathway, checking all the buildings. He stopped outside the lodge, staring up at it. Yirella used her direct meld with the civic net to pull basic information on the stranger. His name was Horatio Seymore. According to his file he was a London resident, captured in 2231, re-bodied a couple of years ago, and currently working as a therapist for newly restored kids—the most difficult cases.

She watched him glance around, then open the iron gate and start up the front path. "We have a visitor," she called out.

Dellian glanced around from the hanging fire in the middle of the room. It was a Scandinavian design—a metal saucer with a copper top, suspended by an iron flue. She'd included it in the lodge more as an aesthetic statement than anything practical, but it threw out a surprising amount of heat. Not that the logs Dellian was shoving in were real wood, of course; these cylinders were a self-oxygenating burner that was CO_2 neutral, After all, nobody wanted to disturb the delicate rebalancing of Earth's climate now that the ice age had been coaxed into retreat.

Dellian used a poker to rearrange the logs, lunging as if he were fencing with a far more skillful opponent. "Who?"

"Don't know him."

"Saints!" A shower of sparks erupted from the fireplace, and he started stomping on them as they bounced across the polished parquet flooring.

The door sensor sent her a polite notification of presence. "I'll go find out." She held back a frown as she walked past him. As usual, Dellian was in his constable's uniform, which wasn't the most welcoming for guests, but there'd only be an argument if she mentioned it. Again.

Yirella opened the front door and found it easy to smile a greeting at Horatio Seymore. He was very handsome, and taller than Dellian, but it was more than that; something about him just made her feel comfortable. She knew he'd be perfect for helping troubled kids. *Shame he looks so troubled himself.*

"I'm really sorry to intrude," Horatio said straight away, "but I'm looking for my wife, and you're the only person on Earth who can help."

Yirella hesitated. "I'm afraid I'm only a part-time advisor to the Alliance alien assessment committee these days," she said. "I have no official status. And anyway, you'll need the family tracing agency for that."

"No, I don't need to trace her. I already know where she is."

"Where?" she asked automatically.

"Sanctuary."

"You'd better come in."

They settled on a long couch facing the fire, Yirella and Dellian cozying up close at the end nearest to the fire and Horatio at the other end, straight-backed and tense, ignoring the Darjeeling tea a remote had poured for him.

"If you've been in a cocoon since 2231, how do you know your wife is in Sanctuary?" Yirella asked.

"Gwendoline was on the Pasobla when the Olyix came," Horatio told them. "It portaled out of Delta Pavonis and became one of the exodus fleet. They established a string of generation worlds."

She felt Del's arm tighten around her at the mention of the Pasobla. "That's the same exodus habitat Emilja and Ainsley were on," he said.

"Yes."

"Wait—" Her meld extracted a whole batch of files. "Gwendoline Zangari? She was your wife? You're Loi's father? Loi who was Saint Yuri's assistant, who stole the entanglement node at Salt Lake City?"

Horatio nodded. "That's her. And my boy."

"You were snatched by the Olyix once, years before the invasion. Yuri found you."

"Yep."

"You're practically a saint yourself," Dellian said in admiration.

"Hardly," Horatio said. "I've spent every waking second since I was re-bodied reviewing files. There are tens of thousands of public records. But with filters, I've managed to build a strategy. The key was Lolo Maude."

"The Factory warship?"

"Yes. You see, I knew Lolo as well, back in the Blitz2 days."

"You're kidding!"

"No. Sie used to come to a community kitchen I helped run."

"Wait! If you knew Lolo, you must have met hir boyfriend, Ollie, as well. Ollie Heslop?"

Horatio frowned. "I don't think so. Lolo's boyfriend was Davis Mohan."

Yirella grinned in delight. "That was Ollie's alias! He was on the run during Blitz2."

"Oh. Okay."

"I'm sorry. It's just— You're living history, you know. We learned all about this in school when we were taught about the Saints."

"Right. But the point is, Lolo obviously made it to the Factory. After that, sie became a warship like Ainsley."

"I know. We picked up Lolo's signal on the *Morgan*."

Horatio leaned forward, his eagerness overcoming lingering apprehension. "Once I learned about Lolo, I ran checks through the *Morgan*'s records. Ainsley said something to you."

"His granddaughter," Yirella exclaimed. She smiled down at Dellian. "Remember? Ainsley said that when the Factory alliance broke up, his granddaughter joined the Katos mothership to establish Sanctuary."

"That's Gwendoline," Horatio said.

"Of course. He told me she was there when he transferred his consciousness into the warship." Her delight faded. "I'm sorry, Horatio. You're right, Gwendoline must be at Sanctuary. But—"

"They called it that for a reason," Dellian said firmly. "Best guess is that it's hiding between the stars, the same as a Neána abode. A place the Olyix could never find. Nobody can."

"But nobody's looked," Horatio said. "Not really. And you're the greatest expert on it, Yirella."

"It was a hobby for a while, that's all. I accessed what files there are, which are mostly stories. There are no solid facts—not one. Our knowledge of Sanctuary ends when the Katos ship left to build it; the humans who went with them were very thorough deleting information from the records. From then on, all we have are secondhand recollections that became our legends. I can give you a list of everything I found, and you can access them, too."

"We can do a lot more than that."

She gave him a quizzical look. "Really?"

"Yes. We can ask people who were at the Factory."

"Ainsley was there, but he didn't know anything, or he had his memories edited for security. And the only other person we know for sure was at the Factory was Captain Kenelm, and sie's dead."

"You're wrong," Horatio said. "There is someone else."

"Who?" she asked sharply.

"The Lolo Maude."

Yirella stared at him thoughtfully. "We don't know where the Lolo Maude went. Sie never showed up at the neutron star."

"Has anyone searched for hir?"

"No," she agreed reluctantly.

"Then that would be a good place to start, would it not?"

"I . . . Well, yes, I suppose so."

"It was thousands of years ago," Dellian said. "And those Factory warships could travel fast. That gives you a very large volume of space. Nice idea, but not practical."

"Sie would have flown to the enclave," Horatio said. "And by now, sie will know the Olyix were defeated. The Alliance is broadcasting a lot of messages out into space to contact lost humans."

"Conjecture," Yirella said, wishing she could sound more confident. *But he's right, it makes sense.*

"And that's why I came to you," Horatio said. "The corpus humans will build you a fleet of ships to search for Lolo Maude if you ask. You're the genesis human. You created them, then you saved them in the enclave. Am I right?"

"Well," she said slowly, "that's a condensed version of events."

"Hundred percent correct," Dellian said proudly.

"I'm asking you to consider my request. You don't have to join me, but if you could just get me a single ship, I'd be eternally grateful."

"If Gwendoline is alive and living in Sanctuary," Dellian said, "she will have been there for millennia. Have you thought about that?"

"I have," Horatio said. "At the end, I gave up everything I'd done on Earth, abandoned people who depended on me, just so I could be with her on the Pasobla. Then the Olyix caught me before I could get through a portal. She knows how much I love her. And she knows I was cocooned, that I'm not dead. I just want to see her again. I want to know she's okay, that she led a good life after—"

Yirella had to look at the floor so she didn't have to see the tears in Horatio's eyes. "Let me think about it," she said.

"You'll think about it?" Dellian said once Horatio had left.

"Well, what else could I say? The poor man clearly loves her."

"And I remember their story, how Saint Yuri got Horatio back after he was snatched by Olyix agents. She loved him, too."

"Well, there you go."

"Over twenty thousand years ago!"

Yirella slumped back into the couch and put her head in her hands. "If it were you, I'd find you."

He sat beside her with a sigh and slipped his arm around her shoulders. "Me too."

She couldn't look at him. Guilt still haunted her mind, that she didn't quite trust him enough to confide that her original aspect had left to go hunting the God at the End of Time. And trust was such a huge part of unconditional love. Then there was the knowledge she could never get over, that this her was the clone. Not the person Del had grown up with and fallen in love with. That she was an imposter—however well-intentioned.

Would he be flattered or horrified? Would he laugh it off, or walk out of the door? She never wanted to know.

All that shame hung between them, the specter he couldn't see—couldn't be allowed to see—holding back what would make him truly happy: a family, children, everything they'd dreamed would belong to them once the war was won. She just couldn't do it. Not until she knew for sure that they were truly safe. *Because I know the war isn't over, let alone won. Saints, do I know.*

The Alliance had established wormholes and portals across nearly a third of the galaxy. Not every star, of course; that would require a colossal—and unnecessary—network. But thanks to the corpus ships racing ever onward, their coverage was comprehensive. Alpha Defense was receiving many reports of clashes with the remnants of the Olyix, but so far, the Alliance was undefeated.

But the galaxy isn't safe. That it could ever be so was a foolish belief, rooted in their childhood, where fear of the *other* lurking outside the Immerle estate fence had been indoctrinated right from birth. *And knowing it is a false belief should allow me to reject it. I am rational above all else.* Yet she was scared to have a child. *What might happen to it if the Olyix returned?* So very, very stupid.

She kissed him and ran her hand over his neat constable's uniform. "What are you doing tomorrow?"

"Huh? Well . . . I've got another batch of meetings with the I and M policy board tomorrow."

"So what's up with Implementation and Monitoring?"

"Nothing much. How do we best encourage compliance with laws when people are struggling with re-body trauma and disassociation?"

"Carefully, I'd guess."

"Yeah. But some constables are being attacked, because they're the authority figures. So there's an argument for light armor when you're on street patrol. They want my opinion on increased unarmed combat training, and maybe some non-lethal peripherals."

"That sounds paramilitary."

"Yeah, but ordinary people who have recovered are entitled to a degree of safety from their neighbors. The alternative is segregation based on mental status. That's too stigmative."

"Sounds like what we need is more therapists."

"Yes, but that's not Implementation and Monitoring. It's not too bad with populations from the exodus worlds. But—wow—people from Earth? Their norms are very different."

"So are you looking forward to it?"

"Am I . . . You're kidding, right?"

"You're bored senseless, aren't you?" She watched his face struggle to expel the guilty expression.

"Maybe," he conceded. "This is not what I trained for. It takes some adjustment, that's all. I'm no different from anyone else. I mean, are you enjoying the assessment committee?"

"Never have, never will."

"Ah. So?"

She held both his hands and smiled contentedly, her nose a centimeter from his. "You want to get out of here?"

"Saints, yes!"

"I'll call Immanueel. They can start designing a search ship for us."

"Oh, Saints, thank you!" He kissed her. "Hey, maybe we can find your tachyon signal while we're looking for Lolo Maude."

Yirella twisted her lips in an awkward grimace. "Maybe . . ."

YIRELLA1

DEEP SPACE

The domain was spherical, which Yirella had found somewhat disconcerting at first. A globe five kilometers in diameter, an almost unbroken green from the luxuriant jungle landscape. At its heart far above, eight tiny bright stars whizzed around one another in circular orbits, moving so fast they appeared as solid lines—electrons in a classic atom model.

She had no idea why corpus humans always favored a tropical climate. Something to do with having a neutron star as your home sun, maybe? But the warm and humid domain was peaceful, and gave her time to come to terms with everything that had happened. Endless time, if she needed it. Time when reflection eventually passed into resolution. She used her morning walks through the gently steaming vegetation to banish doubts. Afternoons were mostly spent reviewing memories the armada had extracted from the oneminds. Then there was yoga, which was calming—especially now. And she learned how to prepare food that had actually grown—on plants. Not that she'd abandoned printed meals, but there were days when she found cooking therapeutic.

Then there was the news. Immanueel's ship scanned space through a wide array of sensors, with a baseline over a thousand AUs across. There was violence out there; they'd seen it. Huge battles had been fought, powerful enough for their radiation aftermath to shine brightly across a thousand light-years—corpus fleets falling upon Olyix outposts. Every time they detected the embers of those mêlées, she was reminded of the squad—of Tilliana and Ellici, of Alexandre. Of him. Of the loss.

This is all for you, she told the memories. *So you can be safe.*

The course they'd flown since leaving the enclave had not been straight. They'd stopped every few centuries to mine and refine new material reserves from the planets in lifeless star systems; constructors formed new warships for Immanueel's ever-expanding number of aspects. So eventually it was a modest flotilla of copper-skinned vessels that flew with her on her quest. The trajectory and pauses meant she'd eventually seen the supernova they'd caused—a gleam that outshone the incredible swirl of the core stars. She'd spent hours in an observation dome, staring at it with her naked eye, feeling no regret at the cosmic cataclysm. It was a beacon to all newly emerging species that they had nothing to fear from the stars. Almost.

That was weeks ago, domain time.

Immanueel's biophysical body arrived at her home as she was finishing a lunch of avocado salad and (printed) salmon. She smiled up at them. "What have you come to tell me today?"

"Genesis human, we have found it," Immanueel said. There was a level of pride in their voice she'd not heard before. A hand went instinctively to her belly. That which she had done was unforgivable. But she had given up her life and love for this quest. She was entitled to some part of the joy that could have been. "Show me!"

It was the same observation dome where she'd watched the destruction of the Olyix homestars. Now, though, the cluster of Immanueel's ships was stationary in interstellar space, with the galactic core gleaming off to one side. Ahead was an unnatural indigo glow as if a miniature monochrome nebula were suspended out there in the darkness. Except there was no dust, no wisps of gas animated by radiation.

"The tachyon beam," she whispered. Tears threatened to emerge, but then she was so emotional right now.

"As it passes through this moment in space-time, yes," Immanueel confirmed.

"Can you determine its direction?"

"We have. It is not quite what we expected."

"Oh?" She turned to them, frowning. "Then where does it come from?"

"The origin point is in orbit around this galaxy, inclined eighty degrees to the ecliptic."

"Close," she said.

"Yes. And, genesis human, the message was sent from sixty thousand years in the future."

"That's not the end of time. Not even close."

"No."

"Okay then." She grinned in malicious anticipation at the enigmatic glimmer of Cherenkov radiation. "Let's go kill us a god."

CAST OF CHARACTERS

2206

MORGAN CREW

DELLIAN . . . . squad leader
YIRELLA . . . . strategy advisor
TILLIANA . . . . tactician
ELLICI . . . . tactician
FALAR . . . . squad member
JANC . . . . squad member
URET . . . . squad member
XANTE . . . . squad member
MALLOT . . . . squad member
OVAN . . . . squad leader
TOMAR . . . . squad member

KENELM . . . . captain of the *Morgan*
WIM . . . . bridge officer
CINREA . . . . bridge officer

IMMANUEEL . . . . corpus human

TIMELINE

1901 . . . Guglielmo Marconi transmits radio message across the Atlantic Ocean.

1945 . . . First nuclear explosion (above ground).

1963 . . . Limited Test Ban Treaty signed, prohibiting atmospheric nuclear bomb tests.

2002 . . . Neána cluster, near 31 Aquilae, detects electromagnetic pulse(s) from atomic bomb explosions on Earth.

2005 . . . Neána launch sublight mission to Earth.

2041 . , . First commercial laser fusion plant opens in Texas.

2045 . . . First commercial food printers introduced.

2047 . . . The US Defense Advanced Research Project Agency reveals artificial atomic bonding generator—the so-called force field.

2049 . . . US Congress passes act to create Homeland Shield Department, charged with building force fields around every city.

2050 . . . China forms Red Army's City Protection Regiment, begins construction of Beijing shield.

2050 . . . Saudi kingdom installs mass food-print factories. Twenty percent of the kingdom's remaining crude oil allocated for food printing.

2050 . . . Russia starts National People's Defense Force; its shield generator project starts with Moscow.

2052 . . . European Federation creates UDA (Urban Defense Agency)—builds force fields over major European cities.

2062 . . . November: Kellan Rindstrom demonstrates quantum spatial entanglement (QSE) at CERN.

2063 . . . January: Ainsley Baldunio Zangari founds Connexion.

2063 . . . April: Connexion twins portal doors between Los Angeles and New York, charges ten dollars to go between cities.

2063 . . . Global stock market crash, car companies lose up to ninety percent of their share value. Shipping, rail, and airline stocks fall. Aerospace stocks rally as space entrepreneur companies announce ambitious asteroid development plans.

2063 . . . November: Space-X flies a QSE portal into LEO on a Falcon-10, providing open orbit access. Commencement of large-scale commercial space development.

2066 . . . Astro-X Corporation's mission to Vesta. Establishment of Vesta colony.

2066 . . . Connexion Corp merges with emergent European, Japanese, and Australian public transit portal companies to form conglomerate. Major cities now portal networked. Noncommercial vehicle use declining rapidly.

2066–2073 . . . Thirty-nine national and commercial colony/development missions to asteroids (the Second California Rush—so called because of the number of American tech company CEOs involved). Large number of World Court injunctions filed by developing nations and left-wing groups against exploitation of exo-resources by for-profit companies.

2067 . . . Globally, thirty cities now protected by shields, two hundred more under construction. Start of decline of conventional military forces. Phased air force and navy Reduction Treaty signed at UN by majority of governments. Armies reconfigured as counter-insurgency paramilitary regiments—numbers cut substantially.

2068 . . . Seven corporations established at Vesta. Astro-X completes its Libertyville habitat colony. Houses 3,000 people.

2069 . . . First solar powerwell portal dropped into sun by China National Sunpower Corporation. Five-kilometer-long magnetohydrodynamics chambers built at Vesta, positioned on large asteroids, outside Neptune orbit

2070 . . . Armstrong resort dome assembled on Moon. Similar resorts under construction on Mars, Ganymede, and Titan.

2071 . . . All major cities on Earth linked by Connexion stations—except North Korea.

2071 . . . UN treaty forbidding nonequitable exo-resource exploitation. Any asteroid or planetary minerals mined for use by commercial companies must be equally distributed among all nations on Earth. US, China, and Russia refuse to sign. European Federation awards treaty Principal Acknowledgment status; starts to draw up its own nonexploitation regulations, where "excess profits" of asteroid development companies will be channeled into Federation foreign aid agencies. Commercial asteroid development companies re-register in non-signatory countries.

2075 . . . Seventeen self-sustaining habitats built in asteroid belt. Construction of Newholm starts at Vesta (by Libertyville)—fifty kilometers long, fifteen kilometers in diameter. Takes three years to form, two years to complete biosphere.

2075 . . . Fifty-five percent of Earth's energy now comes from solar powerwells. Decommissioning of nuclear power stations begins, radioactive material flung into trans-Neptune space via portals.

2076 . . . Increasing number of asteroid developments become self-sustaining and Earth-exclusionary. Start of habitat independence movement.

2077 . . . Interstellar-X launches first starship, *Orion,* propelled by QSE portal solar plasma rocket. Destination: Alpha Centauri. Achieves .72 light speed.

2078 . . . March: Global tax agreement signed by all governments on Earth, abolishing tax havens.

2078 . . . August: Nine space habitats declare themselves low-tax societies.

2078 . . . November: First Progressive Conclave gathers at Nuzima habitat; fifteen billionaires sign Utopial pact to bring post-scarcity civilization to humanity. Each launches asteroid colony expansion, with an economy based on AI-managed self-replication industrial base.

2079 . . . China National Interstellar Administration launches starship *Yang Liwei.* Destination: Trappist 1. Achieves .82 light speed.

2081 . . All Earth's energy supplied by solar powerwells. Connexion largest energy consumer.

2082 . . . Major national currencies now backed by kilowatt hours. Global de facto currency is wattdollar.

2082 . . . Interstellar-X–led General Starflight Accord signed between all starfaring organizations (capable of building starships) and governments, ensuring open access to new stars and no duplicated star missions.

2082–2100 . . . Twenty-five portal-rocket starships launched from Sol to nearby stars.

2083 . . . *Orion* arrives at Alpha Centauri. Psychroplanet discovered 2.8 AU from star, named Zagreus. Too expensive/difficult to terraform. Eleven government missions transfer into Centauri system and establish asteroid manufacturing bases, along with eight independent asteroid companies. Construction of multiple portal starships at Centauri system begins.

2084 . . . Last car factory on Earth (in China) shuts down. Connexion hub network serves ninety-two percent of human population, including space habitats.

2084–2085 . . . Twenty-three starships launched from Centauri.

2085 . . . Utopials launch starship *Elysium*.

2086 . . . Alpha Centauri asteroid manufacturing stations abandoned. Small joint-venture solar rocket plasma monitoring station maintained in orbit around the star, providing drive plasma for the starships.

2096 . . . Chinese starship *Tranage* arrives at Tau Ceti, exoplanet discovered.

2099 . . . Chinese begin terraforming of Tau Ceti exoplanet, named Mao.

2107 . . . US starship *Discovery* arrives at Eta Cassiopeiae. Exoplanet discovered.

2110 . . . US begins terraforming Eta Cassiopeiae exoplanet, named New Washington.

2111 . . . European Federation agrees to terraform exoplanet at 82 Eridani, named Liberty.

2112 . . . *Elysium* arrives at Delta Pavonis. Terraform-potential planet discovered, named Akitha. Construction of habitat Nebesa and extensive orbital industrial facilities. Terraforming of Akitha begins.

2127 . . . The *Yang Liwei* arrives at Trappist 1. China begins terraforming two Trappist exoplanets T-1e and T-1f, Tianjin and Hangzhou.

2134 . . . New Washington terraforming stage two complete, open only to American settlers.

2144 . . . Olyix arkship *Salvation of Life* detected 0.1 light-years from Earth as its antimatter drive is switched on for deceleration. Communication opened. Four-year deceleration to Earth-Sun Lagrange 3 point opposite side of sun from Earth.

2150 . . . Earth population 23 billion; 7,462 space habitats completed, population 100 million.

2150 . . . Olyix begin to trade their biotech with humans in exchange for electricity to generate antimatter, allowing them to continue their voyage to the end of the universe.

2153 . . . Mao declared habitable. Farm settlers transfer from China, begin stage two planting—trees, grass, crops. Fish introduced into ocean.

2162 . . . Neána mission reaches Earth.

2200 . . . Eleven exoplanets now in stage two habitation. Large-scale migration from Earth. Twenty-seven further exoplanets undergoing stage one terraforming. No more being developed; fifty-three marked as having terraform potential. Portal starship missions ongoing, but reduced.

2204 . . . Portal starship *Kavli* arrives in Beta Eridani system, eighty-nine light-years from Earth. Detects beacon signal from alien spaceship.

EXPLORE THE WORLDS OF DEL REY BOOKS

READ EXCERPTS
from hot new titles.

STAY UP-TO-DATE
on your favorite authors.

FIND OUT about exclusive
giveaways and sweepstakes.